THE LIMBERLOST
REVIEW
A LITERARY JOURNAL OF THE MOUNTAIN WEST

*"Hemingway" (Paris, Key West, Cuba & Sun Valley) by John Bertram,
cut paper on canvas collage, 24" x 36," 2018.*

FROM LIMBERLOST PRESS

How to Sleep Cold
17 Poems & Related Writing Prompts from the Outpost Writing Workshop at Billy Meadows

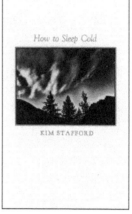

By Kim Stafford

"This book speaks from a place in far northeast Oregon, where time runs deep with stories. Wallowa County was the original home of the Nez Perce Tribe, and anyone who visits there will see, and feel, why it was, and is, sacred homeland. It is a place where the mountains are steep, the rivers clean, and history is yet a compass for navigating the mysteries of modern life."

Thus, from the "Foreword," Kim Stafford describes the place in 2009 where he met for a time with 15 "sterling companions" in a writing workshop they called the Outpost Writing Camp at Billy Meadows. Without electrical power or phones, many sleeping on the ground, the group immersed themselves in the writing craft for a week in a remote landscape, eating Dutch oven meals and exploring nature when not deeply engaged in writing. *How to Sleep Cold* is Stafford's collection of 17 poems, all written at the Outpost Writing Camp, inspired by the writing prompts (also described in the book) that guided and inspired the group of participants throughout their time at Billy Meadows.

Kim Stafford is the current Poet Laureate of the state of Oregon. He is the author of more than a dozen books of poetry and prose, and the director of the Northwest Writing Institute and the William Stafford Center at Lewis & Clark College in Portland, where he has taught since 1979.

Letterpress printed in a limited edition of 500 copies on
Mohawk Superfine paper, folded and sewn by hand into
Thai Chiri endsheets and Stonehenge wrappers.

$20 *(plus $3 Media Mail shipping; Idaho residents please add 6% sales tax)*
from www.limberlostpress.com, or send check to: Limberlost Press,
Rick & Rosemary Ardinger, Editors, 17 Canyon Trail, Boise, Idaho 83716

FROM LIMBERLOST PRESS

Wild Dog Days
By Gino Sky

In this long poem, published in honor of the poet's 75th year, the indefatigable **Gino Sky**, author of the novel *Appaloosa Rising: The Legend of the Cowboy Buddha* (Doubleday, 1980), reflects on history, memory, and the power of poetry in bringing an end to the Vietnam War.

Publishing a 1960s underground literary magazine called *Wild Dog* that the FBI took notice of, Sky tells a story of all that swirled around the magazine during an eruptive time in America. First published by the poet Ed Dorn in Pocatello in 1963, *Wild Dog* was handed off to Sky who moved it to Salt Lake City and then to San Francisco's Haight-Ashbury District right at the moment of the counter-cultural revolution. Sky exuberantly chronicles the time, the place, and the peace movement with hallucinogenic clarity.

Illustrated with photos of some of the poets who helped hand-crank the small press literary movement, *Wild Dog Days* is dedicated to "every man, every woman, every kid, every dog who marched for peace and stopped the war."

Gino Sky has published two novels, a collection of stories, and a dozen books of poetry (including *Hallelujah 2 Groundhogs & 16 Valentines*, also available from Limberlost Press). *Appaloosa Rising* and his novel *Coyote Silk* (North Atlantic Books, 1987) have been translated and published in Korea. He and his wife Barb Jensen live in Salt Lake City.

Letterpress printed in a limited edition of 400 copies.

$15 *(plus $3 Media Mail shipping; Idaho residents please add 6% sales tax)*
**from www.limberlostpress.com, or send check to: Limberlost Press,
Rick & Rosemary Ardinger, Editors, 17 Canyon Trail, Boise, Idaho 83716**

www.limberlostpress.com

THE LIMBERLOST REVIEW

No. 1, 1976 *No. 2, 1977* *No. 3, 1977*

No. 4, 1977 *No. 5, 1978* *No. 6, 1979* *No. 9, 1981*

No. 13, 1984 *2019* *2020*

The Limberlost Review

A Literary Journal of the Mountain West

Edited by
Rick & Rosemary Ardinger

A publication of Limberlost Press
Boise, Idaho
2021

THE LIMBERLOST REVIEW

A LITERARY JOURNAL OF THE MOUNTAIN WEST

2021 Edition

Editors
Rick & Rosemary Ardinger

Contributing Editors
Chuck Guilford
Bob Bushnell

Sports and Social Media Editor
Jennifer Holley

Layout and Design
Meggan Laxalt Mackey, Studio M Publications & Design

Cover Illustrations
Front Cover: "Late Summer Morning Run at Military Reserve"
by Rachel Teannalach

Back Cover: "High Mountains" by Fred Ochi

Limberlost Press
17 Canyon Trail, Boise, Idaho 83716
www.limberlostpress.com

THE LIMBERLOST REVIEW *is published annually by Limberlost Press.*
This issue Copyright © 2021 by Limberlost Press, with all rights to the individual
contributions returned to the authors and artists.

ISBN 978-0-578-92640-7

This journal features some of the best writing from the Mountain West and
beyond, including poetry, fiction, memoir, essay, translation, commentary about
books we come back to again, interviews, artwork, and more. We welcome the submission
of manuscripts, but can not accept responsibility for lost items or electronic correspondence
problems. For copies of THE LIMBERLOST REVIEW, *please email*
editors@limberlostpress.com or visit our website: www.limberlostpress.com.
Printed in the United States of America.

LIMBERLOST LETTERPRESS

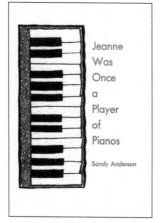

www.limberlostpress.com

LIMBERLOST LETTERPRESS

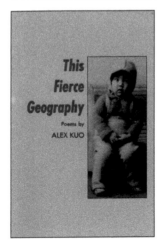

www.limberlostpress.com

TABLE OF CONTENTS

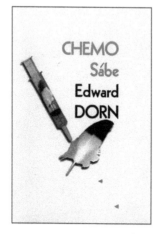

www.limberlostpress.com

"Mother Nature Makes the Best Crowns" by Didi Sharp, paper collage,
8" x 10."

EDITORS' NOTE

Reconnecting and Remembering

This 2021 edition of *The Limberlost Review* appears in an atmosphere of great relief and apprehension—relief at the outcome of the 2020 presidential election and the availability of COVID-19 vaccines at long last, and apprehension about the impact of pandemic mutations and the persistent ignorance and belief by national leaders in lies and conspiracy theories that threaten health and Democracy itself. Tentative steps forward from our isolation are precarious. Words matter. We look for inspiration in the work of writers, artists, poets, historians, journalists, teachers, communicators, true believers to map a way forward.

Since the appearance of the 2020 *Limberlost Review*, we lost several great writers and friends of Limberlost Press. Though we did not lose the following to the pandemic virus, we mourned our losses in isolation. In the last year, we lost poet Judith Root in Portland, Oregon, three days before her 81st birthday. Her gentle, modest delivery reading her work was betrayed by her hearty laugh. We'll miss her poems. And we'll miss her phone calls too. She had poems in the 2020 *Review*, and we thought we'd give her the "Last Word" in this edition.

We lost Peter Bowen of Livingston, Montana, whose historical fiction about Yellowstone Kelly and long string of novels following Montana detective Gabriel Du Pré were historically playful, wildly engaging, and sentence-by-sentence steeled with hammer-strong certainty. Peter was his own man who didn't suffer fools. We'll hear more from him posthumously, but we'll miss his phone calls to catch-up on the lives of friends he left behind in Boise when he left the city for Montana again several decades back, always asking us to give his friends all his best.

Having finished printing a new chapbook by Sherman Alexie, Covid summer of 2020 (photo by Marcia Franklin)

We'll miss William Kittredge of Missoula, whose personal story of growing up on a vast ranch in eastern Oregon in *Hole in the Sky* said more about place and ownership and displacement and rootedness in the West than shelves of histories. His story on the page has a bite to keep you reading, and if you ever heard him give a reading, gripping the podium and delivering a distinctive cadence to his narrative, you will never forget what a force he was as a writer, editor, teacher, mentor, to so many.

Larry McMurtry, born in Archer, Texas, and dying there 84 years later—what can we say? Over drinks recently at a Boise bistro patio with a couple of vaccinated friends, we lamented his loss, remembering *Horseman, Pass By, Terms of Endearment, Lonesome Dove*, imagining the seminar table of Wallace Stegner Fellows at Stanford in 1960 (where McMurtry worked with Wendell Berry, Ken Kesey, Peter S. Beagle and others), McMurtry's love of rare books, his screenwriting career. What a shelf of books he gave us.

On Christmas Day, we lost Barry Lopez, whose exploration of natural history was inspirational. His *Of Wolves and Men* is a book we remember where we were and who we were when it appeared in 1978. The earth seems to move when certain works appear, and this was one of them. He went on to win a National Book Award for his *Arctic Dreams* less than a decade later. His view of natural history and anthropology gave the fields new meaning. We'll hear more posthumously as his work is collected. It has been good to live in his time.

Poet Lawrence Ferlinghetti, at 101—and having published a novel just the year before. Through his own poetry and his publishing of so many others, his impact on 20th century literature will resonate for generations—especially his interest in making poetry accessible in volumes for less than a dollar, the first edition of Allen Ginsberg's *Howl* in 1956 selling from his City Lights Books for 50 cents. He traveled the globe, introduced us to poets from other cultures by overseeing publication of numerous translations, while his bookstore in San Francisco became a cultural landmark. His agenda was international, and yet he remained accessible to letters from young writers and small presses in such far away places as Boise, Idaho, where Limberlost letterpressed a broadside and two of his chapbooks. At an International Ezra Pound Conference in Sun Valley, Idaho, in 2003, also attended by Hugh Kenner, Robert Creeley, and Pound's daughter Mary deRachewiltz, his repeated refrain was memorable: "Dissent is not un-American." It could have been the banner for the conference as it was for his bookstore. We'll miss his large presence in this world.

And at press time, we learned of the passing, at 81, of our Idaho poet friend Tom Bennick, papermaker extraordinaire. After teaching high school English in Mountain Home, Idaho, for more than three decades, Tom "retired" to his passion for making paper from sagebrush bark, desert grasses, milkweed blossoms, and more. On the education roster for the Idaho Commission on the Arts, Tom demonstrated papermaking in school classrooms and at art fairs, involving participants in gathering sheets of pulp onto screens, and even while deafness encroached more and more into his world, he continued to send out his "pops"—seasonal haiku-like poems letterpressed onto his homemade paper. They arrived with seasonal regularity, with his suggestion that those of us on his mailing list hang them somewhere outside so the paper could return to the elements, to the earth. Though we did that with a few of his pops over the years, we just could not do that with these little handmade, heartfelt missives, and we share here his last four pops...

Tom Bennick's last seasonal "pops," 2020

* * * * *

This edition arrives in the summer of 2021 as we all begin to venture forth with vaccinated confidence and a need to reconnect. Over the past year, we had time and distance to read, and the stories of what we read this past year would make a great issue in itself. If there was some benefit to the lock-down months, it was our renewed correspondence with each other. We encouraged readers to contact writers in the last edition, and some writers re-connected with writers published here after many years. If there was a side effect to this awful year of daily casualty tallies, it was our reconnection with so many good folks who reached out, said hello, sent along work they had finished.

We shared reading lists. We feature 10 Re-readings in this edition of memorable books we come back to again and again—or should: Robert Penn Warren, William Faulkner, Virginia Woolf and Elizabeth Bishop, Lawrence Durrell, Robert Pirsig, Ivan Doig, Kenneth Patchen, Sherman Alexie, Thomas McGuane, Thomas Hardy—this section of the *Review* is renewing. Let's keep this going. We want to hear about the books that moved you to believe, to re-live your life re-reading. Who were you and where were you when certain books struck a chord, like an epiphany. We've already received several re-readings for the 2022 edition and we welcome more.

Since last summer, we've letterpressed several projects, including a new chapbook of poems by Sherman Alexie, *A Memory of Elephants*. And as this issue goes to press, we're at work letterpressing *Burning Time*, a chapbook collection of poems by Annie Lampman, of Moscow, Idaho. Annie had poems in the 2019 and 2020 editions of *The Limberlost Review*. If you have not purchased a copy of her new novel *Sins of the Bees* (published last summer by Pegasus Books), you need to do yourself a favor after all these pandemic months and pick it up.

We've said the artwork that appears in these pages is what makes *Limberlost* readable. And in this edition the work is stunning, from our cover by Rachel Teannalach, to work by Mike Woods, Dennis and Ginny DeFoggi, Fred Ochi, Didi Sharp, Janet Wormser, Rod Burks, John Bertram, and Lorelle Rau. And along with artwork, we must thank Meggan Laxalt Mackey for her design and layout of this edition, done while completely immersed in moving and still renovating a "new" home purchased at the end of last year.

The deadline for material for the 2022 edition is October 1, 2021. We look forward to reading work that might have come out of this last year of isolation.

Here's to a summer of reconnections.

—*Rick & Rosemary Ardinger*

"Sunrise on the Palouse from Kamiak Butte" by Rachel Teannalach, oil and wax on linen, 36" x 48."

JIM DODGE

Open Moments

Sometimes a moment opens
and you slip through

into the raucous outraged shriek
of a pileated woodpecker interrupted
stealing walnuts fallen from a tree
behind the barn;

the doe down at the woodland's edge,
her gaze touching your check,
your throat;

the blond coyote ghost
vanishing over the ridge;

redwoods hushed by moonlight;

and then you're back sleeping,
or buttering toast,
or just standing there watering the garden
as if nothing
had changed forever.

Apogee

Walking the harvested fields,
Winter, mid-morning, sun warm enough now
The earth softens,

Frost-melt wraiths
Rise from the corn stubble,

Then detonating like a golden grenade
A rooster pheasant hidden near your feet
Explodes into flight,

Taking your stunned heart with him
To the top of his cackling climb

Where in a silence as sudden as his turn
He banks hard left, levels out,
Sets his wings, and glides.

Through the tattered shroud of your last breath
You follow his motionless flight,

No longer anything
You recognize
As flesh or feather,

Imperceptible shudder
Between air and wing.

On Destroying My Third Refrigerator
in Seven Years Defrosting It with a Filét Knife

True accidents are never senseless.
If nothing else, the slaughter of large appliances discourages cupidity,
And the brain-mushing pamper of convenience is surely deterred.
The gods appreciate a smile when you accept your fate:
Not every blossom becomes a peach;
So few of us reach the pure state of relentless stupidity.
True accidents are never senseless.
If nothing else, the slaughter of large appliances discourages cupidity,
And the brain-mushing pamper of convenience is surely deterred.
The gods appreciate a smile when you accept your fate:
Not every blossom becomes a peach;
So few of us reach the pure state of relentless stupidity.

Owl Feather

I have no doubt there are powers far beyond us
Because the grey-and-brown barred wing feather
From a Great Horned Owl that I found this afternoon

While walking the old logging road above McKenzie Creek
Seemed beautiful beyond the ability to behold it
And certainly beyond any capacity to create

The ruffled back edge of the feather
That muffles the sound of the owl
Launching from an oak's dark limbs

And renders its glide into the talon-strike
So utterly silent it seems a sovereign overture
To the implacable raptures of death.

The Wisdom of Rivers

The thing you have to understand
is we're all just trying to find our way through,
to get to our deaths without too much
damage, compromise, loss,
with some grace and faith redeeming
our failures, calming our fears—

and sure, it's mostly bumble and fluster,
and—of course—fuck-ups galore
(we're human beings,
the depth and complexity of our ignorance
virtually unexplored)
but if we cinch down our dead-mortal lock
on the obvious, take the seats that age
has earned us on the Dead Pecker Bench
or in the hot-flash center of the Circled Crones,
where everyone is awarded
a gold-plated cracker barrel
in front of the all-too-general store
where we're allowed to expound our guessed-at data
along with all the other village explainers, poets,
and point-walkers leading the Insight Patrols,

because we've all been born with the bare sense
that Nature provides the least of its dickey birds,
for don't we all truly and deeply know
the best course when lost is always to follow the river,
splashing along stagnant miles of frog water
or bashing through the churned chutes
squeezed into chaos by sheer canyon walls,
our woeful asses occasionally wrapped around boulders,
hanging on to the very notion of hanging on,
for even the most hapless morons know in their souls
that every rill and rivulet will find a river,
and that every river eventually takes you to sea.

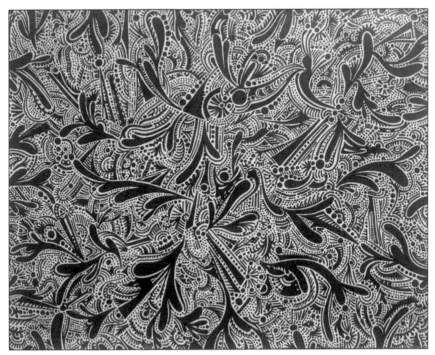

"Untitled" by Jinny DeFoggi, ink on paper, 11" x 14."

SHERMAN ALEXIE

Elegy

The apple tree
in my grandmother's

backyard died.
So did she.

I asked my father if
My grandmother's pallbearers

Were going to be the ghost
Of that tree and the ghosts

Of its apples. "Of course,"
My father said as he pulled

A raven down from the sky
To serve as feathered priest.

The Gospel According to Frequency and Wave

In Welsh, there is a word, "dim,"
Pronounced the same in English
       as it is in Welsh.

In Welsh, it means "nothing,"
Though it can also mean "anything"
       based on an idiom

I don't understand. But that Welsh
       dichotomy helped me realize
       that "dim" in English

Can mean "nothing" if we see dim
       as an encroaching
       half-dark

And it can also mean "anything"
       if we see dim
       as a burgeoning

Half-light. But we can also see
       the dim dark
       as enigmatically

Beautiful and the dim light
       as obviously plain.
       What should we do

About these oppositions?
Let's walk together into the dim
       and ask God

To deliver us nothing or anything
And give thanks for whatever light
       or dark that we might receive.

Midnite Mine

In the uranium days,
My tribe sent us cash—
Two thousand dollars
Twice a year. What

Did my family do with
That money? Used cars
And booze. Fast food.
Weekends in motel rooms

Off the reservation.
And new shoes for us,
The kids. We bartered
Immediate gratification

For future cancer—
For tumors of lung
And pancreas. Often,
As a fifty-something man

Quickly on his way
To an elderly life, I study
And count my skin moles.
It's a task that takes more

Time than one might think
Because I have 73 moles
Randomly distributed over
My body and face. The mole

On my right forearm is
Shaped like a heart. Maybe
You don't believe me.
But it's true. There's a heart-

Shaped mole on my sleeve.
Thank God that it's still
Smooth around its edges.
It hasn't changed size since

I was born, so it's assuredly
Not cancerous. But I still
Monitor that mole and worry
That, one day, my heart

Will grow ragged, larger,
And darker along its perimeter.
I worry that underpaid miners
Will arrive to dig the uranium

From my skin. When I think
About being Indian, this is often
What it means. Some kind
Of soldier, preacher, or politician

Rides a horse that glows in the dark.
He's coming to steal from me.
He's coming to break promises.
He's coming to cancerize my heart.

JERRY MARTIEN

Water & Power

flowed from el rio de neuestra señora la reina de los angeles through la
zanja madre the mother ditch dug by the city's first mexican settlers in
1781 for the gardens and wash houses of the pueblo till lifted by anglo
water wheel to the town's plaza 1857 the ditch then privatized and
covered to keep out trash and dead dogs and occasional drunks until
taken over and replaced by iron pipe belonging to los angeles department
of water from which

flowed power to acquire rights that became 1913 mulholland's
hydrological dream bringing the owens river 180 miles south to the
san fernando valley where by the 1940's it was considered insufficiently
healthy and parents had mountain spring "juvenile water" delivered in
bottles to our house on greenfield till the hollywood marriage failed and
we moved to grandmother guadalupe's house in redlands believing the
water that came from her kitchen tap

flowed from san bernardino mountain snow melt and great-grandfather
joaquin's ill-fated gold mine into bear valley creek dammed 1885 to
create big bear lake to supply mormon settlers and their orange groves
till 1910-12 the new dam for which my grandfather drove wagon
bringing up construction materials but by the time I was a kid the lake
was so low we could stand on the old dam to fish not knowing the water
we actually drank

flowed from upper santa ana's mill creek beside the old mentone highway
where I pedaled in the morning dark with lunch bag and fishing pole to
meet my friend eugene where we caught rainbow and built dams and
drank like thirsty animals but never connected it to the stone-lined ditch
that I crossed every morning on the way to school and was told was dirty
and never play in it the sankey everyone called it the old zanja that once

flowed into the gardens and groves of the franciscan asistencia dug 1819
by serrano people which the friars hoped would divert them from the
cattle and goods of san gabriel mission and remains california's oldest
and most litigated irrigation project which I played in for years till
our remnant family migrated 30 miles south to perris valley where the
colorado river

flowed into the scrubbers of potato sheds from metropolitan water
district created 1928 to pump and tunnel from parker dam through three
mountain ranges and lace with chlorine to wash potatoes grown with the
same subsidized water tumbling onto conveyor belts and graded by rows
of women and spilling into burlap sacks we jigged and sewed and loaded
for farmers who when the price went up to something near its actual cost
moved to oregon and idaho and the river

flowed instead of orange grove and field into subdivision and imaginary
towns over older towns blurred along the interstate imaginary inland
empire stretching south and west taking rivers with it till they all
connected and ladwp could spend millions of rate payer dollars to buy
millions of acre feet of mwd's colorado river to pump north to flood
the former site of owens lake which had become a major source of air
pollution and a visible sign of the miracle civilization has brought
to the west:

made a garden into a desert
& turned water into money and dust.

Following Water

I hadn't heard from Bobby in more than thirty years. He's Bob now,
says he found my number in the book. He's retired, driving up the
coast in his motor home. Says his wife died the year before on a trip
to Mexico. I think he must be on some kind of pilgrimage. Sure, I say.
Let's get together. I'm surprised that he remembers me, then by the
flood of memory.

Late one August night, toward the end of the 1950's, Bobby and I are
on the open road. From Riverside, east on Highway 60, we're driving
across the southern California desert.

Maybe we've heard of Jack Kerouac—probably not. Hill country kids,
a couple of years out of high school, neither of us has been anywhere.

Bobby has an aunt in Phoenix.

The only thing I know about Arizona is that Bobby's high school sweetheart was sent to a college there, not far from Phoenix—mostly to get her away from Bobby. We used to double date sometimes, me in the back seat of his '50 Lincoln with a girl whose father also hated me.

I don't know why we didn't take the Lincoln. Maybe I want to show off the '52 Ford I've just bought at an auction, thinking I got a great deal. It turns out to be a road test for all of us. A few hours out, as we approach the Arizona border, the Ford is making an ungodly noise. We're about to throw a rod.

We clatter into Blythe, leave the Ford in back of a gas station, decide to hitchhike. In the faint glow of dawn we walk the couple of miles to the border, cross the long two-lane bridge over the Colorado, head out into the Arizona desert with our thumbs out.

After an hour or so a guy in a pickup stops. Ain't going far, he says. We don't hear the cautionary note in his voice, cheerfully jump in the back. Just as walking seems better than standing by the road, we figure any ride will beat walking.

Then we're several miles deeper into the desert, watching the pickup disappear northward in a long cloud of dust. Sand and rock and sage in every direction, the highway a narrow black ribbon across it. Sun getting higher. No hats. No water. Bobby in brand new Levis. The rides far between and moving fast. We walk till the sun is overhead and the pavement melting under our feet. Then, our thumbs still out, we walk back to California.

At the edge of Blythe a sign by the phone booth says The Friendly Place To Stop—which is lucky because Bobby's brother can't come tow us home till day after tomorrow. By now the highway is like a frying pan, the swampy river air too hot to breathe. Bobby walking bow-legged. We blow most of our travel money on an air conditioned motel room, but hunger soon drives us out. A plague of crickets has descended on the town, flying and crawling on cars and store fronts and sidewalks. We can't help but crunch them as we walk.

We spend our remaining money at the town's drug store soda fountain, a couple of long afternoons of drinking Cokes and talking to the young waitress. Dropping nickels in the juke box, Fats Domino wanting to know what we're gonna do when the well runs dry.

The journey was a clue to the lessons life had in store for us.

It was our first summer away from home. We shared a little rental in Riverside, where we'd be going to school next year—Bobby at the JC studying engineering, me at UCR thinking I would be a rocket scientist. His parents owned the house, gave us a break on the rent, even provided jobs.

They lived out in the Gavilan hills on a few cleared acres crowded with large vehicles and machinery—including a well-drilling rig and sewer-pumping truck that we'd be paid to operate.

Bobby's dad was a little guy, hunched over, wire glasses and a welder's cap. With one lung, he chain smoked Camels and worked relentlessly. The Mom was big, like Bobby and his brothers. She'd bring food to town, leave it in our fridge. It was hard to be homesick.

The well rig had a 20-foot derrick supporting a heavy cable that lifted a ten-foot steel shaft with a 500-pound bit screwed onto it, then dropped it. And then lifted and dropped it again. And again. Basically pounding a hole in the ground.

All that fall and into winter, on weekends or after class, we'd drive the dozen or so miles out to the well site, pound a few feet deeper into the decomposed granite. The work had its compensations. Looking out over the Gavilans, guiding the cable's rise and fall, getting paid six dollars a foot—ten after we hit rock.

The pump truck's return on our labor was about what you'd expect.
Poking holes in suburban lawns. Digging, opening the tank. The
home owner standing around, the big hose throbbing with his life's
excrescences. You can keep all the rubbers you find, he said.
The rock slowed the drilling more than the extra dollars added up.
Even cheap gas and free time cost something. But it diverted me from
the confusion of differential equations and dating girls. I even played
bongo drums and wrote beatnik poetry.

We never got through the rock. I was relieved when we quit at 50 feet.
Bobby had played varsity tackle all four years of high school and could
absorb the extra twang of the cable when the bit hit granite. I bounced
around like a fly on a banjo string. And it felt like our luck was bad.
Another driller, just over the hill, dowsed and hit artesian water at
30 feet.

These might have been the most necessary failures of our lives.

We did eventually get to Phoenix. It was hot and humid and nowhere
near as memorable as not getting there. Like most of the things we tried
that year—white lightning whiskey, home-made fuel injectors—it was
dumb as two right thumbs. But we laughed a lot. And we were
changed by it.

I turned into an English major. Bobby quit school, went to work, and
the following summer got married. Not long after, I married a girl I'd
gone steady with in high school. Once we all spent a weekend together,
water skiing on the Salton Sea where he was installing water and septic
systems. I was headed to graduate school. We never saw them again.

Bob stays a couple of days at an RV park in town. We meet for dinner
twice, same restaurant. The waitress is old enough to be patient with
a couple of guys trying to locate their past. After we remember Blythe
neither of us knows what to talk about. Then he heads north to Oregon,
where the old girl friend is living now.

He'd been very successful, serving the water-starved culture we grew up in. My marginal life—a solitary poet in an old house on a remote spit of sand—must have looked to him like the decisions we made when we were young. Maybe he wouldn't be far off.

With our thumbs out, walking into a flawed idea of the world. Walking it back. Crossing the river, crossing again. And from there our ways divided, flowed into different worlds.

He spent his life bringing water to the desert. I live where it falls from the sky.

Leaks

It began with a trowel.
Digging out the meter.
Watching the little dial turn
when all our faucets were off.

It began with the water bill.
The panicked human brain
re-tracing all the places
money and water goes.
Nothing.

So it didn't actually begin till my
neighbor remarked that the grass
on his side of the fence was strangely
green and I remembered our lots once
were one. Water came to both homes
from the pump house near the road
till the water district extended its
lines to our neighborhood and the
owners replaced the old iron pipe
with ¾" black plastic connected by

hose clamps back and forth across
the property line which wasn't there
till they divorced and the guy who
bought our house built a fence with
a concrete footing which the leak
turned out to be under.
The thing that makes humans do this
is a leak we are unable to fix.

So you could say it began
when the black pipe broke the first time
and I only replaced it as far as the break.
Original sin. Western civilization.

It began at the meeting of two rivers.

We have dug ourselves a ditch
and the neighbor and I are standing in it.
We're on his side of the fence where he
had also been meaning to replace his line,
me digging at one end, him at the other.
Then I dig by myself
under the fence and footing
to where I stopped ten years ago.

The neighbor's ditch has square corners,
runs straight along the fence line.
I quote my friend Tom, who'd say
when he was painting a house,
"I'm not very good—but I'm slow."

I'm more worried about the money
than the water or the ditch.
When the line broke before
the service district gave me a discount
but I'm not sure they'll do it again.
The district leaks. Influence. Effluence.
Logging upstream leaks silt into

our river which is no longer
fit to drink. For years the local nuke
leaked radiation into the bay and
onto the nearby elementary school.
Two pulp mills leaked hydrogen sulfide
over Eureka and up our valley.
The mayor said he'd never smelled it.
The slow drip of power
may be the hardest leak to fix.

Plumbing is a long odds bet we can
control the earth's essential liquidity.
Civilizations go broke repairing leaks.
I realize that these days of digging
are just my small contribution.
Now I feel better about the money.
As I shovel the dirt back in the hole
I think I might start singing.

Somewhere a meter is turning.
Somewhere the grass is green.

MARY ELLEN McMURTRIE

From Here to Texas

Telephone wires hang like a giant
cat's cradle all over this big old country.
One hooks to a box on my back door
and loops through the linden tree
to the alley. It wanders across State Street,
down Fairview and up the hill till
it can ride the freeway to the open desert air.
Except for a dip across the Snake River
it doesn't make much of a bend
all the way to Wyoming. And that flat
prairie of a land can let
a length of wire blow full tilt
forever to slice the Continental Divide.
It's a pull up the Rockies
but a smooth grade going down.
Ties in somewhere in Oklahoma
before it angles south to Texas.
And finds you there in Dallas sobbing
so hard, I can just barely figure out
he is ignoring you and making you feel
ashamed of yourself in a way
I never wanted a daughter of mine to know.
How long between your sob
and what I hear? Maybe generations
because I have forgotten what it's like
to hang your star to the heart of a man
who ends up having no soul,
and you forgetting you had one without him.
I wonder if that long loopy line bulges
just ahead of your words and they race
latitudes of states I need a map to name.
And does it ripple the perch of a crow watching
each eighteen wheeler crest the horizon?

Stafford's Deer

This one is an elk
at dusk.
Still breathing.
Slowly.
In and out.
The Jeep ahead—windshield broken
us behind—whole with help.
The old man stumbles back to us.
She just come out of no where, he says.
I know, I say, they never warn you.
She's bad, ain't she?
Yes, I say, she's bad.
None of us has a gun.
And then we hear the cry
off in the snow where it's too dark to see.
Her calf asking what's keeping her.
Blood shines on the black road
I bend close.
Call her mama.
Tell her it's the last chance.
A driver going down canyon
will call from Hill Top
and Sheriffs carry guns.
I position her front feet
then I push,
talking low and meaning it.
Pavements slick for her effort.
Another question beyond the lights,
we look at each other
and agree there's no choice.
I hold my breath and push.
In one great heave
she stands.

We pull onto the darkened road
watching her trot through snow
and head for home.
I've never touched an elk before
my daughter says.
She hands comfort
to the back seat
for her baby.

Grandmothers

hold us
on their laps
like bowls of grain
ready for tossing
chaff to the wind.
We listen to the weft
weave among the warp
of their stories
and nestle closer
to visions of
peacemakers
changebringers
wrongrighters.
We stick licked fingers
in the sugar bowl
and wait to see which
shuttle threads us
into the design.
Ancient is the truth
tied round their middles
with apron strings.
The world should be
governed by a tribunal
of grandmothers.

"Rolled Hay Bales" by Mike Woods, mixed media, 31" x 39."

GAETHA PACE

I Don't Know

The huge dumpster appeared across the street at dawn. Linda slipped into her sweats, washed her face, ran a brush through her hair and made a pot of coffee. The next day the front-end loader would arrive. Best thing, she said to herself.

Nancy's house was being torn down and the acre lot would be used to create three small cottage homes. Andy, the resident developer, had given Linda permission to dig the pink and magenta peonies and other plants that lined Nancy's back path for the garden club sale. The old "pass along" plants had withstood years of neglect and, in Linda's opinion, deserved new homes.

"You're welcome to any of it," he'd said, when she asked if she could go into the house. "Be careful. It still stinks to high heaven."

The obituary in the paper months before had spoken of Nancy as a domestic goddess, kind to her children and a rock during times of poverty and disappointment.

Andy had purchased the property from the heirs. Most of the proceeds had gone to the state to reimburse Medicaid. He said Nancy had been cremated and her ashes sent express mail to one of the children.

Linda had been thinking about that obit all week, thinking about the list of Nancy's children, one name significantly absent. So much of our historical record, she thought, has always been spin and that was the opinion of a well read fourth grade history teacher. The one who writes the history gets to tell it his own way, she'd told her classes. She suspected Helen had taken her comments into consideration when she'd written her mother's obituary.

Linda's son, Harry, on his last visit to have coffee and to check up on her, told her to quit obsessing. Linda hadn't responded to that piece of wisdom. But all in all, she was tired of men, young and old, telling her what to do. She could live the remainder of her life without that aggravation.

"If you want to know the truth," she could see that he didn't. "Speaking of age," she'd said. He hadn't been listening. That's what she meant. When you're an old woman you can say what you want because no one is listening. "There are too damn many interfering know-nothing politicians. I don't know why people put up with it."

Her son nodded absently. He was on the county commission and in the fall would be running for State Legislature. "Better watch out, Mom. You might wake up a Libertarian."

"Don't get me going," she said.

He shook his head and said he had to get to the bank before eleven. He answered his phone as he pushed open the screen door. "I don't know what set her off," he said.

"You don't want to know," she yelled to his back.

Then, later that day, when her daughter-in-law brought over a couple of free weights and suggested that lifting a few extra pounds might ward off osteoporosis, Linda's irritation spread to include Amy.

"Lifting unnecessary weight isn't something I'm interested in," she said.

"You're only in your seventies," Amy said, "and too skinny."

"Indeed, and I have no intention of devoting one ounce of effort to delaying the inevitable. I've been pulling above my weight for most of my life." Linda had been widowed as a young woman. Amy left shaking her head.

Linda gathered up a shovel, a few buckets and a spading fork and put them in the back of her Kawasaki mule. She steered down her long drive, across the street and into Nancy's dried up yard. These days she drove her new toy all over their small town, had traded her husband's antique truck for it.

Bob Murray, the local sheriff, joked she'd have to get it licensed soon. She'd taught him in fourth grade. "When you make your Dad get a license for his golf cart."

Linda came to a stop beside the peonies, got off and dug a few, shook off the excess dirt, hoisted the buckets into the back of her ATV, glanced about, unsure about what she expected to find in the house. Andy told her that the key was under the rock by the spirea.

She opened the door to the stench of years of cat feces and urine. Filth and neglect had destroyed what had been a nice bungalow: two bedrooms, fireplace, bay window, screened in porch and wood floors. After Nancy had gone into the care home, her youngest daughter had become a cat hoarder. Andy said that after the house was torn down, they intended to scrape the ground, take the first layer of dirt to the dump and replace it with new soil.

Surely someone had searched the house but she had to look anyway. She pulled on her gardening gloves and began to look, drawer by drawer, cupboard and closet, under piles of rotting clothing and stinking debris looking for hiding places. She sneezed violently and thought the wrecking crew should consider hazmat gear.

Someone had tried to fix the back roof with a blue tarp but that was rotting, too. The studs were exposed where the plaster deteriorated from the moisture. It was no use. There was nothing to find.

Young Bob stuck his head in the front door. His shirt was pressed and clean. Unlike his father he made a dapper sheriff. His father had been more slap-dash, in Linda's opinion.

"You're not going to find your things, you know."

"You looked?"

"Of course. Dad searched the place back then and again after Rachel died. I think he even dug up the basement. I looked when Nancy passed on. Nothing was found. Go home and take a shower, Mrs. Maxwell. Andy shouldn't have let you inside."

"There's no 'letting' to it, Bob. This situation involved an agreement between two consenting American citizens. Last I heard they hadn't carved out an exception for skinny old women still in possession of their faculties."

"Really?" He raised his eyebrows and touched his chin.

She walked out with him. "If you don't mind, I'll finish digging the plants before I go."

"I wonder why she did it?"

"I don't know," Linda said. "Want to help me dig?"

But by the time she finished her sentence he was lifting himself into his county truck. That kid never had been one for wrinkling his trousers. She returned to the project, dug the remaining plants. What did she expect to find after all these years?

Linda's home had been burgled a few weeks following her husband's death. The theft still rankled. Food had been taken from the pantry and her grocery money stolen from the kitchen drawer. Her mother's pearls and the small silver heart pendant her husband had given her the anniversary before he died, and her mother's engagement ring intended for Harry's wife when he married, were all taken. The thief had come in through the back unseen and had left the same way. Linda sat down on the bed that day and cried until she couldn't cry any more. It had been too much to bear. When ten-year-old Harry came home from baseball practice he had called the sheriff.

It took the town four more robberies to realize Nancy had been keeping her children home from school on robbery days and that the children had been breaking into homes when she knew the families were away. Linda knew Nancy put them up to it but she couldn't prove it. What would make a woman do that to her kids?

Bob's father had been sheriff during those years. He finally cottoned onto what was happening when he saw the children on the street when they should have been in school. When he tried to stop them, they dropped a bag of groceries, a watch and small radio and ran. The thieves had been maybe seven, eight and ten at the time. The toddler Rachel was disabled with cerebral palsy and at home with Nancy when the robberies happened. They hadn't recovered the money, the pendant, ring or the pearls although they checked the pawn shops for several years.

Still Linda had a job and help from her family. She worked hard to make a life for her son and pay the mortgage. She didn't begrudge the stolen food or money, if it had been used to feed the children. Nancy had help from the churches and the government, and had inherited the house from her parents. Her children remained with their mother, ill-clothed and thin. They had no friends. Linda often saw them outside of the house, waiting for their mother, who seldom left the home, to open the door for them.

"Why don't they go inside?" Harry would ask.

"I don't know," Linda always answered. It seemed best not to guess.

She spoke to the children when she saw them on the street but they moved away from her, their faces downwards and their hands behind their backs.

After she called the law the first time and they were ushered into their home at the Sheriff's insistence, they waited out of sight on the west side of the house or in back. The sheriff reported that there were no bruises or broken bones, no physical signs of abuse.

In the summer following the robberies Linda would see them in the yard, waiting for whatever they were waiting for. That fall she had Helen in class. The girl seemed thin and lethargic but held her chin up in fierce determination. The school cooks put extra food on the children's plates. Everyone knew they were going hungry.

One windy winter afternoon about two years after the robbery, when Harry had the flu and Linda stayed home to care for him, she saw the children's feet protruding from behind the back shed.

"Damn," she said. "I'm tired of this. Why aren't those children in school where they at least can get a decent meal?" She called Child Protective Services. The agency assured her that the Sheriff had been inside the house and that it was warm and clean. The children had no injuries.

"I'll keep calling, you know I will. I've had about as much of this as I can take."

Finally, a week later, Bob's father asked how long she would keep at this harassment of her neighbor.

"Until someone checks in every room of that house, sir, and finds out what's going on. Something's not right. Why are those children afraid to go inside their own home? Is she locking them out? I'd break in but she doesn't leave the house."

To his credit, Bob, Sr. had been on Nancy's door step many times. It wasn't just Linda who was upset about the state of things. But he didn't feel he had enough to push his way in. "You, of all people, should understand. In this country you can't just force yourself into another person's home. She has a sick child in there."

He said that he would stand at Nancy's door and wait while Nancy beckoned her children inside. Bob said it was plenty warm in there. Nancy told him that the children had been outside playing of their own accord. It appeared to him that they didn't want to go inside. "She's a mean talking woman," he told Linda. "I wouldn't want to spend much time with her myself."

"They don't play. They just stand there. Please find out why she makes those children stay outside while she's sitting in there on her butt. You wouldn't treat a dog that way. It's awful, awful. Do you realize that it's 20 degrees today and the wind is blowing?"

He had been fully aware of the wind and the temperature. The Sheriff had become angry, too, angry at Linda and her interference. He did push his way past Nancy, searched the whole house. He found Rachel in the corner of the children's bedroom rolled into a fetal position. There hadn't been much left of her. The coroner said that from what he could tell she had been starved and could have been dead for a couple of years. Linda couldn't get the image of the child out of her head. She made herself look at that house every day for months wondering what else she could have done.

Nancy spent six months in the mental health unit of the regional health center. Helen and her younger brother went into foster care in another county. The youngest girl went too, but returned when she was 18 and lived, slow and heavy like her mother, in the bungalow until a few years after Nancy entered the care home. No one saw the youngest girl after that and no one knew where she went, but Linda thought she'd probably gone to Helen. Helen, the one Linda suspected of authoring the delusional obituary, the story she could one day show her children. That's what made Linda so mad—glorifying Nancy in the obituary. Good for Helen, bad for history.

That evening, after Linda drove her little rig into her garage, she undressed in the laundry room, threw her clothing into a trash bag, took a long hot shower, washed and curled her hair, tidied the house and puttered thoughtfully in the kitchen until Harry and Amy came by with Linda's youngest grandchild. They were going out with friends and Linda liked to babysit. Harry was telling Amy the neighbor's story as they were coming in the door. "I wonder what really happened, how could she do such a thing?" Amy asked Linda.

"I don't know, dear," Linda said, as she took her grandchild by the hand.

Two days later, after the peony roots were cleaned and separated into $3 bags, and after watching the crew destroy the rickety shed and move the last of the rubble from the lot and the blade drop deep to remove the polluted ground, Andy crossed the street to visit. A few minutes later Bob Murray pulled up at the site to visit with the heavy equipment operator.

"It appears we've found Nancy's stash," Andy said.

"Imagine that," Linda said and took a deep breath.

The next day, Bob came by with photos of things that had been buried in the dirt under the floor of Nancy's shed. "We've found most of the small stuff," he said, and over $1000 in cash. You'll get your things back as soon as the office is through with them. Why would a woman with money let a sick child starve?"

Linda sighed.

"Dad said he thought she was trying to kill them all and might have got it done if you hadn't been so damned interfering. What was going on in that woman's head?"

"I've run out of ways to say I don't know, Bob. But I'll tell you what, I'm glad to see that house torn down." ∎

"Blue Note" by Janet Wormser, oil on canvas, 12" x 16."

MARTIN VEST

Demolished

for a building

There was nothing friendly about it. The community
bathrooms a brown fingerpaint of malnourished slurs,
foul scenes, promises of violence. Perfectly good light bulbs
disappeared, then turned up again as perfectly good
meth pipes. The neighborhood watch photographed needles
and broken bottles, marched their findings to the mayor.
They forbade their children from walking past
its taped windows. In the courtyard was a garden
of stationary bikes planted by tenants with big plans
of going nowhere. It was a place of occasional
murder, halls that smelled of canned sex, always the crawl
of smut. Still, it kept the rain off when no one else would.
It was a sorrow you had to weep to understand.
It was a drink of darkness when all light failed.
The crenellated pigeons flew and returned like a crown.
The key-carved walls stood for us like mothers.
The hearts among the curses were proof
that once we'd loved.

Philia

For L, RIP
"Absurdity is king, but love saves us from it."
—Albert Camus

At the park, a mother pours candies into her two boys' hands.
One of the boys, whose keen eye quickly notes a disparity
in the number of pieces, protests—*No fair! I only got four!*
Hold on! I'm not finished! barks the mother.
She drops a fifth candy into the boy's hand.
But then it's the colors that bother him.
Red is *his* favorite color—not his brother's.
He wants more red ones.
I'm that way, indignant, incapable of grace, a child.
When I think of all the people for whom every hour
is another million dollars, another epiphany, another red candy,
another chunk of time well spent with a lover
in a field somewhere among the butterfly migrations,
I want to remind them that we're all going to die,
that no matter how many butterflies you see, you will unsee them
one day while putting on a shoe, or gumming broth in a home
to which you've been sequestered by children, or traveling
to the store on a Wednesday afternoon that would be typical,
if not for the war. And no matter what you wish
to have done with your remains, eventually, they won't remain.
Everything becomes dust, even dust.
And when I look at my brother's face, I see a ring
of chocolate around his mouth, and I see that he sees
the same ring around mine. And all of our candies are gone.
And sometimes, I admit it, that's the only reason I love him.

Soon the Horses

You're married, still, but to what you can no longer say.
You're unemployed, burning through floors, sofas, friends.
Soon you'll be off to the courthouse for crimes
that would be amusing if you were still twenty-one—
public urination, trespassing, resisting arrest.
But now it's just shameful when your name makes
the police log. Soon chained dogs will sound
their tattle cries when you bed down in the weeds,
a yellow vapor of skunk scent hanging
in the darkness like a lantern. Soon the drunk tank;
soon the psyche ward. But tonight you're on top
of the world, knocking back boilermakers.
Tonight the Molotov, car bomb, redheaded cocksucker,
the old crow leaving its feathers in your throat,
the grave digger dragging its shovel down your spine.
A white horse for foresight. A black horse for hindsight.
Tonight the burning bush reveals the face of God.
Soon you'll awaken in a hospital bed,
tubed, diapered, indigent, swearing
the man in the moon was real.

As if Your Life

First, Love should never be hard-boiled. It is not an egg.
When Love poaches you with its two-headed arrow you will fall
from a cradle of purest world. It won't be easy. There will be
times when you need to kill Love with rhetoric and poison
apples and rock slides. There will be times when it needs
to kill you with stingrays and O rings and mysterious
brake lines. Love comes back like a season, like a zombie,
like a creature of habit. Love rises, makes the furniture
float, has no anchor. It drifts Coriolis and trade, is anchor,
a doldrums, an eye wall. Love is a dinner fork with one tine bent,
a wakeful insight, a quarrel gone to bed on. In the spring,
put your Love on a hill and bury it in a jar for twenty-nine moons.
Don't touch it. On the thirtieth moon release it and now it is a frolicking
goat. Feed it thistle and garnet, watch it grow into song. Discourage
nothing. Perhaps it will leper among the stars. Perhaps a soldier.
You don't know. How should you know? When Love vanishes
without a note of explanation, let it quickly return carrying
fresh produce and dairy. Greet it at the door as if your life
has been taken. When the kiss comes crushing
the bags between you, let one of the eggs be broken.

E. ETHELBERT MILLER

What We Live For Is What We Die For

They came for me last night.
I was tortured and finally confessed
that I loved you. What else could I do?

Morning

There are love notes
in the kitchen.
Just heat and serve.

Black Orpheus II

1.
When you turn around there is no one
pushing your wheelchair.

2.
Memory is the bad date you try to forget.

3.
When she steps out of the shower it
begins to rain again.

4.
The blues will pull you underground.
Never make love in a coffin.

5.
Everyone wears a mask.
Wash your hands after every breakup.

GAILMARIE PAHMEIER

Hole Punch

Primary Use: punching holes in leather and other tough materials,
for example to keep a belt in service after dieting.

Secondary Uses: punched dots of leather or Naugahyde can be glued
on the bottom of craggy lamps and vases so they won't scratch your
grandmother's antique table.

How to Use: mark the locations of the future holes...

Before the new girl in junior high school,
the one who'd come to your small city
from a place you imagined had charm,
had class, before she said aloud how tacky
it was, so deeply red and rubbery,
you thought the Naugahyde sofa your dad
had won, grand prize at the company picnic,
was the coolest thing in the whole house,
the only item not gifted by grandmothers
and distant aunts. You thought it mod, thought
it groovy, thought it said something about you,
that you could be different, could stand out.
But the new girl noted how the sofa clashed
with the heavy wood rockers, their leather
seats splitting under the weight of your clan.
When your dad came in from feeding his hounds,
sat first on the porch to smoke, rubbed the ash
into the knees of his Wranglers, when your
mother called for supper, served white bread
and fried potatoes, when the new girl said
she'd never eaten two starches in one meal,
something that had been glued, had been tough,
had been both wondrous and familiar,
that thing got punched, left a perfect hole inside
you, big enough to locate your future.

Random Orbit Sander

General Description: a handheld power tool…when powered up, rapidly rotates an abrasive disk in an interesting rosette pattern. The random orbit sander is bigger than your doubled fists but smaller than your head.

How to Use: to assess the smoothness of a sanded surface, look at it under angled light, which reveals defects by their shadows. Lightly stroke the surface with your fingertips, which can detect defects the eye cannot see.

Tool-Kit Minimum: anyone who wishes to refinish will not regret investing in a random orbit sander.

On the college campus where you teach,
nearly every student has beautiful skin.
It's not just the unwrinkled surfaces,
the blood flushes of hope, of potential.
It's the perfect lack of imperfection.
What, you wonder, has happened to acne,
where has this gone, so common in your own
school days that nobody really minded much
the ever-present scent of medicated
creams, masked only modestly under
Love's Baby Soft or Old Spice cologne.
Is a diet of quinoa and string cheese,
of power bars and bottled water
the key to clear complexions? Your own
college meals a memory of macaroni,
of scrambled eggs and Smoky Links,
lima beans in a butter bath, sweet tea.
You carried a thermos of black coffee
to class, where on a humid spring day,
you met the girl from Osceola, the one
who, over many beers and a semester,
trusted you enough to tell you her lovely
skin was hard bought, a year's tuition,

a trip to Little Rock where a plastic surgeon
sanded her face down to its smooth finish,
the pitted layer, her daddy's legacy,
gone, the whirring tool under the angled
light a sound she won't ever forget, will
forever stroke her birth face, lightly,
forever searching for defects no eye
could see. You sort of miss her, have heard
she moved to Tucson, married someone
who wooed her with miniature roses,
bunches of them. She's been outside your orbit
for decades. Just thinking of her, of skin,
of smoothing scars—this cannot be random.

Mask

General Description: a paper or fabric hemisphere or cup about the size of your closed fist.

Habitat: found among sanding and painting tools.

Operating Principle: the rim of the mask should make a tight seal around the wearer's mouth and nose (not easily accomplished if the user has a beard).

1963-1969:

Every Halloween for the six years of grade school
she was a princess, costume of thinnest
fabric, all sparkle and wand, the flimsy
box bought the October before,
Saturday sale at Katz Drug Store,
Route 66, St. Louis, Missouri.
She has no knowledge of the lunch counter
sit-ins at the Katz in Oklahoma City
but she knows the song of this highway,
how her mother hums along, the promise
of kicks, passing through a pretty
Oklahoma City, toward the real West
where possibility and potential seem palpable.
Yes, she was always a princess, just wanted
to be pretty, to be blond, a face hard
enough no one fist could bruise.

2020:

Her husband's
beard has become unruly, tangle
for tortilla chips and other sharp-edged
crunches. On the second day of her state's
reopening—this is Nevada, fraught
in its own history, but far from the old
road that led her here—she's in search
of razors and scented candles, senior
discounts at Ross Dress for Less, anything
to pretty up a bit, return to days
of delicate adornment. She's masked.
The women who block the fragrant aisle
are not, are young blondes, take turns twisting
the caps of waxy lipsticks, unsure which one
will call out, will say *Princess*, will say *fear me*.
She knows they expect her to go away.
Instead she rolls her cart forward
toward the opening door of this fragile world,
a place where a fist, when raised, is beyond
pretty. It's goddam beautiful.

Funnel

General Description: the space between the spout and mouth is called its neck.
The mouth may be fist-sized to about head-sized; indeed, inverted funnels
have been worn as hats in such movies as The Wizard of Oz.

How to Use: listen to the gurgle, whose pitch rises slowly as the container fills,
then rises sharply just before it overflows.

Tool-Kit Minimum: one funnel for each class of fluids—don't pour gasoline
through the same funnel you use for wine.

If you are of a certain age, you might
remember Easter Mondays as the day
you played *Wizard* on the playground, the movie
shown each Easter evening, family sprawled out
around the Magnavox, bellies full of ham,
scalloped potatoes, some sort of cream pie.
The movie is one you've nearly memorized,
will dream of flying monkeys for decades,
nightmares which begin with benign whispers,
escalate into guttural groans that wake
your lover, who's smart and brave and mostly
kind. Back in grade school, he'd have been called upon
to play the Tin Man, the handsomest of the trinity.
You could have played Dorothy, *click, click, click,*
but the most coveted role was that of Toto,
and everyone wanted to be her, the freedom
to frolic all afternoon, to howl and bark,
to have your lunch served in a bowl inside
the coat closet, permission granted
by teachers who allowed one full day
of otherness, one full day to be whatever
you could inhabit, to be that thing entirely,
to funnel your whole self into a growl
worth hearing, worth raising a glass to.

KEN RODGERS

Post Traumatic

I sipped black coffee and glanced at Lindy Lou's tight little butt as she poured her javvy, spooned sugar and fake cream into the pink cup with the blue butterflies—as if she wasn't sweet enough.

She wandered from my office to her desk in the scale room. I followed and peered over her shoulder as she spun dials so as to balance the truck scale. I liked the way the gears and beams clicked and clanked.

I wanted to say, "I already did that," or "it's already taken care of," but I didn't. She'd say, "Oh, I know. I just want to make sure. It's my responsibility."

I walked back into my office and studied delivery receipts for loads of calves that had come that morning from Oklahoma.

As I wrote dead slips to mail to customers, she hummed a song I'd heard on the radio, but not my kind of music. I don't like rock and roll.

A white and yellow truck with a full load of manure drove by the office, and I scribbled a note to see how the crew was coming on cleaning the pens.

Our order buyer in Texas had bought several loads of calves in Amarillo so I wrote drafts to pay him.

As I hurried to the boss's office for his signature on the drafts, I heard a truck pull up on the scales. I turned; another grain truck with a load of milo.

Nodding at one of the drafts, the boss said, "These calves worth the money we're paying?"

I didn't think so but said, "Who knows? They look like good cattle."

I exited his office and glancing at the scale room, recognized the only truck driver I couldn't stomach.

He leaned over the counter, chatting on the company telephone. A jolt of bile shot all the way into my nose. I ran down the hall and, before I could yell, "Put that phone down," he waved me away, saying into the phone, "Hello, hello."

I yelled, "No! No! Use the pay phone down by the mill. No, damnit, no!"

But he didn't quit.

As I slid to a stop at the scales, he grimaced. "See you later today, honey. Love you and love to the kids."

I grabbed his arm, "What the hell do you think…"

He yanked his arm away and I would have expected him to say something like, "Don't you ever touch me." Instead, he blurted, "It was a collect call. I called collect." He pointed to the phone. "I called collect."

With my index finger I stabbed the handwritten sign posted on the wall. Rule One: Truck Drivers Will Not Use the Company Phone Under Any Circumstances. Period.

He avoided my eyes.

The door to the outside opened. In her right hand, Lindy Lou gripped the probe we provided for drivers to sample grain, as wet or damp grain can heat and explode.

In her left hand she carried the rusty half-gallon can the drivers put the grain in after sampling. She looked at me, then the driver, then back at me. Lindy Lou nodded, "Man, Bill, your face is really red."

I wanted her to say that about the driver. She giggled and stood the probe in the corner and placed the can of grain on the counter. Ladling part of the sample out of the can, she dribbled it into the mouth of the moisture monitor.

She nodded and smiled.

He left and I said, "I told you to stop doing that jackass's work for him."

She stiffened.

Maybe I shouldn't have said what I said next but something pushed. I barked, "Goddamnit, I'm the boss."

She said, "You are just an employee."

"But I'm your boss and I'd appreciate it if you did what I said."

She glared. Not like the homecoming queen we all drooled over back in school. "He's disabled. He wears an appliance that allows him to evacuate his feces. It might bust when he jumps off his trailer."

"What?"

She stomped her foot on the floor. On her feet were new pink Ropers. I liked that.

Slowly, like I was stupid, she said, "He got shot in the guts in Vietnam. He almost died. His intestines were irreparably damaged and they had to give him an appliance."

Jungle grass, the musty scent of dampness and somebody talking on a PRC 25 shot into my brain all at once, and I shook my head to throw the images back where they came from.

I took a deep breath and glared out the window at a cotton field across the road. I said, "How do you know all that and who told you that and…and…an appliance?"

She laughed. Not a funny laugh. She raised her arms like she wanted to fly, then slapped them against her sides. "He told me. The appliance is called a stoma appliance."

She sucked a deep breath and leaned towards me. "Here's how it works. The doctors take whatever is left of your intestines and cut a hole in the abdomen and then sew the end of the intestines to that hole which they call a stoma. Then they can attach the appliance to that and the feces are evacuated."

I must have looked dumbstruck because she stuck her hands out like my kindergarten teacher did when she tried to teach me my letters.

"Then, when the bag gets full, you can go empty it in the toilet."

"Did he tell you all that?"

"No, my grandma has one."

I nodded. I knew her grandma; when I was a little fellow, she doled out cookies and candy to the neighborhood kids.

I said, "Sorry for your grandma."

She smiled. "Me, too."

I decided not to say anything else until the driver returned from the mill to get his truck's tare weight. Then I'd talk to them both.

Through a window in my office, I noticed the jagged teeth of the desert mountains.

His air brakes hissed and the scale moaned as he pulled on. As he stepped from the truck, he closed the cab door with a clunk. I stood, made sure my shirt looked neat, walked into the scale room and watched Lindy Lou. She stamped his ticket, signed his manifest, and handed him his copy. I cleared my throat. They both looked in my direction.

I pointed at him like I shot a pistol. "If you are going to haul grain into this feedyard, you have to do your own work. We don't get paid to do your work."

He shrugged. "Hey man, I got a problem…well, I got more than one problem," he chuckled like a clown trying to pull something over on me. "I got shot in the guts in Nam and…and…ah, shit, man, I…"

That's when Berry showed up, in my head, whispering, "Please, please, God, please don't let me…" I wrestled that memory down.

I don't know how long I stood there before I said, "Shit, that's what this is all about, ain't it? Shit, or not being able to shit."

He stared at me.

Choppers flew over the office and I glanced up to see where they were going. Something I'd never seen out there at the feedyard. Choppers. But then they disappeared, fragments of my imagination.

I said, "I was in Nam."

He said, "Where?"

I felt sweat on the palms of my hands. "Doesn't matter."

He jerked his head like I'd shocked him with a cattle prod. "Ha, man, it matters to me. I think about it every day. Where I was, when it was, how it happened." He pointed at his abdomen. "I am not going to forget this."

I wondered what outfit he'd been in. "You Army?"

He nodded, "You?"

All this time I sensed Lindy Lou watching.

I stood tall. "Marines."

He snorted. "Gyrenes, damned gyrenes."

All Army guys hate Marines. It's a fact.

I pointed at him, "Our employees will not do your work. If you can't do your own work, best find something else to do."

Halfway to my office, I turned. "And best forget about what happened in Vietnam. Worrying about the past gets you nowhere. Move on."

The rest of the day the memories battered me. Bad C-rations, and cold, foggy nights, the leeches, good God, the leeches on your feet and your armpits and groin. And Berry, four of us, each on a corner of a poncho, hauling him to the medevac chopper.

I sat there and wondered if he had made it home alive. His guts hanging out when we last saw him and…I scolded myself, this is not going anywhere. Get on with life.

Lindy Lou didn't speak to me that day. Or the next. I'm sure she said something to the boss, because later he summoned me, "Go light on the guy who craps in a bag."

I never argue with the boss. I wanted to. About him sticking his nose in my business. I think he sensed that because he started talking about sending me to Newport Beach and a cruise on his yacht down to Guaymas.

I've been to Southern California and the world of the Pacific, and I don't need to ever go back.

I saved most of my anger for Lindy Lou.

I didn't say anything to her and when Shitbag—that's how I saw him—would show up with a load, I'd hurry outside and drive around the pens checking feed bunks. Sometimes I'd find a cowboy to yell at about sick calves that needed doctoring, or a buckaroo building a loop to rope a calf, practicing for the Saturday night steer roping contest. Rule Number One for cowboys: Don't rope the livestock unless necessary.

Something I learned in the Marine Corps. Rules are made for the 10% who can't get with the program. Rules saved a lot of us in Nam. I wondered if this guy, this shitbag, was one of the 10% and got his guts blown apart because he couldn't follow rules.

I thought, no. So long to all that.

I thought Lindy Lou was kind of sweet on me. That's why I hired her and here she was acting high and mighty like Shitbag was more important. In high school, I cast the swing vote that got her to be a cheer leader and I made sure she got to be a candidate for Girl of the Year.

Now she defended him.

In the coming days, even though I promised myself, I couldn't keep my jaws shut. I needed to get past the differences between Lindy Lou and me, but I wasn't sure what to do.

She mostly ignored me. Once, when I knew it was Shitbag's truck she'd weighed, I said, "Still kissing up to that whiner?"

She snapped, "Oh, grow up."

I smiled to keep up a front.

I couldn't let it go. "For once, I wonder if you would just do as instructed."

She shuffled papers. I stepped right behind her. She barked, "Back off."

I whispered, "I don't want to fight with you."

She didn't respond.

I said, "I've always thought you were real special."

She relaxed. I looked at her neck, the little blonde hairs swirling. I leaned, my mouth close, blowing a soft wind.

She swirled around, arms flailing and one of them caught my glasses, sent them skidding across the white vinyl tile, stopping at a filing cabinet.

Instead of getting angry, I thought, *good thing I have a spare pair in my desk.*

She hissed, "Don't you ever touch me, you pig."

You'd think words wouldn't matter. I used the excuse of picking up my now-busted glasses to figure out how to deal with this sudden hurt. I returned to my office, acting as if I was fixing my glasses.

I put on my spare pair, rose and walked into the scale room and said, "I'm sorry."

She didn't look at me.

I walked closer. "Please excuse me for being a pig."

She sighed and shook her head. "Just leave me be."

I said, "I don't see why you have to give special attention to that…"

She stiffened and I thought about how a bayonet appeared when you didn't want to see it coming. She said, "Jeez, Bill, give it up. The guy's got a serious handicap and I'm just trying to help. Don't you care about helping people?"

Her words slammed into me like the typhoon that smashed our combat base in Nam.

The word "help" bothered me. A thought wounded me. *Did I care?*

As if reading my mind, "Bill, do you care?"

When we'd been in Nam, I didn't want any new friends after Berry, and when the new guys arrived, I stayed away from them and when they died, tough shit. Better them than me was my philosophy.

She said it again, "Do you care?"

I squirmed. I couldn't escape.

She said, "Come on, Bill, I know you saw a lot of bad shit in Nam." She took a step towards me and said, "I knew you really well then and I know you, kind of, now. Not the same guy, Bill. Not at all."

She took another step and I took one backwards. I stared at her and tried to keep bloody guts and heads smashed by incoming from taking over.

"You really need to think about what happened in the war, and..."

I threw my right arm out as if slicing someone in half, my hand a machete. "No. No. And hell no."

Then I sliced from top to bottom. "There's no need to relive all that shit. It's history. Very ancient history, and we all just need to head on into the future."

I'd had all that crap stuffed. I was doing good. Now....

She frowned as a truck rolled onto the scales. Shitbag's rig.

My stomach burned. "We can't change the past. We just need to look ahead. Put one foot in front of the other."

She said, "You need to talk to Jimmy, that's this truckdriver's name, and see what he does to help..."

I yelled, "I don't need any help from Shitbag."

I guess I'd never used that name around her. She yelled, "Shitbag, shitbag? Is that what you said? I swear, Bill, you are horrible."

Horrible. That's what I was, or what she thought I was, and I wondered if I shouldn't be horrible. I mean, because she was Lindy Lou, I let a lot of things slide and I could really tighten the toggle if I wanted to. Maybe I would have, but the boss told me to tone it down. When I asked him if Lindy Lou had been whining about me, he said, "Everybody knows what's going on between you two. I like you both. Don't make me pick."

I liked my job but I had my pride, and they tussled with each other for over a week.

Early one morning before Lindy Lou arrived, his truck pulled onto the scales.

I watched Shitbag climb out of his cab and the way he stepped down—well, I'd never noticed it before—was timid. He clutched his papers in his left hand and he shuffled to the door, pulled it open, and stepped in. He started to say something, maybe it was "Good morning," or "Top of the day to you," or something else.

I thought I heard someone holler, "Halt," and then I felt the snap of a round as it went past my head.

He muttered, "Oh…it's you."

I didn't want him to see me react to that, so I smiled bigger than necessary and without talking, handed him the sample bucket and pointed to the probe standing in the corner.

He glared at me and no shit, he bawled. Maybe he didn't bawl but tears rolled from his eyes.

He opened his mouth, but I stopped him, my hand like a .45 caliber pistol. "Don't start, mister. Get on the trailer, get a sample and bring it back. You. You do it."

He shook his head, "No, man, I got this damned thing," and pointed at his right side.

I shook my head, "If you can't get me a sample, then pull your truck off the scales and get your ass on down the road."

He stood there, staring at me, then left.
A landing ran alongside his trailer on both sides, allowing him to work around his trailer, probe for grain, or to tarp and un-tarp the load—that's something I hadn't thought about. Who tarped and untarped his loads? He must have finagled someone at our mill to do that part, too. He pulled a corner of his tarp loose and managed to get the probe in and then filled the bucket with milo.

His carcass wasn't long enough to ease from his trailer to the ground, so he dropped down and shouted as the probe clanked on the concrete. I winced. What if the probe broke?

He bent over. Tears streamed down his face.

My stomach erupted and my ears rang as if a hand grenade had exploded next to my head.

One of the maintenance crew driving the big yellow backhoe pulled around the corner and headed north. The bucket swung like a limb in a windstorm and I made a mental note to chew his butt.

Shitbag staggered in, reminding me of Berry.

He seemed lost, like he'd been popped with a morphine syrette.

He whispered, "Please, can I use the bathroom?"

I thought about my drill instructors at boot camp. I put my hands on my hips, spread my legs as I leaned toward him. "Louder. I can't hear you."

He shook his head and moved towards the main office.

"Hey, Shitbag. Ask me louder."

He ran towards the back with his hands holding his guts.

"Hey, stop. I said, 'stop.'"

But he didn't and worse, he veered into the wrong hallway, towards the boss's office and the women's restroom.

I took off at a trot. Little balls of shit had dribbled out of whatever mess he had for guts.

I caught him, thankful I hadn't stepped on one of those dung balls.

I yanked him around. "Wrong hallway, maggot."

That's what my drill instructors liked to call screw-ups like Shitbag.

He rasped, "Oh, man, I broke my stoma apparatus."

I grabbed his shirt collar and half-dragged him to the men's room as I kept repeating, "Don't you dare lose any more of that shit."

My biggest fear: that I'd have to police it. When I returned to the main office, Lindy Lou was cleaning the mess.

I said, "No. Let that jackass clean up this crap."

She sneered and went about grabbing little balls of shit with a tissue.

I thought the top of my head would blow.

Bent at the waist, Shitbag returned and stopped when he noticed Lindy Lou.

He shuffled close to her and touched her hand. He said, "Thank you. God bless you."

I said, "God doesn't have a damned thing to do with any of this. Get your truck off the scales and out of here."

If I'd have been him, I'd have wanted to kill me. But he didn't. He looked like he felt sorry...shit man, that hurt.

He said, "Can't drop this load. Need to get somewhere where my bag can get replaced or repaired or..."

She grabbed his arm, drew him close and whispered.

Shitbag shambled out but didn't get in his truck, and I suddenly felt like all the energy had drained out the soles of my Tony Lamas.

Lindy Lou dumped the fecal mess into a metal trash bucket.

I said, "How can you do that?"

While rushing towards the back of the main office, she said, "What in the world is wrong with you?"

"Absolutely nothing. If he wants to be out in the world, he needs to be able to deal with what comes. It's not our responsibility."

As she stomped out the back door, she shouted, "I'm going to haul Jimmy to the hospital."

In my office, I stood in front of the window, scoping the feed pens. Two cowboys built loops, planning to rope a steer that looked like it didn't need roping. I marched towards the door so I could chew their asses.

Outside, Lindy Lou's Pontiac pulled out onto the highway. Her tires burned rubber as she hit the accelerator. In the pen where those cowboys played rodeo, manure dust boiled.

A steer bellowed somewhere near and it made me think of Berry. All the way from the bloody trail into the LZ, he bellowed about his mother and his guts and God.

The dried manure those cowboys roiled invaded my nose and throat and burned my eyes. ■

WILLIAM JOHNSON

Reach

Over cutbank gravel, on the heat-wicked wave
    of a mirage, dreamlike, it floats
toward me and away. Bumper-flung
    apparently, neck-snapped and spine-crushed
where I drive to work, this buck muledeer
    who gazes the way it came. I'm a child
in a room alone, sprawled on the bed slapped
    cold, the curt brute back of a hand
a headlight's heart-breaking blaze. How it swims
    or wishes it could, a foreleg's dislocated stab
at grass up the bank I reach toward for us both,
    its rack a diviner's branch probing gravel.
See how I run, won't you? There's a ghost in this.
    What lost forest, what road far from home?
How eyes shoo-fly the poem of dying alive
    so that after weeks of shrunk fur-sloughed
break-down, bones arc like consonants
    robbed of a vowel. What I leave by the road
stretches for a cud of green impossibility,
    the bank no less than earth itself,
a cellophane mirage I float away on, dust if that
    suddenly flung back, hands at the wheel
as I take the next leg, driven to work of my own.

Covid at Cache Creek
Snake River, June 2020

A family of mergansers paddles evening
into slackwater off the dock,
the river laced in shadow on its way to dark.

No caretaker at the cabin now, the visitor center
locked. Grape-leaves on the yard's long arbor
lift silent applause. And the trees, pear and apple

fruits half ripe, heedfully pruned and seasoned.
Old locusts harbor furrows of an iron age
and turkeys, fat longnecks umber-feathered,

run the place, its acre or more of grass mowed
by a visiting stranger, who, given sheds, stumps
and fences, leaves well enough alone. And my son

near his prime past forty, and my grandson
who led me into the history sleeping here.
Drowned in tangles of blackberry, Cache Creek

chuckles off rocks on its way to the big river.
Shadows of bereavement fall from cracked basalt
into Hell's Canyon, the heart of a dark water.

JOHN NEAL WILLIAMS

Best Apple Pie

I learned the best apple pie
from grandma Josephine rolling dough
every Saturday using only butter and
refrigerated water to flake crusts
around pared and peeled apples
sprinkled with the only spice
her cupboard held   cinnamon
drenched apples and bracing second crusts
eaten every Sunday after services
by uncles and cousins enough
to add leaves to the table and
sending children around cardtables
to living rooms waiting on adults
and dessert with never any left-overs

and I continue tradition every year
at fair time baking pies for
that golden apple "best of fair" trophy
with my name spelled correctly
on the reader board
so everyone will know and remember
a boy grown man can bake the county's
best apple pie

Ten years I've entered
thirty years of practice and her patience
only to come in second each time
reading judged comments of too much
cinnamon   I don't understand too much
cinnamon when that is the only spice i've ever
known to taste and grandpa never said
too much cinnamon when he ate that first slice
of Sunday's dessert his bride had set aside lovingly.

"Winter Sun" by Dennis DeFoggi, oil on canvas, 24" x 20," 2018.

NANCY TAKACS

Remnants

After saying our rosaries at early Mass,
some Saturdays Aunt Ginny and I
took the hour-long bus ride
to Manhattan's garment district.

I'd help her sort
through messy bins, pick out
yard or two of paisley challis,
a piece of shimmering shantung
she found alluring.

Single, prim, devout,
she was so good
at her own designs
and invisible seams,
she became loose with pleasure
as our palms felt the prickles
of weave, our wrists the feathers
of selvage.

Over our arms
we hung watered silks
and sheer chiffons
she would conjure
into blouses for herself,
my mother, and me.

Here was where
I learned about luxury
for almost nothing, how to eye
the sharp store owner,
and bargain
bitterly
for whatever I love.

Why I Became Black Dragon Canyon

I needed the spit of crow-wings,
a heron flapping in tree-pose on my shoulder,
a cougar on alert under my pinyons.
I needed sun to scheme through my bodies,
the beige earth of my openings,
the wind to sheer off chips of me,
then amethyst my bones.
I wanted to be carved out of aimlessness.
I needed my other side to finally
shadow me, shuck me, as I waited
in silence for the manna
of planets, the icy blossoms of stars.
I needed paintbrush and mallow
to whisk up through my toes.
I wanted a waterfall for grasses
to thicken: be green, then go gray
at my knees. I needed to let my faces
become varnished persimmon.
I needed that juniper to touch me.
I wanted to drink rain
from my own stones.

JOHN D. LEE

[My father's father fought in WWII—]
An excerpt from IN/Desiderata, *a long poem in-progress*

1.

My father's father fought in WWII—
saw the bodies line
the Battle of the Bulge
& may have helped to put some there

he must've known
the smells of toxic gas   the unwashed bodies—
heard the bombers' engines echoed
in the muddy groans of not-yet-corpses—

he must've known the klaxon wail   the Luger snick
        the Granatwerfer mortar thump—
the stomachwrench of silence—
he never talked of these

but we know he knew the child
who dreamslept in his Texas wife—
who would be there living
if he made it home

we know this
because we kept his letters—
ink   sweat   hope
on military-issue yellowed paper—

but there are gaps between his hope   his terror
because the censors opened every letter—
cut out words   phrases—
his letters looked like inverse target practice sheets—

he made it back—
lived another forty years—
just long enough
to see his grandson

& in between
he ran a high school—
taught the kids back home
            what it means to be at war

in the end
cancer cut its holes through lung   liver—
left behind
a shredded leaden soldier

but the dreamsleep child
he waited for lived on—
grew   wed   had a son

2.

The battlefields
have healed of course—
nature threw her skirt
across her scars

the grass grew back
the seeds erupted into tree   into flower
& the soldierblood that spilled
sank into the ground   fed the roots

Omaha & Utah beaches—
like any beach—
have bikinied tourists who lie on laundered towels
            & mince across the seawashed rocks

in the Ardennes
the rubble piles were cleared away—
used to build the steeples
that point the way to Sunday morning prayer

we've concealed our scars so well
        that all those who've seen the damage are dying

but wreckage has a way of rising—
so decades later
a woman planting flowers in her garden
unearths an unspent hand grenade
or a city drains a swamp for land
& finds the remnants of a tank

& though it doesn't often happen
sometimes what comes crawling back
curled around its splinted bones
is us

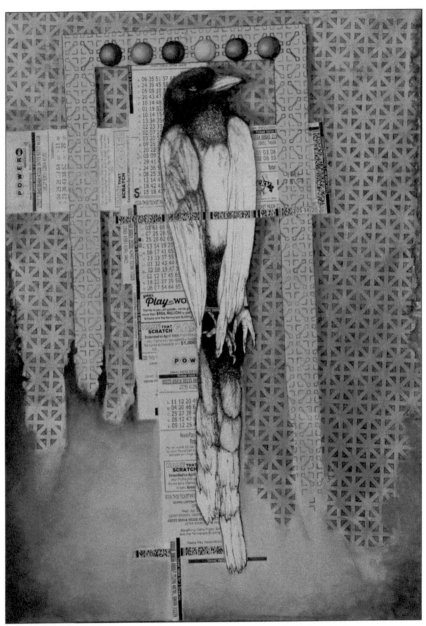

"Lottery" by Rod Burks, mixed media paper on panel, 17" x 24."

PETER ANDERSON

Well

Author's Note: The following excerpt is the opening sequence of a novella called Well. The novella traces the last days of an eastern born and bred man as he prepares for his death in a small Idaho town. The story is part of a group of novellas, collectively called The Spring Quartet, *set in the fictional farm town of Spring, Idaho.*

I t rolled into my hands with a cascade of floury chips and loam pouring through my fingers. I dropped the heavy pickaxe and clutched at the object as it slid, flashing from my first perception, a small glacial rock, to my second. As it tumbled, an image flickered across, the image of a face. I caught the object in my hands. I hefted its lighter-than-expected weight and rotated it slowly. There, eye sockets, and cheekbones, and a row of soil-roughened teeth. The reluctant fact: this thing in my hands was a skull.

At first, as a startled person does, I sought tangents of possibility: it was the skull of an animal, a cougar or bear or sheep or some other such round-headed creature; it was a fragment of a dinosaur, one of the multitude which wandered vast expanses of Pleistocene marsh, whose fossils emerge in the peeling shale and sandstone of the buttes; it wasn't a skull at all but a carving or a remarkable yet randomly-formed piece of bleached tree root or pale pahoehoe. But no, the shape was too familiar, too obvious, though I had never actually held a skull in my hands. All those images from film and books blurred into the solitary truth. This had been someone's head.

I hefted the skull above my eyes. Sand poured from the openings in cool, soft streams over my arm. As it drained, it lightened. I shook it eggshell gently and final pebbles rattled and escaped through the nasal conchae and orbital sockets.

Emery-board surfaces along switchblade cheekbones and wide eye-sockets caught my fingerprints. I held the skull at arms' length directly before my face to study, to introduce myself. A glare returned. Perhaps the annoyance of disturbance. The forehead was not tall. The teeth were not good. I ran gentle touches over mastoid ridges and sphenoid hollows.

I set the skull on the left extremity of the pit I had dug. Here, up a sloping gully from a dry meadow, in the lee of a billow of willows I had begun a hole into the earth, an exploration for water. Above, a black forehead of old lava rock cleft into hexagonal piles hung under the long ridgeline. The willows implied a spring, though no honest water showed in this meandering, earthy fissure between the hills. Coolness emanated from the spot, a scent, clean as a breeze when I climbed the sandy alluvium from my tall, unfinished log house, shining in its sagey hollow out on the flats.

I'd built my house of hewn and hand-peeled Douglas fir logs over the past two years on the ashes of a homesteader's cabin. The house was the terminus of my work, my final goal.

The house had its own well, of course, a sump sunk one hundred and eighty feet into the old sand and lava. But if I found a spring up this draw, I would dig a shallow well here, too. This hand-well would bring icy water from the shoulders of the mountains to the gardens of my house, in my chosen, narrow margin of the west where no one ever visits. Nor would I care to have visitors.

Though the blazing wreckage of August hung over the valley of the great river, I had begun to dig here in the destroyed old earth. I leaned into my shovel and pickaxe.

And then, on this morning, it broke loose and rolled into my groping hands, a small awakening, the object which now sat, propped on flat stones, on the rim of my waist-deep excavation.

The skull had loosened as I'd excavated into a flat, mulchy area the size of a dinner table below the bushes. It had been buried shallowly, lazily. Now, I dug further into the light, gritty soil with my hands, clearing down through layers, an inch at a time. I used one of my leather gloves as a brush when I came to more traces of bone.

Sand fell away in stuttering streams. Here were ribs, and a curve of winged vertebrae, paired ulna and radius still clinging, phalanges like pebbles and sticks, palm-like scapulas. Patches of fabric, blackened and sere in the alkaline soil, emerged around the edges.

The body lay head downhill. It lay shallower than the dense roots of the willows.

Under my fingers, the moose-antler pelvis emerged wrapped in the stiff, crusty band of a leather belt. The buckle of the belt was brass, and black, a plain, brass disk, with no markings.

The lower jaw, dis-attached from the skull, lay stuck in a glue of grit across the breastbone. I tugged at it gently. With a light clatter, clavicles and handfuls of ribs fell into the pit below. Startled anew, I dropped the mandible, and it clicked into the pit also, flickering a couple of gold teeth in the sunshine. I lunged to stop the flow of sand with my hands. The hole's upper edge gave and collapsed. Half of the person remained stuck in the earth uphill. Cool sand and bones rustled into a knee-deep pile around my legs where I stood in the shallow pit of my well.

I remained thus for several minutes, thought-bound. Why here in this odd place, protected from the outwash and winds by this leaning, matted mausoleum of willows? Then too, I wondered whom to tell. The local sheriff seemed not the right choice, him with his hip-slung radio and gun, shouting and shaking his pinched and crudely-cropped head, his thermos of reeky soup, his enormous Bronco with outsized tires and antennae and rack-lights. But someone needed to be shown what I had found.

I couldn't leave the body in two halves as it now lay, one half exposed in the sediments uphill and the other jumbled in the hole. So, I pulled at the bones in the earth above. I scraped away the sand. The bones came gradually free, femurs and tibias and fibulas, and finally a pair of shrunken black boots wearing rusted spurs and filled with tiny foot bones. I brushed ever so gently and the bones in their blankets of pale sand cascaded gently into the hole. The lower half rejoined the upper.

I picked and shoveled at the earth I'd previously dug from my well and tamped it down over the pile of remains. I hoped to stave coyotes and ravens. I set the jawless skull carefully aside. This I would take with me. I skidded several flat rocks down from the embankments right and left into the flattened area to protect the sandy soil from the sawing wind.

The clumps of living bushes, with a pile of rocks at their feet, bore now the aspect of a wilderness chapel.

With the skull in one hand, I shouldered the pick and the shovel with the other and started down the broadening alluvial fan, through

the sedges and grasses, into the deep sage beyond, under the limit-
lessness of that basin of sky. And as I walked, a feeling of certainty
welled up in me, that kind of knowing which can spring from lack of
fact. I trod slowly, meandering, among the sage, a pallbearer's pace.
I tried to remember. I cast aside recent memory for ancient, as sometimes happens in episodes of emotional disquiet. In this reverie between
fragments of old memories and the prosaic tableau of the new, I grappled
with this odd feeling of certainty, sureness. I thought I had last known
that feeling as a child.

But that wasn't quite true.

For only a few days earlier, Otto Bottom came running to me.
He had barreled up the dusted two-track ruts toward my house in his
leaning, once-white Chevy truck. I stood in the bony grasshopper front
yard of my house in my jeans, shirtless and slick with sweat, resting
against the handle of an axe among heaps of fresh-split ponderosa.
An honest August sun like a molten anvil hung above the land and the
dust-coated cottonwoods and my pile of ponderosa, some split and
shining and some only blocked and waiting.

The roar of Otto's truck growing from afar up the valley. As he
closed the distance, his incomprehensible yelling rose, Otto leaning out
the window of his bouncing truck and waving an arm. He had burst
suddenly into the enormity of afternoon cicada-song quiet in which
I stood with my down-turned axe.

His truck banged across the cattle guard and into my yard and he
came spilling out, galumphing and shouting toward me.

"Help," he called out to me as he approached. "Help me, Will.
Help me." I dropped the axe into the woodchips where its polished
head became a small sun. "My daughter Lila's having a baby, I think."
He gasped. His thick body heaved.

I rode with Otto back down the valley toward his small cluster of
dilapidated buildings two miles distant. Otto and his daughter were my
nearest neighbors. We swung up to his farm and I leapt out while we
were still rolling. From the driver's seat, he called after me, "She's in
the barn."

There I found her. Gold-streaked blades of light sliced the
splintered roof, angled through rafters and touched the floor just to

her bare feet. She hunched in deep shadow beside the stall of a cow. She lay in a wallow of fetid straw. Remnants of her dress encircled her waist; her knees were drawn up; her broad kneecaps touched at the ends of big, blood-spattered white thighs.

In her arms, against her chest, lay a small, red baby.

I reached to the baby. The girl shook with fright and pain. But under my palms I could feel its tiny stir.

I asked Lila a question or two. Her broad face gazed back at me, unmoving and soft. I had only spoken to Lila once in the past when I stopped by Otto's farm to drop off a jack he'd asked to borrow. She hadn't responded to me then, either. Her face now amplified the vague bewilderment and fear I'd received then.

"Are you bleeding?" I glanced quickly between the legs of this woman. The baby was still connected to a mess of placenta she covered with her legs as if in embarrassment.

"Don't worry," I said, "Be calm." Lila had gazed down at the baby and then up at me with her udder-like, haloed face as if to say, Look!

I drew out my pocket knife. I glanced around and saw a piece of baling twine nearby. I tied off the slippery umbilical cord a foot from the baby and then cut it with my knife. Lila made a noise as she watched me cut the cord, a noise of protectiveness. Sitting there in the shadows, holding her baby, her eyes shone, black, wide, animalistic.

Otto came into the doorway at that moment gasping and phlegmy. He stood in the entrance of the small barn, blocking much of the light, casting his long shadow down the cracked and tilting concrete floor, his storm-tossed hair clawing. He lifted his cap and wiped his head.

"Did you call the paramedics?" I asked, but he only stared at me with his throbbing face. Saliva strung from his lips between gummed and gapped teeth.

I ducked past him to the house and called and then hunted through the shambles and rubbish in the kitchen for towels. I drew a bent pan full of water from the corroded faucet. Sloshing water from the pan, I ran back into the barn, past Otto still standing in the doorway, and gave Lila a drink. With one of the towels, I gently washed parts of her quivering body. I dabbed at the mucous and cow manure on the baby. The baby flexed its tiny ruby limbs and hands.

Then Otto spoke over my shoulder.

"I didn't know about it. I just came out and here she was. I never even knew she was pregnant. I don't know how it could've happened. She just snuck in here and did it."

He broke free of the threshold and walked up and down the floor of the barn, tugging at the straps of his overalls. Manure dust rose around his feet. "I guess I better go outside and pray," he said at last, and stepped out into the sunshine.

Lila's fear-filled eyes followed him, tugged from her baby to his outline in the wavering heat. Her father's presence clearly terrified the girl. Her face fell blank and she stared. She shook. I washed her face with cool water and touched the body of her baby, its blood-streaked face. I drew the edge of her dress over her knees. I sat with her in the old straw on the floor of the barn for long minutes until at last across her eyes had risen again some lighter expression.

I rose and moved to the door of the barn. Otto stood now near a corral. I entered the burden of the sunshine and came to stand beside him. He said nothing for a while; he scuffed one foot in the manure on the ground.

I listened and watched across the long, dusty distances for the sound of an ambulance coming from town. Only the sound of the cicadas and Otto's scuffling foot rose to us.

He spoke at last. "I didn't know she was going to have a baby," Otto said. And then he added, "Jesus won't like this" as if he and some form of deity were both gazing, arms folded disapprovingly, at the girl hunched in the barn.

The two of us leaned against the rail fence ovalling the corral. His bulk had ceased shaking. He now only sweated. Each of us stood with our forearms on the uppermost rail and one foot resting on the lowermost. Our shadows lay before us like x-rays on the ground.

"Why did this have to happen?" he asked. Though perhaps a question, the tone was declarative, and bore finality.

"I don't know," I said, after considering.

"Why does it have to be this way?" he asked, unhearing, feldspar eyes swerving again and again to the barn to our right and its dark open doorway. "Why didn't she tell me anything about it? Why did she have to keep it a secret? Cause you know," he said looking into my face for the first time with his close-set eyes widened under the brim of his cap, "it's a sin for people to keep secrets."

I reached a hand to this man. I patted his shoulder lightly, briefly, touching him though I understood the lying.

The two of us there waiting under the transfiguring sun; a third and fourth waited in the stinking heat and shadow of the barn, each of us alone, all of us together. We waited for small town help which never seemed to come.

"I don't think that's true, Otto," I said. An eon passed. "I don't think that's true at all." ∎

"Seven" by Mike Woods, mixed media, 33" x 41."

SHAUN T. GRIFFIN

Driving into the Rainbow

hard wind, rain in the
creosote bushes—the
long climb into the Sierra,
and my mother, alone
in her room with Ida and Rod,
caretakers whose care
cannot undo the weakened heart,

how she holds her cold,
thin hands to mine
and moves the pale
light in her window,
the brief respite in the
rain, family on her bed,
this small uniform of
grief attends her now—

reticulate,
in the failing hour
as I leave for this highway
into the high desert,
snow at the window, my
wife trying to drive
the icy black—what we
tell ourselves to return:

the fluorescent arc will
follow to the other side.

After the Election in the Desert South of Hawthorne

Almost to the iridescent bloom of the Wild Cat Ranch,
a red Chevy out front like a rose in the dust,
and farther still, the snow on Boundary Peak
cuts the horizon from earth. Would you lie with her?
I ask myself, with no answer but the sullen pose of monogamy.

November, post-election, in these few hours of caramel light,
and what of us in this fresco of burnt color, of the woman
in the trailer, hidden like an outpost of affection?

The cold hands of morning reach to still the darkness.
On the road edge, the last moisture frozen before dawn,
staring into the mouth of tomorrow, each mountain,
a light of sage, devil's breath, and salt bush.

Crossing into Esmeralda County, I leave her in the mirror.
The frost remains, but as Patchen asked, is it enough?
A crow answers at Redlich Summit, and I descend
into nothingness, somehow reminded of the brown country below.
I will name it for her, burnished daughter of paradise.

Today a senator said all we need is a gun, a horse, and
a plain to ride—whose legs have been parted now?
It's almost make-believe until I understand
the desert is a place where rocks cry and a
woman bleeds in the palm of what is left behind.

O. ALAN WELTZIEN

Hold Me

Alec, four, capers as we enter
the old folks home, find our
way to my step-grandmother's
semi-private room where he

bounces while the roommate
gestures for me to clutch then
empty her piss bag. I soothe
feeble Gram Barb with

platitudes as Alec,
bright smile, stretches the dull
room beyond its flimsy privacy
curtains. After his quick hug

we retreat to the lobby,
walkers and wheelchairs
in random assortment
that occasionally shift as do

limbs, jaws or eyes. When Alec
passes out of my clasp, eyes
draw close, moths to small
flame, and desire reaches stilled

arms as though hands touch
his warm skin and active limbs.
They yearn to hug him and remember
the surge of skin on skin.

Tumbling with Sons

When they were toddlers
a decade apart both sons
waited to "wrestle" with me
so I lay on the floor
and they crawled over me
and I extended my legs or arms
or tossed them up until I
couldn't and we kneeled
and bumped and I rode them
around the room, bucked
and jerked, and they hooted
and giggled. And asked
for more until they trudged
off to "play adventures."
Soon enough in their
lengthening they no longer
asked and sometimes I
remember our entwined
bodies, their hot skin
on mine, and I know
this is as good as it gets.

MARGARET KOGER

The Hike

In the Great Basin National Park
I stand at the foot of Wheeler Peak
where ancient bristlecones survive
on glacial moraines 10,000' up

my feet aching from the climb

fingers tracing striated limbs
solid beneath a blazing sun
where the dense wood shuns
insects, fungi, rot, fires. disease
and sub-zero nights

killers all for me—

minor gods who grow no rings
in years of extreme weather
mates to the howling wind
their claw-like scales on cones
ready to guard seeds for saplings
ready for another 5,000 years.

Drink Starlight

Light pours down the Big Dipper—
Ursa Major. Stars of the great
she-bear's flank trace the bowl,
stars of the dipper's handle ready

to your command as you come
thirsty through the night to the well
grasping the long-handled dipper
from the nail beside the cistern.

Hold the cup beneath the spout
lever the pump arm up down
and as the cold water gushes
catch a splash before the rest
pools in the pail.

Raise the dipper to your lips
drink starlight, clean and spare.

Peer into the pail below
starlight, crystal white:
the bear stars rippling kiss.

GARY GILDNER

Stormy

eremy when he was younger loved being a Boy Scout. Loved being in the woods, even when he got wet. But here's the truth: he never liked shooting a gun. Didn't even like touching one. He could put up our tent in the dark. I was not surprised he was seeing Breeze. She saw lots of men. She never said *dated*. "I am dating Jeremy now." No, never said anything like that about any of them. Ezra, Adam, Tad. And then Jeremy. Who didn't fit our game. Ezra, Adam, and Tad almost always spelled *eat, ate* or *tea*, depending on the order they came knocking. Jeremy messed that up.

The first time he kissed me was behind the trailer. He was setting up the hibachi for Breeze. I was all sweaty from running. I love to run. "You taste like cherry cough drops," I said. He laughed. Jeremy could laugh. I wasn't sure about being kissed like that. But I sure enjoyed hearing him laugh. So did Breeze, who thought he was crazy, but in a funny way.

No, I was not present when he said he asked Breeze about taking me camping. I was out running. But one night in our tent when I asked what did she say about me going with him he said, "You know Breeze." Well, I guess I did know her. Still, that was not an answer to my question. I may have been only fourteen. That didn't mean I had to be treated like a kid. I was almost fifteen. In fact I turned fifteen the day we first suspected we were being followed. Jeremy said, "Happy birthday, Stormy, that's a cop chopper over yonder." Then he laughed.

Okay, I realize people thought Jeremy was missing one or two screws. Take his laugh. I know now, after talking with all these experts, that it was partly nervousness, partly a way of saying *that's the way she goes* or *oh well*, and partly his way of punctuating a sentence. The rest was confusion. He was not an idiot. I said no, I did not want to get married and he right away said, "Hey, I understand." Had nothing to do with me being taller.

Of course Jeremy and I were running away. "Being scarce," as Ezra liked to say. I really thought Breeze would accept Ezra's offer to come live in his big house by the ocean, me included. She'd open a can of V-8 juice, pour some in my glass, the rest in hers, plus a shot of vodka, and we'd talk about it. We'd each have our own room to decorate as we wanted. Breeze liked purple. I really didn't care for that color all around me—plus on the ceiling. She said she couldn't help it, she was a fool. Said it went back to her childhood, liking that particular shade because other people *didn't* like it. For a whole room. She was raised in one of those personal conversion churches. Pacific View United Holy in Jesus. One of those.

"But nope," she decided. "Ezra for all his money is too lame." By lame she meant on the dull side. He knew almost nothing about music, for example. Once he brought me a CD of *oldies*. He put his hand over the front and said, "Guess who." I said, "Elvis?" "Oh, no," he said. "Jerry Lee Lewis?" "No, no," he said. Then he showed me the cover picture—it was a dude in a suit and granny glasses holding a *trombone*. Glenn Miller.

The crazy part was I came to kind of like Glenn Miller. Breeze said, "You are one weird kid."

"I like him at certain times," I said.

"Certain times," she said.

"When I have cramps."

"You mean the curse?"

"He calms me."

One of the craziest things I've ever done was head out for Ezra's house when the shooting was about to start. As if I could get all the way to California on foot from those Idaho mountains. He wasn't such a bad guy. And he could cook. Breeze couldn't cook anything except hardboiled eggs. Jeremy could cook too. Build his own fire, everything. I don't know about Adam or Tad. I didn't care for either one. They didn't care much about me, either. I thought they were zombies. I honestly don't know what Breeze saw in those two creeps. Other than drugs. And she was getting better. Doesn't make any sense.

Did I think it was strange that Breeze only wanted me to call her Breeze? I don't know. Maybe, at first. I guess I was around five, starting school. All these little kids hugging their mothers goodbye. Some saying, "Mommy, don't go. Don't go." Breeze took me aside, bent down to my level, and said, "Listen to me, Stormy. Never call me mommy, mother, or mom. I hate those names."

"What should I call you?"

"You know what my name is."

"Breeze."

"That's right. Breeze. Learn to spell it."

I did okay in school. All the way to eighth grade I received *Excellent* and *Pays Attention* and *Eager to Learn*. My letter grades were almost always A's, a few B's. I liked sitting up front and raising my hand and making a straight line and the hot lunch. I loved meatloaf and mashed potatoes. I never got meatloaf and mashed potatoes except at school and at Ezra's.

Jeremy said he loved school, too. One time a kid punched him in the nose, made it all bloody, and he never told. It was on the way to school. He didn't want to go back home and hear his mother scream. He ducked into a gas station bathroom and cleaned his face with water and stopped the bleeding with toilet paper.

In eighth grade I shot up like a thistle, as Breeze said, except I wasn't prickly like her. I did get her long legs. I was also a natural redhead, not that carrot color. And, to be honest, there was only one boy in my class who could run faster than me. Chester Boyle. But not much faster, and they all knew it, that's for sure.

Not counting my teachers, Ezra was first to compliment me on my running, and Jeremy was the last. He was still alive when I took off. I was going out to search for firewood and saw these men crouching down with guns. I just ran. Later, I remembered his last words to me. "It's going to be a pretty day, honey."

The conservation officer's wife was the first one I could talk to. Paige. I like that name. She was so pregnant. I said, "Are you having twins?" She gave me hot cocoa and a warm piece of apple pie fresh from the oven. She put a slice of cheddar cheese on top. I just couldn't talk to her husband about anything right away, but especially not about Jeremy. Paige said I was safe now. I drank the hot cocoa and finally stopped shivering. Then I ate the pie. She had a really nice smile.

"Yes, I *am* having twins!"

"Do you like Glenn Miller?" I asked her.

"Who is Glenn Miller?" she said.

We both had a laugh straightening that out. And twins. Wow. I don't recall every little thing that happened to me, but what I do remember is usually very clear. Jeremy could make pancakes and catch fish and clean up our campsite as if we'd never been there. That was the whole point, he said. Make it look like we'd never been there. "Why is it called the River of No Return Wilderness?" I asked him. He said everything needs a name. I thought to myself, Well, I would like to return to school. Then every so often, to tell the truth, I thought I would not mind staying in those mountains a long, long time. Maybe forever.

I thought about how I kept all my report cards from school in a shoebox. Breeze would look at them when I brought them home. "Well, well, well," she'd say, "aren't we the good little girl." Which sounded sarcastic, but I knew it wasn't. I wondered if she was okay. I wondered because of the way Jeremy would answer my questions. The closest he came to saying what I found out later was, "You don't want to live alone, do you?"

"What do you mean?"

"I'm the only one who cares about you now."

"What if I want to go back? I mean, sometime?"

"Just tell me when," he said.

Then we'd get busy putting up the tent or something. That conversation was early, in June. We had the whole summer. Late August, when school would start up again, was a ways off. I would be in ninth grade, in the high school building. The thought of that thrilled me and scared me a little.

I wished I had brought my shoebox. I trusted Breeze not to mess with it, but I did not trust Adam or Tad. They were so shifty. In the box I had three birthday cards with a silver dollar Scotch-taped inside each one, from my grandmother. I also had pictures of Breeze and me from when I was a baby. I don't know who took the pictures. When I asked Breeze she said, "Who remembers crap like that?" I had blue ribbons for winning races, all my report cards going back to kindergarten, and the two personal letters from Mrs. Groth, the principal, for being on the Honor Roll in both seventh and eighth grade. I only put the best stuff in my shoebox. I didn't care if Adam and Tad stole those silver dollars. Well, I did care. But if they messed with my other keepsakes I would be sick.

My grandmother moved around a lot. She had a white food truck and sold foot-long hotdogs out of it. Breeze said when you let down the long side window it made a shelf to hold the napkins and catsup and relish. Plus the cold drinks—Coke and stuff—from a cooler. "The Original Foot-Long Dog" their sign said. Breeze went with her and liked it. She never said so, exactly, but I could tell she did from her comments. At night they slept on cots inside the food truck. They traveled to county fairs mostly, sometimes to big parks by the ocean. But then Grandma made Breeze stay home with Harold and go to school. He was also the minister of their church. I don't think Breeze liked him. My grandmother sent me those silver dollars starting in fifth grade. Before then she didn't know where we were. "Here you go," Breeze would say, " a birthday present from Grace."

Jeremy and I were camping beside this beautiful lake inside the River of No Return Wilderness—Morehead Lake—when I thought about leaving my shoebox behind and wondering about Breeze. If she was okay or what. Jeremy gave me a pretty gold ring with a gold heart on it for my birthday. But it was a little bit loose and I was afraid it would slip off when I wasn't paying attention. I thought I'd better put it in my shoebox as soon as I could. Then all those other thoughts happened, like they do.

We actually circled back to Morehead Lake three times, because we liked it so much. Also it was easier to pitch a tent there than on the side of a mountain. And we could catch such beautiful trout. But looking at that really blue lake, I'd suddenly wonder about Breeze. It was our second time there when I said, "Is Breeze okay?"

Jeremy just shook his head.

"What does that mean?" I said.

"I don't know."

"What did you mean when you said, before, that you were the only one who cared about me now?" I was thinking about her, Jeremy, Adam, and Tad all being in the trailer at the same time. Jeremy didn't care for Adam and Tad either.

"I really do not want to talk about Breeze," he said. "Or her friends. They have not been nice to you or to me lately. Have they?"

"Maybe not."

Jeremy, as I said, was shorter than me. Shorter than everybody. Adam and Tad made fun of his health problems. How his eyes could water, and his heart get to racing. Which was why he never made Eagle Scout. Also, his parents babied him. He even said so. He hated being babied.

He wasn't weak, though. He broke off the biggest branches when we covered up the car. So no one could easily spot it and maybe steal it.

I hadn't said goodbye to Breeze because Adam and Tad were at the trailer. I knew that and I did not want to see them. Jeremy said he had to see her regardless. I asked him to pick up my jean jacket then. Yes, I was mad at her, it was not a secret. For letting Adam and Tad come over after she promised me, "No more. I'm clean and I'm staying clean."

She'd better. Or she'd lose another good job. She flipped off I don't know how many. One thing about Breeze, though, she could walk away from one good job—or be fired—and walk straight into another one. I know Ezra spoke up for her, a lot, but she was also very personable when she wanted something. And her looks didn't hurt. She could have been a twin for the actress who played in *Baby Doll*. Ezra got a copy of that movie so we could watch it when he had us over. I watched it with them maybe twice. They seemed to love it. I thought it was okay.

I cried in front of everybody when I learned what had happened, which was unusual for me.

We were planning to go somewhere that weekend, to get away from San Diego and Breeze and her druggie friends. But not way up to Idaho. We kept driving, though, and whenever Jeremy said should we see what was next up the road, I said why not? Made kind of a game out of it. Then we stopped at a good place to put up his tent and built a fire and that was fun. So we did it again the following night farther up the road. We'd stop at a Walmart or some other big store and load up on jerky and apples and energy bars, also hot dogs, which I liked to cook over a fire. Before I knew it we were in the middle of all these tall trees.

Paige and her husband Jake offered to let me sleep in their extra bedroom until I felt better. At first I said no, I needed to get ready for school starting up soon. Then we talked and I decided to stay. Paige was nice. Jake was too. They were going to have girls. They were planning to name them Margaret, after Paige's mother, and Jane, after his mother. Paige had a college degree from the University of Montana. She was actually younger than Breeze. It's too bad Breeze didn't have a friend like

Paige. Or at least one woman friend. Jake graduated from the
U of Wisconsin. Both majored in Forestry. Which is how they met
later, working in the woods. That's so cool. I wondered where I would
go to college.

I also wondered where Jeremy went finally. I honestly was not
interested in Adam or Tad. If that sounds mean, then I'm a mean
person. Was Jeremy buried? Cremated? I tried calling his parents,
but all I ever got was a recording to leave a message. I left three
messages and gave up. Grandma said maybe I was lucky not to know.
I could make up my own ending, she said. I don't want to make up my
own ending. I know where Breeze is buried, and when I leave her, after
visiting, and go for a run, or to the library, or come home, nothing is
made up. I mean that was my routine when I lived with Grandma and
finished high school. She has a small stone that says: *Ruth Ann (Breeze)
Monday 1981-2013. She was loved.* ■

"Listening to Mondrian" by Janet Wormser, oil on canvas, 12" x 16."

BARON WORMSER

The Bodyguard

He—it is a largely male occupation—spends a lot of time
Waiting in cars where under the pale
Interior light he reads long novels by women.

His boss, a quiet preoccupied executive,
Has never asked him a question about himself
As a human being.

That is okay.

His feelings are not hurt.

He is free to move from one page to another
Like a snail or beetle.
His admittedly pudgy fingers meditatively
Considering the textures of time.

Women give it away, he was told by other men
And in the novels there is
A scrap of truth to that saying.
Things are said about longings and confusions
That did not have to be said,
That could have stayed in the bureau drawer
With the hairbrushes, lotions and scarves.

He lifts weights, goes for long walks
With Gus, his Golden Retriever, has been dating a woman
For three years.

They circle around one another
Like fish, then they hunger, then they circle again.

Out in the distance someone is ready to kill his boss.

He must be ready to die and thinks about it now and then
While idling at a light
Or starting up the car in the morning.

Is that what men know?

He wants to ask his lover
What she thinks but is ashamed.

He consults another page.
A woman in an apartment is shouting
Into a telephone after a man has hung up.

Time for his boss to be leaving the building.

The bodyguard exhales.

His breath lingers in the air,
Palpable as a plum or a peach.

He dreams about unwariness and he
Wants to embrace her.

BOB BUSHNELL

?s

who is the i in me?
what is the o! of u?
u suit me 2 a t.
r 2 of u a w?

i m bluer than the c,
what m i 2 do?
where m i 2 b,
if i cannot b with u?

Icarus' Brother

Recently returned
from our quest
to the rising sun,
I am the one
who turned back,
who feared to test
the limits of the wax,
who will never know
how close Icarus
came to the sun,
and whose name
will be forgotten.

Midnight

. . . and I wake
to the clatter of a skateboard
as it click-clacks over cracks
in the hollow alley,
the same rhythm
the night train made
on nearby tracks
when I was a boy,
listening from my bed,
staring at the ceiling,
yearning for adventure.

I hear my son's key
in our backdoor.

He's late, of course,
and I should be angry,
but I lie still,
hoping to hear
the whistle.

SAMUEL GREEN

Unexploded Ordinance

for Mona Lydon-Rochelle

> "We must learn to live with bombs
> Shaking the sky
> And the heavy smell of gunpowder . . ."
> —Duc Thanh, Soldier Poet

We grew up on the March of Dimes, the president's face
on a ten-cent piece, the threat of polio real as the braces
on a classmate's legs, the cost of a carton of milk.

My mother pasted Easter Seals on cards
& letters, bought red paper poppies outside
the supermarket door. On white cane days

we threw our pennies into buckets for the blind,
or the bell-ringers at Christmas, brought canned
food to school for the holiday poor.

1.
My father's mother sold her extra milk & butter,
eggs, old hens for the pot. She kept her
coins in baskets or empty Folgers cans. Each
month she made a count & set aside a share
for Father Flanagan's boys. Another
portion went to needy kids in Ecuador.
A neighbor helped her buy the money orders.
It wasn't that she practiced what she preached,
because she wouldn't preach to anyone.
There was a Boys Town calendar on the wall
beside her phone. Photos of Maria, Rosa, Juan
arrived in letters with exotic stamps on frail
paper. For herself, she made do, got by
with little. If asked, she'd say she was just fine. OK.

2.
It's nineteen sixty-nine, the DMZ
at Cua Viet, & I am knocked to the deck
of my ship's signal bridge by shock
waves from the battleship *New Jersey,*
half her guns engaged & sending shells
in-country more than twenty miles
to cool down a landing zone, stop
an enemy mortar team, maybe keep
a recon squad alive. Not one man
on a gun crew would think about
a live round waiting in the dirt
for more than forty years. And me? My hand
dropped a hundred grenades over the ship's side
into the river at Cat Lo. They didn't all explode.

3.
In Quang Tri the school kids study a new
three Rs. *Recognize*, they chant,
& run through the roster of UXOs: 'bombies,'
mortars & mines, artillery shells, grenades,
old ammo. They learn to read shapes, what hides
in rust, a pile of stones or the laced roots of trees.
Retreat, they say, meaning go back, don't
touch, watch each foot, don't squat to view
it closer. The weight of a spider could set
it off. Just call their friends & go, get
an adult & *Report*, tell someone, right now,
what doesn't add up. They already need to know
the ways of thirty-seven poisonous snakes,
as well. Their daily world is a dangerous place.

4.
Cluster shells are the worst. They came
in metal pods that opened in the air,
six hundred metal spheres the size

of softballs, each a separate bomb
designed to rupture, pierce, shred, tear
up anything soft, whatever grew, grazed,
flew, crawled, ran or simply stopped
in place. Sometimes when they dropped
they didn't open, buried themselves deep
in the ground, got caught up on limbs
or smothered under elephant grass, became
a nest of metal lumps, corroded, fused in a heap
you might pass safely year by year by year,
until–one lightest step–they do what they were made for.

5.
Yes, there was a loan arranged by Commune Worker
Nhi to buy two pigs for Mrs. Thi, whose leg a mine
blew off, whose husband died, whose only daughter
had to work, whose two grandkids can finally go
to school. And yes, it's true that Dang Van Han,
who nicked the skin of a mine in his field with a hoe,
can tend his crops of peanuts & peppers with much less
hurt. Ms. Nhi set him up with a surgeon. And, yes,
it's a fact that now Le Huong has two cows to help support
his family, new skills to manage pain from yet
another hidden mine. But, listen, this is also true:
Young Le Quynh Nhi was first to sit with a cup of tea
steeped from lemongrass & say, *I want to hear you
share your story. Sister, Brother, there is time. Tell me.*

6.
Simon tells his late-night AA group he thought
he saw his best friend waiting for a red light
to change, & a charge went off in his own chest:
fifty years, but his buddy Lee from boot was still a kid,
eighteen, eyes full of boogie, restless
fingers tapping the steering wheel, head
shaking a little to a beat–some 'sixties tune,

no doubt—as though he hadn't put his big foot down
on a homemade mine, right leg off above the knee;
as though the corpsman stopped the blood & Lee
was on a chopper *di di mau* & safe. Because there he
was, man, rolling down the window of a cherry
red car, lobbing change toward the held-up paper plate
on which Simon had scrawled: *Please Help a Vet.*

The same small village blacksmith who takes the steel
shards of shells & bombs to forge a hoe or batter out
a cow bell in a shower of sparks on a homemade anvil,

can also conjure a monk's begging bowl. It takes eight
strips of scrap steel cut & pounded together with heat,
a copper & herb paste melted to seal the seams, twenty

thousand hammer blows for the final shape. Imagine it
done, held before the poorest of the poor in silent asking,
& how a single grain of rice might make the metal ring

Shoveling the Outhouse on Gary Snyder's Birthday

"Light that shines on dung
is not part of the dung."
—Rumi

Because we pour our piss in the compost,
there's only the smell of must & damp
stove ash from a thousand fires. Everything

is dry. I built hinges into the floor,
so it lifts with only a little scraping. When light
angles in, spiders the size of a fingertip wake

from their daily practice & find whatever cracks
they can in the cedar shakes, or simply curl back
into themselves & wait. The shovel is an old one,

long-handled hickory slick with a coat
of linseed oil, the blade a little bright
at its tip. In two hours, ten wheelbarrows

of song-bird phrases, owl calls, the smoky flourishes
of breath on frosted mornings, go to fill a bowl
in the ground near a rotted nurse log, shades

of brown, black & gray combed & leveled, nothing
like the patterns a monk might make with a kumade,
a wood-tined rake, no cloud patterns, no currents

of sea or wind-wiped lake. Star flowers there
next spring, heal-all, fringecup & another two years
of space to use & leave the self behind

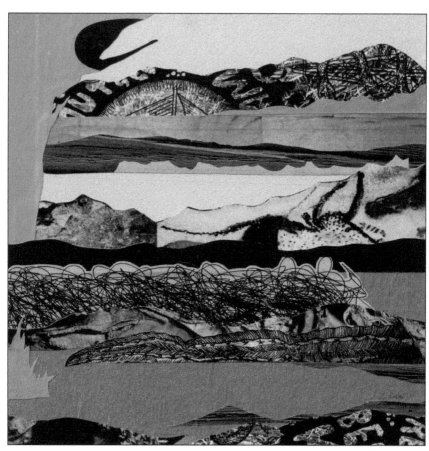

"Chaco Canyon" by Lorelle Rau, cut paper on panel, 12" x 12," 2013.

JAY JOHNSON

Roadhouse

H is firm grasp on the steering wheel did not explain all the tension through his neck and shoulders. Mike Smithson concentrated on the curves of Highway 14 and headed to the roadhouse at Garnet Creek. It was a night designed for black ice, and the highway was unforgiving. His Ram was set up for winter, tires changed over, but confidence would be a killer here, and fear could be a life-saver. He could see the trails of the anti-icing liquid on the blacktop. The county road boys had been picking up some overtime that evening. His brow furrowed, he examined the road almost fiercely.

Mike Smithson knew it was too late, and he was too tired and too lonely. The house was going to be cold for hours, and he didn't feel like going home to fire up the two wood stoves that had once seemed practical and romantic, warmth from the nearby fruits of the earth. He wanted the comfort of a warm hearth, the comfort of a warm bed and a bedmate. He was proceeding, and he wished he were receding. He sensed his tension, so he breathed deeply and forced relaxation, but that crept away quickly.

None of the newness of youth would welcome him at Camilla's Place. Young people, maybe, but they would be a generation away from what was new when he was young. There might be the warmth of people he had seen before, warmth of whiskey, and even a fire at a real hearth. Nice. The Ram eased through the final S-curves of the river-tracking grade, and the old neon was still lit, Camilla's Place. Camilla herself had passed on years before, the neon sign had failed, and a new owner found an artist a hundred and twenty miles away in Camp Joseph who could duplicate it, and re-charge and fire up the sign. Camilla's was still lighting up the night. The orange-red glow of the sign reflected off snowbanks.

Friday night in the country, out in the county. The computerized jukebox would still take money rather than a plastic card, and there would be a few loggers and a couple of cowboys and maybe a couple of Nez Perce, and a half-dozen women with their men out on a date, dinner at the roadhouse—a grilled steak and a Washington red wine.

He coasted into a parking spot and rested in his seat for a couple of minutes. What was this all about? He had done this many time before, he was well-practiced. There was nothing that this would improve. He set the brake and got out, left his briefcase inside and did not lock the cab.

When she was seventeen, looking like she was twenty-four, his Sweet Pea had defied him and gone to work out here at Camilla's. She was too young to legally serve drinks, but it was too far and out of the way for such a law to be enforced. Too long ago. Penelope Smithson, smart and saucy and too damn confident for a woman that young, had decided she wanted a job, after school and into the evening, and he had said no, for what precise reason he did not know, but he knew the roads were bad in the winter and the seasonal help in the kitchen was sketchy, and the loggers would flirt roughly with her and not give a damn who her daddy was, and she wanted something that wasn't just ordinary stay-at-home and didn't want to deal with dopey dad. She had seemed to do just fine, despite the later and later nights. He had suspected the kitchen help brought the drugs, enticed her, and she embraced the whole scene. She survived that bar, back then. Penny graduated, moved on to nursing school, moved on to two bigger towns before she got popped for pinching her patients' meds. She never looked back to when she was seventeen, and he found it difficult to look forward again.

He walked to the door and entered.

Inside, a fire burned in the big circular fireplace in the center of the room. To the left stood a little raised stage area that had not been used in the twenty years he had patronized the joint. Enough light to see, sconces all around. The bar filled the far right wall. As he approached, he recognized two men, apart from each other. Ronnie Lodge sat on a barstool; he was a former client who once long ago had been sentenced by Judge Gordon, who was sitting alone at a two-person table. Smithson would not have crossed the street to say hello to either of them. Gordon saw him and seemed to look through him. Ronnie Lodge looked him up and down and beckoned him over with a nod of his head. Smithson waved limply at Gordon and walked over to Lodge. They shook hands, and Lodge introduced Smithson to his date, Jillene.

"So, Mike. Okay if I call you Mike?" he asked.

"Yeah. Call me anything you want. I'm okay with anything," Smithson replied.

"What's the matter? You look like you lost your dog and your woman in the same afternoon."

"No. Different afternoons."

"Oh. Huh."

Jillene smiled at Mike. "So, how do you guys know each other? You're kind of dressed up."

"Yeah. Should have taken my tie off before I came in. People will think I'm a doctor or something."

"All they got to do is talk to you and they'll know better," said Lodge.

"What, I don't sound smart enough to be a doctor?"

"Didn't say that. Man, you're awfully touchy. What's going on?"

"Yeah, and you didn't answer my question, you know," the woman said.

"I was gracefully avoiding it," Smithson said.

"Mike here was my lawyer. Got me out of a little scrape once, when Jimmy Collins was the sheriff here in town. Not that that mattered, really he was all right. Doing a hard job, I guess. I wouldn't want to do it."

Yeah, that's a tough job. Jimmy was all right, for a country sheriff. Hard to have to go around enforcing the law on your friends." Smithson glanced back and forth. "I need a drink, excuse me for a minute." The girl with the serving tray rounded the fireplace then, saw him, and stopped.

"Hey," she said, smiling. She smiled just like she knew him, like he was an old friend. "Hey, Mister."

Hey, Sister," he said as if he were on auto-pilot, then realized his overfamiliarity and was embarrassed. He did not know her. She sure smiled nicely, pretty-enough-not-beautiful but a really charming smile, one of those genuine smiles. He looked at her quizzically.

"I don't think we've met," he said. "I don't think you are one of my clients."

"No, I don't think I am." She smiled. "Are you a doctor or something?"

"No, I'm not." He managed to smile back. "Not a doctor," he said. "Doctors have patients, and that doesn't describe me at all."

"Well, no matter. You're kind of dressed up. At least for being in here. Do you want a drink, or what?"

"Yes, I want a drink. You're kind of dressed up yourself."

"Well, what do you want?"

"If I told you, you'd slap me," Smithson said.

"Maybe so. How about if you tell me what you want to drink."

"Okay. I want an Alaskan Amber."

"Okay then, you're in luck," she said.

"Not too much. Not enough luck. Wish I'd get lucky tonight. You are about the smartest woman in here."

"Oh, shush. Where do you want it?"

"You keep asking things that beg for a smart-ass answer."

"That's on you, not me." She rolled her eyes and wrinkled her nose. Small, refined, uplifted nose, like Sweet Pea's was. "Where do you want the beer to go?"

He unzipped his coat, shrugged, and smiled again, weakly. "Over there with the judge."

"I don't know who that is."

"That older man over there."

"Okay. Didn't know he was a judge."

"That's okay. He might have forgotten, himself. He's getting on." She moved off, and Mike went back to Lodge and the woman. Lodge had not offered to pay, and Lodge's own glass was empty. Lodge's old bill with Smithson was probably sixteen or seventeen years old, but it was still an unpaid account. He'd be damned if he'd buy Lodge a beer. "I'm going over to join Gordon over there," he said. "Good to see you again. Gordon looks pretty tired."

"Yeah. He's tired out, I think. Things got a little easier for us all when he retired." Lodge finished his beer. "Didn't make a lot of friends in this county, at least out in the sticks where we live."

Smithson moved over to the judge, waited for the old man to acknowledge him, and nodded toward the vacant chair. "Mind a little company?" he asked.

"No," said Gordon. "That's what I came in for. Truth be told." He looked up at Smithson. "Who are you?"

"Name's Mike Smithson. I had some cases in front of you."

"Yeah? Trials?"

"A few. I won them all." Smithson smiled, and Gordon smiled back.

"Yes, now I remember. The defense attorney who never lost a case. Mythical. Unforgettable, although obviously I have forgotten." He looked at Smithson, up and down. "What brings you around here?"

"On my way home. Thought I'd stop in."

"This is not on the way to anyone's home. This is just a roadhouse."

"Only one in the neighborhood," Smithson said.

"So you live in this county?"

"Yeah, pretty far out. Got some acreage on the west side of the county, and I'm going there. But I hadn't stopped here in a while."

"Looks like to me you haven't had the right kind of feminine company for a while, and that's why you stopped in here."

Smithson looked at him, somewhat startled. "Seems like you're just as blunt as you used to be, only you haven't got a black robe on. I thought that was the only reason you got away with it."

"Yeahhh. People kind of put up with me. I come here for the feminine company. Don't get your hopes too high. I never brought anybody home from this place."

"I don't have any expectations, other than somebody will say 'hi.' I didn't expect to see anyone who'd recognize me," Smithson said.

"Hell, I didn't recognize you. I don't even count."

"Lodge did."

"He was working you for a free drink."

"Thanks for the insight."

Both men stared into their drinks for a few minutes, uneasily shifting their vision from to time to time. Gordon raised and pointed his glass at Smithson. "So, remind me what cases you had in front of me."

Smithson thought for a minute. "Well, there were a bunch that settled, of course. Then there was a DUI trial, the truck-driving kid, part of the construction family, McIver family. One-day trial, went into the evening while the jury debated. Made them think, came back guilty. Jury was out late, until nine o'clock.

"And then there was an agg assault case, the old guy who was damn-near completely blind, out there at the old garnet quarry which was a swimming hole, with some dirtball friends, and some young punks, and some scuffle, and then the old guy— I can't remember his last name, first name was Robert, I remember, because of the punch line—the old guy has a handgun, and he's mouthing off to some young drunk kid, who takes the gun away from him and promptly shoots him. People out there picnicking, kids and dogs and lot of alcohol, and this old fart gets shot. I represented the young guy, I was appointed. The Public Defender on that case for the county was conflicted. Guilty verdict. No, it was agg battery, not assault. My guy got a few years, you gave him a few years."

"Yeah. He was a punk. Was not going to amount to any good."

"Yeah, sure enough. Especially if you send him to prison." Smithson smiled at the old man.

"Shot a guy. Shouldn't shoot people. Wasn't self defense, even though that's what you wanted those people to believe. He took the gun away, fair and square. Should have been the end of it."

"What if the old guy had grabbed it back. Then what?"

Gordon laughed. "Well, that might have been a different story. But the old guy was about completely blind. Couldn't find his own ass with both hands."

Smithson smiled. "Could have happened."

"You're mad you ended up with a conviction on those facts?"

"No."

"I remember that. He had some gal with him, the old guy did, and she had some other younger guy, and they were doing something fishy regarding the old man. It was like she was servicing the old guy—Robert —and sleeping with the other guy, seemed like, but it wasn't relevant to the facts, except the old guy was kinda cranky about things, and then when this other guy—your client—gets mixed up somehow, something to do with a dog fight, something about that intelligent, Robert gets pissed off and gets his peashooter pistol out of his camper trailer that they had dragged up there to camping with, and your guy—"

"Alvarez, I remember now."

"Yeah, Alvarez, some fourth generation Mexican, good-family-bad-kid syndrome. Anyway, there's some stupid mix-up, dogs and drunks and a gun, shoots Robert—some generic last name, Hudson or Hopper, something like that, doesn't matter any more—and the dolly who was down dipping her toes in the water with the other younger fella, she hears the shot, comes running, and hollers, 'Robert, are ya daid?

Robert, are ya daid?' And I thought the clerk and the court reporter both were going to die laughing. They're supposed to keep their courtroom decorum, but they were struggling. People in the gallery were laughing."

"Yep. They were laughing, the jury was laughing. I thought we had them then."

"Yeah, you might have won that one, even with those facts."

"Might have."

"Yeah. Would have been an injustice, though, wouldn't it?"

Smithson laughed at that. "Nope. Would only have been what the jury found, and in that case justice would have been served."

"Bullshit."

Gordon's eyes focused on his drink, and his face relaxed, submitting to the gravity of age.

"I think it was a colorable self-defense," Smithson said.

"Colorable with crayons only. You couldn't have even colored that in with a PowerPoint. Computer would have rebelled, gone up in smoke."

"Well. There you have it. The old fart was asking for it, and he got it. And the dumb bastard got a Rider—'Retained Jurisdiction,' or 'prison-lite' as you used to call it—and you did it. You must have been influenced by something."

"Didn't have anything serious in his record up to that point," Gordon said. "Of course he was practically too young to have done anything serious. Put him on a Rider, see if the State can re-parent him. That's what all those things are, see if the State can re-parent the bastard."

"Not always the parents' fault."

The Judge took a deliberately long pull on his drink. "That's right, not always the parents' fault. And the parent isn't found guilty. But if the damn parents were paying attention, many of these cases wouldn't happen."

"You know my daughter went on a Rider, back in Minnesota. They don't call it a Rider, but it's the same thing."

The judge peered up from his glass. "Yeah? No. No, I didn't know. I heard some gossip, but I didn't believe it."

Smithson looked at the old man, hunched over a drink in a dark dive of a bar, inspecting him as if he had caught a liar in cross-examination. The muscles under his eyes tightened, piercing; whatever the effect was, his cross-examination countenance was intended.

"Rumors were true. She had a rough go, got out, landed in California. Santa Rosa. For now."

"Drugs?"

"Yep." Smithson drained his beer and scooted his chair back, getting ready to move on. Where was the waitress who had called him Mister? Why was he stuck talking to some old worn-out retired curmudgeon, who only could be sociable when he was digging at a festering wound? "Got too personal for now. Sorry, going to visit."

Gordon nodded in response, and as Smithson rose from his chair the waitress appeared with another drink for the older man. No money was exchanged, and Smithson smiled genially. "You are like the daughter I never had," he said to her.

"Yeah?" she replied.

"He has a daughter, for Christsakes," interrupted Gordon. Smithson just looked straight at the waitress.

"Yeah, but she wasn't like you. She wouldn't ever bring me a drink, at least not after she was about twelve or so. She listened to her mom."

"Go on, go visit with Lodge," Gordon said. "This comely young lass is going to serve me a drink. I think."

Smithson moved off, shifted directions to the men's room, and as he did so he noticed Gordon gesturing to the waitress to sit across from him, where Smithson had been. He went into the restroom. It was dank and sour-smelling but overly bright. He rinsed off his face, then relieved himself, then examined himself in the mirror. He forced a smile, swept back loose locks of hair, and tried to make his face just a tad bit prettier.

"Exit, stage right," he murmured to himself.

Lodge was still there, and Smithson approached again. His glass was still empty, and Smithson gestured towards it. "No matter, lost the waitress," said Lodge. "But thanks."

"What are you having?"

"Busch Light."

"Lady friend?" Smithson asked.

"Same."

Smithson nodded slightly and said nothing, and approached the bar to get his own service, and saw the girl rear back her head in laughter, and the old judge looking at her straight ahead. After a minute wait, he got the three beers and headed back to Lodge. The waitress remained planted.

He and Lodge talked about the local logging economy, weather, trucking logs in the weather and how spotty the work was, compared to what the work paid when it was going strong, and how it wasn't sensible for a man to try to make a living working any more, and they each had another beer for themselves and shot of well whiskey for Jillene. The crowd had thinned, and Smithson looked at his watch. Late, pushing midnight now. Time had gone, and beer had been poured. He headed off to the restroom again, and then he saw the waitress walking back to the judge's table, putting on her coat as she moved. Gordon put on a long heavy black coat, suggestive of a judicial robe. He offered his arm to the waitress, and she took it. Smithson stopped short for just an instant, continued, returned to his place with Lodge, and then stared at his half-full glass, somber as an undertaker.

Lodge looked at him and laughed.

"Looks like you shifted personalities in the john. You bipolar or something?"

"No. At least I don't think so." Smithson glanced over to where the old man and the girl had been.

"Ah. Aha. You're wondering what that old fucker has that you ain't got. Ain't that it? He left with the cute young girl, and here you are with an old drunk guy and the old drunk guy at least has a woman, and all you got is a little bit of beer left to drink. Old judge guy worked his magic. You ain't got the mojo he has."

"Yeah. Maybe. Beat it."

Lodge looked at Smithson and laughed again. "Yeah, I'll beat it."

Lodge went to get his coat, and the woman traipsed after him. They walked back past Smithson, and Lodge said, "You know that old goat is just an old goat, and he's got money, and sure as hell he ain't got a plan or a hard-on left in him. Yet you're standing here wondering what the hell just happened. That girl is on her way somewhere with him, and he's laughing at you. Right now, he's laughing at you."

"Yeah? Why's that?"

"Cause you're wondering about all kinds of stuff, and he's causin' you to wonder, and you can't figure out who's going where with who. You're just wondering what the hell happened."

"Yeah, and what I'm wondering about is why that would happen. What did I do to deserve that?"

Lodge looked at him, his eyes half shut, and the woman with her eyes closed, pulling on his sleeve of his Carhartt coat.

"You worry too much, Mike. And that's why you're lonely in this bar on a Friday night. You worry too much."

Smithson looked up at him.

"Don't worry. She's fine, and he's fine, and you gotta let some of that come to you. You all right to drive?"

"Yeah. Besides, you just told me I worry too much. I'm okay."

"I wasn't offering a ride. Hell, I'll get in an accident, you'd sue, and I wouldn't have any money. I was just checking if you had learned not to worry so much."

"Lesson learned. I'll never worry again."

He had never taken off his coat. He caught an image, a flash of memory of the waitress and her laughter, head tipped back and joyously laughing. *Don't worry,* he thought, *you worry too much.* He zipped the coat, jammed his hands in his pockets and stepped outside into the cold, and noted the sparkles on the asphalt. *Who was doing okay now,* he thought, *Gordon, or the waitress, or Lodge and his woman? Smithson? Sweet Pea?* Didn't matter, except he was going home alone, just lectured to by people who mystified him by their contentment. *Stop wondering.*

He walked to his pickup, opened it and clambered in, and started the engine. He wished he had his spare keys so he could warm it up while he went back inside.

Then he noticed the briefcase—it had been tampered with, opened up and the files disturbed. The laptop computer was still there, and he breathed a sigh of relief. He got out of the truck and walked around to the passenger door to inventory the contents. His breathing was quick and shallow, and the cold clouded the vapor of his breath. He flipped the blower motor switch to "high" and pulled out the contents of the briefcase.

He was carefully stacking files on the seat of the truck when he noticed the additional business cards in the pocket of the briefcase, and he pulled one out: "Jerry Gordon, mediator and arbitrator," with a Camp Joseph address and phone. On quick examination, he knew that nothing was taken, just additional cards left there. A small smile crept across his face. He did not understand why, but he understood that the old man had just been screwing with him. Left his cards on purpose, and rifled through the contents and left it messy just to tip him off. He reassembled the contents into the briefcase neatly.

I don't think I'll be needing his mediation services anytime soon, he thought. He imagined the old man walking to the truck, waitress in tow, and deciding it was Smithson's. He could see the man testing the door, opening it, seeing a briefcase, and then just deciding to leave a calling card. Just for the—what? to show off? And the young woman would be quizzical but amused. Antics of old men, whom she could get to treat her, but whom she would not understand until she herself grew older. Old men, seeking company of others, prettier ones than those who had tired of old men, those who had left them as they raged into the storm, raged into the cold, raged about the inexplicable. And Gordon had joined forces with the arbitrary forces of the aether, random acts of not-even-kindness, just acts. The woman would have wondered and laughed a charming laugh, and hooked her arm in his to drag him away.

He pulled his laptop out of the case and powered it up. It was slow, slower than what he should endure, but it came on and asked for a password, and he typed it in and everything looked normal. No, the old fart wouldn't know how to screw with that, and Smithson did not suspect more malice than a weird joke. He shut it down and fit it back in its slot in the case.

Then he imagined the rest of the scene: The older man nodding gently and closing the pickup door, and walking the girl to her car and patting her heavily clothed buttocks, and nodding again before shuffling off to his own rig. She wasn't going home with him, she was just getting up to leave and played along with a fantasy for just a bit. They were players in a scene, but the scene ended peacefully. Except for him, with a stuttering heartbeat.

Smithson set the briefcase on the floorboard and slammed the door, then walked around to the driver's side and got in. The cab was warming up now with the high-speed air, and he couldn't see his breath. He drew out his handkerchief and wiped his face and laughed silently into his hands. That briefcase stunt was something his Sweet-Pea might have done. Never mind that if a cop had seen it—well, everyone knew there wasn't a cop for miles. You pretty much knew what would happen at Camilla's. Gordon screwing with him in such a whacky fashion, that was unexpected and weird. No harm, no foul, and then some relief from too much thinking.

Lodge pulled out of the lot, driving a Ford F-350 with lots of diesel exhaust. The woman was squeezed up tight against him, and Lodge had to be over twice the legal limit. Lodge rolled down the window, gave him a big wave and hollered, "Hey, hey, Mikey! You worry too much, man!" In turn, Smithson rolled down his window and waved back, middle finger extended, and grinned. Lodge mimicked the salute.

Smithson tossed the handkerchief aside and pulled the Ram into gear and headed back onto the highway, looking for black ice. ■

SANDY ANDERSON

Border

No visible line in sand
        invisible yet enforced
        by guns
A line across which
        you change language
        you change dress
A tear gas line
A barbed wire line
A line in the middle
        of a river
An imaginary line
        known to vigilante,
        to border guard
        to refugee
A line you can be
        shot
        for crossing
A line unknown to fox,
        coyote, wolf
        prairie dog
        rabbit
        tarantula
        lizard
A line of boredom
        which has nothing to do
A reason-defying line
        across the desert
A non-humanitarian line
A starvation line
A line not at all like
        a breadline
A covenant line
        to nationalists
A line that means nothing
        to the land it crosses

and everything
to those who cross
A line identifiable only
to politicians
to the paranoid
to racists
A minefield across the desert
that keeps those without
without
and those who have
from being infected
by withoutness
A filter of people
A hot spot
with no dancing
A fearful line we cannot
speak to
nor understand
nor hear
A borderline that brothers
cannot reach across
A fusible line when attacked
by armies
A tongueless snake
without rattles
A corrodor of countries
of selves
A line that separates us
A line we set up
within
ourselves
to keep us from touching
The line we maintain
to keep us from being human
A line that protects the borders
of self
from expanding
A limit

Cigarette Universe

The cigarette ash fell off the end of the cigarette and landed in her lap.
It was hot just a second. She was too busy typing to do anything about
it. In another scenario she could have been in bed reading when the ash
fell into the sheets, and smoldered until the bed exploded in flames. This
went through her mind, and she smiled, annoyed. She paused to brush
away the ashes, but a black smudge remained on her lap. Sooner or later
this all had to stop. She knew this. But she didn't want to do anything
about it. She wanted the world to continue as if there were no flames.
The thought of these things made her fretful, so she lit up another
cigarette, took a long draw and watched the glow in the twilight. And
this time the ashes fell down the stream of stars, fell up the milky way,
made a gray mist around the stars. It was easier to go on smoking. Even
if the smoke made her eyes water, her throat ache, even if she missed
the star for the ash. She pounded the typewriter faster, trying to erase
these thoughts. But another ash fell, and she stopped to brush it away.
She slowly ground out her cigarette in the ashtray; lit a new one. In the
morning the ashtrays were always full. This happened to them in the
night. It probably had something to do with her, and the stars hidden
behind the shroud of the milky way, but it was nothing she could touch
a finger to. If she touched the cherry, it burned, and she had to pull her
finger away. That's what she did now. And she went on as the pages went
up in smoke, as the sheets ignited, as the smoke rose in a ring like a halo.

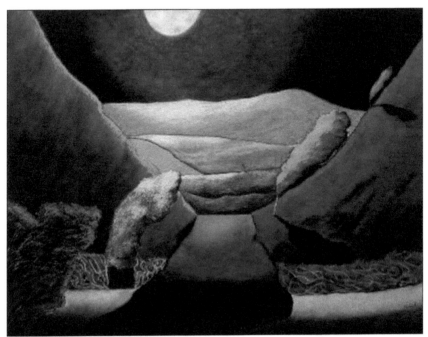

"Camas" by Mike Woods, oil pastel and graphite, 41" x 33."

BRANT SHORT

America's West in Three Takes

Communities

Phoenix is a diesel-fueled Caterpillar D9 bulldozer that never stops,
never sleeps, always marching toward an unknown finish line in the desert

Seattle is a fashion model, tall and lean and angular, looking for
a new runway to strut her stuff and make us want more, just a little more

Salt Lake City is a factory buzzing with worker bees who share a
communal history that can be ignored but never forgotten

Portland is a flute player who wears a different hat each day and plays lyrical
melodies that can be both beautiful and harsh, always demanding our attention

Los Angeles is a crossword puzzle that can never be finished because
clues and answers change every minute of every day without pause

Albuquerque is a shuttered adobe church being repurposed as a coffee shop
for the upwardly mobile, retirees, and local pilgrims searching for sustenance

San Francisco is the neighborhood rich kid with a fast car, a beautiful girlfriend,
and multitudes of acquaintances but who can't escape the dull ache of loneliness

Las Vegas is a haunted house, designed by overly creative high school seniors
with only one goal: maximum stimulus, maximum response, repeat

Denver is a 1972 split level Brady Bunch ranch style house that is adding
a new garage, a new deck, a new bathroom, a new dining room and on and on

Oakland is a middle-weight champion from a time when boxing mattered
who spends his days dreaming of the past and planning his return to greatness

Wisdom, Weiser, Roundup, Sisters, Panguitch and all the small towns in the
American West are magpies, who awaken each morning and practice the same ritual:
find some food, tease one another, watch for predators, take flight to survey their world,
and chirp and cackle at the alarm clock of conquest that urbanites set for 5 a.m. every day

Coyotes

Some memories hide in the basement
out of sight for good reasons
but a sound, a smell, an image rips that door wide open
when you least expect it

That TV commercial with a shivering dog begging for help
transports me to an afternoon visiting my step-father's buddy Wally
A coyote laying on cold concrete chained by the back door
"Don't go near him, he'll bite you"
"Wally found him as a pup and keeps him for protection"
I saw that coyote when I was 12 years old, I can see him now

If I had three wishes from a benevolent genie
I would return to Burley Idaho in 1968
I would ask for courage to free that coyote
I would put Wally on the chain for day or two
Enough time to satisfy my human need for vengeance
Not enough time for all the coyotes who have suffered by the hands of God's lesser creatures

Cowboys

True story, no fooling, but I know a cowboy
an honest to god hard work cowboy and a poet
who drinks tea instead of coffee
who prefers sangria to rot gut
who reads the *New York Times Sunday Book Review* for pleasure

The cowboy is an endangered species, that's the story
Real life, horse-savvy, dusty boot wearing cowboys are hard to find
Not pickup truck jockeys with gun racks and ball caps and bulging belt buckles
And attitude
Big time in your face attitude
An attitude that old John Wayne would kick sideways to Sundays

My friend writes long lyrical poems about love and loss
that rip the breath from your lungs but keep you wanting more
He works the feedlot range of central Oregon and waits for his chance

to share his work with lovers of language
and English majors who listen with their bodies and not just their ears
and possibly a beautiful thoughtful woman who thinks
big thoughts in a shrinking world and who does not care
one damn iota about saddles and hats and spurs
but who understands that poetry is the ticket to finding one's soul

Cowboy poets who listen to Dave Brubeck and Leo Kottke
Hard to swallow, I think, and so do you, if you're really honest
Poets who are cowboys who drink merlot and eat gouda and
gaze upward late in the evening and think of the beyond
Now that makes sense to me

"Just Another Sunday in Storyland" by Didi Sharp, paper collage, 9" x 12."

GINO SKY

Riding Out from Anomie*

That's where I was born. In
Pocatello, Idaho, in 1935. At
the tail end of Everyman's Depression.

The next eighteen years
were a cold war between
landscape failure and scenic enemas—
the going rate of exchange at the time.

Raised Mormon—
I refused to partake in the transmigration
of seagulls—reincarnated
Jewish prophets or not.

I keep trying to go back
but I couldn't speak
how they see it.

There is a word for it, and it's suddenly like
being able to make it fit somehow.

Anomie. There's a lot of us lost
out there who can
never return
even for the Anomie Reunions.

I changed my name
so that I wouldn't have to be reminded
that way. I used to be Buddy. As in
My Buddy, or Good Old Bud . . . or
for God's sake, the beer.

Gino was the name of a rowboat
on Lake Lugano, where I was convalescing
from all those years in Idaho.
I rowed out as Bud and returned as Gino.

It was one boat load better than Bud. Or
Burt Gail, or that one who gave the invocation
at the senior class commencement
and then disappeared for good.

Gino Sky is now president of the University
of No Where, and Everyman and Woman.
I exist only in poetry
Drunk or sober. That's where

I am in case someone wants to know. Just
start with Buddy Boy and take it
all the way from there.

*Anomie—the state of alienation by an individual or class
[Greek: lawlessness, from anomos, without law.]

—1971

THE STAGE

coach
to believe
your own
body
is one
night's ride
deep
within
beauty

Five Aces on Christmas Eve

5 card draw at the Cowboy
Buddha Hotel—

Jesus,
Buddha,
Moses,
Coyote.

The Great Mother
was dealing.

Also smiling
to have most of the rooms
filled
for the holidays.

For old times
sake,
Jesus
asked for
his old room
out back.

CHUCK GUILFORD

Owyhee August

What's under all this
bunchgrass

and this sand?
High, folded hills where

memory runs on
like feldspar
from footprint to ridgeline

and no sudden creek,
reflecting my image

but deeper than I imagine,
pulls me back out.

Is there only this one
hard release?

Only mud rivers cracked
and warped, rock doves

lifting in waves
from hundred foot cliffs,

under morning sun
until rock drops
off to nowhere

and the nothing
starts to speak.

Out here you see it all
in stark relief.

At Winter Solstice

Too long since we've walked
these silent hills, climbed up
from the rich black bottom lands,
bright fields of winter wheat,

Bent with the weight of the whole
world's need, past fences shouting —
It's mine. Keep out. Beyond the muddy
year-round streams, past the last
now unused gate.

Along the dried creek bed,
latticed limestone overhung
with burr oak—twisting, broken branches
tugging at our shirts.

Until even the brown tipped cedars stop
and the land fans out below,
around, on every side.

And a dry wind slips
over the spikes of the prickly pear
in tough, unignorable silence.

JIM HEYNEN

Red Toyota

She is so pretty that she scares me. But when I hear her say "wuss" for "was" and "hiss" for "his," I know she isn't from around here. With just two hundred kids in our high school, word spreads fast that she is an exchange student from Iceland, and, no, she won't be around town after school because she lives with her uncle and aunt on a farm six miles out.

Her name is Brynhildur Gunnersdottir. I heard a teacher call her Hilda, but I haven't met her yet, so I'm not sure what I will call her if such a sweet occasion ever comes to pass.

I am eighteen and a senior. Brynhildur is taking tenth-grade classes, so I guess she is about sixteen. I see her glittering smile as she strides through the hallways with other students who obviously have gotten to know her and like her a lot. I am the shy type, all right, at least on the outside. On the inside, I am full of plans that I don't know how to act on. I am doing great in Advanced English. I am on the debate team. I am a member of the drama club. But when I'm not on stage, I am pretty tongue-tied. Sometimes when a teacher calls on me in class, I can't catch my breath and just sit there red-faced and speechless.

Now just seeing gorgeous Brynhildur move down the hallways takes my breath away. Those flashing blue eyes. The sweep of her long blond hair. No way on earth would I dare to walk up to her and say, "Hi, I'm Johnny." Maybe there will be a happy accident, like if she trips and falls in front of me and I can say, "Oh no! Let me help you!"

Brynhildur has long legs but moves with the ease of someone who has never tripped on anything in her whole life. I'm not sure exactly what it is, but there is something bold and confident that makes her stand out from everyone else. And she is the only pretty girl I've ever seen who acts as if she doesn't know how attractive she is.

Then one Monday morning one of the guys says, "Hey, Johnny! See your mug shot in the window at Bodner's Studio?"

I think it is one of those teasing guy-jokes, but it turns out that the photography studio that took our high school pictures is displaying the head-and-shoulders shot of me in their downtown studio window for all the pedestrians in the world to see.

When our history teacher comments on that fact, I know it isn't a joke! I run the four blocks to Bodner's Studio during noon hour, and there I am. They have enlarged my face to something much bigger than my real face and put it on some kind of pedestal in the middle of the display window. My portrait is center stage, with a couple of smaller baby and family pictures off to the side! The studio folks have changed the color of my tie, but they are the pros so I have no issue with that. Looking at my face displayed for all to see is embarrassing. It is also the most thrilling moment of my eighteen years on earth.

Back at school, the teasing starts. One of the hefty jocks says, "That picture makes you look like Rock Hudson," and then the laughing because everybody knows Rock Hudson was gay. "Looks like you're wearing makeup in that picture," and a few more pathetic jabs like that.

The attention I get from the girls almost cancels out the boys' teasing. Everyone has wallet-size school pictures, and no fewer than thirty girls ask to trade pictures with me and ask me to sign mine to them. I order more wallet-size pictures to keep up with the requests.

I study my school picture, trying to see what the girls see, and I do see it—the perfect wave in my dark hair, those full lips with just a hint of a smile, the earnest blue eyes, the prominent chin. Yes, I do see what the girls see. It is hard for me to believe, but I really am good looking. Darn good looking.

The debate topic for the year is on the question of whether the US should work harder on energy independence. I am sitting in the lunchroom going through my flashcards on the topic when I hear a clear girl's voice say, "Excuse me" but she pronounces "excuse" to sound like "excoose." It's Brynhildur.

"Want to trade pictures?" she asks.

She lays a wallet-sized school picture of herself in front of me. She is as beautiful on paper as she is in real life.

I nod and reach for a wallet-sized picture of myself.

I hand her my picture. My hand is not shaking.

"Would you sign it to me?" she asks.

"Yes," I say. My voice is clear and confident. This is like being on stage. "My pleasure," I say.

"My name is Brynhildur," she says. "I'm from Iceland."

"I know," I say. "My name is Johnny."

"I know," she says. "Should I tell you how to spell my name? Or you can just write 'Hilda.'"

"I like Brynhildur," I say. I know how to spell it." I write, "For Brynhildur." But should I say anything more? My heart says, sign it "With all my love, Johnny," but I stop myself. I write one word, "Johnny."

"Would you sign yours?" I ask. I hold it toward her and try to smile.

"Love to," she says.

She sits down next to me. She has her own pen. There is a confident manner in everything she does and says. She writes, "For my friend Johnny, Yours truly, Brynhildur."

The ink from her pen is lavender. She leans her shoulder against me as she hands me her picture. She is so close that I can pick up the scent of her. She smells like clean clothes. I wonder if she is picking up on my aftershave.

"I hear you're a good student," she says.

"I don't know about that."

"You're in drama club."

"Yes."

"And on the debate team."

"We've just started on the topic for the year." The words are coming easy for me. Being able to talk to Brynhildur is even more wonderful than having my picture on display at Bodner's Studio.

"You doing any extracurriculars?" I ask.

"I can't do after-school stuff. I live on a farm. I have to catch the bus."

"That's not fair," I say. "So you can't even come into town for a movie?"

"Nope," she says. "Nobody can have everything. My uncle and aunt can't drive in at night because they are busy with evening chores. Cows to milk and stuff." She says "cows" so that it sounds like "couse." She says "chores" so that it sounds like "chorse."

I like the way she talks.

"I could drive out to get you for a movie," I say. After I say that, I can't believe I said that.

"You have a car?"

"Red Toyota Corolla SR5," I say. "Perfect driving record."

Just like that I have a date to take Brynhildur to a movie.

I pick her up at six-fifteen for the seven o'clock movie, a romantic comedy.

"My uncle and aunt asked how old you are," she says as we drive off from the farm where she lives.

"I'm eighteen," I say.

"I know," she says. "I told them."

"You're probably fifteen, right?"

"Turning sixteen in a month," she says and gives me her glittering smile.

"Did they think I was too old for you?"

"They were glad you were older," she says. "They thought that meant you'd be a safer driver."

"I'm a very safe driver."

"I can see the speedometer," she says.

"Fifty-six. One mile over the speed limit."

"My uncle drives seventy on this road. Scares me." There is her beautiful pronunciation again: "drives" was "drifes" and "scares" was "scarce."

I am driving too slow for the car behind me. It whizzes around us at what must be seventy-five or eighty.

"That's even faster than my uncle drifes," says Brynhildur.

"That's a red Toyota Corolla just like this one."

It really is the same year and model, though short on the shine.

"Oh!" shouts Brynhildur in a voice I didn't know she had.

A ginormous pickup truck has just run the stop sign from the gravel road to the left and broadsided my red Toyota twin. The Toyota pinwheels around on the blacktop road as the clunky pickup ricochets off into the weedy ditch on the other side of the road.

There is dust in the air and two ripped-up vehicles, but the only thing we see is a body splayed out in the middle of the blacktop.

I have my Toyota under control and ease off onto the shoulder. I put the car in park and set the handbrake. I turn on my emergency flashers and look in the rearview mirror. There are no cars coming. There are no cars coming from the other direction either.

"Oh, my god," says Brynhildur. She jumps out of the car and runs toward the splayed body.

When I try to undo my seatbelt to get out there with Brynhildur, something is wrong. I'm not sure if it is my hand or the stupid seatbelt latch. It won't come loose. My hand vibrates. I put my other hand over the shaky hand.

What if I had driven into a river? What if my car was covered with water and I couldn't get my seatbelt loose?

I get out of the car, but my legs won't move. Yes, they will. I'd make them move to help Brynhildur who is very busy with that motionless woman. I do move. I move straight toward Brynhildur and the woman on the road. My legs feel awkward and heavy—but I do move!

The motionless woman looks to be maybe twenty, beautiful lips—but she is spouting blood from the side of her head. Maybe her left arm too. Brynhildur moves her hands from one blood eruption to another. The woman on the blacktop has an immense amount of long brown hair that looks as if it is plastered to the road with blood. There is blood all around her.

I stand over kneeling Brynhildur and the splayed body.

"I can't," I say.

"You can't what?" says Brynhildur.

"Stand the sight of blood."

I wake up on a stretcher in the back of an ambulance.

"Where am I?" I ask.

"You fainted," says Brynhildur. "I tried to catch you. I got my hands under your head." She holds up her hands. Her knuckles are scraped, but they aren't bleeding.

"You did?"

"Yes," says Brynhildur. "I just wanted to make sure you didn't hit your head on the highway. At least I managed that."

"Thank you," I say.

"You're welcome," says Brynhildur. "I couldn't get you to wake up. I slapped your face but that didn't do anything."

Her face is kind and beautiful as she looks down at me. This is the image I wish I could see in the window at Bodner's studio. Her long blond hair touches my shoulder. I see its touch but don't feel it. There is a blood pressure band around my arm. An ambulance attendant sits beside Brynhildur.

There is no siren sounding off on the ambulance and we are not going very fast. I must not be an emergency.

"How are you feeling now?" Brynhildur says and puts her index finger to the corner of my lip. I know she must have touched me before because she said she slapped my face after I fainted, but this is the first time I can feel her touching me. It makes me remember the time I touched an electric fence that was meant to keep cattle from breaking out.

Brynhildur wipes her finger on the blanket that is over my legs.

There is a visual echo of the blinking red of the ambulance as we drive along, little bursts of red light into the darkness. It is comforting.

"Where is the woman who was on the road?" I ask.

"She's in a different ambulance," says the ambulance attendant.

"Is she all right?"

"She didn't make it," says Brynhildur.

"She what?"

"She died," says Brynhildur.

"You did what you could," says the ambulance attendant. "You did what you could." He puts his hand on Brynhildur's arm. I don't say anything.

"She was gone when the ambulance arrived," says Brynhildur. "I had to make sure you were all right."

"You were almost choking," says the ambulance attendant. "She did the right thing: she had you on your side and had moved your tongue so you could breathe."

So Brynhildur has touched me more than once already and I didn't even know it.

"But that other woman," I say.

"She didn't have a seatbelt on," says the ambulance attendant. "She went through the windshield. Multiple lacerations. Serious lacerations."

"I couldn't stop them all," says Brynhildur.

The ambulance attendant looks back at Brynhildur. "You did what you could."

I look up at Brynhildur. She doesn't look at me. She looks toward the front of the ambulance out onto the road where we are riding. "I tried to get a response from her," says Brynhildur. "I asked her what her name was. I was hoping I could talk to her."

"But she was unconscious?" I ask.

"No," says Brynhildur. "She said her name but I didn't catch it. That's when I tried to wake you up."

Brynhildur puts her hand on my shoulder. "I'm glad you're awake now," she says.

We cruise slowly up to the emergency room of the hospital. Another ambulance is already there and has its emergency lights turned off. I sit up and lean toward Brynhildur.

"You don't feel faint now, do you?" asks the ambulance attendant.

"No," I say.

Brynhildur and I watch through the front windows of our ambulance. They are taking a body out of the other ambulance, a body covered with a sheet. Two people from the hospital carry the body toward the emergency room, and a man walks beside them, shaking his head and weeping. The body under the sheet must be the woman from the blacktop, and the man walking beside her, shaking his head and weeping, must be the driver of my Toyota Corolla twin.

"That's the woman's dad," says the ambulance attendant. He turns back to me and Brynhildur. "We should wait a couple minutes before we go in," he says. We all sit still in a moment of reverence for the dead woman and her father.

"You feel all right to walk?" asks the attendant.

"I can walk," I say.

Brynhildur and the ambulance attendant take my hands as I step out of the back of the ambulance.

"You need to go inside to be checked out," says the attendant.

Inside, they don't even ask for my identification. A nurse walks over, stares intently into my eyes, and asks me what day it is.

"It's Friday," I say.

She holds up a finger and asks me to follow it. She shines a light in my eyes.

"When is your birthday?" she asks.

I tell her.

"May I see you walk?"

I walk.

"I think he's fine," she says. "Have you fainted like this before?" she asks.

"Couple of times," I say. "I can't stand the sight of blood. Last time it was from a chicken I saw being butchered. On a farm. They just chopped its head off and blood went everywhere."

"Does it bother you to look at that?" she asks and points at Brynhildur.

There isn't any blood on her hands and arms, but her jeans are caked with dried blood. So is her shirt. There is dried blood on the ends of her long blond hair. There is dried blood on her left eyebrow.

"That doesn't bother me," I say.

"Do you think you can drive a motor vehicle? You've got the red Toyota, right?"

"Yes," I say. "I feel okay to drive. I'm a good driver."

"He's a very safe driver," says Brynhildur. Her shoes have dried blood on them.

"I left my Toyota parked on the shoulder of the road," I say.

"And you left the keys in it," says the ambulance attendant. "Sheriff's deputy drove it to the hospital. Parked right over there."

We don't talk as I drive Brynhildur back to the farm. I walk her to the door. I stand staring at her. I smile. I feel that good on-stage confidence. "A good-night kiss?" I say.

She smiles at me. It is a sweet and forgiving smile. "It doesn't feel like that kind of night, does it?"

"Not really," I say, and leave.

We don't go out again, but Brynhildur is always friendly to me in the hallways. I encourage her to join the debate team, but she says she really can't stay after school. Before I know what has happened, the school year is over and Brynhildur has gone back to Iceland.

All of that happened forty years ago. I never saw Brynhildur again, but not one day passes that I don't think about her. Our high school alumni newsletter likes to boast about her as if she were one of us. She went on to college and then graduate school in Denmark. She's a doctor, a hematologist working through the University of Copenhagen. Her research is focused on blood disorders in people of Icelandic ancestry.

She's married to a Swedish doctor, also a hematologist. They have two boys, both of them on track to become doctors too. None of that really means anything to me. What I remember and think about is the Brynhildur who held my hand in the ambulance forty years ago. I have never again felt that kind of love, though she never told me she loved me.

Me? I graduated with honors from our little high school. Big deal. Of course, I went to college, but in my sophomore year I dropped out. Nerves got the best of me. I just couldn't take it. I was getting about two hours of sleep a night. My doctor said I had to change my life or die. I didn't want to die, so I dropped out. I moved to Portland, Oregon, where I wouldn't know anybody and where I could get a fresh start. I got a job with the US Postal Service. I've had the same delivery route for over 30 years now. Perfect driving and delivery record. Great benefits.

No, I never did get married. I do have a dog, Gretta, a beautiful golden lab. It's not as if I don't like women. All kinds of women, old, young, pretty, ugly, smart, stupid, gay, straight, it doesn't matter. Something in me is just programmed to like women, and it all started with Brynhildur. It's a burden and a blessing, I guess. I'm relieved that it is unfashionable for men to be too overt in their attraction for women today because I still haven't learned to be overt. I just live with a mild but real love of women. I know it's all about Brynhildur. I still don't know how to put the feeling into words or action, so, yes, I'd have to say I'm pretty lonely. But that's all right.

Sometime in the past, I lost the school picture of Brynhildur. Oddly, I still have a picture of my red Toyota. When I look at it, I think of Brynhildur in the seat beside me. And I do have Gretta, who is lying at my feet right now, looking up at me with her kind eyes in a way that tells me she knows exactly how I feel. ∎

"Shadow Play with Potato" by Mike Woods, mixed media, 28" x 34."

DAVID LEE

Acceptance
Silver City, September, 2016

Today Fred Swanson's rattlesnake
killing cat that the Vet told him
Quit calling her Cat
give her a name that
will let her feel endeared so
he named her Sweetie Pie, our self
designated neighborhood welcoming committee
left a cottontail rabbit
dead on our doorstep
lying on the face
down welcome mat
which I found
incidentally
on my way outside
the Domes on the Rock with
my coffee cup
steaming
as I made my way
around behind the little brown barn
to take a crisp Sierra sunrise
first morning likewise steaming
leak
while the night
finished its unbuilding
and our new day
took its glorious shape
in this place we
are learning to call home

75: *A Memory Walk Through the Hill Country*

Ripeness is All my ass

my two Williams, S & K

At the outer edge of January
sauntering an earth hillocked
with snags and stumbles
Spanish Oak branches stiff
brittle-brown as the bones
long dead of cardinals
Windstir the last hanging leaves'
only song clings
like life itself to
September's memory
pouring a perfumed reminiscence
that flutters with the dark wings
of rising turkey vultures—
the mind clutch realization
of the rites of passage
foot-trapped in the race
between two millstones
and the headgate lifting

Year of the Sequestration Idyll
Seaside, April 2020

Rapt in the armchair of study
light Oregon mizzle
masked by the ever lingering wind
long late afternoon silence

suddenly through Prospero's soliloquy
before leaving Ariel and the island
the lovely returning home call
of a Canadian goose

"Visitation from the Imaginal Realm" by Didi Sharp, paper collage, 9" x 12."

BETHANY SCHULTZ HURST

Afterlife: Brothel Abandoned in 1986 and Re-opened Later as a Museum

Pink packing peanuts suggest bubbles in the bathtub
around a mannequin's yellowed leg. The kitchen drawer
is crammed full of worn-out egg timers that once tracked
the procured time. We've become both the canyon
the town was shoved into and the mountains, bored through
with silver mines. The high school marching band
that paraded in gleaming costumes purchased by the madam:
We're the gold cord dripping from their shoulders.
The one stoplight they marched beneath. And the joystick
on the floral velveteen just out of a nightgowned
mannequin's reach? We're her favorite Atari game.
A bright 8-bit graphic on the screen. Her lamp shade's
cascading silky beads. Remember how that cartoon duck
could swan-dive in and out of riches, how he alone
could pass through gold coins like they were liquid?
We're a pin-feather gaining purchase. The spring
inside the wound-up timers that one by one would ding.

Guardian

My father's brother has taken to standing watch
all night on the patio because he knows
the invasion will come at dark. He scans

the sky. He'd prefer a shotgun over his lap
but his guns have been taken away. As of Friday
morning, he is no longer guardian of himself.

Meanwhile, I'm on a roadtrip, an unfolding display
of all the places I might have had a home. The sky
is screened with wildfire smoke. Air tankers

zig-zag over, dipping low to drop retardant.
They're almost in formation. At a truckstop diner,
we watch through the window

as three hippies scurry barefoot in and out
of a broken-down car. From the looks of it,
they won't be leaving soon. With them

is a tiny kitten, a string tied around its neck.
The youngest hippie bounces between truckers
in the parking lot, always holding out her hand.

I hold my breath, not wanting to lose sight of her
in the rows of idling trucks. Finally one trucker
brings them all inside. "They were out there

with no food," he announces as they enter, as if
we're all to blame. I can't tell their age. The booths
are stenciled with inspirational quotes and specific facts

about Oregon. After a while, it's hard to tell which
is which. Should we be uplifted by the height
of Multnomah Falls? You can't see the bottom

in all of that mist. This side of the fire, crop dusters
buzz by. Pesticides drift in low clouds beneath
them. Later, when I go to wash my hands,

one of the girls appears from a stall, dragging the kitten
behind her. She gently admonishes him for meowing.
That string worries me, but I say nothing,

just run my finger around his neck to check
it's not too tight. We drive away. The kitten
becomes my fault. The hippies. My once-gentle uncle

will live in an institution 45 miles away so he can't
hurt his family or himself. He used to scour
junk shops for Prussian glass and teacups. What's

the difference between disarmed and empty-handed?
The tankers drop an orange line between what's burned
and saved—then they retreat with hollowed bellies.

ROBERT WRIGLEY

Falling off a Log

It must have been the shadow
of the golden eagle landing
on the shadow of a snag that sent
the hare from the safety of its spot
beneath the fronds of a sword fern:
It was hard not to root
for the hare, imagining
its terror, and equally hard
to resist the fierce nobility
of the eagle. Then the hare veered
more than ninety degrees left,
directly at me, where I sat
on a fallen tree. And the eagle
banked into a dive
at both of us, or so it appeared.

The look in the eyes of one, the look
in the eyes of the other,
and the look in the eyes of me:
I do not know if the others
took note of me at all,
but I closed my eyes then
and let myself fall
backwards off the log, easily,
but onto a painful blunt stob,
which caused me to squeeze my eyes
shut even tighter
and open them an instant later.
When I did I was alone in a little meadow
by a narrow spring creek
under an empty cloudless sky.

Savor

Often but not always
it involves the mouth,
or in this case the beak
of a brown and gray bird,
feasting, yes, feasting
on a long visitation
of Japanese beetles,
with the odd leafy palms
at the ends of their antennae
and their many-spurred legs.
Mostly unflying today
they are seized and gobbled
when, surely, they ought to be
savored. But savor
must be a human construct,
an artifact hunger
suffers not to be.
                    Oh, not so,
not so, even in the bird's hurry,
that nugget of beetle lusciousness—
the thorax—is consumed, while
legs, heads, and antennae
are dropped, abandoned
like cosmic insectile lingerie
on a wild riverbank boudoir
fifty miles from cell reception
and sixty from the power grid.
We've been out here 15 days now.
I have no idea what is Japanese
about Japanese beetles,
but my mind wanders
among their weird carnage
and vows to begin
as early as possible

to ransack such memories
as I still remember
for any vestige
of lusciousness
I have lived through,
until I can taste them all.

INTERVIEW

Mary was born in Lewistown, Montana, to rancher Albert Hogeland and mother Doris Welch Hogeland in 1939. She is pictured here in 1943 with her grandmother, father, and younger sister in Montana.

THE WALTZ AND EVERYTHING ELSE: AN INTERVIEW WITH

MARY CLEARMAN BLEW

Joy Passanante and Gary Williams

lthough a film has yet to be made from any of her works, Mary Blew's aura is synonymous with the state of Montana. Her works body forth the geography and iconography of the Last Best Place, as surely as Norman Maclean's do, even if there's a minimum of fly fishing in them. The great empty high prairie of central-northern Montana has never minted the coin of scenic wonder, of sportsman's paradise. In *This Is Not the Ivy League*, her 2011 memoir, she speculates that newcomers to her part of the state are likely to be "stunned, then appalled" if mountains are what they're expecting. *"People really live out here?"*

Well, yes, they do, and have, including Mary and her ancestors going back to her homesteading great-grandfather in 1882. That's twenty-seven years before the Maclean clan arrived from Iowa. Mary's late good friend Ivan Doig was born the same year she was, in a similarly unfashionable part of the state. But unlike Ivan, Mary made her adult life for many years in the state of her birth, and only for a few years during and after graduate school has she lived more than a day's drive from the now-gone cattle ranch on the Little Judith River that was her formative landscape.

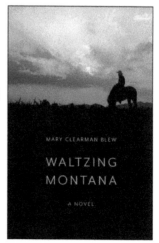

It wasn't, and isn't, glamorous in any sense. "If anything in my experience seems permanent, it is the prairie, with its pale turn of seasons, the quiet cycle of the grasses, the shadows of the clouds," Mary writes in one of the beautiful essays in *Bone Deep in Landscape*. Pale, quiet, shadowy . . . except that the people and lives that populate this terrain in Mary's work are the very last thing from pale or quiet or shadowy.

You have to be tough to live where she has lived, and where her characters make their lives against some substantial odds. These characters include real people like her grandmother, who lived alone on a ranch, pregnant and with two small children, without seeing another woman for eighteen months—carrying all her water from a spring a quarter of a mile away. Or like her larger-than-life second husband Bob Blew, Montana oil man, big spender (when he had it to spend), big liver, a man of "diamond-blue eyes," a man with "a grasshopper's delight in the sunlit present." The riveting story of his breakdown and Mary's nighttime flight with her youngest daughter to the "golden Palouse" makes the title essay in *All But the Waltz* one of the most powerful short memoirs of the contemporary West. Or like Corey Henry of *Jackalope Dreams*, "temper like a bad windstorm," charged with figuring out how to make a new life in her late fifties and finding that her talentsand internal resources are more than up to the task. Paul Wilner in the *Los Angeles Times* called Corey's story a "small masterpiece," deserving "the attention it makes a point of not seeking."

Mary herself is tough—though, meeting her casually, you might take a while to apprehend the steel that under-lies her congenial social self. Need a chocolate angel-food cake or the region's most prized cheese-cake? Mary's on it. How about a quilt? Mary has made around fifty full-sized beauties as gifts (including one begun by Gary's mother's cousin in the 1920s that languished for almost a century as 3,456 stacked pieces in a falling-apart box until Mary rendered them whole, fifteen stitches to the inch, as a gift to Joy on her retirement).

Or a bourbon-drinking companion? Couldn't find a more affable one. Accordion-player? Yup. The person at a party who can recite from memory "Ode on a Grecian Urn" and any number of lines from Shakespeare (although she claims she'd never give in to requests for such performances).

The steel has been visible over the years in various ways. Steel in her determination to finish college and a master's degree at the University of Montana despite an unexpected baby, a frazzled husband, and near-universal opposition from family, neighbors, and the local minister. Steel in managing to earn a Ph.D. at the University of Missouri while teaching four sections of first-year writing every semester for five years (and now there were two toddlers, and a husband with a full-time job, and a professor who wondered why she wasn't "working up to [her] ability"). Steel in her resolution to accept a job offer from Northern Montana College, which brought to an end both her first marriage and her pursuit of a scholarly life (but propelled her toward writing fiction again and produced *Lambing Out and Other Stories*). Steel in rising to the challenge of caring for her dementia-afflicted Aunt Imogene while single-parenting her young daughter Rachel in a new terrain and with a new job in Idaho. It's also work-ethic steel that has generated the almost incredible productivity of her recent years: three novels written and published in the five years since she retired from the University of Idaho in 2015, and a fourth currently in the publisher's hands.

But to backtrack a little. Mary's breakaway from Havre wasn't just an escape from a no-longer-tenable marriage, but also from academic administration. She'd been quickly commandeered into management at Northern, starting just three years after her arrival as chair of the English department. Before long she had found herself appointed, perhaps a bit improbably, as a dean charged with upgrading the nursing program. Her seven years at Lewis-Clark State College (1987-94) provided new opportunities to help nascent writers gain confidence in telling their stories and to offer the kind of support she herself had seldom received. Those years also gave her mental space to launch a second book of short fiction (*Runaway*) and the two books that made her a national figure in Western writing—*All But the Waltz* and *Balsamroot*, both published by Viking. She also garnered two Pacific Northwest Booksellers Awards in those years. Mary's decision to move to Moscow in the fall of 1994 was a momentous occasion for the University of Idaho's English department. The first faculty member ever to be hired at the full professor level with tenure, Mary joined Ron McFarland, Lance Olsen, and Tina Foriyes in designing the state's first graduate creative writing degree program, which opened its doors two years later.

And thus it happened that Montana Mary became also one of the gems of the Gem State. When we got to know her in the early 1990s, she had already been appointed to the Idaho Humanities Council, and soon became its chair. Half a dozen years later, she received the Council's Outstanding Achievement in the Humanities Award. A bunch more accolades followed, most notably a Lifetime Achievement Award from the Western Literature Association and a Western Heritage Award from the National Cowboy Hall of Fame.

For us, her University of Idaho colleagues, a much-valued highlight of Mary's twenty-one years at the University of Idaho are her collaborations with others to promote new writing about the west. She and novelist Kim Barnes produced a landmark collection called *Circle of Women: An Anthology of Contemporary Western Women Writers* (2001). And as she mentions below in the course of our chat, one of her prized projects was an edited essay series tackling the Elements. The first, *Written on Water: Essays on Idaho Rivers by Idaho Writers*, was a solo endeavor, after which she was joined by Phil Druker in turning out two others before Phil's untimely death—*Forged in Fire* and *Borne on Air*. These three volumes deliver work by over sixty Idaho writers, including a dozen or so who were nurtured in the University of Idaho's MFA program. The dedications of these collections also tell a critical part of the story of writing in Idaho—Water is "for the godparents of the Idaho writers, Keith and Shirley Browning"; Fire is for Rick Ardinger and the Idaho Humanities Council; and Air is for the memory of William Studebaker.

This interview with Mary happened on the back patio at what we've taken to calling Chez Passowilli, in the early summer of 2020 and in email exchanges for a month or two as the Coronavirus reshaped our socializing practices. It could have gone on for a few more months, from the interviewers' point of view: this subject is inexhaustible, prolific (18 books and counting, and don't forget those quilts), absorbing, astonishing, and about as affable as they come.

Williams: *First, Mary, thanks for sitting down with us in the time of COVID, at a distance, outside, to talk about yourself. It's not something you can be inveigled to do very often, and we're honored. So let's start by going back a long distance and ask when you first realized you wanted to be a writer?*

Blew: I can't remember a time when I didn't know I was a writer. I've always thought in terms of story, of something happening that leads to something else happening. My early years were on a remote ranch, deep in the sagebrush country of central Montana, and perhaps the compulsion to create stories came from the scarcity of books in my childhood. I was perhaps three years old when someone gave me a copy of *Raggedy Ann and Raggedy Andy* and the *Camel with the Wrinkled Knees*, which I begged to have read over and over to me. When the story invariably ended in the same way, I decided to write my own. I had learned to print in capital letters, so I printed up a full page and took it to my aunt to read it to me. "But honey, I can't read this! It doesn't say anything," she protested, and I felt my first frustration as a writer.

When my younger sister was old enough to talk and play, I invented complicated fantasies for us to act out, with an assortment of dolls and a cat in doll's clothing as minor characters. As I recall, some of these fantasies involved a couple of pioneer women and their children (the dolls and the cat) traveling West in a covered wagon and fending off all the perils I could think up. Occasionally the action became so fast-moving that I forgot to narrate it aloud, and my sister would implore, "Talk! Talk!"

Mary, her sister, and dolls in Lewistown, Montana, 1947

Passanante: *My sisters were roped into the same role! Do you remember the first time writing made you feel, as some might say, transcendent?*

Blew: Those early fantasies, if they can be called *writing,* lifted me out of dull daylight reality of the ranch in the sagebrush and into an alternate world, one I was certain existed somewhere, in which lives were action-packed and exciting. I had no idea that some might view my humdrum life of horseback riding and cattle-tending as exotic, even romantic.

Passanante: *So after the sister-fantasies, when you were old enough to read, how did your reading habits form? What were your favorite books from the early days?*

Blew: I had learned to read at a young age, in that I had been taught to sound out the words and struggle through a sentence, but I clearly remember the afternoon I read fluently for the first time. I think I was six. None of the adults in my family had time to read to me, so I picked up the book my grandmother had begun reading to me the night before and wandered outdoors. The unfinished story was calling to me, so at last I opened the book and told myself to try. Try turned out to be the right verb. After a few hesitations, I found myself reading easily down one page, then another, skipping any words I didn't understand and continuing until I had finished the book. Later that day, when my grandmother finally finished her day's work and offered to read my book to me, I said, "Oh! I finished it," and saw adult glances exchanged over my head.

But I never had enough books. Many of the ones I did have were outdated textbooks my grandmother and aunts brought home from the rural schools they taught. I still have one of those books, *Our Little Neighbors at Work and Play*, which told of children and their doings from around the world and also from American history. I seem to remember a story about two Puritan children, but the one I liked best was about Bear Claw and Bright Star, who did fascinating work like tanning hides and, in Bear Claw's case, making bows and arrows.

Mary, 1947

A bow and arrows—I could do that! I'll come back to the question in a minute, but I'm remembering a follow-up to my reading the story about Bear Claw. I borrowed my mother's paring knife and cut a good long and springy branch from the willow tree by the lane, as well as several short branches. I tried flaking arrowheads, as Bear Claw had, from road gravel, but he apparently knew more than I did about the process, so I finally gave up. But I strung my bow with what everyone called store string, the heavy white cord that in those days was tied around packages of purchases. And I notched an arrow. I was all set! All I needed was a target. Just then I spotted my grandmother walking out of the barn with a bucket of feed in each hand, and I took aim, let fly, and hit her right in her stomach.

I tell myself now I couldn't have hurt her—not with a willow twig less than a foot long—but it certainly surprised her. She dropped her buckets, and I dropped the bow and the rest of my arrows and decided to put some distance between her and me. From the other side of the ash pile, I watched as she picked up the bow I had dropped and fitted an arrow. Unfortunately, she didn't understand the mechanism and turned the bow backwards and shot herself again, just as my father came from the barn and burst into laughter. She turned her wrath on him, and I made myself scarce!

Passanante: *Remind me of other early books you read and loved. I know we share many of these.*

Blew: All of Laura Ingalls Wilder's *Little House* series. A lot of Zane Grey, whose novels tended to be found lying around ranch houses and bunkhouses. And Mary O'Hara's Wyoming trilogy. *My Friend Flicka. Thunderhead. Green Grass of Wyoming.* All of these books told me that the real West was in the past, probably in Arizona or Texas, or, if contemporary, in Wyoming. Certainly not in dull central Montana.

But then—I must have been in high school by then—I pulled a book from the library shelves called *Chip of the Flying U,* by B.M. Bower. To my astonishment, the novel's setting was a ranch near Chinook, Montana, on the Montana Highline, and when I read a few pages and discovered a character reading the Great Falls *Tribune,* I was struck by a revelation. Montana could be written about! Real towns, real newspapers, could appear in fiction! My Montana suddenly shone with a new light.

Another book I must have found on the library shelves was Mildred Walker's *Winter Wheat,* which I came to love and return to. Less "action-packed" than Bower's novels, *Winter Wheat* depicts a young girl on a small Montana wheat ranch who learns some painful lessons about herself and her parents and grows in the process. I've had many a good talk with the late Ivan Doig, who read *Winter Wheat* at about the same time I did and spoke lovingly about the influence it had had on him. High school girls often had syrupy religious novels like *The Robe* or *The Big Fisherman* thrust upon them, or the so-called "older girls" novels, whose plot followed a formula: girl has ambitions for a career, but wisely gives up her silly dreams to marry the boy next door. I remember a classmate of mine bragging that she had read every book on the "older girls" shelf except for the ones written by someone named "Jane Ever."

Passanante: *Funny! She meant* Jane Eyre, *yes? And did you also read these "syrupy" books? It's a familiar formula from those days, of course…*

Blew: Yes, I think my classmate meant *Jane Eyre*. And yes, I read everything, including *Anne of Green Gables*, which angered me: I realized the family illness that prevented Anne from attending college was a choice of the writer.

Williams: *This makes me wonder if, when you were young, you had anything like a changeling fantasy, believing you might somehow have been prevented from living the life that ought to have been yours?*

Blew: It was clear that boys were preferred in ranching culture, and I was encouraged to act like a boy. I helped my father break horses, round up cattle, brand calves. But also I wanted to be a part of the great romantic *elsewhere.* When I read news stories about Wallis Simpson living the high life with the Duke of Windsor, who had given up his throne for her, I was transfixed. How much Wallis Simpson had dared! Could I dare as much?

Mary and pony in Montana, 1949

Passanante: *Well, clearly you did! But support helps when you determine to dare something. Which particular teachers or other adults validated you as a talented person?*

Blew: I was home-schooled until I was eight. One of the first adults to recognize my potential was the county superintendent of schools, a friend of my grandmother, who administered a placement test when I finally was enrolled in a rural school. When the test showed that I was reading at the 12th grade level and doing arithmetic at the 3rd grade level (I'd forgotten how to do long division, which my mother had taught me), the county superintendent told my parents I was gifted and that they should provide me with special resources, like a typewriter, which they shook their heads over. For the sake of the teacher, who already was teaching eight children in six grades, I was placed with three other children in the fourth grade and spent my next years whipping through my reading assignments, then being bored and drifting into daydreaming.

I started high school in Lewistown, Montana, in the fall of 1953, a time when expectations for girls were low. All girls took an obligatory year of home economics, where we were lectured on preparing a budget and cooking for the family we soon would be starting. And I remember that, when a geometry teacher heard I planned to go to college, he asked me if I was going after my MRS degree. When my English teacher gave my class a test on our reading speed, he was startled to find me clocking in at 3,000 words a minute with excellent comprehension, but he gave no extra encouragement. On the other hand, the biology teacher, a Mr. Robinson, praised my work in his class and encouraged me to do my best. I still have the biology notebook I kept for him, with drawings and text.

However, both of my parents and my grandmother were supportive of my further education, my grandmother's mantra being that every woman should be able to support herself. She had helped her daughters through the minimum two years of what was called normal school to qualify as rural school-teachers, and the plan for me was to do the same. My parents apparently were unaware that the full four years of college were by then required for a teaching certificate. And I had higher aspirations for myself, which I couldn't have articulated.

Mary, 1956

Williams: *Even if not quite formulated, the aspirations probably depended on attending the University of Montana, right? How did that happen?*

Blew: My high school guidance counselor had decided that I should enter the elementary education program at Eastern Montana College (now Montana State University-Billings), explaining to my parents that it was close to home and best suited to their means. When scholarship tests for the University of Montana were sent to his office, he selected two other students to sit for them. It turned out that the University of Montana sent three, not two tests to him. "Can Mary take one?" asked one of the selected students, a friend of mine. When he agreed, she ran downstairs and stopped me before I could board the school bus for home. As it turned out, she didn't win a scholarship and I did.

Passanante: *So what did you study?*

Blew: As a freshman at the University of Montana in 1957, I signed up as a drama major, in keeping with my exalted ideas, and I also registered in a first-year Latin class. After my freshman year, at the age of eighteen I married Ted Clearman, from Helena, Montana, who planned to become a high school English teacher in good hunting and fishing country. He convinced me to change my major to English, where I began the honors track in writing along with coursework in literature and, eventually, creative writing classes from Robert O. Bowen, Henry V. Larom, and Leslie Fiedler. I wrote fiction that was published in the department's creative writing journal, *Venture*, and I also continued with Latin, having fallen in love with the language, graduating with a double major in English and Latin.

At some point I took the Graduate Record Exam and received high marks, which led me into the department's MA program and eventually to the PhD program at the University of Missouri-Columbia. By this time, Ted and I had two children, Jack and Elizabeth. Ted taught at Jefferson Junior High School in Columbia while I studied and taught undergraduate classes. While at the University of Missouri, although I was in the literature track, I wrote a short story called "Lambing Out," which won a prize for fiction that enabled me to purchase an electric typewriter, and earned me praise from Professor William Peden, who headed the creative writing program.

Williams: *So, your PhD in Renaissance Studies would seemingly put you on a track to become a literary scholar, but even while in school you were nurturing two talents. What nudged you toward imaginative writing instead of literary research?*

Blew: I had never really stopped writing creative work. It's true that when I finished my PhD program, I thought of myself as being on the track to literary scholarship and research. I had recently published my first scholarly article, "Aspects of Juvenal in Byron's *English Bards and Scotch Reviewers* in the *Keats-Shelley Journal* and was working on a similar article that would have tracked influences of Juvenal through Hamlet's lines when Polonius asks him what he is reading: "Why, slander, sir. For the satirical rogue says here that old men have gray beards . . . ." I was arguing that the "satirical rogue" was the Roman satirist, Juvenal, and that Hamlet was reading Juvenal's Satire XV, sometimes called "The Vanity of Human Wishes."

"A note on *Hamlet* would be very exciting," my dissertation advisor, Professor Donald Anderson, encouraged. But I was graduating and— as was expected in those days—following my husband to a suburb of Seattle, where he had found a job teaching in a junior high school. I spent a year searching unsuccessfully for work when I spotted an advertisement for an assistant professor at Northern Montana College (now Montana State University-Northern) in Havre.

I called the number in the ad and to my astonishment almost immediately was invited to an interview. When the chairman of the English department learned I was from Montana and wasn't alarmed by distances, he offered me the job. After discussing it at home with Ted, we decided I should accept the position and, with our two children, go to live in Havre while he continued to teach in the Seattle suburb until he could find a position near us.

Passanante: *Was this a difficult discussion, and decision? What year are we talking about now?*

Blew: It was the fall of 1969, and yes, it was a difficult decision. I would be living on my own, getting an eight-year-old and a six-year-old ready for school in Havre, while beginning a new teaching position in a remote rural college, while Ted visited on occasional weekends. But I simply could not continue doing—well, nothing.

During my first week at Northern, I learned that the college lacked a library that came anywhere near to my research needs. With no internet, only a slow and undependable interlibrary loan system, I turned from research to writing fiction again, publishing in literary journals like *The North American Review* and *The Gettysburg Review*, and eventually in a collection, *Lambing Out and Other Stories*, as part of the Breakthrough Series at the University of Missouri Press in 1978.

Williams: *Finding a venue in such prominent journals must also have assured you that you'd chosen wisely. So, your publishing life took off with short fiction—and then in 1991 you nailed (and in fact helped define) the personal essay/ memoir form with* All But the Waltz. *What generated that switch?*

Blew: I think all prose writers of my generation began with short fiction, which, then as now, was what was taught in creative writing classes. During my years at Northern, I began a couple of novels, but fell back on short fiction, which I could write in the bits of time I had between working and caring for my children. (By this time, my marriage had failed). But in 1987 a financial crisis overcame the state of Montana, which in turn riddled the budgets of colleges and universities.

My position, by that time Dean of Arts and Sciences, was slated to be eliminated. Although I could have fallen back on my tenured position as a professor in the English department, thereby forcing the firing of a younger faculty member, I began the search for another job and found an advertisement from Lewis-Clark State College, in Lewiston, Idaho, for a professor of Shakespeare. I applied and was given the position almost immediately—in part, I later learned, because the faculty spotted *Lambing Out* and realized that, in addition to my teaching classes in Shakespeare, I could help to develop their program in creative writing.

Passanante: *So did you offer LCSC's first creative writing classes?*

Blew: No, not at all. Bob Wrigley had been teaching poetry classes at LCSC for several years before I arrived. He and Hugh Nichols, the Dean of Arts and Sciences, hoped to develop a BFA degree in creative writing. Keith Browning had been running Confluence Press and publishing a literary journal, *Slackwater Review*. After Keith's retirement, Jim Hepworth took over Confluence Press and taught composition and publishing arts. Jim knew an editor at Viking-Penguin, Dan Frank, with whom Hepworth had negotiated the re-releasing of a book of essays Confluence Press had just published, *Having Everything Right*, by Kim Stafford. Hepworth was prescient—we were about to enter the 1990s, the decade of the personal essay—and he continually urged me to try my hand. I read *Having Everything Right* and *A River Runs through It*, by Norman Maclean, and also *Owning It All*, by William

Mary in Lewiston, Idaho, 1989

Kittredge. Particularly after reading *Owning It All*, a memoir of Kittredge's growing up on a remote cattle ranch in eastern Oregon, which mirrored some of my own early ranching experiences, the thought drifted up: I could do this.

And so I began the essays that soon would become *All but the Waltz*. Jim Hepworth had negotiated a contract with Dan Frank and Viking, who gave me an advance of $10,000, and I felt as though I had been discovered on a soda fountain stool in Hollywood! A few years later, Dan Frank also published my memoir, *Balsamroot*, about my aunt's experiences with dementia at the end of her life and my experiences in caring for her.

Passanante: *At that point—this was thirty years ago now—your writing began directly to engage your family. Could you talk a bit about any challenges you felt then in making your family your subject? I know that several of your books are dedicated to family members.*

Blew: I believe only three of my books have been dedicated to people other than family members: one to Keith and Shirley Browning, one to you two, and then *Sweep Out the Ashes* is dedicated to the Palouse Writers (for the record, that's you, me, DJ Lee, Pete Chilson, Rochelle Smith, and Jeff Jones).

Most of my family and friends have praised my personal essays, although my mother used to sniff and remark, "You ought to take that out," until she would have reduced the text to a skeleton. On a sadder note, I lost a close friend when I wrote an essay about her late mother, a distinguished novelist, and remarked of her life, "It was as though she was two women." My friend cut all contact with me and complained to other friends and to her own editor that I had stolen her idea. Nothing came of her complaints on the professional level—as my own editor remarked, "It isn't really such a remarkable insight." But I grieved the loss of the friendship for a long time.

Williams: *All writers, of course, put something of themselves in the work.*

Blew: Madame Bovary, c'est moi, as Flaubert famously said. But hopefully all family members don't take Flaubert's remark as literally as my first husband, Ted, who was certain he was being portrayed, thinly disguised, in my fiction, which he tried to read over my shoulder as I wrote. When I started a never-finished story about a widow, he remarked sadly, "I see you've killed me off this time." However, we were long divorced before I started publishing nonfiction. In later years, talking with other women writers, I learned his reaction was common, "From a heightened sense of privacy," as writer Patricia Henley put it. As for my children and grandchildren, they have been supportive. My oldest daughter, Elizabeth, remarked after reading *Balsamroot*, "I don't remember some of these scenes the way you do, but it's your story to tell." And when, recently, I told my fifteen-year-old granddaughter that I was naming a character in a new novel for her, she said very little, but her mother reported that she hurried home, screaming, "Grandma Mary's putting me in a novel! I've wanted to be in a novel all my life!"

Passanante: *I've taught* All But the Waltz *in more classes than I can count, and Gary's taught* Balsamroot *several times. The narratives in both these works seem to spin out in a harmoniously coherent way, as if they required no attention to technique to arrive at their final form. But were there other nonfiction writers whose work impacted your strategies in those early days?*

Blew: I've mentioned Norman MacLean, Kim Stafford, and William Kittredge. I can add Linda Hasselstrom, the South Dakota writer and rancher. As more memoirs about life in the American West began to appear, I loved and pondered over the work of my friend Annick Smith, who began writing nonfiction about the same time I did, as well as that of Terry Tempest Williams and Teresa Jordan, who wrote a little-known book called *Cowgirls* and has since turned to watercolor art.

Williams: *When you joined the University of Idaho faculty in 1994, plans began to launch Idaho's first MFA in Creative Writing program. What do you remember about those earliest days? Your first classes in the program? How has teaching in the program affected your own writing?*

Blew: We opened the MFA program for the first time in the fall of 1996 to seven graduate students, of whom one, Paula Coomer, has continued to write steadily and publish her work. As you know, the outlines of the MFA program, the first in Idaho, had been shaped and seen through the state approval process by you, Gary, as chair of the English department then, and by Lance Olsen, recently hired to teach innovative fiction. All of us were feeling our way in those days, designing classes and making assignments that fit around those early students. I remember those times as filled with endless demands: meetings, counseling of students, experimentation with curriculum, debates about the program within the creative writing faculty (there were four of us during that first year—Tina Foriyes, Ron McFarland, Lance, and me—with Lance on sabbatical). It also was a time of excitement, the feeling that we were creating something that was growing as we worked, something with enormous promise. And I found myself drawing energy from the energy of my students.

Williams: *Yes, I think the whole faculty felt that energy, because the MFA program put its students in lots of literature classes as well. But now let's move forward about twenty years from that point and talk about your shift to the long form. In recent years you've won an impressive amount of acclaim for your novels. Can you talk about your evolution from short to long fiction? How did your work on* Jackalope Dreams, *your first novel, begin?*

Blew: For years, beginning during my years at Northern Montana College and continuing through the years at LCSC, I had tried and failed to write novels, although I preserved the drafts. However, my first successful long work was *Jackalope Dreams* (unless you count the novella "Sister Coyote," which was included in the collection *Sister Coyote* published in 2000). I think the shape of *Jackalope Dreams* grew out of my experience with nonfiction. *Balsamroot*, for example, is not a collection of linked essays, but a continuous narrative that patterns a novel. Like *Balsamroot, Jackalope Dreams* moves back and forth between present time and the past, exploring the effect of the past on the present.

The idea for *Jackalope Dreams* was sparked by the life of a woman, Evelyn Cole, who ranched on the prairie near Chinook, Montana, during the mid-twentieth century. Apparently from her girlhood she had yearned to become an artist, and somehow she managed to attend a term at the Minneapolis Institute of Art, where she experienced the clash between contemporary art practices and her own Western representational paintings. Disillusioned but determined, she returned to her prairie home and made a local name for herself as a painter and sculptor.

In the 1970s, I had lunch in a Chinook café which featured her murals of stiff ranching scenes with all the figures outlined in black. She came to statewide attention when she entered a contest for a sculpture of the cowboy artist C.M. Russell to be placed in the Montana capitol. "One of the entrants in the C.M. Russell contest is a woman," read one newspaper headline. Also in the newspaper was a photograph of the statue itself, a strange monolithic figure that looked as if it belonged on the tomb of a pharaoh of Egypt.

What, I wondered, had led this woman, whose life resembled that of my early years, to imagine herself as a sculptor? That thought led to another: what might have become of my creative drive if I had been an obedient daughter and gone on living on my parents' ranch while teaching in rural schools? My answer was that the creative drive would have refused to be stifled and might have emerged in unexpected, even bizarre form. And so was born the central character of *Jackalope Dreams*.

Williams: Jackalope Dreams *appeared in 2008, and then it's almost a decade before the next novel,* Ruby Dreams of Janis Joplin. *Those weren't empty years, of course, but your attention turned to editorial work for a period. How do you feel about that phase of your publishing life (which also included another memoir,* This is Not the Ivy League)?

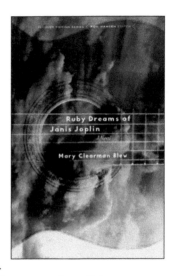

Blew: My years of living at the confluence of the Snake and Clearwater Rivers had awakened me to the beauty of Idaho's rivers. As the late poet William Studebaker had pointed out, Idaho is the great state of rivers. It occurred to me to showcase this wonderful resource by editing a collection of essays about those rivers. "Choose a river, any river for an essay," I asked friends and colleagues, who responded enthusiastically. "I own the St. Joe," I remember Ron McFarland replying. Soon the collection, *Written on Water,* was published by the University of Idaho Press. Shortly afterward, my colleague Phil Druker stuck his head around my office door and remarked, "You've done water. How about the other three elements?" And Phil and I went on to co-edit *Borne on Air* and *Forged in Fire,* essays by Idaho writers. We talked of a collection of essays about the fourth element, earth, but Phil's illness and untimely death intervened, and I didn't have the heart to continue.

Passanante: *Tell us about your extraordinary productivity since retirement.*

Blew: I retired in June of 2015 but returned to UI during the spring term of 2016 to teach a graduate seminar in the art of the personal essay that had lost its instructor. I had never taught that seminar, so the preparation was intense, as were the needs of the students under the stress of having lost one professor and changing stream with another. On the other hand, it was one of the most stimulating classes, with some of the most outstanding students, that I ever had taught.

At the end of that semester I turned in final grades and went home, finding myself for the first time in my life without the demands of full-time teaching and hands-on single motherhood, yet keyed with the excitement of the class I had just finished. I opened a new computer file, dragged out the failed draft of a novel I had written during my LCSC years, and began, not revising, but reimagining. In thirty days I had a complete new draft of *Ruby Dreams of Janis Joplin*, which saw publication in 2018. Almost immediately I began a new draft of what would become *Sweep Out the Ashes*, published in 2019, and another, *Waltzing Montana*, in 2021. A fourth novel, *Think of Horses*, also borne of previous failed work, currently rests on my editor's desk. If I do say so, not a bad run in four years!

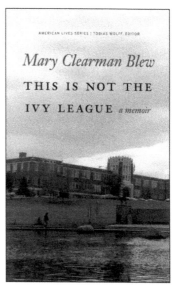

Passanante: *Can't help smiling here. Mary, what an understatement! So, taking a long retrospective view, what have been your most significant challenges in forging your professional life?*

Blew: Being a professional woman during my time and place has been a challenge which I explore in my novel *Sweep Out the Ashes*. But a larger challenge has been living as a single mother—I have raised three of my birth children as well as a foster-daughter—while teaching full-time, often with heavily weighted class assignments.

Williams: *And now, even though you still take an active role in raising grandchildren in your home, what are your plans for the future?*

Blew: If another novel comes along and taps me on the shoulder, I'm here. ∎

Mary Blew, summer, 2020

BY MARY CLEARMAN BLEW

Stories
Lambing Out and Other Stories (University of Missouri Press, 1977)
Runaway: A Collection of Stories (Confluence Press, 1990)
Sister Coyote: Montana Stories (The Lyons Press, 2000)

Novels
Jackalope Dreams (University of Nebraska Press, 2008)
Ruby Dreams of Janis Joplin (University of Nebraska Press, 2018)
Sweep Out the Ashes (University of Nebraska Press, 2019)
Waltzing Montana (University of Nebraska Press, 2021)
Think of Horses (University of Nebraska Press, forthcoming)

Memoir
All But the Waltz: Essays on a Montana Family (Viking, 1991)
Balsamroot: A Memoir (Viking, 1994)
When Montana and I Were Young: A Memoir of a Frontier Childhood,
        by Margaret Bell (edited and with an introduction by
        Mary Clearman Blew, University of Nebraska Press, 2003)
This Is Not the Ivy League: A Memoir (University of Nebraska Press, 2011)
Writing Her Own Life: Imogene Welch, Western Rural Schoolteacher
        (University of Oklahoma Press, 2004)

Essays
Bone Deep in Landscape: Writing, Reading, and Place
        (University of Oklahoma Press, 2000)

Edited Anthologies
Circle of Women: An Anthology of Contemporary Western Women Writers
        (Ed. with Kim Barnes, Penguin Books, 1994)
Written on Water: Essays on Idaho Rivers by Idaho Writers
        (University of Idaho Press, 2004)
Forged in Fire: Essays by Idaho Writers (Ed. with Phil Druker,
        University of Oklahoma Press, 2005)
Borne on Air, Essays by Idaho Writers
        (Ed. with Phil Druker, Eastern Washington University Press, 2009)

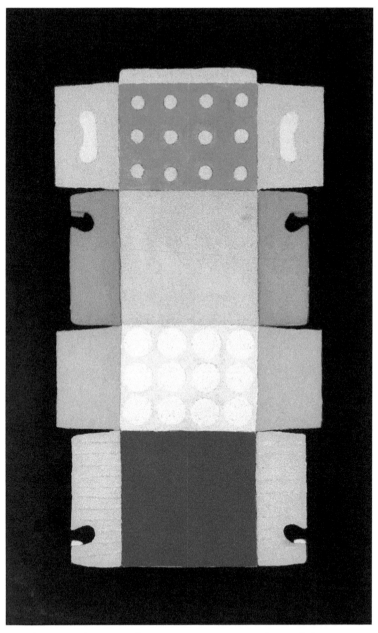

"Half a Case of Corona" by Dennis DeFoggi, acrylic and thinset on panel, 43" x 23," 2020.

ESSAYS & NONFICTION

University of Wisconsin Oshkosh
Historical Marker

Black Thursday

On Thursday, November 21, 1968, 94 African-American students occupied the offices of Wisconsin State University-Oshkosh President Roger Guiles, demanding that the University improve its relationship with black students. As a result of their protest, the students were arrested and soon thereafter expelled. Many never returned to the University. Others continued their education elsewhere. The students' actions led the administration and the entire Wisconsin State University System to examine their commitment to the black students they were actively recruiting. The sacrifices of the following 94 students brought several reforms to the campus, including the creation of the Multicultural Education Center and a diversification of the faculty and curriculum.

Ernest Abbott	Stephen Coulter	Gay Howard	Kenneth Owens
Barbara Adams	Barbara Dallas	Donald Jackson	Dorothy Palmer
James Allen	Glen Davis	Esther Jackson	Gloria Palmer
Delores Banks	Noreen Debnam	Joel Johnson	Bernard Patterson
Mary Barnes	Gregory Doby	Lyna Johnson	Essie Reed
Floria Bell	Jarden Eckles	Rita Johnson	Lamont Robbins
Margaret Bell	Glenn Ferguson	Shirley Johnson	Bettie Rodgers
Sadye Bender	Rufus Finner	Charles Kimble	Elliott Ross
Jerry Benston Jr.	Rhonda Foulks	Ruth King	Glenn Ross
Karen Berkley	Edward Franks Jr.	Caleb Leggett II	William Sinclair Jr.
Vincent Bevenue	Ruth Frausto	Martha Leonard	Carolyn Staples
Darryl Bevly	Wanetta Fullove	Jerrel Malone	James Tatum
Judy Braggs	Michael Gordon	Robert Martin	Bradley Thurman
Janice Brazil	Susette Gordon	Vickie Marzette	Carolyn Warren
Henry Brown, III	Phyllis Graham	Loretta Mattox	Ervin Weatherby
Richard Browne	Yvonne Gransberry	Betty McCadney	Leonard White Jr.
Anthony Brunson	Ross Grant Jr.	Geoffrey McCreary	Karen Williams
Sandra Calvin	Katie Gray	Sandra McCreary	Robert Willis
Celeste Campbell	Irma Hall	Thomas Miles	Ruth Williams
Carl Caroll	Robert Harris	Jesse Miller III	Avera Wilson
Michael Carufel	Vada Harris	Milton Mitchell	Susan Woodruff
Henry Clay	Robert Hayes	Juanita Moore	Lonnie Woods
Manuel Cockroft Jr.	Samuel Henly	Sheila Morgan	
Gladys Coleman	Joyce Hunter	George North	

Dedicated February 2011

Plaque honoring student social reform attempt on "Black Thursday," November 21, 1968, at Wisconsin State University-Oshkosh.

ALEX KUO

I Wanted to Write a Story

Plain and simple. Although I was born in Boston, I spent most of the Second World War in Japanese-occupied Shanghai. Toward the end of the war, we were bombed almost daily by American B-29s. The sound of the thunderous roar of the Wright engines in those Boeing bombers still haunts me: first the air raid sirens and a rush to duck under furniture, then moments later the deep, thunderous roar of the massive engines, followed quickly by explosions, shattered windows, choking smoke, body parts in the streets, and dead birds everywhere, the air sucked out of their lungs by the explosions. Death by friendly fire. I don't remember any of the horrible crying, and there had to have been a lot of it everywhere, in the alleys, hallways, churches.

Like Jim in J.G. Ballard's autobiographical novel *Empire of the Sun* at the end of this war, I too saw the reflection of history's first deployment of a weapon of mass destruction, *Little Boy*, over Hiroshima on the early morning of August 6, 1945. Ballard described it "as if the sun had blinked, losing heart for a few seconds." In my autobiographical novella "White Jade," I described it as "an unearthly blue light throbbing in the distant sky beyond the east window, as if the sun for a few seconds had been displaced by a pale, blue sheen covering everything, everything."

Over a long, eighteen-year circuitous journey between Shanghai and Oshkosh, I had decided that I wanted to be a writer; but it was not until the events that took place at Wisconsin State University-Oshkosh on Black Thursday*, November 21, 1968, that I started to learn what kind of writer I wanted to be and what kind of story I wanted to write. Up to that point, for about a decade I had been playing the role of the writer: got a MFA from Iowa's Writers' Workshop along the way, publishing here and there in "littles," writing easy, obscure and deferential poems of no particular significance or of any personal interest to me, making things up, as it were, and the brutal exploitation of technique, technique, technique, as if I had to repeatedly demonstrate a technical confidence that I could write a poem about anything at all, crop the line, trim the image and craft a crisp ending, the kinds of thing a good creative writing student remembers later for tenure in an academic career.

This realization that I really wanted to be a different kind of writer started about a week before Black Thursday, when one of my freshman composition students asked me to be the faculty advisor to the Black Student Union with its 130 members, 1.86% of the 7,000 student body, or about one fifth of one percent of the town's population. Joyce Hunter had asked me because, as she put it, "You're the closest to being colored" among the faculty.

That made me different, an outsider, and I learned quickly that that essential difference is what writing is all about.

Bye-bye to the assimilation model. I refused to be destroyed by the American academic life, the institution that had been both a prison and bane for Chinese intellectuals and writers and artisans for more than twelve centuries, a location that ultimately compromised them and turned them into grifters, con artists running scams, courtiers, "phonies," as Holden Caulfield would have called them.

Somewhere in here I must have understood what kind of writing I was about to do, because I started taking pages and pages of field notes of Oshkosh, its culture and its politics, in the process archiving documents, and paying attention to everything happening in front of me and trying to remember everything as it was without changing a word of it, just in case it might be useful later, even when I didn't quite understand what I was witnessing at the time. That included this description of a cracker at the Howard Johnson's bar celebrating the Black students being expelled from the university: "Silent hunks of people, displaced or not, from Belgium, Holland, Russia, and always Germany, the first illegal aliens, uninvited, who didn't know the language, religion or customs. These translucent men came in unending numbers, their wide-chunked bodies filling their social clubs, churches, and assorted animal lodges**. Always good with their hands, they now chisel their epitaphs in agonizing fonts and serve fresh bear stew to everyone up at Fuzzy Thurston's Left Guard Restaurant in Green Bay when the Chicago Bears come to town."

Some of these events were later included in my recently published novel *The Man Who Dammed the Yangtze*. It included the names of several key Black Thursday participants starting with political science department chair David Chang, Green Bay Packer left guard Fuzzy

Thurston, president Roger E. Guiles, vice-president Sherman Gunderson, judges Sitter, Miller, Channey, and Horowitz, Miss Wisconsin Sharon Singstock, Oshkosh area Chamber of Commerce's Robert Yarbro, Sigma Pi fraternity's correspondence secretary Timothy Morrissey, vice-president Ray "Rocket" Ramsden. In this novel I used their real names because I believed it was important to get the facts right, especially in a work of fiction. But mostly because like Dante and Joyce, I believed the guilty must be held accountable for their actions, and using their real names reflected my authorial bookkeeping.

I also kept the names of the people who did the right thing, especially for the right reason, for the record, so to speak. Head of student government David Frank, Federal District Judge James Doyle, Milwaukee State Rep Lloyd Barbee, Father James Groppi the White Knight, and the names of all of the 98 students who were hauled away from Dempsey Hall that morning to the jails in Winnebago County, Neenah City Police, Fond du Lac County, Outagamie County, and Waushara County.

Somewhere here in the late 60s, I started to write fiction, perhaps influenced in part by Vine Deloria Jr. and Luisa Valenzuela's argument that fiction is a more effective political instrument, and realizing after teaching Melville's *Moby Dick*, that it was a startling political novel, moreso than Conrad's *Heart of Darkness* or Malraux's *Man's Fate*. This is not to deny that poetry—especially poetry as witness, as in W.H. Auden's "September 1, 1939," Carolyn Forche's "The Colonel," Anna Swirszczynska's "Building the Barricade," or Joy Harjo's "For Anna Mae Pictou Aquash" that were based on political events, or imagined political events as in Dante's *The Divine Comedy*—does not provoke a substantial and significant response from the reader. Of course it does. Just maybe the difference between fiction and poetry lies in that imagined dialogue with Margaret Atwood in which she'll convince you of those differences and when they cross over in so many words.

After resigning from Oshkosh on the same day that I received my tenure notification the following spring, my writing turned more and more to fiction, as if there were a connection, at least a determination. The beginning was slow and halting, as I went through a decade of university administration during which my colleagues thought I was taking anal, copious notes of meetings, when in truth I was actually writing down their profiles for future use.

It wasn't until I finally retired from university life [the first time] and Boulder, Colorado, that this determination resulted in completed work, written on the old Lexitron VT 1303 a set of four stories published almost immediately in the *Chicago Review* while I was teaching in Beijing right after the Tiananmen Square incident. That semester I saw the willful, ideological distortion by American journalists reporting on the events of that political spring, especially that iconographic photograph of the Tank Man waving a bag in front of a column of four Type 59 tanks, who *Time* magazine later elevated from a heroic student to one of the most important people of the 20th century no less, when in reality he was a senior security agent tasking these tanks. That's the story I had to write, how American journalism faithfully perpetuated the one-hundred-and-eighty year history of seeing and reporting on China through self-serving and myopic narratives. (This episode is explored in my current novel-in-progress, *shanghai.shanghai.shangha*, the last in the Ge trilogy.)

I was very disturbed by my country's racist coverage of news events in the country of my parents, and tried to resolve it by affirming that fiction, literature, art, had to provide a critical and counter voice to that late-capitalistic perception of the world, and proceeded to write short stories, novels and essays about the lives of the people in Beijing, their dreams, wishes, lies. This determination culminated in the collection *Lipstick and Other Stories* that received the American Book Award in 2001, and also in the recently released essay collection, *My Private China*, and other work in between.

It has not been easy, taking huge chances along the way, the space between my non-fiction and fiction often blurring, and the distance between the story-being-narrated and the editorial me looking over and occasionally stepping into the narrative just enough to be uncomfortable for most readers. To complicate things further, I continue to believe in the transformative power of words, and place great emphasis on language and its beauty, taking on huge risks with the form and shape of my work.

Since I believe that writers are not joiners, I have avoided net-working, especially the Association of Writing Programs, and have suggested mostly unsuccessfully to my best writing students to stay away from the MFA and get a real life. I detest the consumer-driven memoir, and vampires, and have refused to deliberately write anything that'll make the reader cry.

And I do not make up anything, unless it's true, as in my narrative of the November 21, 1968 events in Oshkosh.

I continue to write in this way, trying to write only of things that are important that I care about, and to satisfy my personal curiosity. In this process my work has earned the admiration and respect of some of my friends, agent and publishers, but sometimes I can hear them whispering "that's not commercially viable," while other friends pretend they do not know I'm a writer. I cannot think of another life that I would want to have pursued. This is the story I wanted to write. ■

*For taking over the office of Wisconsin State University-Oshkosh's president Roger E. Guiles's office on the morning of Thursday, November 21, 1968, 98 members of the Black Student Union were carted away in rented U-Haul trucks by the city police, and later 104 of them were summarily expelled without a hearing. They left behind a bewildered president, a trashed telephone, a busted IBM Selectric typewriter, a couple of broken ashtrays, a chair with a cracked arm, and a knocked-over filing cabinet during an otherwise peaceful one-hour occupation in which they presented a list of demands. They had the nerve to ask the university to academically and culturally reflect the diversity of Wisconsin and the nation.

**Elks, Moose, Lions, Eagles.

The White Savage Apartments, a 1910 building in Boise that Alan Minskoff helped renovate in the 1970s.

ALAN MINSKOFF

The Discreet Charm of the Small
An excerpt from Three-Quarter Time, *a memoir-in-progress*

A seventy-four-year old lapsed Jew, born in White Plains, New York, has lived the better part of fifty years in Boise, now on Loggers Creek. I have a mild case of epilepsy, am addicted to coffee, fancy wine, exercise sometimes to excess, lost my gardening mentor but continue to fill my raised beds with tomatoes and herbs. Live in the red brick house of my dreams with my best pal and wife of not quite four decades, Royanne. A seventy-four-year-old transplant who has spent most of my adult life in Idaho as an editor, teacher, writer, who has traveled to Idaho's out-of-the-way corners to find things small writ large. Still teaching after all these years, a septuagenarian reared in Westchester County, I write in long hand in bound notebooks on quadrangle sheets. A medium blue liberal in crimson Idaho. The boyhood fears—ice, heights, water immersion—stick like wet sweat. My body assures me daily it feels used: it aches, creaks, bruises, retreats awaits orders and routes.

Living by the Boise River on Loggers Creek, I am an exile from the big city and the big time, moved west to roost by the moving water, out of the rains, away from the noise, detached. Except.

II

In the summer of 1970, I had recently divorced, was anything but certain about my academic future as a grad student at the University of Chicago, and was mentally off kilter. When Calvin Jensen, my friend and fellow grad student, offered me the opportunity to come to Boise for a month and help out renovating an old building, the grand dame of north end residences—the 1910 White Savage Apartments—I got a plane ticket and headed west.

The old building, then owned by Calvin Jensen and Ray Allen, had a handsome exterior of white painted bricks and bark brown wooden porches facing 13th street. The inside held a different story: the apartments had wobbly Murphy beds tucked in the walls; pitted plaster, antiquated wiring; kitchens that seemed pre-World War II. The units were coated with the dust and grit of the past. The first facts of fixing up old buildings: history reveals itself in crinkled up old newspapers buried in the walls, layers of old wall coverings, two-by-fours that actually measure two inches by four inches, wavy glass windows and tongue-and-groove oak floors. By the time I left, I decided to invest in the building, move to Boise sometime in the not too distant future, and reinvent myself.

III

What drew me to live in Boise and later to investigate small town Idaho? When I moved here in the early 1970s, everything about Boise and Idaho was different from what I had known. The clear dry air, the imposing mountains, the transparent rock-strewn streams and vast fields were so different from what I knew—packed parkways, noisy streets, museums, literature, indoor life. The long drives with steep pitches, the seductive encompassing darkness, the bracing air, the more modest human mark, silence, here was a place to evolve into, to take in, to stay.

I came to Boise a privileged city kid, a naïf, who had never hammered a nail, painted a wall, had no idea what sheetrock was, no less how to hang it. That hot, dry August fifty years ago, I reset my clock, cast my line at a different angle. I knew Idaho would become home.

Two years later I moved here permanently. I expect like many who came of age in the charged particles of the 1960s, I saw a value in acting impulsively, followed my own bent and between the summer of 1970 and the spring of 1972, I decided to take a leave from grad school at the University of Chicago, first to live in Italy then to move to Idaho in June of 1972.

IV

My backstory. I grew up in the gilt-edged suburbs of New York, the youngest son and potential scion of a real estate family that went back to the late 19th century when my grandfather Sam Minskoff, immigrated to the country. SM, as he was known, began as a plumber's assistant, and within a generation rode the Horatio Alger special becoming a plumbing contractor, general contractor then owner builder. He built apartments, hotels and shopping centers. He died from heart failure when I was three, so I have no real memory of him. My father, the second of six children and his younger brothers Jerry and Myron ran the business after his death and focused more on office buildings by the mid-1960s. They were one of a handful of New York builders featured in *Fortune Magazine*.

While I never really saw myself as the heir apparent—majored in American Studies in college, history of culture in grad school—I wanted to write like John Dos Passos. The glitter and gloss of running a family business was off and on my magnetic north. However, I was a screw-up, a drop out, wannabe writer. I remember (though I have been able to locate it) watching a PBS interview of James Baldwin, who when asked what he would recommend to the aspiring writer, answered, find a city of about 50,000, go there, learn all you can about it and write. Boise was a modest and isolated capital city of about 75,000 people. Boise fit.

V

My family resources gave me options: to spend time in Italy, drop out, ultimately invest in White Savage and move to Boise. The pull of Idaho, the independent life of renovating old buildings and living in a vast state with a small population beckoned. And on a Saturday in June of 1972, a white-hot afternoon, I became a full-time White Savage resident and partner. I pulled up in my VW Squareback and parked on 13th and moved into my apartment on the second floor across the hall from Jack Gish. He grew up in north Idaho, was a GI who married his German girlfriend Ludmilla, played guitar and wrote haunting folk songs. Many a night we stayed up to the pale gray hours and sang Bob Dylan, John Prine and Jack Gish tunes.

The old building became home, workplace and spiritual center. We did demolition, which can be very satisfying and is the necessary first step in renovating. I lived alone, could fall out of bed and be at work. Everything we removed was worn out and old. We recycled, renovated and refurbished, left the historic details and look of the building intact, but removed the old Murphy beds, dropped them off the porches to the side yard. We pulled out the plaster, the board and batten walls, upgraded the electric system and plumbing fixtures. We also added some singular touches: alder butcher blocks in the kitchens, sprayed the woodwork with semi-gloss oil-based paint and rolled the walls with regular water-based, sanded and refinished the oak floors. Each unit was unique. One morning, Grocery store magnate Joe Albertson, wearing a suit and a fedora, walked the few blocks over from his 16th street office, and asked, "what are you boys doing?" We gave him a tour and he approved.

VI

Nineteen-seventy-two was an election year and that summer we all supported George McGovern's hapless campaign. He did well at the White Savage. Cal, Ray and I were young, left leaning, counter-culture supporters, pot smokers who were trying to change the city one old building at a time. By then we had another apartment building, the Paterson on 12th street (I lived there for a time too) and on a snowy May afternoon had found, and soon purchased a ranch 25 miles north of Boise city in Boise County.

Never more than a half-assed carpenter, I pursued writing and was lucky to meet and get freelance work from the old-school editor Sam Day, whose *Intermountain Observer* was an alternative (liberal) weekly before the genre existed. My byline appeared along with Alice Dieter, Perry Swisher and a small group of independent minded journalists. After a small article or two, I took on urban renewal and wrote three long pieces entitled "It's Not Too Late," advocating for saving the city's late 19th and early 20th century local sandstone and red brick historic buildings then threatened by an irrational overreach—one iteration would have destroyed 50 blocks of downtown—of a redevelopment plan. By then I had joined forces with local planner and preservation activist John Bertram (who's still fighting the good fight), and we founded Friends of Old Buildings. The organization existed to preserve the city's historic core that happily now has more than its share of historic buildings that form the retail, entertainment and cultural hub of downtown Boise. Ironically, we were aided in our battle by a returned native son, bound on setting the record straight.

VII

Author L.J. Davis blew in town on a fast-talking, high octane wind to gather information for his forthcoming *Harper's* article, a deconstruction of his hometown, entitled "Tearing Down Boise" that appeared in November of 1974.

We sat down in the annex to the White Savage (also the headquarters for Friends of Old Buildings) and Davis, who had gone to Boise High, then Stanford, was a comic novelist living in Brooklyn. A speed talker with lots of breathy *uh uh uhs* in between his questions, he was getting started as a nonfiction business writer and shared his singular interviewing method—pretend to not know a thing, come in *tabula rasa*—believing he gained the confidence of his subjects more easily that way. He did know that I had written three articles on the future of downtown for the *Intermountain Observer*. And he even used— unattributed—my description of the then-new Bank of Idaho building (now Key Bank) as "looking like nothing so much as toaster ovens piled on top of each other" in his piece. We became friends and when I called him on this, he blamed the copy editor for taking the attribution out. Over the years, L.J. introduced me (a New York native) to Brooklyn, where he lived but I had only visited once. He also wrote a fine piece for the initial issue of *Idaho Heritage Magazine*—the magazine I founded in 1974.

We were both members of the Nancy Stringfellow Admiration Society. Nancy had been the

Idaho Heritage *Magazine, 1974*

manager of The Book Shop on Main in Boise and the written word never had a better friend. After retiring from bookselling, she lived in a cabin right below our mountain ranch, 25-odd miles from the capital, beneath a wall of basalt rocks, smoked Lucky Strikes, grew eight varieties of thyme, was surrounded by books shelved two deep that filled her living room and always had a pile of books beside her. I got to know her son Jim and her talented daughter Rosalie Sorrels, the singer/songwriter who would come through town in her old van and regale us with her tales of the road and stories of her five children.

VIII

By the time L.J. Davis came to Boise in 1973 (both John Bertram and I were interviewed) to examine how the city was self-destructing through urban renewal, he could fairly describe the center city looked desolate, empty, forsaken and write an irony-laden evisceration with the ardor of a prodigal son sickened by what had happened to his hometown. Published in *Harper's* in November 1974, the piece galvanized locals and helped our cause. Far from coastal urban America, Boise existed blissfully, peacefully in one of the least known states in the union. "Tearing Down Boise" hurt community pride and more people began to listen to us. It did give me an unexpected opportunity to get published in *Harper's*, when on a trip to New York, I brought the art director photos that she used in the story. I handed her a brief article on removing false fronts and revealing historic facades; it made its way to the editor and was published in their wraparound section in April of 1975.

Fortune also grinned on those of us who bought and fixed up some of the capital's icons. Joan Carley, whose grandfather started Idaho First National Bank, led the way renovating Old Boise. Ken Howell, who later developed the Idaho Building and the Idanha Hotel as affordable, began a long and successful career renovating and later as a developer. Architect Charles Hummel championed historic preservation. And we put together a group and purchased the 1901 French Chateau-style Idanha Hotel on 10th and Main. A story goes with it.

IX

Near the time of purchase, our group was short of funds. We needed what is called a bridge loan—financing to close the deal. The bank asked for collateral. My parents were in town visiting, and we entreated my dad. They loved the old hotel, but at that time my dad was in an extremely difficult financial position—having lost his major tenant in the largest project the company had ever done. So, he was strapped. Things look gloomy, except my mom had very valuable jewelry with her that she put up as collateral. We got the loan, secured construction financing and she got her rings back.

In the following years, White Savage Associates, as we called our business, owned the 1865 Miner's Exchange Saloon in Idaho City, the Idanha, the Paterson Apartments and an apartment building in Glenns Ferry (70 miles east of Boise)—all classy old buildings. Then the dark night of the soul came: We became investors, and managers of the then Plantation Country Club (more on this twisted tale later).

For a time, we would say we supplied a lot of the fun for the valley. At the Idanha Hotel, Peter Schott, a fine Austrian chef, opened his restaurant; the great jazz pianist Gene Harris played piano in the lobby and the Idanha became a jazz scene not seen before or since. The Miner's Exchange was a classic mountain town saloon with live bands, stiff drinks and the open-ended appeal of a getaway. Every weekend, flatlanders, as we called them, drove up from the Treasure Valley to drink, dance and romance. It had its flickering of fame when in 1976 Senator Frank Church announced his run for president in tiny Idaho City, and the national media set up in the bar. We spent the previous night making food for the event. I concocted a salmon mousse diligently following what I remember as a NY Times cookbook recipe—and it turned out. As an owner, I occasionally tended bar, more often danced until closing and in the parlance of the time, occasionally got lucky (sometimes unlucky).

Once an only slightly tipsy lady, sidled up to me at Boise's old Bouquet bar and asked, "Are you a Jew?" I snapped right back, "Are you a bigot?" We spent a good chunk of the summer in an affair. Impulse control went on hold. Like any experimenting post adolescent, I let go:

smoked weed daily, snorted coke, tried acid a few times, inhaled what I was told was blue morphine and once while back in New York, after smoking opium, stopped at a light on St. Mark's Place for 30 minutes (or maybe two hours of my life), immobile even as the chaffed NY drivers went around cursing and flipping me off.

X

My most award-worthy drug-addled scene came on a drive back from Jackson, Wyoming, with my great and good friend, Pocatello-born novelist and poet Gino Sky. We had ingested some mushrooms and on a stop at Craters of the Moon, I spent some serious time staring very closely at the lava rock, saying to Gino, "look at all the colors" then had the chutzpah to tell him in the car that the mushrooms had no effect on me. Now Gino has more than a touch of the imp of the perverse and a sense of humor big as a Yellowstone sky and for many years later at moments would say to me deadpan: "Did you see all those colors?"

Gino Sky (left) and Alan Minskoff, at City Lights Bookstore in the 1980s (photo by Royanne Minskoff).

For a couple of years, I acted as the opening act at Gino's readings, I was the barely lit fuse before his grand explosions. He was an extra-ordinarily theatrical, gifted writer and funny reader. His imagination never quit. Though on more than one occasion, post reading he would tie one on and a slightly darker version emerged. On these occasions, when Gino, misconstrued some remark and the alcohol talked and he was neither imaginative nor funny, I helped smooth the waters. But we always survived and prevailed. I never had better company or more fun. Gino, who liked to give people new symbolic names called me Dr. Flood. Years later when in another one of my *why-not-be-a-* this time a small press publisher and join the lexicon of aspirational ventures that I have tried. I did three books, a collection of Gino's short stories, *Near the Postcard Beautiful* and a volume of Rick Ardinger's poems, *Goodbye Magpie*. I am still proud of all three books. Gino thought of the publishing company's name, Floating Ink. A name that was baptized with Gay Whitesides' brilliant and spare poetry collection *The Station Plays a Lusty Song Good Morning*, that Gino and I co-published,

XI

So, I chose Idaho to have a first and last name. When your family moniker graces a Broadway marquee, and they have been builders for generations, a separate identity was something I craved. The Gem State hooked me with wide bluebird skies, brief but engaging state history, accessible people, endless ranch and farmland and its small, forgotten towns. I first experienced switchbacks and roads so steep that you could crest a hill and be airborne. Of course, my minimally powered VW, made every trip a deliberate journey and downshifting struggle. Jack Gish and I wrote a song together driving on the Old White Bird Hill south of Lewiston, which took the measure of my Squareback and produced a melancholy tune that we had plenty of time to perfect on the way up north.

A New Yorker off the avenues, away from Manhattan's steel and glass wallpaper, I was (am) a displaced New York Jew escaped, gone west to start anew, to see what's what. To pass. Then I drove up alone to North Idaho in October of 1973 and my past (genes), something pulled me…. Israel, the Jewish state, was attacked. Somehow, I needed to help. I volunteered and spent three months on a kibbutz, witnessed a country at war, and as abruptly as I had arrived, I left the land of Israel and returned to the States. I arrived in New York just in time for my pal Andy Tananbaum's January 27th, 1974 wedding, gave a schmaltzy toast about Israel and friendship, pretending that the wedding alone led to my impulsive exit from the Holy Land.

Idaho beckoned. Soon enough I returned to Boise, where when I disembarked, was met (in those days people met you on the airport tarmac) by a contingent of my friends, one of whom said, "you won the war and came home."

The war taught me much: My time on the kibbutz remains a pivotal experience. Being in a country at war has an electric urgency. The Israelis were tense, you had a job to do and Americans, Australians and the English were volunteers who worked, played, maybe learned a little Hebrew, but were outsiders, who never really understood in our bones what was at stake. So, when a desultory American passed through and passed around a hash pipe, we all got high, then got caught, and were called before a meeting of the entire kibbutz to explain and apologize. I talked for the group. We were allowed to stay. I left soon after: to extricate myself from an impossible relationship, the pull of Idaho, to attend Andy's wedding or something of all three—I'll never know. Like high school, college and grad school, I dropped out early.

XII

Nineteen Seventy-four revealed Watergate. I too had a busy year. An acquaintance, the late J.M. Neill, a fellow Boise preservationist and the executive director of the state's US Bicentennial Commission, told me about a summer job in Idaho City for the Historic American Buildings Survey. In theory, I was still a graduate student and did have a serious interest in preservation, so I applied, was accepted, rated as a GS-7 and joined a group of architecture students who worked measuring, photographing and sketching. As the project historian for the Historic American Buildings Survey, I spent much of the summer in the County Recorder's office tracing the provenance of the half-dozen buildings that our team of young architecture students were measuring and drawing. I scoured publications of all sorts, pored over 19th century articles, read old *Idaho World* newspaper articles to learn what I could about the people who built the Miner's Exchange Saloon, the Masonic and Oddfellows Halls, the Catholic Church, the Merc, the historic school among others. [You can look up these histories on the HABS website to this day]. I did the buildings' histories, I perused the antique ledgers firsthand, determining when the ownership shifted and comparing the floral 19th century signatures and dates.

Reading was my constant, so the Idaho City gig gave me the rare opportunity to get to know the state's earliest histories, peruse the brittle old *Idaho World* papers and *Idaho Statesman* microfiche, ask old timers what the place was like decades earlier. Besides I got to play on the Idaho City softball team, drink at O'Leary's and walk up and down the boardwalks, notebook in hand, joint hidden in my jeans. ∎

Gray whale in Baja Mexico (photo by Steven Nightingale)

ROBERT LEONARD REID

What Wondrous World

On a chill and overcast day in early March, I joined a group of friends at San Ignacio Lagoon in Baja California. Each winter, several hundred gray whales make their temporary homes in the lagoon. From late December till early February the females deliver their calves. By early April, most of the animals have departed on the longest migration undertaken by any mammal, a 6,000-mile journey north to summer quarters in the Bering and Chukchi seas.

Over four days, riding the deep waters of the lagoon in nimble eight-person fishing boats, my friends and I saw scores of grays. Sometimes in the distance, their location betrayed by misty, ten-foot-high, here-I-am blows; sometimes, amazingly, alongside our crafts, allowing us to touch them, even encouraging us to touch them: 60,000-pound creatures, curious and playful, accompanied by their 2,000-pound newborns. A calf may measure 17 feet in length at birth; during its several-month sojourn in the lagoon it may drink 50 gallons of mother's milk each day. If all goes well, a typical gray will grow to a length of 40 feet or more and live to an age of 60 or 70 years.

The species faces enormous challenges. Illegal hunting is one. Global warming. Loss of habitat. Nevertheless, grays are arguably better off than they were a century ago. Following the invention of factory ships in the nineteenth century, the gray whale population plunged to some 2000 individuals in the early 1900s. The species hung on precariously until 1946, when, in a move of shocking foresightedness, hunting was outlawed. In 1994, grays were removed from the Endangered Species List. Today, the population is back to pre-whale-hunting numbers, some 25,000 individuals.

On the final evening of my visit to San Ignacio Lagoon, the members of our party gathered to reflect on our experiences. Sometime during those reminiscences, a line from an old Shaker hymn popped into my head. The lyric as originally rendered was "What wondrous love is this." Somehow I heard it in slightly altered form: "What wondrous world is this." In that moment I recognized something I'd known for a very long time in my brain and in my bones, but that, all too frequently, I'd failed to hold in my heart and to manifest in my behavior: the wonder that we are, all of us—human, whale, fox, willow, bluebird, oak tree, leaves of grass—

That we are, all of us, wondrously, one.

In everyday mode I process that understanding dutifully, welcoming into my world caribou or rhino or monkey-faced bats or whatever the species of the week happens to be. From my home in a valley south of Carson City, I'm five minutes from a trail into Humboldt-Toiyabe National Forest, where I've generously shared the terrain with a great horned owl that decided to build her nest at the top of my favorite juniper; and where, without interfering in their business, I once watched a team of badgers extricate an unfortunate ground squirrel from its den. I welcome the cry of coyotes and I once stepped aside, so to speak, to allow a mountain lion to pass.

At the evening gathering with my friends at the lagoon, my benevolence was turned on its head. What I registered in a single moment was not pride or satisfaction or amazement that during my hours-long adventures on the choppy waters of the lagoon I had welcomed gray whales into my world. It was, rather, shock from my realization that, across those many hours, gray whales had welcomed me into theirs. That they were the hosts, and I the guest.

The generosity implicit in that reversal—the goodwill we normally appropriate for ourselves—cannot be overstated. Given the horrors that gray whales have endured during their long association with humans, no one would have blamed the local members of the species for unceremoniously squelching any suggestion that they show up for four days to entertain us very fortunate people—breaching, blowing, rolling over two or three times, allowing us to pet them and, for crying out loud, kiss them! Yet show up they did, bringing with them a gracious and cheerful message: "We've been waiting for you. What took you so long!" Thereby inspiring hope that healing of our scarred relationship has begun, that forgiveness of monstrous wrongs of the past may follow someday as well, for gray whales, for red fox and cutthroat trout, for mountain gorillas and the Amazon rain forest, for all that is alive.

I love the story of Francisco "Pachico" Mayoral, a wise and compassionate fisherman who, plying the waters of San Ignacio Lagoon one day forty years ago, did something unheard of: he reached out and touched a whale. Gazing back across the decades, it's hard to comprehend how daring, how revolutionary, how inspired that act was. At the very least, as I see it, Francisco Mayoral deserved a Nobel Peace Prize. "Francisco 'Pachico' Mayoral," the citation might have read: "Visionary, myth wrecker, hope builder, who understood what wondrous world is this." ■

Henry and Theresa Nuwer

HANK NUWER

Polonia

My pregnant mother Theresa waddled into Louise de Marillec Maternity Hospital in Buffalo, New York, and rolled out in a wheelchair with me in a blue blanket.

Born in 1946 exactly nine months after my parents wed, I heaped responsibilities on a father back from horrific fighting in Europe and North Africa, his best friend killed by a shell near him while the two took a smoke break. His love letters that I found and read in part until my mother caught me and yanked them away, declared his wish for a normal life after five years killing men of his ancestry.

At the hospital, one of the Sisters of Charity screwed up while helping my mother fill out my birth certificate. I am my own father, married to my mother, my name written where Dad's should be. Hankipus Rex *c'est moi*.

Henry Robert Nuwer went from driving a tank nicknamed Lonely for General Patton to driving a Downtown Merchants delivery truck. He thought his job delivering dresses to housewives in the suburbs gave his family security.

Not so. The malls put Buffalo's hometown department stores downtown out of business, and his company failed when housewives took their mall purchases back to their cars. The city condemned our first house on Riley Street and tore it down. Our second on Fillmore Avenue was a dump thrown up for returning dogfaces called "The Buffalo Veterans Project." My parents resorted to turning up the volume on their vacuum-tubed radio to drown out the vicious arguments of our neighbors.

I watched our neighbors escape the project to move to better and safer homes. When I was four years old my girlfriend Linda kissed me on the lips, which thrilled me until she cried and said she had come to say farewell.

Little Hank Nuwer

Linda was my only friend in that complex where the projects harbored abusive older boys reared by their mothers while their fathers hunkered in foxholes. We didn't have much money, and my hand-me-down, old-fashioned flat hats, knickers and bunched sweaters worn twenty years earlier by my uncles made me an instant target.

"Am I a D.P., Ma?" I remember asking, a reference to the displaced persons from Eastern Europe crowding into Buffalo after the war.

"Who called you that?" she demanded, and I checked off the names. To my shame I recall her taking me to Sattler's Department Store in Polonia and buying me new shoes and better clothes than I needed or she could afford.

Outside my peaceful home, savagery rose like a heat wave off the broken, weed-grown sidewalks. A bully named David smothered me in a mud puddle until my father pulled him off like a tick.

After I threw up mud and breakfast in the bathroom, Dad gave me a mandate to fight back and showed me how to throw a punch. Thus, when I caught a teenager stealing my basketball, I chased after him screaming bloody murder as he loped away. My mother cried twice after she found me. The first was because I had gotten disoriented and lost in a dangerous part of the city. The second was because I told her the thief had been "some cocksucker." When my father came home he had to endure a "talking to" about his continued use of Army profanity.

There were other lessons. My kid sister Louise and I learned that snitching was verboten. "I'll punish you both so that I know I have the right one," my dad liked to say, putting us nose to wall-paper. "You'll stay there until I learn you a lesson."

But he only spanked me once. I had tracked black goop on my shoes over his brand new linol-eum. Before I could cry he picked me up with his

Playing in the Buffalo, New York projects

large hands. I saw fear in his face over using his own great strength. I never again saw that fear until one time when he had major surgery, and he squeezed my hand while hospital tubes penetrated his body like St. Stephen's arrows.

I never interpreted his gentleness as weakness. The weaklings were the angry brutes the neighbor boys had for fathers. My Dad could make me laugh and stop inappropriate behavior at the same time using one of his funny expressions. "I'll tear off your arm and hit you with the wet end," he'd say, trying without success to hide a smile while I giggled for minutes.

The worst thing my father called anyone was a "bullshit artist," a slang term reserved for labor fakers, con artists, and Buffalo mayors. He wasn't joking when he used that expression. Contempt narrowed his eyes and made the corners of his mouth twitch.

My mother became the family disciplinarian, spanking me when I threw a fit. All I had to do was accompany her to church and she too became controllable. The Catholic Church meant everything to families like ours in the 1940s and 1950s. Other people's photo albums had dogs with the family; our family photos had priests in them. We had no money for luxuries, but Ma spoiled her children with pineapple upside-down cake made every Saturday.

My mother, Theresa by name, was four years younger than my dad. She was born in the 1919 great influenza epidemic that killed thousands in New York State. Living but one mile from the Nuwer farm, she spun an early crush on my father and taunted him in the St. John's schoolyard with doggerel: *Hank, Hank, turn the crank; his mother came out and gave him a spank.*

Theresa's father, Josef Lysiak, was a Pole and an orphan. He wed Stella Mary Golota, whose own parents had emigrated from that part of Poland wrested away by Germany. He made it to America in 1913, working for Pierce Arrow in Buffalo until he could afford his eighty acres, supplementing his income by bootlegging vodka with his own potatoes. Before emigrating, Josef and an older brother had been conscripted into the Russian army for life. They deserted and were nearly caught. "We ran with bullets all around," my grandfather said, his accent thick as porridge.

Thus, my mother's people hailed from captured lands. Then and now I admired my grandfather for choosing to flee rather than submit to life in a tyrant's service. By the age of five I knew he could sing in English and in Polish the fiery national anthem of an enslaved Poland:

Poland has not yet succumbed.
As long as we remain,
What the foe by force has seized,
Sword in hand we'll gain.

In time my family also had enough saved to escape the projects. Although my father wanted to put down a house on the family farmland that now rented out to tenants, she nagged my father to buy a small house in the Polonia section of Buffalo. The move to St. John Gualbert's parish proved too soon after the war for a boy with a German last name. A Felician nun told the class that my forbears had enslaved Poland. Male classmates caught on and for them I became the Kraut.

Hedwig Street stank of cooked cabbage, scalded duck feathers and Old World memories. The women tied their hair in a carapace under babushkas. Many men had worked in the steel mills, and they had missing digits to go with their pensions.

I hated the new neighborhood. Like my father, I wished for a move back to the family farm, but my mother put her foot down. She wanted no return to patriarchal rule and the threadbare way of life.

To me the farm was a pastoral haven with acres of woods where red fox built their dens, and I imprisoned butterflies in jars. Grandfather Josef taught me to guide a plow behind a team of horses, to sharpen an axe on a stone wheel, to turn an errant cow with a wave of a switch, to pull an egg out of a hen's nest without getting pecked, to scrape the hide off a butchered, boiled hog and to set out salt blocks as a treat for the milk cows. Grandma Lysiak was a large woman with rolled-down stockings and flowered dresses. She spoiled her grandchildren and introduced me to a bookcase lined with board games, adventure books and Montgomery Ward catalogs.

But all through grade school, the nuns made me feel like a marginal being, never belonging in Polonia. After I won a school-wide spelling bee, the nuns conferred and sent the second-place winner, the son of the funeral director, to represent our school in a Buffalo-wide competition instead of me.

I stood similar insults for years. But when Sister Mary Archangel teaching seventh grade went too far with her anti-German insults directed at me, I retaliated before class one day by chalking caricatures of her on the blackboard. After she moved my desk to the hall outside the classroom and I became a real outcast, some older boys—the perennial "held backs"—believed they had Sister's permission to go Kraut hunting.

The bullies waited to pounce as I walked to and from school, and the bruises on my face inspired my stay-at-home mother to walk with me when she could. When she could not, I took on opponents up to thirty pounds heavier. I hurled rocks and ice chunks to level the playing field.

When a walleyed redhead named Jim, later to spend time in prison for theft of mail, punched me brutally in the arm as he walked by in class, I seized a hard-cover textbook and battered his head as he sat trapped behind his desk by the cloakroom. Sister Mary Archangel came to his aid, slapping me with her robe-covered hands like a crow flapping its wings.

As the fighting intensified, my protective mother ordered me not to leave Hedwig Street except to go to school. This meant I could not join my baseball-playing buddies in the city park until my constant pestering made her relent a few weeks before my twelfth birthday.

One Saturday afternoon, finding no game at the park, I walked to a dairy store to ask for a paper cup of water. A tall, broad street predator blocked my way. I knew this Dale August belonged to another parish and that he was already in high school. The boys on my Little League team called him Psycho. He was destined to die young and unloved.

"Where you think you're going, Lips?" Dale said. He wrestled away my baseball glove and bat and threw them over a concrete wall behind the dairy. They landed by a smelly, polluted stream of water we boys had nicknamed Shit's Creek. I vaulted over the wall as did he, and I picked up my bat.

Dale bear-hugged me, my nose pressed tight against one foul armpit. The stench made me retch. Strong as a bull, he threw me to my knees and ordered me to use my mouth. He cooed an expression I had read as graffiti in the school restroom.

From the concrete bridge above the creek, an old woman in a cloth coat and a scarf on her head shouted at us, "What are you boys doing, what are you boys doing?"

Dale cursed her. His words directed toward an adult shocked me. Frightened and taking advantage of the diversion, I jabbed the knob of the bat into his opened zipper. He seized the bat from me, slamming it into my arms, chest and head.

With one eye on the shrieking woman, he zipped up, vaulted the wall and strode away.

After picking my glasses up out of the dirt, I too slid back over the wall. I planned to thank the old woman, but she ran at me screaming. "Shame, shame."

Blood freckled my clothing, and I brushed past her. I went to a lavatory in the city park to wash up, but I could only get so clean.

My mother stepped onto the porch as I walked past the dying elm on our sidewalk. She took one look and yelled at me for getting into what she assumed had been another fight. She gasped when she viewed the bruises where Dale had squeezed and battered my head. "How can you keep doing this to me?" she asked.

Days later Dale August walked toward me on the asphalt road running through the park. I thought of running, but in my neighborhood that was not an option. I stood my ground but Dale delivered a twisting martial arts punch to my sternum, knocking the wind out of me. The unspoken message was that I was not to tell anyone about the first attack, but I did anyway.

My confidante was Frank Szachta, a powerfully built boy with a greaser's spitcurl. A fellow altar boy and baseball player, he had lost his father from a heart attack, becoming one of the poorer boys in the parish.

I told him about Dale. "What does 'Blow me' mean?"

"He wanted to put his dick into your mouth."

Revulsion went through me. "You mean he wanted to piss in my mouth?"

214

Frank said that what would come out was called jism. I turned vermillion. Some had begun coming out of me nocturnally, humiliating me because my mother made my bed.

My friend, to my knowledge, never told anyone in the neighborhood. For sure he never threw his knowledge back in my face.

The next year, responding to the badgering of the Polish nuns who wanted Frank and me to see if we might have a "calling," we enrolled at the Diocesan Preparatory Junior Seminary, a high school and a community college.

"You have nothing to lose," the nuns said to me.

They were misinformed. I risked losing my mother's pride in me. If I failed to graduate I would deprive my mother of her sudden status in our parish. I knew from the rapture on her face that she envisioned me in full vestments preaching from the pulpit and serving her communion.

School began and I knew I had made a bad decision. The priest-teachers made us stand at our desks and repeat by rote pages of textbook copy. My grades were D's and F's except in English class where bald and beaming Father Cyril Trevett allowed me to write funny stories instead of dull compositions.

Religion class was the worst torture for me. A red-haired priest named David Doyle resented questions he considered impertinent. Actually, I really wanted to know everything I asked. One question took him aback. *How could he be sure Mary and Joseph had not had relations before the birth of Jesus?*

Father Doyle ordered me out of class and into the library in solitary as punishment. The next day he brought a watergun to class and shot me in the face when I raised my hand.

Our group health lessons were absurd. A short, plump visiting priest addressed a roomful of us freshmen on how to wash our penises without sinning. "How does he find that tiny dick of his?" I stage whispered, causing even the college men around me to scream with laughter.

Unprepared for high school, I wrote classmate Len Kaspyrzak's themes and book reports in exchange for his math and science homework. He traded with someone else who was good at Latin and Religion. Len got caught with three copies of the same homework assignment, and he was expelled. So was a big fellow named Tom

Hubner caught one noon hour stealing a Coke. Jim Bursey, an amiable African-American student who had taught me to wrestle, was next to go when a priest caught him doodling a bare-boobed girl in his notebook.

Then Frank quit, the tuition too much for his widowed mother.

I went on borrowed time. Father Daniel Duggan, my Latin One teacher, put me in the Bad Boy row next to the open windows. "Easier for us to throw you all out," he said.

One day near the end of my first year, I decided to bait him. "Will you teach us in Latin Two?" I asked him during a class break.

"Oh, yes, I taught Cicero."

"That explains all those wrinkles of yours, Father," I said, enjoying the mirth of my classmates as he marched me to the library for another afternoon "in the jug."

The priest I could never please was my algebra teacher. The Rev. Paul Belzer was destined to gain national fame late in life as the testy parish monsignor and counselor to the family of Oklahoma City bomber Timothy McVeigh.

One day when Belzer left the classroom for a moment, I opened a window to make a snowball and took aim at Vincent Gidzinski. The snowball went high and landed on the old-fashioned ledge above the door. All eyes in the class watched it as Father Balzer stepped into the room and the snowball dropped on his head. All my "I didn't mean its" carried no weight, and I spent another week in detention.

At the seminary, my connection to a relative haunted me. The priests compared me to the family hero, Monsignor Roman Nuwer, and found me wanting. Monsignor Nuwer was a writer and priest and head of Our Lady of Sorrows in downtown Buffalo. He had filed dispatches from the South Pacific in World War Two for Buffalo's Catholic newspaper.

A chaplain in both World Wars and a general in the Second, he was a personal friend of two popes. He once spirited the remains of the martyred St. Joseph at past guards in the Russian sector of Vienna while costumed as a coal deliveryman. He helped the exiled von Trapp Family of *Sound of Music* fame make their way to America, and Maria praised him in her autobiography.

To me at fourteen years old, however, Monsignor Nuwer was like a pimple on my butt. His heroics made my own deficiencies all the more apparent. "We think he is gifted-disturbed," the Rev. Paul Juenker, school Spiritual Director, told my mother on Parents Night.

I'll pass on the gifted, but if I was disturbed the problem might have been that I had bought my father's early advice that you avenged all wrongs done against you. So when Tom Turici put a chocolate bar in a side pocket of my only suit jacket to melt, I felt justified in clobbering him until strapping Father Anthony Caligiuri picked me up and dangled me like a puppet.

My doom was sealed on Family Day.

I hid in an empty classroom slurping tongues with the older sister of a classmate. All at once the rector threw open the door.

Monsignor Roman Nuwer

Monsignor Ralph Miller summoned her upset mother and pissed-off brother to the classroom to witness his tirade. He put me on final probation. Sure enough I got into a second fight a week later, this time in chapel, and Monsignor Miller broke it up.

It took but a few minutes for the rector to write up my dismissal papers and those of the boy I fought with. He stood by me with folded arms as I cleaned the smelly gym clothes out of my locker. I walked in disgrace through the gates of the seminary and boarded a Buffalo bus. I stayed on to the end of the line and refused to get off and face the music. I went back again twice for return trips until the driver parked the bus and marched to the back to order me off at my stop.

I broke the bad news at the dinner table. My mother sobbed. I had humiliated the family, and my father used plain English to tell me so. "I hope you're proud of yourself because I'm not, Bullshit Artist," he said.

This disgrace of mine at fifteen for my parents was good practice for them, however. It foreshadowed what they needed to endure from me for many, many more years. ∎

Ha Long Bay, Vietnam

ED MAROHN

Going Back to Nam

The aircraft's window revealed the morning overcast engulfing Hanoi. At 7:50 a.m. on January 15, 2009, the pilot landed the Airbus A321. It had been a long international flight with multiple stops, starting on a Boeing 747-400 China Airline in Los Angeles at five in the evening on the 13th. Unlike my first trip in 1970, I was now a civilian traveling with my wife on a plane dominated by Asians coming back to their ancestral homes to celebrate Tet, the Vietnamese New Year, from the 25th through the 30th.

Flying to Hanoi instead of Saigon, renamed Ho Chi Minh City, plopped us into former North Vietnam and the civilians and soldiers who had fought the Japanese from 1940 to 1945, the French from 1946 to 1954 and then the Americans from 1955 to 1975. I didn't know what to expect. How would they react to me, an American, who battled against them? Would there be hatred, acceptance, or indifference?

During the flight, I reflected on my combat tour, when at age 24, I had left my young wife and six-month-old son to go to war for a full year. The book *Flashbacks: On Returning to Vietnam* by CBS reporter Morley Safer of *60 Minutes* fame is written from his perspective of the Indochina War during his correspondent years and his subsequent return to the country after hostilities ended. He succinctly wrote everyone who had served there had memories peppered with conflicting truths. What would my scattered recollections reveal in the present-day Socialist Republic of Vietnam so many years later?

*****

When I first shipped over, I was a Field Artillery captain on a plane with over 250 US Army personnel. The contracted United Airlines flight took off from Oakland in July 1970, with us in starched and neatly creased khaki uniforms. Regulations prohibited traveling in fatigues on commercial flights even for deploying troops. We became the next wave of newbies as the ones already serving in the Vietnam War would soon call us. The continuous turnover due to the completion of the one-year tours, or from the increasing death (over 58,000 Americans would die), or from the evacuated wounded required new bodies. It was my turn. In the states, rumors ran rampant about the attrition of company grade officers: the life expectancy in combat for lieutenants was given as seven seconds; for captains maybe a minute. Of course, these tales changed as did the various people telling them. Call it sick military humor.

The enlisted, noncommissioned, and officers on board represented most Army branches. But it would be the combat arms who faced the brunt of the reaper's daily needs as he accompanied the units into battle on the landing zones, on the fire bases, and in dark jungles.

In a middle seat with a Quartermaster major on my left by the aisle and to my right a Signal Corps captain, who outranked me by two years, I reflected on my recent promotion. In the military pecking system, I was junior to these two having just been promoted days before I boarded the jet at Oakland. Naturally, I drew the least desirable middle seating.

The military bureaucracy had little patience for stateside ceremonies. At the Fort Sill Officer Personnel Building I was handed my promotion papers along with my travel orders to Vietnam from a Department of the Army civilian-—a young attractive woman surrounded by a room full of other women. The female aspect gave a morale boost: they could sympathize with us over the directives for going to war, unlike the hardcore male staff. The 1st Lieutenant next to me received the same orders. As captains on paper, we decided to promote ourselves before departing; we entered the men's restroom and with the flushing urinals as the background music we pinned the captain railroad tracks on our uniforms after reading out loud our promotions. We saluted each other and left the facility as new captains, the twin silver bars reflecting in the Oklahoma sun, headed for Nam, as GI's called Vietnam. A major walking past advised us not to miss the transportation to the airport and our plane for California. He disappeared into the building.

My captain friend shrugged and said, "What are they going to do if we miss our flight, send us to Nam." That moment I smiled and forgot the war.

The trip took over 21 hours from Oakland to Juneau to Guam to Tokyo where the plane topped off with fuel for the last leg. The pilot announced an immediate turnaround for his craft once we deplaned with engines running: the reason for refueling. When we landed just after midnight at Bien Hoa airport, near Saigon, we had morphed into tired and anxious beings, wearing wrinkled and sweat-stained uniforms. Facing separation from my wife and son for a full year, and with the uncertainty of war, my mood soured as an exhausted and apprehensive stewardess made announcements to deplane immediately and follow the guides to the nearby processing building; its walls and roof thick with sandbags, with open-air windows to reduce injuries from enemy mortar or rocket explosions.

We moved fast, emptying the aircraft from forward and aft doors, encouraged by the replacement clerks to hurry while unloading our duffle bags from the airplane. I heard the United jet taxing for takeoff, trying to erase being a target for the enemy. The craft rushing down the runway jolted me back to the reality: I was here for war—no going back until the tour was completed, one way or another. In those early morning hours, segregated by rank, we processed and loaded on open-air buses, window openings without glass, covered with mesh iron screens and driven to Long Bien Army Base and our billets to wait for unit assignments. Being in the artillery I knew I would be headed into the field, the jungle. The staff sergeant in charge of officers found me the next day and handed me my assignment paperwork to the 25th Infantry Division.

His single advice was to discard the OD issued boxer shorts I received with my fatigues, boots, socks, and combat gear. I must have looked confused because the sergeant said, "To avoid jungle rot in the crotch and as important if you catch a bullet in the abdomen area the medic has less shit to cut through to access the wound. Besides those god-damned boxers ride up your thighs in this heat and humidity and strangle your privates." He winked. "Why give yourself a wedgie."

After trying the underwear for one day, the NCO was correct. Days later wearing my fatigue pants sans undershorts, called commando style, I left my dozen pairs of shorts stacked on the cot in the temporary billets and caught the supply convoy armed with an M-16 rifle and decked out in a flak vest. In the moist heat of South Vietnam, I was grateful I had taken the advice. My jeep driver followed the transportation commander as we headed through the disfigured earth of the Iron Triangle, the Bo Loi Woods, and by the nearby Cu Chi Tunnels; American units engaged with the Viet Cong in these areas but had never eradicated them.

On the drive to the headquarters of the 25th Infantry Division, the war started to be a series of events, a kaleidoscope of colors and emotions, twenty-four hours a day, seven days a week.

Cu Chi represented a stateside post: PX, NCO and Officer clubs, barracks, hot showers, and hooch maids to clean the billets. A US Army division consisted of 15,000 personnel, but only 5,000 in combat arms deployed into the jungle. It took the remaining 10,000 to provide support and logistics for the field operations. From Cu Chi, I joined my battalion at Tay Ninh, aka Rocket City, on the Cambodian border. Despite President Nixon's assurances that the US would not invade Cambodia, the US military had already done so.

A few weeks later I went through my first mortar attack at the Combat Support Base Dau Tieng. The thumping sounds as the rounds launched from the surrounding jungle told everyone to seek cover; the next noise would be the explosion in our area. Hurling myself into the bunker I slashed my right rib cage against a protruding two by four board. The ground attack that followed was repulsed with the capture of a Viet Cong sapper clad in black silk pajamas. It was my first encounter with the enemy. He was lanky and taller than the average 5'4" height for an Asian male. Covered in dirt and sweat the POW showed both defiance and a stoic resolve to his fate, a peasant indoctrinated to fight in a war, believing in the ideology for unifying Vietnam that Ho Chi Minh espoused. With a South Vietnamese Army officer to translate we tried to interrogate him but garnered little and placed him on a helicopter to transport him to a prison compound in Long Bien. My gut sensed he would not live long as some of his countrymen wouldn't hesitate killing POWs. The joking expression "The only good commie was a dead commie," used by soldiers had a macabre reality to it.

Being the battalion's assistant operation officer, I spent my time running the tactical operations as troops deployed into battle and I flew aerial observation missions adjusting artillery and airstrikes as the grunts slugged it out with the Viet Cong. We operated near the Michelin Rubber Plantation, designated a No Fire Zone for political reasons. The VC, hidden among the trees, launched ambushes against our units knowing that to get clearance to shoot back into the area took time.

Vietnam was and is still a beautiful land with lush vegetation and terraced rice paddies. But war's destruction permeated through the idyllic picture. I flew over the contrasts of bombed-out jungles versus the untouched areas. B-52 bombers used in tactical air strikes dropped 500- and 1000-pound bombs, creating hundreds of pockmarks which, due to the high water table, filled with turquoise water, reflecting in the warm sun. The craters with reddish tint where a VC or NVA unit had been destroyed took away from the scenic view.

LZ Binh Dinh

CPT Marohn

C Btry FM-FSB Brick

Ed Marohn in Vietnam

CPT Ed Marohn

FSB Bastogne

RTO and driver

Still, I needed a war command to cement my original plans to make a career in the army. All the 25th Infantry Division's slots had been filled for the immediate future, but up north in the I Corps area of operation, by the Demilitarized Zone, the 101st Airborne had been doing heavy fighting with high officer attrition, opening up company-grade positions. Soon I had orders to Camp Eagle, near Phu Bui, the base for the Division, where I took over a 155 mm battery.

We battled the NVA in what was then South Vietnam. Hanoi, far north of the DMZ, existed as the warring capital and was regularly and heavily attacked by US Air Force and US Navy planes. In the ground war, my field artillery unit hopped from one LZ (Landing Zone) to another, airlifted by helicopters. My mission along with the infantry was to stop the foes from infiltering the south through the A Sha Valley, often called the Ho Chi Minh Trail. I conducted 25 air assaults on my tour.

Vietnam became a part of my life in a 24/7 environment. Sundays occurred any day the Chaplin flew in to bless my men before we loaded up on the Hueys for another assault. I experienced the ugliness of war, it's brutality. The killing fields, the jungles, impacted me in so many ways. The forests of Nam held me and the soldiers I commanded, physically and mentally: We lived in its afternoon rains, surrounded by its decay, its parasites, its leeches, its snakes, its monkeys, its bugs, and its mosquitoes. But above all we could never shake the fear that crept from its gloom where the enemy waited; in there existed a nightmare that we didn't want to face but did anyway. In the novella *The Heart of Darkness* by Joseph Conrad, the protagonist said these oft-quoted lines: "The horror! The horror!" Kurtz immersed in a Congo jungle feared much. For it set the stage of remorse for his actions against the natives, losing his sanity. In Nam, we had a term for that: the thousand-yard stare. Soldiers who constantly faced battle and burned out acquired a blank and unfocused gaze. That look to this day haunts me.

In the end, the dangerous A Shau Valley and its environs became my home. We battled in the steamy growth and on the plateaus, enmeshed in the pungent jungle, grit melding with unwashed bodies, enduring the heavy humid air, hearing the forest creatures in their domain, seeing death regularly-—friends and foes grotesquely molded in their final poses.

My exposure to the South Vietnamese populace or their military was minimal; I participated in combating the VC and the NVA, in the bush, in the jungle, and on the hilltops. This was my yang phase of Taoism.

The ARVNs were often seen as poorly trained and unmotivated led by corrupt officers, more concerned about the material wealth that the US had than fighting, as the growing black market of military supplies showed. We had more faith in the Montagnard and Bru people, the ethnic minorities discriminated against by the majority of Vietnamese. They fought for the Americans and proved to be fierce warriors. At the Strategic Hamlet of Mai Loc, I used them to cover my field artillery battery flanks knowing they would never abandon their American allies.

This loyalty did not always exist with our southern allies as some fled when under attack. In the campaign, Lam Son 719 the 101st Airborne had to be inserted as a blocking force along Laos to allow demoralized ARVNs to retreat from the battle against the more professional NVA. It would have been a total rout otherwise. Still, it became a disaster as some of the ARVN units were badly mauled. I knew then that South Vietnam would never be able to stop the enemy if American forces ever withdrew.

But it would take my return trip in 2009 for me to comprehend the Vietnamese people; to understand their psyche; to grasp the impact on all who fought and died on both sides.

*****

Deplaning at Noi Bai Airport, Hanoi from the jet we caught in Taipei, Hieu, our private guide, greeted us. Vivacious and friendly she introduced herself and said, "Welcome to the Socialist Republic of Vietnam." About five-foot-four she represented the typical height Her English was perfect.

Downtown Hanoi, 2009

On the drive to the Hotel Nikko where we would rest from the travel and prepare for our week of private tours, we passed by Truc Bac Lake in downtown Hanoi where John McCain crashed his damaged navy plane and was rescued from an angry mob by NVA soldiers. Hieu's stoicism, is typical, accepting life's

Truc Bac Lake—"John McCain's Lake," Downtown Hanoi

good and bad, the yin and yang of life, reflected in her telling of the rescue and capture. When he was elected as US Senator he earned celebrity status with his former foes; he had survived five years in the POW prison camp which the Americans called the Hanoi Hilton. The Vietnamese admire the endurance of character; their own harsh life is one of eking out an existence on the rice fields, on the farms, and in manufacturing plants. It's this stoicism that allows them to accept a former enemy. I would see this trait in the days ahead; during the war, we begrudgingly complimented the tenacity and sacrifice of the NVA. They were admirable soldiers. I got to know them better than the South Vietnamese because we confronted them regularly.

Some tense moments occurred as she explained the impact of the American Indochina War: her father-in-law died of wounds and soon after the mother had been named a national hero for losing all three sons in the fight against the Americans. Hieu even linked back to the French conflict and how her travel agency manager's father perished fighting and defeating them at Dien Bien Phu in 1954.

Hieu's father, an NVA officer, fought in South Vietnam, and then against the Khmer Rouge in 1979, ending that repressive regime and its mass killings of over two million Cambodians. He served for over 10 years, away from family and loved ones with no trips home.

Then there was the starvation that set in after peace due to the poor management of agriculture by the government and the devastated land. The ongoing cost to the people remains to this day, long after the conflict ended. In 1986 policies improved food production but before that the people struggled to survive. She told how her family hid and raised a pig in the bathtub in their flat, to have something to eat.

As we toured Hanoi and nearby areas, the openness of the former North Vietnamese allowed for frank discussions. On the junk in Hoi Long Bay, one of the crew, Chuong, explained how his NVA father was wounded during the final invasion into South Vietnam in 1975. It seemed everyone had casualties from the fighting.

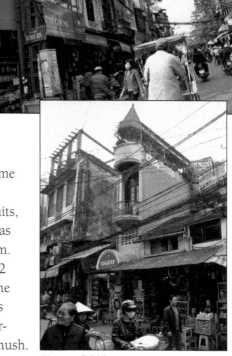

I also met war veterans, some very old men, who told of their struggles attacking American units, and then hiding after the battle as US jets dumped napalm on them. Or losing their comrades to B-52 bombs dropped in the jungle, the concussion of the 500-pounders exploding, blowing out their eardrums, turning their brains to mush. Tears welled as they remembered

Hanoi, 2009

mercy killing a mortally wounded comrade because they lacked medical evacuation. Was it any different when a US medic eased the pain of a dying soldier by injecting heavy doses of morphine, his intestines spread over his fatigues?

By the time we flew to Da Nang, which was part of former South Vietnam, another perspective arose. Because they supported the Americans and the Saigon regime, the Socialist Republic of Vietnam imposed a three-generation moratorium against them before they could

227

work for the government, police, or military. Those who had served in the armed forces were also imprisoned in re-education camps, to become "loyal citizens." Families split much like in the American Civil War, brothers fought each other supporting opposite causes. The stories continued about the other devastation: Agent Orange still lingers in the soil and is blamed for the high percentage of birth defects and deformities seen around the countryside.

In the Museum of the Cham Sculpture at Da Nang, I became intrigued with artifacts from My Son historical site of the Champa people, saved from the extensive bombing by the US in 1969 because the VC and NVA operated near the ancient temples. It took international outrage to convince Nixon to stop the destruction. As the curator talked I sensed the emotions over so much loss of the history of the people, who survive today in smaller populations.

Hoi An, probably the most beautiful city in Vietnam has become a tourist attraction with premier hotel resorts along the beach, palm trees swaying, providing a tropical paradise. Immaculate golf courses have sprung up, luring the Aussies only a short flight away, as well as the French and Germans to an inexpensive vacation wonderland.

In Ho Chi Minh City, I experienced the revitalization of the former Paris of the Orient with its skyscrapers, restaurants and night clubs, and its masses working through traffic jams. Forty years ago Saigon was a vibrant metropolis but a very dangerous one, with ground attacks and bombings. Today the youth walk the streets, laughing, little concern on their faces. For them, war is not a personal memory.

We drove to the Michelin Plantation and I had the driver stop to take a picture of me among the rubber trees, near where the enemy ambushed my troops. The No Fire Zone

Ho Chi Minh Memorial

designation for acreage that allowed such ambushes roiled me during the war but now it is a distant thought and I have grown to accept it. Who would have guessed that after I served my military time I would be working for the Michelin Tire Corporation?

Cu Chi was off-limits to tourists since it is an army base for the Socialist Republic of Vietnam. I never anticipated this outcome. The greatest power in the world had to admit it no longer could win in Indochina, forced to evacuate and leave military and air bases for the invading forces. Trying to see where I served in the bush was impossible, the jungle took care of erasing the memories by growing over the battlefields that cost Americans lives, terrain that meant nothing more than a place for a battle to be won. We fought without front lines; a 360-degree environment all around us. Seen as invaders and exploited as such by the successful North Vietnamese propagandists, we became pawns in a war of attrition of the NVA and VC: success related to high enemy deaths, often erroneously inflated. General Westmoreland would brief reporters daily at the Rex Hotel in Saigon. Called the "five o'clock follies," he used charts with the escalating body counts of the opponents, trying to convince the press and himself that we were winning.

The truth existed somewhere in between. For instance, 274 US Marines died at Khe Sanh, eventually abandoning the base and units of the 101st Airborne Division fought and took Hamburger Hill, of little strategic value, losing 72 soldiers, but left the hilltop to nature and our foe to reoccupy.

We never understood the nationalistic cause by the North. Their beliefs stayed strong, even during those long years of fighting various foes before the Americans. Ho Chi Minh, who died before seeing the unification of the southern and northern parts into the Socialist Republic of Vietnam, said: "You will kill ten of us, we will kill one of you, but in the end, you will tire of it first."

John McCain agreed: "The US never lost a battle against North Vietnam, but it lost the war."

Upon my return, my flashbacks, my memories of its dark and wet jungles, faced me. Much like the ones that Joseph Conrad described, they represented darkness for me. However, as I mingled with former allies and foes a certain peace, a lightness of emotions evolved.

The Vietnamese had been battling invaders for centuries, beating back their enemies, time and time again. It was appropriate that they could now live without daily war for future generations; it was time to regain their nation and their lives.

However, after America abandoned its embassy in Saigon in 1975, the Socialist Republic of Vietnam still had little peace as it went into Cambodia to eliminate the morally heinous Khmer Rouge which was supported by the Chinese Communists. Although China allied with North Vietnam in the conflict with the US, it invaded the new country in 1979 to support its Cambodian puppets. The Vietnamese Army stopped the Red Army after four weeks of fighting and secured its northern border.

I do believe that the Vietnamese accept Taoism as a philosophy of life; its dualism with the concepts of yin and yang. The yin is often seen as the dark and the negative side of life. Whereas the yang is considered the bright and positive side. The yin and yang are essential to them and made life and war bearable for over 2000 years against the Mongols, the Chinese, and of course the Japanese, the French, and the Americans. By becoming a peaceful and modern unified country it has melded its yin and yang: its wars complete the life cycle with peace.

My two trips exposed me to this dualism of life. Like day and night, these opposites compliment—dark versus bright, negative versus positive, death versus life. The American Indochina War was my yin—the death and destruction on the killing fields—and Vietnam in peacetime became my yang: the light and the positive. Just as the country has reached the end of its wars, my return in 2009 brought me closure; my yin of darkness is now in harmony with my yang of peace. ■

Returning to Vietnam, decades after the war, brings Ed Marohn (below) some peace.

LIMBERLOST LETTERPRESS

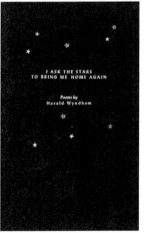

www.limberlostpress.com

Idaho artist Fred Ochi was well known for his iconic "Red Barn" watercolors.

THE DEMOCRATIC VISION OF
FRED OCHI

Rick Ardinger and Jennifer Holley

He was prolific, most known for his plein air watercolors of remote western landscapes, but he was an artist who also experimented in sepia and monocolor abstracts and mid-20th century tonal statements worthy of a serious art historian's attention. A gifted portrait artist, his paintings typically are devoid of people, radiating absence and impermanence through stark images of empty fields, weathered fences, and structures seemingly abandoned against a vast and formidable horizon.

There was a time in the later half of the last century when the artwork of Fred Isao Ochi (1913-2007) had a ubiquitous presence in Idaho and the Intermountain West. During his long life he produced a body of work that was accessible and affordable, and in his way he was the most democratic of artists. Perhaps remembered most for his paintings of "red barns" in all seasons—some paintings as small as four-by-six inches for folks at summer art fairs—Fred Ochi is known for his perspectives on Idaho's iconic landscapes: Sun Valley's Mt. Baldy, the Tetons, the Sawtooths, ghost towns, rivers, and barns again in spring, summer, fall, and nearly obscured in snow-storms. When he died in Idaho Falls, Idaho, at the age of 93, he left a legacy as an artist, teacher, business leader, and activist for ethnic and racial diversity, and he left an archive that awaits a long-overdue retrospective.

Artist Fred Ochi

Fred Ochi was a Japanese American artist who made his way in a politically conservative region of the country during the second half of the 20th century. He witnessed and navigated through some of the nation's most shameful years of racial discrimination. He endured because of who he was, surviving even the dark years of World War II outside of a concentration camp while more than 100,000 other Japanese Americans on the West Coast were forcibly relocated to camps throughout the nation's interior between 1942 and 1945. It is not a stretch to say Fred used his art to broaden awareness and acceptance of ethnic diversity during an extreme time of racial discrimination.

Born in Watsonville, California, in 1913, Fred grew up the son of sharecroppers in an area that today is the heart of the Silicon Valley. His mother died when he was only eight in 1921, and his father decided to send him and his older brother Tom to Iwakuni, Japan, to be raised by their grandparents. Their father stayed in California to farm.

Though the boys did not speak, read, or write Japanese, they made their way as students in Japan, where part of the curriculum schooled the boys in the meditative art of calligraphy and brush painting. For Fred, the importance of his education in Japan cannot be overstated in terms of its impact on his future working life as an artist.

After three years in Japan, however, the U.S. Congress was about to pass the 1924 Immigration Act that set quotas on European immigrants coming to the U.S. and excluded Asians altogether. Fred's father, fearing

"The Tetons," watercolor

his sons could be stuck in Japan, decided to bring them back to California, and because the boys were born in the U.S., they were allowed to return. Fred was about 11, his brother 13.

Back in California, Fred and Tom worked again picking strawberries on a place called the Webb ranch near Stanford University, about 40 acres sharecropped by five families. Throughout his life, Fred reminisced about picking strawberries as a boy.

His father remarried, and in 1930, he and his new wife decided to return to Japan. By then of high school age, Fred and his older brother chose to stay in the U.S., and when they parted, the boys never saw their father again.

Out of high school, Fred attended the California College of Arts and Crafts for a time, his education in Japan greatly influencing that experience and his versatility. To make a living, he found work painting butcher paper banners of the daily specials and sale prices for grocery stores and other shop windows. That experience of quick daily work led to a three-year apprenticeship as a graphic display artist for a chain of 17 movie theaters in the Bay Area.

Movie theater signage required quick work, most often on short notice each week when the theaters learned their new line-up of films and shorts. Each movie theater would need a different display, and so he developed the skill of speed to attend to the theater marquees in nine cities. Though he was not paid as an apprentice, he became a highly skilled graphic display artist by the end of his apprenticeship.

"To watch him lay out a poster was a spectacle of speed," Fred's son Jon says. "He would just lay down the paper, put down the ruler, find the center, mark the center line, then take the yardstick as a measuring device, go down three inches, and he'd say, 'OK, in this space is where the wording goes, and maybe a graphic illustration over here. He did it so quickly. It was really pretty phenomenal."

For the theaters, he often worked through many nights, not just lettering window posters, but painting large, quick portraits of movie stars and marquee scenery.

"It was all done by hand," his son Jon says. "He learned to do portraits really fast. He used to say 'Oh, I did Greta Garbo, Clark Gable, Buster Keaton, Jean Muir'—who was later blacklisted in the McCarthy era. They might get photographs of movie stars from the film distributors, and

Ochi's pencil line drawing of film star Jean Muir done in 1934.

my father would have to paint much larger poster portraits from the photos, all very quickly. Often the theaters hosted big special openings that might be attended by movie actors."

Working around Menlo Park just prior to WW II, Fred in 1941 became the first president of the San Mateo Japanese-American Citizens League during a time of growing unease, participating in patriotic events and penning numerous letters to newspapers proclaiming the loyalty and patriotism of Japanese Americans.

After Imperial Japan attacked Pearl Harbor on December 7, 1941, however, the atmosphere for persons of Japanese heritage in the U.S.became hostile.

It is often assumed and mistakenly reported that Fred came to Idaho because he was part of the forced evacuation of Japanese Americans from the West Coast and that he spent years in the Hunt concentration camp (or the Minidoka Relocation Center as it was known by the federal government), in south-central Idaho. But in February of 1942, about a week after President Franklin Roosevelt signed Executive Order 9066 prohibiting anyone of Japanese ethnicity from living on the West Coast, Fred and his brother left California on their own and moved to Ogden, Utah, to relocate near relatives. That quick decision to move saved them from three years of incarceration in one of the camps in the interior.

Living near Salt Lake City, Fred found work again with the regional chain of Fox West Theaters doing promotional movie illustrations and signage for theater lobbies and marquees. Because of his talent, and quick versatility, his work took him to southern Idaho theaters.

After seeing Idaho Falls, he decided to settle there in 1943 and start his own commercial art and sign shop. On the side, he continued his work for the Fox West Coast theaters in Idaho Falls and traveled to theaters across the state in southwest Idaho, until an incident in Nampa where he had to be escorted out of town by the Idaho National Guard due to threats to the lives of Japanese Americans.

He met his Idaho-born girlfriend Yoshiko in 1945, and they married a year later in the Methodist church because Methodists allowed Japanese Americans to join as worshipers when other religious congregations banned Japanese from becoming members. For the rest of their lives, Idaho Falls would remain their home, where they raised five sons.

One can only imagine how two Japanese Americans made their way through these years of intense racial prejudice and bigotry in a region of the country that was not at all racially diverse. But to be accepted, Fred and his wife purposely became involved in social organizations and community clubs, and they volunteered their services for numerous community events and good causes, proving their status as loyal Americans and productive, engaged members of the community. Fred became a member of the Idaho Falls Chamber of Commerce and he never missed a Kiwanis Club meeting in more than 40 years. Yoshiko was involved in the PTA, the Cub Scouts, and political organizations.

"He had a way of diffusing potential racial confrontations," Jon says. If he were walking up to a business to do some sign painting and someone who appeared to be a belligerent or rough character would walk toward him, my father would say something like, 'Hey, you look like you know your way around here, you must be the mayor.' And he'd quickly diffuse tension. He had a way of sensing potential confrontation, and

he'd break the ice with humor. He was very charismatic and people were always fascinated watching him work so quickly and so adeptly. He always said to us kids, 'I have no enemies . . . everyone is my friend.'"

And in addition to joining community organizations, he often took the lead on starting things he felt the community needed, such as helping found the Idaho Falls Arts Guild in 1948 as a way to bring artists together and to take their art to the public. He later became president of the state-wide Idaho Art Association.

"He always volunteered time to help out community events and good causes by making promotional signs and banners for organizations like the United Way," Jon says. "He did posters for events sponsored by both political parties, and if the governor or some other speaker came to town, he'd paint promotional posters with their portraits on a banner. Over the years he painted portraits of Presidents Truman, Eisenhower, Reagan, of Idaho Governors Robert Smylie and Cecil Andrus, and many other state and national political leaders who visited Idaho Falls."

"Red Barn," watercolor

"Waterfall," watercolor

His business had him creating signage for commercial vehicles, designing logos and letterhead for businesses, and other things that required a skilled hand in graphic arts, teaching his sons the business along the way.

And while Fred was busy making a living, he devoted his off-work time to painting watercolors.

"As a plein air painter, he'd take us kids out to these landscapes so he could paint, and he'd set us up with our own brushes, while he'd do his work," Jon says. "And we'd do ours and then we'd get bored and throw stones at pheasants and run around while he focused an afternoon on his painting. He was a very serious artist. That's how as kids we saw so much of Idaho."

As his five sons grew more adept in the family business, he devoted himself more and more to his art full time. In 1979, Fred's son Jon took over the family commercial art business, and Fred was free to fully commit himself to his painting. He matted and framed his own work, displayed in gallery shows and art fairs and made his work available to all who wanted something original. As he grew older he began to receive deserving accolades, such as the 1998 Idaho Governor's Award for Excellence in the Arts.

He was invited to teach watercolor classes at universities and arts organizations in Idaho, Montana, and Wyoming. He welcomed Idaho Falls art students into his studio to demonstrate his calligraphy and to teach them his distinctive brush stroke and spray techniques.

People remember walking over puddles of dried ink and paint on the floor. Fred would always be set up in a local park, painting and displaying his work for purchase at public events.

For Idaho's 1990 statehood centennial, he was honored among 100 Idahoans "who made a difference" to the development of the state for his cultural contributions, in part for his artwork, and in part for his work promoting acceptance of diversity.

He continued to work until the last weeks of his life, and when he died in February of 2007, his family estimates he left a legacy of thousands of paintings in galleries, museums, and in private collections across the United States. Jon says he and his brothers are wrestling with documenting a large archive of work and at some point may entertain the idea of a Fred Ochi retrospective.

"Sheep Wagons," watercolor

"Snow on Bald Mountain," watercolor

* * * * *

This profile goes to press at a time of an alarming rise in white supremacy sentiments across the nation and, particularly, a dramatic rise of violence against Asian Americans. Given his personal experience in his lifetime, how Fred Ochi would have confronted this time in our national politics is worth imagining.

The democratic approach he took to his art is in part reflected in his representational focus, which establishes a common connection with so many viewers, sharing a common experience with landscapes we know in the West, a familiar experience with non-judgmental nature. We can imagine that reaching that intimate connection with viewers was intentional. It was what he sought in his everyday life, in his commercial art business, quietly and subtly *insisting* in his friendly way that he and his family and people of diverse heritage be accepted. It was part of making his way in a largely white, politically conservative world. It is why his paintings of barns, of familiar mountain peaks, of ghost towns, of abandoned windmills, shacks, and farm equipment are still so appreciated.

In addition to offering simple visual pleasure, his art shares an intimacy of knowing a place, a region, a geographic or geologic land-mark, a shared viewpoint, an experience, as a way of bonding with the viewer. His art is a bridge to recognizing what we share together equally in the natural world.

Fred Ochi approached his watercolor art with the business sense he had for his commercial art business. A criticism by some in his time was that Ochi's repetition of themes and scenes in his work was commercial, popular, and therefore somehow less exceptional. But it is precisely the empathy between artist and viewer that Ochi sought to achieve, extending shared, quiet acceptance in nature, as if the experience of art—a balance of discipline and imagination—offers a sense of love and justice in a fragmented world. Rather than having something deep inside him to "say" about equality, he expressed himself through his artwork, offering a sense of wonder about the natural world as something to be imagined among equals.

Out in the wild, alone with his easel and brushes, a vast and stun-ning landscape before him, we can imagine the simple peace Fred found in his meditative focus. It is hard not to think of the challenges he faced as a Japanese American artist in mid-20th century Idaho, and it is hard not to think how we'd all benefit from sharing in that meditation. ∎

"High Mountains," watercolor

LIMBERLOST LETTERPRESS

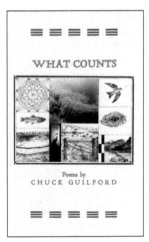

www.limberlostpress.com

Kenneth Patchen

LARRY SMITH

Coming to the Writings of Kenneth Patchen

Growing up a working-class kid in an Ohio Valley steel town, not unlike Kenneth Patchen's Warren and Niles, Ohio, I was struck deep when I first read one of his poems. It came in a college survey of American Literature in 1962. By then I already knew of poet James Wright who grew up 20 miles south of me in Martins Ferry, Ohio. My response to both was, "Wow, there can be poetry like this, about mills and working people!"

That I even found a Kenneth Patchen poem in an academic setting then was fortuitous since he was always regarded as a maverick writer, existing outside of the accepted critical world. The poems, brought in by a fine teacher, Ralph Church, must have come on one of those mimeograph sheets that served to supplement our *American Poetry and Prose* leftist-leaning anthology edited by Norman Foerster. Anyway, one of the poems was in Patchen's humorous vein, the other was "The Orange Bears: Childhood in an Ohio Steel Mill Town." It knocked me over for its raw and real portrayal of the predatory life facing working people, my people. I had found an ally for life.

> The Orange bears with soft friendly eyes
> Who played with me when I was ten,
> Christ, before I'd left home they'd had
> Their paws smashed in the rolls, their backs
> Seared by hot slag, their soft trusting
> Bellies kicked in, their tongues ripped
> Out, and I went down through the woods
> To the smelly crick with Whitman
> In the Haldeman-Julius edition,
> And I just sat there worrying my thumbnail
> Into the cover. . . .

I knew these people. They were family. Their struggle and sacrifices were real to me. I had worked alongside my father in the steel mill to earn money for college. Here was a writer to acknowledge this world.

My pressure to "fit in" at a conservative Presbyterian, liberal arts college, could not and would not confine me.

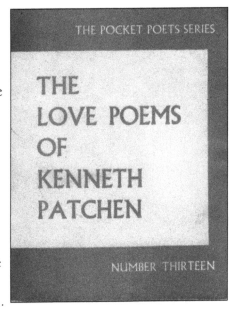

Soon I found my way to the City Lights Pocket Poets Series of booklets by Patchen, *Poems of Humor and Protest #3* and *The Love Poems of Kenneth Patchen #13*. At a conformist college in the early 1960s, such writing took me out of the classroom into a discovery of the Beat Movement and writers Lawrence Ferlinghetti, Allen Ginsberg, Gregory Corso, Diane di Prima...

et. al. My own poems took on new energy and purpose as witness and protest. Such writing led me further to the books of James Laughlin's New Directions Publishing which I found fully displayed along a whole shelf in the Campus Bookstore in Kent, Ohio. I began picking them off one by one starting with *The Collected Poems of Kenneth Patchen*.

Though I was a teaching fellow at Kent State University (1968-1970), my real education and awareness continued outside of the classroom. So, when it came time to choose an original dissertation subject, I thought of connecting the two worlds. Standing in line to pick up my books for the next semester at the DuBois Bookstore, I spotted a striking book cover, *The Journal of Albion Moonlight* by Kenneth Patchen. I quickly added it to my stack and as quickly dove into reading/living this apocalyptic world which Patchen envisioned at the brink of WW II. I was then sharing a similar dark world during the Viet Nam War. That book and the government-sanctioned shooting of students on my campus forever changed me and my wife Ann to become activist advocates for peace and justice.

After much struggle to find an advisor and a committee who would accept Kenneth Patchen as a dissertation subject, I completed my study as well as one of the first books on Kenneth Patchen in the US Authors Series done by Twayne. At one point, my advisor Sandy Marovitz called me, "The Patchen Man," and I was surprised yet proud to carry that banner and watch his international reputation grow.

The book I would focus on in this re-reading is the *Love Poems of Kenneth Patchen* (City Lights Pocket Poems #13, 1961). As his widow Miriam once pointed out, "Kenneth Patchen never wrote the same book twice." His diversity was Promethean. He dedicated each of his books "For Miriam." His love poems rise out of each era of his work to share and celebrate a deep and abiding intimacy. A personal and universal love is his main theme, from his earliest poems, through his avant-garde prose, and into his poetry-jazz, his poems-and-drawings and finally into his picture-poems.

In some 40 poems, *The Love Poems* weaves images and emotional tones to create a world in which two brave lovers share a vision of deep and abiding caring. Perhaps one of his most loved poems is this auto-biographical poem of their early life in Greenwich Village. They had just returned from working for James Laughlin and New Directions at Norfolk, Connecticut.

23rd Street Runs into Heaven

You stand near the window as lights wink
On along the street. Somewhere a trolley, taking
Shopgirls and clerks home, clatters through
This before-supper Sabbath. An alley cat cries
To find the garbage cans sealed; newsboys
Begin their murder-into-pennies round.
We are shut in, secure for a little, safe until
Tomorrow. You slip your dress off, roll down
Your stockings, careful against runs. Naked now,
With soft light on soft flesh, you pause
For a moment; turn and face me—
Smile in a way that only women know
Who have lain long with their love
And are made more virginal.

Our supper is plain but we are very wonderful.

251

Moved by the slow deliberateness of this declaration, one senses devotion as the key element of the Patchens' relationship. Those who knew the couple recall that Kenneth was never forcing Miriam into their humble existence, but rather that it was typically Miriam who was supporting and leading him.

Kenneth and Miriam Patchen, 1946

While researching my biography of Kenneth in 1989, she insisted I move from my fleabag hotel in Berkeley to live with her in Palo Alto. We would interview in the morning, I'd type up those notes, then re-interview in the evening, checking for accuracy. She confided that one day during those last years when Kenneth was laid up from a broken back and in pain much of the time, he told her he was going to quit writing, that he had already said it all. And she, knowing his need to connect, reminded him, "No, Kenneth, you mustn't. There are so many others who need your voice and action."

Dispelling any belief that theirs was a romantically idyllic bond, I learned of the practical side of their life. While Kenneth would be working at writing, Miriam with her red flowing hair and piercing blue eyes would be out scouring Greenwich Village for a cheap but livable apartment which she would turn into a studio. Picture one with Kenneth seated in the bathtub pecking a typewriter on a desk of boards. She also confided that once after she had come on a little too strong favoring Leon Trotsky at a Hollywood gathering, Kenneth had told her, "Miriam, you know you could just stop and think before you speak." She told me, "I thought it over a few moments, then replied, 'No, Kenneth, I just couldn't do that.'" They both laughed, as did I. Interviewing her was the delight of my research and the first step in a long path toward completing the book begun at the "Kenneth Patchen Literary Festival" in Warren, Ohio (1989) when Miriam and good friend Joel Climenhaga tapped me for the job.

Another fortuitous event came about while I was staying with Miriam Patchen that fall of 1989. City Lights Books had called to tell her that they were no longer going to be publishing books from their older Pocket Poets Series including Kenneth's two books. Later that night I proposed that Bottom Dog Press pick up the *Love Poems of Kenneth Patchen* and enlarge it with the more than 50 other love poems I had found not included in *Love Poems*. She was relieved and joyful, and I was delighted to be going home to Ohio to work on such a project. As my co-editor I chose my daughter Laura who was about to graduate from Bowling Green State University. Perhaps it was Miriam who suggested the title *Awash with Roses: Collected Love Poems of Kenneth Patchen* from one of his poetry-jazz love poems.

Awash with Roses contains 106 love poems including those from his periods of poems-and-drawing and picture-poems, thanks to the cooperation of both City Lights Books and New Directions Publishing. My biography was far enough along by that point to include "Kenneth and Miriam: When the Wreath Touches the Heart" a 50-page telling of "one of the great love stories of American literature."
It concludes with "The Patchens found this fundamental 'yes' in each other, and through sacrifice and determination they nursed it into being. This was the true child which Kenneth and Miriam nurtured all of their years. The love poems of Kenneth and Miriam Patchen are a way of remembering and a way of going on."

Throughout life, Kenneth Patchen painted when he was not writing, and combined both passions with his painted poems (Rick and Rosemary Ardinger collection).

Perhaps all of Kenneth Patchen's writing and art can best be seen as a love poem for Miriam and the world, as in this poem:

The Sea Is Awash with Roses
for Miriam

The sea is awash with roses O they blow
Upon the land

The still hills fill with their scent
O the hills flow on their sweetness
As on God's hand

O love, it is so little we know of pleasure
Pleasure that lasts as the snow

But the sea is awash with roses O they blow
Upon the land

Kenneth died in 1972, and Miriam continued to present and promote his works and vision for the next three decades. It is hard not to see them as ideal in their devotion and to cling to the love poems as hope for a better world. Lawrence Ferlinghetti's City Lights Books and James Laughlin's New Directions would come to serve as a model for the Bottom Dog Press which I and poet David Shevin would found in 1985. Now 215 books later, we remain indebted to Kenneth Patchen and his engaged vision of writing that matters. ■

Painted poem by Kenneth Patchen (Rick and Rosemary Ardinger collection)

THE BUSINESS OF FANCYDANCING

Stories and poems
by Sherman Alexie

RON McFARLAND

Re-reading Sherman Alexie's
The Business of Fancydancing

A bout a dozen years ago (spring of 2008) I taught a 400-level course at the University of Idaho on Sherman Alexie, whose semi-autobiographical young adult novel, *The Absolutely True Diary of a Part-Time Indian*, had been released the previous year to considerable acclaim. It won the National Book Award for Young People's Literature and drew the wrath of parents, principals, schools and school boards from Antioch, Illinois, to Yakima, Washington. Predictably, I suppose, that little novel proved quite popular among the fourteen (including four graduate students) registered for that course. Beginning with complaints out of Meridian, Idaho, in 2014, the novel evolved into something between a *cause célèbre* and a tempest in a teapot, but the furor certainly improved sales.

Consequently, when I thought of re-reading one of Alexie's many titles, *Absolutely True Diary* came readily too mind as did his highly esteemed collection of short stories, *The Lone Ranger and Tonto Fistfight in Heaven* (1993), one story from which, "What it Means to Say Phoenix, Arizona," became the basis of his screenplay for the noted film, *Smoke Signals* (1998), which was shot on the Coeur d'Alene Reservation (his father's tribe) in Plummer, Idaho. The Spokane Reservation, headquartered in Wellpinit, Washington, where he grew up, was not so well disposed. I might have focused on one of my favorite stories in that collection, "The Trial of Thomas Builds-the-Fire," if only because in it he takes up the subject of Colonel Steptoe, subject of my book, *Edward J. Steptoe and the Indian Wars* (2016).

Other possibilities on my hit list from the work of this prolific writer in multiple genres include his 1995 novel, *Reservation Blues*, which attracts me, among other reasons, because of its treatment of the Faust theme. For several years I thought of offering a course, possibly at the graduate level, on that theme from Christopher Marlowe's *Doctor Faustus* through both parts of Goethe's *Faust* and the libretto for Gounod's opera and on to such novels as Louisa May Alcott's *A Modern*

Mephistopheles, Thomas Mann's *Doctor Faustus*, Klaus Mann's *Mephisto* (he was Thomas Mann's son), and John Banville's *Mefisto*. I chickened out. Also on my list is Alexie's rather controversial, dark novel set in Seattle, *Indian Killer* (1996), which was the topic of a master's thesis I directed a few years ago. Or why not take the leap of faith into Alexie's ambitious sprawl of a memoir, his most recent book, *You Don't Have to Say You Love Me* (2017), which appeals to me, among other reasons, because of the villanelles he scatters among its 456 pages, and I've long been captivated by that challenging form.

But no. As the title of this re-reading indicates, I've opted to go back to the beginning of it all, to the 41 poems and four very short stories that make up his first book, *The Business of Fancydancing* (1992), which Hanging Loose Press published in Sherman's 26th year, when he was an undergraduate at Washington State University learning the ropes under the tutelage of my old friend Alex Kuo. On the back cover a very young Sherman looks out solemn and unsmiling at his potential reader. It could be a passport photo. Below it, the publisher has quoted from James R. Kincaid's *NYTBR* front-page review that vaulted Alexie into the public eye. Kincaid declared that among the new Native American writers, Alexie's was "perhaps the most commanding voice," and he asserted *The Business of Fancydancing*, his first book, was "so wide-ranging, dexterous, and constantly capable of raising your neck hair that it enters at once into our ideas of who we are and how we might be," conclud-ing (in bold font) **"Mr. Alexie is one of the major lyric voices of our time."**

How could such a claim not go to the head of any young poet, let alone the brash polemicist Sherman Alexie was determined to be? In an essay titled "Sherman Alexie's Polemical Stories," published in a 1997 issue of *Studies in American Indian Literatures*, I proposed that his polemics in fiction and poetry connect him with the Greek origin of the term, which is "war," or for the polemicist, "warrior." He was from the outset, and he remains, a verbal warrior, and words are his weapons.

Especially in his early public appearances, he would lash out at his largely white audiences, who were drawn to his poems and prose fiction, shaming them (us) for everything from Native American genocide to the desolation of life on the rez. We might cringe, we might indignantly stalk out of the room mumbling under our breath that we were not complicit in the Sand River Massacre, *our* forefathers did not dump smallpox blankets on the tribes. Were we offended? Some of us were, perhaps still are. Did Sherman care? Nope. Making us feel indignant was what he has been all about. That's what good satirists, particularly those in the acerbic tradition of Juvenal (as opposed to the gentler school of Horace) are all about. In another of my essays, I described Alexie as "the Native American Voltaire," or words to that effect. Jonathan Swift comes to mind.

Has he gone over the top from time to time? Has he whacked us upside the head with a two-by-four when we might prefer more subtle, understated prodding? Of course. My wife and I were seated among the audience in Tacoma when the Western Literature Association bestowed its 2007 Distinguished Achievement Award on Sherman. Although he expressed his gratitude for that honor, among the first words to flee his mouth were something like the following: "Part of me just wants to say, 'fuck you.'" Mr. Alexie has never associated himself with the Dale Carnegie methodology of winning friends and influencing people. I checked: Carnegie's noted bestseller dates from 1936, and it remains in print. The first chapter is titled, "If You Want to Gather Honey, Don't Kick Over the Beehive." Let it be said now that Sherman Alexie has never intended to go about gathering honey. Remember your primary school report card, that section that rated you S, U, or N on "Gets along well with others"? *Not* Sherman's concern, nor has it been that of most satirists, from Aristophanes and Moliere down to contemporary political cartoonists and late-night television personalities.

Back to the texts from *Business*, I will say that the title poem, a well-crafted sestina, remains among my favorites in all his many collections of poetry (at least ten in number). The terminal words, to be repeated in an intricate pattern throughout the six-line stanzas, are suggestive: reach, fancydance, empty, we, money, promise. The concluding tercet brings those words together (the first line is enjambed with the last word of the final sestet—"reach"):

> for more. A promise is just like money.
> Something we can hold, in twenties, a dream we reach.
> It's business, a fancydance to fill where it's empty. (69)

I would add that the terse end-stops here counter the free flow of the poem, in which only three lines of the 36 are end-stopped with so much as a comma. The syntax flows not only across lines, but across stanzas. The poignant last word of the poem echoes the emptiness of reservation life with its unfulfilled promise.

The front cover of Alexie's first book features a fancydancer in full regalia. I remember asking Sherman after he read before a sizable audience at the University of Idaho soon after the book appeared whether he was himself a fancydancer. He said no, laughed. Sherman was a standout basketball player at Reardan High, but finesse at roundball does not necessarily equate to skill at fancydancing.

In re-reading the poems and stories of *The Business of Fancydancing*, I find that most of my favorites remain so: "Traveling," for example, the opening story, only a little over two pages, which ends in phrasing I find reminiscent of the closing line from Ginsburg's "America": "America, I'm putting my queer shoulder to the wheel." Alexie: "I turned back to the van, put my shoulder to the cold metal and waited for something to change" (15). "Grandmother," in which he portrays her leaving the sweat lodge naked, "steam rising off her body in winter / like a slow explosion of horses" (23). Coincidentally, that simile recalls for me one of Sherman's best ever poems, a fairly long one entitled "Horses," which I heard him recite at a reading in Pullman before this book appeared. I can still not only see and hear, but can somehow *feel*, the impact of that closing refrain:

> I own no horses,
> the Indian was measured before
> by the number of horses he owned,
>
> the exact number, I own
> no horses, I own
> no horses, I own
> no horses.

This poem appeared in Alexie's next book, *Old Shirts, New Skins* (1993), a disintegrating copy of which I have on hand, published out of UCLA in its American Indian Studies series. Not surprisingly, Alexie has scored well as a performance poet, and "Horses" is particularly effective in that context.

I still like some of his postmodern renditions in which historical personages pop up in contemporary settings, as in "Reservation Cab Driver," when at three in the morning he picks up Crazy Horse, who is hitchhiking. "Giving Blood" is also a fav. In it, the first-person speaker tells the nurse that his name is Crazy Horse and his birthdate is "probably" on "June 25 in 1876" (the historic Lakota warrior was killed by a guard in an escape attempt on September 5, 1877). The poem ends when the nurse informs him, "sorry Mr. Crazy Horse / but we've already taken too much of your blood / and you won't be eligible / to donate for another generation or two" (78). In "Evolution" Buffalo Bill opens a 24-7 pawn shop on the reservation. In "War All the Time" Crazy Horse comes back from Vietnam and heads for the Breakaway Bar, where he pawns his medals for beer, and when the bartender asks him why he is "giving up everything he earned," Crazy Horse "tells him you can't stop a man / from trying to survive, no matter where he is" (65). In his story "The First Annual All-Indian Horseshoe Pitch and Barbecue," from *The Lone Ranger and Tonto Fistfight in Heaven*, Alexie offers his often-cited formula:

Survival = Anger x Imagination (150)

In one of the pieces I've turned out over the years, I've proposed that the right side of the equation should be divided by Humor. What makes most of Alexie's often painful poems and stories tolerable is his (admittedly) bitter humor. For the record, I do not presume that Sherman would agree to my mathematical revision of or corollary to his formula for surviving on the reservation, or more broadly for surviving as a Native American (Sherman more often uses the term "Indian").

In *Business* Alexie introduces his readers to a small cast of characters who will appear in his fiction: Victor Joseph, Thomas Builds-the-Fire,

Lester FallsApart, Seymour. Recurring themes involving the speaker's father, distance, and deadly house fire contribute to making this book something of a primer for readers embarking on Sherman Alexie's writings. In my re-reading I found myself drawn unexpectedly to the four short poems titled "Indian Boy Love Song." Each poem runs thirteen lines constructed as tercet, quatrain, tercet, tercet, a reminder that free-verse poet though he may be, Alexie has been fascinated with form from the outset. The concluding tercet of Song #2 seems apposite today more than ever:

> Indian women, forgive me.
> I grew up distant
> and always afraid. (55) ∎

REBECCA EVANS

Thomas Hardy's Spirit of of Influence

Stationed in the military at RAF Upper Heyford, England, I had longed to feel "smart." I made a pact with myself, *devour 100 books a year*. Quota, not quality. Toward the year's end, I chose the easiest reads off shelves. I packed a novel everywhere, snatching paragraphs in small moments. Here I could disappear.

My co-worker, Tony Maycock, a British National, pointed at my heap one evening, "You Americans read crap."

I folded my arms, pushed my chin forward.

"That's not literature," he said. "It's not even reading."

"I read more than anyone else I know."

"If you want, I'll bring you something worthy."

"Sure." It felt a challenge.

The next day, he handed me Thomas Hardy's *Jude the Obscure* and I was lost for always.

*****

After the Persian Gulf War and a bad break-up in 1991, I decided to visit Thomas Hardy's cottage in Dorset, a two and half hour drive from Upper Heyford. After reading *Jude*, I hoped to summon Hardy's energy into my unsophisticated poetry. Maybe I felt the same longing as Jude Fawley, his yearning for academia. Or maybe, due to my recent break-up and the war, I recognized the harrowing impact of Jude's choices: a love lost, a life removed, a relationship failure. In the end, death became Jude's punishment for misplaced love. I could relate, as my heart continuously sought alignment with someone, anyone, who eventually left me or harmed me or both.

Thomas Hardy's cottage in Dorset, southwest England.

* * * * *

At Hardy's home, the sun streaked hazy lines through thick stratus clouds and trees dripped in a silent cry from early rain. I approached the cob and thatch presence, charming, and unbelievably small. The ceilings, low enough I could almost touch them. The rooms, scented with sweet moss, reflected England's aroma. In the center of the parlour stood a hearth that filled most of the room. I imagined Hardy's family gathering—boiling their kettle for tea, preparing food and, sharing stories. I lingered in Hardy's office, originally a scullery, hoping to absorb the beauty of his language. I thought of lineage, traits passed through bloodlines, much like the inheritance of physical belongings. I pressed my hand into his stone floor, as if it held source from another's life, as if I could channel words and wisdom directly from the dead. The tour guide interrupted.

"You know, the room was used by Hardy's father to manage accounts for his stonemasonry business," she told me.

I shrugged.

"Can I venture into the gardens?" I asked.

"There's a walking path. Stay on it," she offered.

*****

I entered Hardy's garden, Thorncombe Woods. The British term, garden, indicates a front yard, or even a back yard, not the American garden bearing fruit or vegetation. Hardy's magical woods held evidence of bats and butterflies, dragonflies and damselflies. I watched for grass snakes, though not venomous, and should I encounter one, I'd try to make friends.

I veered off the trail and into the woods, into the drizzle, following what I believed Hardy's footsteps, much like a child stepping into the footprints of her parent with possibility of filling them.

One of many things I cherished in England throughout my eight-year-assignment were the guided-walking tours. In London, I once strolled through Jack the Ripper's life, visiting murder sites of the legend interspersed with a pub crawl. On the Ripper tour, staged actors reenacted deadly scenes and as my tour progressed so did my intoxication, thanks to gulping half a pint per pub-stop. I felt embedded in 1888, in London's Whitechapel District, and thought Jack himself would escort me home. That didn't happen, and I returned to my base unscathed.

I wished a similar encounter with Hardy, something abrupt: his presence, somehow, some way. Hardy once said ... *in a wood almost every tree has its voice as well as its feature* and I listened. I listened hard. I listened close. I opened my worn journal, which served as a log-book of sorts, the pages dog-eared, many torn away

Thomas Hardy

and burned as if to rid myself of memories. I sketched images, jotted sounds—the peaceful buzz of grazing horses, woodland creatures, and the soft spilling waters at the pool.

I rubbed at my scar up and down. Up and down. Raised and vertical, it initiated at my wrist and spanned midway up my arm. The wrong direction for suicide effectiveness. I knew, at this moment, I wanted to not exist. I wanted, more than anything, to stop my suffering. I felt, I could have easily disappeared, here, in these woods. Later, my journal entries show descriptions of sounds alongside sketches of leaves and branches. The pages during this time held few words and little indication of my state of mind.

Sound seems akin to prayers. The intonations run through, rinse over, as if cleansing wounds. Sound also elicits recollection and these woods held zero triggers from my past, which, on reflection today, most likely saved me.

I had learned that as he walked his woods, Hardy pictured his characters from his manuscripts chasing behind. In my mind, Arabella, the wife who had tricked Jude into marriage, twirled beneath the branches, mocking him. In *Jude the Obscure*, Jude struggled, unsuccessfully, to not love his cousin, Sue Brideshead. I could almost see Sue, as if playing hide-and-seek, behind those trunks as their (Jude's and Sue's) children, swung, hanging by their necks from the branches above. In the novel, the children's half-brother, Little Father Time, (Jude and Arabella's son) murders them, and after, takes his own life. A dark and eerie presence of consequence Jude endured for his heart's misappropriation with Sue, for wrong love.

Though I had hoped for voices, for ancient guidance, I heard no one, felt positionless. Empty-headed and -hearted, I left that well-preserved fragment of land. I drove another 25 minutes to Weymouth, anticipating the sweetness of scones, cream, and tea once I arrived. As a poet and writer, I often credit influences and mentors, mentioning many books. Too many to recall, yet all informing my art, as if every author took the time to behave as my muse. Hardy most likely influenced me the most. Perhaps because his work was the first real literature I'd read, much like a first love. Or maybe I needed his garden to relieve my mind of suicidal thoughts. In any case, I did not take my life that Dorset weekend. Instead, I curled, returning into Hardy's world, this time on the page, re-reading *Jude the Obscure*, feeling Hardy speak to me, advising me: a writer, a woman, a warrior.

"She leaned in to smell the apricot-tinted rose whose petals had just unfolded into a ruffled cup. The scents of lemon, myrrh, and peach floated up, and Sorrel once again wondered why anyone would name a rose." ■

Robert Penn Warren

ALL THE KING'S MEN

RON HATZENBUEHLER

Re- and Re...-reading All the King's Men

I first encountered Robert Penn Warren's *All the King's Men* (*AKM*) in a college history class when I read Chapter 2 ("The Historical Dimension") of C. Vann Woodward's *The Burden of Southern History* (1960), in which Woodward recounts his search as a young college student for the roots of Southern distinctiveness. *I'll Take My Stand: The South and the Agrarian Tradition* (1930) offered one possibility, but Woodward found Southern particularity planted not in an agrarianism based on rigidly traditional mores but rather in the outpouring of Southern novels from William Faulkner and Katherine Anne Porter and, later, Eudora Welty, Tennessee Williams and—above all—Warren (Woodward dedicated *Burden* to Warren). Woodward credited these Southern writers for enriching "our consciousness of the past in the present [...and for giving] history meaning and value and significance as events never do merely because they happen" (39).

Inspired by Woodward's effusive recommendation, I snagged a paperback copy and began reading it. Along the way, I learned that Warren taught for a brief period during the Great Depression at my alma mater, Southwestern at Memphis—now Rhodes College. It was exciting to speculate that Warren may have been working on the novel while he was teaching at Southwestern, which made reading it while I was a student there (especially on my own time) seem like EXACTLY THE RIGHT THING TO DO. I was mesmerized during my first reading of *AKM* by Warren's use of language to evoke emotion:

> There was . . . the cold grip way down in the stomach as though somebody had laid hold of something in there, in the dark which is you, with a cold hand in a cold rubber glove. It was like the second when you come home late at night and see the yellow envelope of the telegram sticking out from under your door and you lean and pick it up, but don't open it yet, not for a second. . . . There's the cold in your stomach, but you open the envelope, you have to open the envelope, for the end of man is to know.

But I was mainly intrigued by Warren's telling of the interactions of the protagonist, Willie Stark (aka The Boss), and the menagerie of personalities with whom he comes into contact:

(I)t is possible that fellows like Willie Stark are born outside of luck, good or bad, and luck, which is what about makes you and me what we are, doesn't have anything to do with them, for they are what they are from the time they first kick in the womb until the end. And if that is the case, then their life history is a process of discovering what they really are, and not, as for you and me, sons of luck, a process of becoming what luck makes us.

Willie's journey of self-discovery takes him from being "Cousin Willie from the country"; to small town lawyer; to County Treasurer; to candidate for Governor in the Democratic primary ("which in our state is the same as running for Governor"); to Redneck hick; back to small town lawyer, except this time "he saw folding money for the first time in his life. He saw quite a lot of it"; to The Boss.

There's also the evolving story of Jack Burden—reporter turned confidant and enabler to The Boss—but Jack's story had too many twists and turns for me to grasp fully until my re-readings of the book. When I re-read *AKM* as a history graduate student, I focused on Jack's coming into possession of letters, account books, a photo, and a man's gold ring on a piece of string that belonged to his great-uncle—or so he initially believed—Cass Mastern. Cass's life story completely befuddled Jack: how Cass owned a profitable antebellum plantation in Mississippi but in 1858 freed his slaves; placed a caretaker on his plantation (rather than selling it to someone who would bring in new slaves to work the land); and moved to Jackson to study law. In 1861, he opposed Mississippi's secession and hoped for peace, but when the war began, he enlisted as a private in the Mississippi Rifles. Although he experienced the Battles of Shiloh, Chickamauga, and Chattanooga, he kept his vow never to kill anyone. Finally in 1864, "the bullet for which he waited" found him outside of Atlanta, and he died from his wounds' infections in a military hospital. Only at the end of *AKM* does Jack begin to understand Cass's suicide by proxy, and in doing so finds meaning in his own life.

Another complexity in Jack's story concerns his tendency when something bad happens to him to drop everything and Go West:

For West is where we all plan to go some day. It is where you go when the land gives out and the old-field pines encroach. It is where you go when you get the letter saying: Flee, all is discovered. It is where you go when you look down at the blade in your hand and see the blood on it. It is where you go when you are told that you are a bubble on the tide of empire. It is where you go when you hear that there's gold in them-tha(r) hills. It is where you go to grow up with the country. It is where you go to spend your old age. Or it is just where you go.

I had never planned to Go West until I was offered a job (for that matter, the only real job offer I have ever had) teaching at Idaho State University in 1972. When I next re-read *AKM*, I especially appreciated the contrast Warren develops between the South's obsession with the past and the West's preoccupation with the future, that "there is innocence and a new start in the West, after all."

My next re-reading of *AKM* occurred when I was teaching a sophomore-level course on historical methods ("The Science and Art of History"). To emphasize the point with my students that the study of history requires knowledge of when and how to use the narrative (to tell a story) or the analytical approach (to solve a problem), I frequently began the course with a historical novel. In various semesters, I assigned Gore Vidal's *Burr* (Aaron Burr's take on early American history compared to that of his nemesis, Thomas Jefferson); Michael Shaara's *The Killer Angels* (pitting the emotional Robert E. Lee against the calculating James Longstreet and Joshua Lawrence Chamberlain at the Battle of Gettysburg); and *AKM*, in which Jack philosophizes about *doing history*. His second historical assignment, to find some dirt on one of The Boss's political enemies, Judge Irwin, perfectly encapsulates the historian's craft—asking questions, finding and pursuing leads (even when they don't pan out), asking more questions, and enjoying the chase:

Robert Penn Warren

> I found it. But not all at once. You do not find it all at once if you are
> hunting for it. It is buried under the sad detritus of time…. And you
> do not want to find it all at once, not if you are a student of history.
> If you found it all at once, there would be no opportunity to use
> your technique. But I had an opportunity to use my technique.

The artistic side of *AKM* is evident not only in Warren's devotion to
detail, character development, and—above all—his poetic interludes:

> There is always the clue, the canceled check, the smear of lipstick,
> the footprint in the canna bed, the condom on the park bench, the
> twitch in the old wound, the baby shoes dipped in bronze, the taint
> in the blood stream. And all times are one time, and all those dead in
> the past never lived before our definition gives them life, and out of
> the shadow their eyes implore us.

All of these elements make the reader—or at least this reader—
want to turn the page, especially at the end of *AKM's* ten, long chapters.
For example, at the end of Chapter 1 (in which, parenthetically, all of the
characters in the novel make an appearance), The Boss, his chauffeur,
and Jack take a late night trip to Jack's hometown (Burden's Landing) to
confront Jack's childhood mentor, Judge Irwin. On the way out of town,
when The Boss tasks Jack with digging up some dirt on the judge, Jack
questions whether he'll find any. The Boss responds, "'There is always
something.' Two miles more, and he said, 'And make it stick.'… Little
Jackie made it stick, all right." Turn the page….

Warren spent much of his life after *AKM* debunking the notion that
The Boss is a surrogate Huey Long and insisted that his books should
not be viewed as history. A few years back, when I was researching my
book on Thomas Jefferson, I encountered another of Warren's books,
Brother to Dragons: A Tale in Verse and Voices (1953). This line in the
book brought me up short: "Historical sense and poetic sense should
not, in the end, be contradictory, for if poetry is the little myth we make,
history is the big myth we live, and in our living, constantly remake." I'm
still working on understanding fully the meaning of that thought, but
it did inform my most recent re-reading of *AKM* three years ago while
I was convalescing from a knee replacement. In fact, it led me to the
conclusion that I've kept the book so close at hand for over fifty years
(YIKES!) in order to marvel at the poetic interludes in the book (Warren
was, after all, the nation's first poet laureate) juxtaposed with the stories
that are wrapped in history. I flatter myself that Warren might approve. ■

VINCE HANNITY

On Re-reading William Faulkner's
Absalom, Absalom!

*"O my son Absalom, my son, my son Absalom! would God
I had died for thee, O Absalom, my son, my son!" (2 Samuel 18:33)*

Like bibliophiles everywhere, I love reading beautifully wrought language—precisely chosen nouns, verbs and adjectives artfully crafted into sentences, paragraphs, chapters, and completed works.

Over the years I have read many books with these qualities, and have returned to many of them more than once. Yet to my mind, no author I have read has so magisterially achieved such artistry as William Faulkner in *Absalom, Absalom!*, published in 1936. Because of Faulkner's masterful control over his art in this novel, I return to it, like a moth to a flame, again and again.

In Faulkner's long-sentenced, repetitive narrative style, events and sequences are interspersed and heaped upon one another from speaker to speaker, event to event, in flashbacks and flash forwards. Words and phrases are repeated—clause after clause, adjective after adjective. One sentence in *Absalom* is famously 1288 words long, nearly three pages. (Faulkner, 148-150)

In *Absalom*, Faulkner applies his dense and evocative narrative style to the story of Thomas Sutpen, a fictional character of the Civil War-era South.

The Greeks would have recognized Sutpen as a hero much like their own. The ancient Greek heroes (Heracles, Achilles) were not necessarily good men, but they were extraordinary ones. They struggled against fate and overwhelming odds according to a heroic code of behavior. Their victories were majestic, their failures tragic. So it is with Thomas Sutpen.

At the macro level, Sutpen's story is, in condensed form, a commentary on slavery in the South. The novel explores how history and information about social mores are passed from one generation to another. It struggles with the meaning of history. It seeks to understand the error-ridden process of coming to know, reconstruct, and finally accept history. (Hobson, Cleanth Brooks, 17-47)

Four Flawed Narrators

Faulkner himself described *Absalom* as "the story of a man who wanted a son through pride, and got too many of them and they destroyed him." (Hobson, 283) He relates this story through four narrators. Each one recalls, opines, guesses or fantasizes about different elements of the Sutpen saga. No one knows the whole story. Everyone's telling contains gaps, misconceptions, and contradictions.

Faulkner once acknowledged that the four narrators of *Absalom* are akin to "...13 ways of looking at a blackbird with none of them right. When the reader has read all 13 different ways of looking at a blackbird and developed his own 14th image of that blackbird, that may be the Truth of the matter." (Hobson, 290)

Quentin Compson, the central narrator of *Absalom*, is a native of imagined Jefferson, Mississippi, where much of the novel's action plays out. He is the grandson of General Compson, who was Sutpen's only friend in Jefferson back in the Civil War era. Now, in the winter of 1909, Quentin is a student at Harvard. He tries to explain what the South is like to his Canadian roommate Shreve by telling the story of the Thomas Sutpen family.

Quentin, although unrelated to Sutpen, seems to believe that the tale has a direct bearing on his own identity and fate.

Shreve to Quentin: "Why do you hate the South?"

Quentin: "*I don't hate it...I don't hate it...I don't hate it he thought, panting in the cold air of the New England dark: I don't. I don't! I don't hate it! I don't hate it!*" (Faulkner, 303)

Miss Rosa Coldfield, the second narrator, is the much younger sister of Ellen Coldfield, Sutpen's wife in Jefferson. To Miss Rosa, Sutpen is a monster. She loathes him and has rigidly maintained her hatred for 43 years. Her story reflects this deeply felt rage.

Miss Rosa on Thomas Sutpen to Quentin: "Oh he was brave. I have never gainsaid that. But that our cause, our very life and future hopes and past pride, should have been thrown into the balance with men like that to buttress it—men with valor and strength but without pity or honor. Is it any wonder that Heaven saw fit to let us lose (the war)? (Faulkner, 13)

The third narrator is Mr. Compson, Quentin's father and son of General Compson. Mr. Compson presents Thomas Sutpen as a mysterious, driven, powerful man determined to see his dynasty achieved. Mr. Compson respects Sutpen's achievement—a man who came to Jefferson with nothing and attempted something great.

Shreve McCannon, the fourth narrator, is Quentin's roommate from Canada at Harvard. He has no personal connection to the Thomas Sutpen story or to the South in general. He serves as a touchstone to normal reality. He asks questions a typical modern reader might ask.

As the narrators intone (not merely speak) the layers of Faulknerian dialogue, you the reader gradually come to understand the character, perspective and limitations of each one. Thomas Sutpen's nature and grand design slowly reveal themselves. You become immersed in Sutpen's heroic power, rage and tragic failures. You absorb rather than simply grasp Faulkner's achievement.

Thomas Sutpen's Grand Design

Of course, you also, gradually and obliquely, discern *Absalom's* plot:

Thomas Sutpen, as a boy, lives with his white-trash family on a plantation in West Virginia. One day he knocks on the mansion's front door, carrying a message. A liveried black slave humiliates him by sending him around to the back door. After this reproach, Sutpen creates and sets in motion his "grand design"—to become, at any cost, a man of wealth and dynastic power. No offspring of his would ever be turned away from any door.

He makes his way to colonial Haiti and marries the daughter of a plantation owner. But in 1831 he abandons his wife and newborn son, named Charles Bon, when he learns that his wife has a strain of Negro blood. He leaves Haiti.

In 1833, Sutpen arrives in Jefferson with a gang of Haitian slaves. There, as dictated by his grand design, he begins to forge a dynasty that will carry on his name. He cheats a Chickasaw Indian out of a hundred square miles of land. He wrenches a plantation and a mansion out of the wilderness, calling it Sutpen's Hundred. He acquires a second wife, a respected local girl named Ellen Coldfield. They have two children— Henry and Judith.

But some twenty years on, the son that Sutpen abandoned in Haiti, Charles Bon, returns to haunt him. Henry now attends the University of Mississippi. Bon also attends the university and becomes Henry's best friend. Bon becomes a regular visitor to Sutpen's Hundred. He eventually becomes engaged to marry Judith.

Henry and Charles go off together to fight in the Civil War. They return from the war in 1865 on the eve of Charles and Judith's wedding. In a savage turn of events, Henry shoots and kills Charles Bon as they enter the gates to the mansion. He does so to prevent Bon from marrying their sister Judith-—either because Charles has Negro blood in his veins, or because Charles is his half-brother, or perhaps because of an even deeper fear.

Charles Bon to Henry Sutpen (as imagined by Shreve): "So it's the miscegenation, not the incest, which you can't bear." (Faulkner, 285) Henry flees into self-exile. Sutpen, who also fought in the war, returns to a plantation in ruins. He's reduced to running a backwoods general store to make ends meet.

But Sutpen's grand design is not dead. He plans to breed yet a third family with Miss Rosa Coldfield, the sister of his dead wife Ellen. But he deeply offends Miss Rosa by insisting that they consummate their marriage before the actual wedding. She rejects his shocking proposal. Sutpen's offense earns him Miss Rosa's deep hatred, which abides until her own death 43 years later.

In 1869, in a final attempt to gain a male heir and complete his design, Sutpen impregnates the teenage daughter of a poor white man,

Wash Jones, who lives on the plantation. But the girl gives birth to a daughter instead of the required son. Sutpen brutally insults her. Jones kills him with a scythe.

Near the end of the novel, Quentin accompanies Miss Rosa to Sutpen's Hundred. It's 1909. There he meets Sutpen's dying son Henry, who has returned to the mansion from self-exile some years before. Shortly after their visit, Sutpen's mansion burns to the ground.

The only descendant who survives to carry on the Sutpen blood is the intellectually disabled grandson of Charles Bon. Thus ends Thomas Sutpen's grand design.

I will read *Absalom Absalom!* again. It's mesmerizing prose. Reading Faulkner is like sinking slowly into quicksand or spiraling down a whirlpool. You read on and on, sucked down and down, immersing yourself in the consciousness of the narrator, until you reach the end of the sentence or paragraph or chapter. Your mind explodes from the pressure of concentrating. You gasp for breath you didn't realize you were holding. It's an experience to be savored. ■

Faulkner, William. *Absalom, Absalom!: The Corrected Text.* Random House: New York, 1986.

Hobson, Fred, Ed. William Faulkner's *Absalom, Absalom!: A Casebook.* Oxford University Press: New York, 2003.

William Faulkner

ROBERT M. PIRSIG

Author of ZEN AND THE ART OF
MOTORCYCLE MAINTENANCE

LILA

AN INQUIRY INTO MORALS

JONAH ANDRIST

The Static Social Course of the Intellect:
A Re-Reading of Robert Pirsig's Lila

I often encourage people to start reading books in their middles. I do not read for plot and I believe that every page of a good book should have its own kind of power. Such is the case with Robert Pirsig's novel *Lila*. Like Pirsig's surprise bestseller of 1971, *Zen and the Art of Motorcycle Maintenance* (*Zen* for short), *Lila* follows a similar structure: Man on a journey ponders the universe. With *Zen*, it's a motorcycle trip across the Midwest. In *Lila*, it's a sailing trip down the eastern shore. In both books this loose-knit structure offers a stage for much personal thought, often making both books seem like philosophical works rather than novels. *Lila* has even less plot-structure than Zen does. In part this is because *Lila* offers a more sophisticated presentation of the philosophy that Pirsig first suggested in *Zen*; and as such, more emphasis and clarity are given to the significance and substance of his thought.

So why read *Lila* as a novel? Pirsig tackles this problem from many angles. He begins his book explaining that he'd wanted to write a work of anthropology, but knew such a notion would be rejected by that scientific community. Pirsig goes on to explain why this rejection is part of the problem he's trying to solve. He is in turn grateful to academics for their interest in ideas, yet confounded by how they refuse to accept the 'values' inherent to their discipline. He calls most academic philosophers "philosophologists," arguing that they do philosophy the same way an art critic does art. The novel—the actions of characters—for Pirsig, gives more freedom.

The lead character of Pirsig's novel is our namesake Lila, a drinking, dancing, mentally ill woman who joins Pirsig's character, named Phaedrus, on his boat. As we've learned from Zen, Phaedrus too, has had a mental break. He is well positioned to understand Lila. In fact, the whole novel is essentially a re-appraisal of what he found so memorable about her, even while (or, *because*) most of society was turning away from her. He tries to answer the question of how Lila embodies "Quality"— Pirsig's own formulation, a value metaphysics that attempts to understand a biological-cultural-intellectual divide. He finds Lila compelling because she is at a point in her life where she sees that line where the cultural subject-object dichotomy starts to fray. Later in the novel he reflects on insanity.

> The scientific laws of the universe are invented by sanity. There's no way by which sanity, using the instruments of its own creation, can measure that which is outside of itself and its creations. Insanity isn't an "object" of observation. It's an alteration of observation itself. There is no such thing as a "disease" of patterns of intellect. There's only heresy. And that's what insanity really is. (*Lila*, 327)

If those sentences don't turn your crank, Pirsig isn't for you. Reading him I'm often reminded of the maxim "it's not *what* you think, but *how* you think." There's something in that *how* which I can understand so clearly. When I read his work I know exactly who Robert Pirsig is—and this hybridization of style, philosophy and character is exactly what I find compelling in a novel.

Authorial intent takes a back seat to 'reader response theory' these days. Yet, personally, I find intention a useful metric to measure a work's poignancy. Pirsig's intentional quality has a striking clarity for our current moment. He begins the book arguing with an acquaintance about his idea of what Quality means. He realizes that there are still some sticking points he needs to flush out. Quality is a concept he explores in *Zen*, 20 years earlier, but it's a project of a lifetime. It's a grand theory about human activity, or, "An Inquiry into Morals" as the subtitle of *Lila* explicitly states.

Like the concept of *Zen* itself, one doesn't need to know precisely what "Quality" means. It's often easier to describe what it isn't. It's not a *socially* enforced, arbitrary, set of rules. Quality is not an imposition of morality. Pirsig lays out for us the Dynamic Quality the intellect has to upend social codes. He details how 20th century intellectualism and degeneracy (the hippie movement) took Victorian morality to task, and he establishes the moral necessity of such thought. He acknowledges that Dynamic Quality is disruptive and that this close relationship with degeneracy is part and parcel of precisely what makes it *dynamic*. Of course a society cannot tolerate all forms of degeneracy, but if society doesn't embrace any then there is an immoral oppression.

Pirsig goes on to establish a kind of moral hierarchy, distin-
guishing between biological morality, social morality, and intellectual
morality. He points out how:

> Intellect has its own patterns and goals that are as independent
> of society as society is of biology. A value metaphysics makes it
> possible to see that there's a conflict between intellect and society
> that's just as fierce as the conflict between society and biology or
> the conflict between biology and death. Biology beat death (the
> static state of non-life) billions of years ago. Society beat biology
> thousands of years ago. But intellect and society are still fighting
> it out. (*Lila*, 265)

In his value metaphysics each level needs a Dynamic moment
that exudes a Quality which 'transcends' previous moral codes. But each
moment of Dynamic Quality also needs a static period in order to retain
the gains from this dynamism. This worries Pirsig at the end of the 20th
century. He sees all around him a fantastic intellectual growth, yet he
has small lamentations for the end of Victorian morality. He knows to
return to such a moral code would be against his value metaphysics,
but degeneracy without some kind of social mechanism to restrain it
is dangerous.

> Intellect is not an extension of society any more than society is
> an extension of biology. Intellect is going its own way, and in doing
> so is at war with society, seeking to subjugate society, to put society
> under lock and key. An evolutionary morality says it is moral for
> intellect to do so, but it also contains a warning: Just as a society
> that weakens its people's physical health endangers its own stability,
> so does an intellectual pattern that weakens and destroys the health
> of its social base also endanger its own stability. Better to say "has
> endangered." It's already happened. This (the 20th Century) has
> been a century of fantastic intellectual growth and fantastic social
> destruction. (*Lila*, 164)

This point about intellectual growth in the 20th century is fascinating. In his essay "Don't Become a Scientist," Jonathan Katz lays out
a simple counter-narrative to the culturally conceived notion of our
intellectual development, noting how today—as compared to the
1970's—many of the practical details about becoming a practicing
scientist have worsened. Katz describes that a physicist in our current

climate and culture probably won't get to pursue *ideas* (to truly engage in the Dynamic Quality of ideas, answering questions for their own sake); instead, you'll be somebody's lackey. Whatever fit the good qualifications for that job in the past—independence of thought, respect for position, wage potential—is no longer in physics departments.

I have a different way of thinking about it compared to Dr. Katz. I think it's remarkable that these kinds of jobs ever existed in that capacity. For most of history, intellectual dynamism has operated entirely on the periphery. In fact, I've found that to be one of the bizarre things about Pirsig. *Zen and The Art of Motorcycle Maintenance* sold millions of copies when it appeared in 1971. When I first picked it up as a 20-year-old, I expected a breezy, popular novel. Instead, I encountered many sections which were as tough to deduce as a Wittgenstein-ian philosophical treatise. I still find it interesting that Pirsig ever got as popular as he was. I presume it had something to do with intellect's reign—destructive reign as Pirsig puts it—in the 20th century. I've often speculated that the 20th century was a remarkable time to be a writer or physicist (in Pirsig's words, to attempt to engage with "Dynamic Quality"). If true intellectual dynamism is at least loosely correlated with the degeneracy of a social idea, then "by definition" those ideas can not be significantly popular. Pirsig's success coincided with a certain societal denigration that can only happen at certain periods of history—presumably, after society has had a static period to retain its intellectual gains.

I have a writer friend who loves to say, "Hemingway wouldn't make it today." And I don't think he's wrong, though I often tell him that I find this statement functionally meaningless. What is or isn't *making it*? Did the 20th century's intellectual growth give us an inflated sense of its importance?

Pirsig notes that "[The 20th century was] a century of fantastic intellectual growth and fantastic social destruction." I think what Pirsig wasn't considering at the time of writing *Lila* was that very soon that growth would need its static latch, the mechanism for retaining its gains. And the way it seems to have done this was by re-integrating society—*society co-opting intellect for its own means.* In *Lila*, Pirsig writes about the cultural movement away from Victorian culture through intellectual dynamism. What was left for modern society but to take such information to heart: to turn itself into a society based on intellect, not how Pirsig might perceive intellect, but intellect as a social idea.

Many of us have been told our whole lives that any and all education is worthwhile. And while to undercut such an idea seems fallacious, to notice that perhaps these were not suggestions about the pursuit of knowledge *for its own reasons*, but, a code of new social values, has helped me to think about it better. If it's the social mechanisms that help us overcome biology, this new century is going to need society to answer our big questions.

I've heard (and basically agree with) the notion that the 21st century will be mainly about biology. Moving to other planets is, in many ways, a biological question as much as a technological one. It will take a lot of minds doing a lot of research. And while it can and should be argued, as Pirsig does, that the Dynamism required for breakthroughs usually come from strange, degenerate and independent places; a social code based on the fundamentals of our intellectual pursuits from the 20th century was the more meaningful way to make progress. Can't build a spaceship by yourself. The more intellects in the world, the more chances there are for discoveries. That's the benefit of society adopting the intellect; that its precepts have spread to corners it couldn't reach before. Yet, still, we cannot confuse the social and the intellectual.

What we have learned from the Theory of Evolution is that life is a series of useful mistakes, that the social code cannot abide by this wisdom is its *obvious* function, as protectorate to the whole. Yet crossing this social divide—letting the intellect engage with biology *for its own reasons*, has proved tricky (social complications in gene editing, cloning, risky medical procedures such as full head transplants. Ideas the intellect might pursue *for its own reasons*). As society has adopted the intellect (being the natural front line of defense against biology) it can often pretend towards dynamism. Most people want to be smart about their lives, but following a social code or idea is not engaging with the intellect. The tool we actually need to answer hard questions—space without public approval and where things are messy and often fail.

Society is not any longer trying to "restrain the truth" in the classic fashion of social codes. If anything, it's sort of weirdly made the truth *too true*. We must never forget that the truth is a consequence of life and not life itself. Because the danger, it seems now, is that the social fear of biology runs the risk of over-whelming or eliminating the potential for Dynamic Quality.

We can wonder if Pirsig would have sold 20 million copies of *Zen and the Art of Motorcycle Maintenance* today. Would his dynamic ideas have the kind of impact they seemed to have in the 1970's? It's impossible to know, but I would guess that they wouldn't. Though the book still has many fans and *Lila* does deserve more. It's difficult to leaf through novels today and find anything quite like it. Hell, it's even hard to find a place *to go* to leaf through new books.

Robert M. Pirsig

But that's ok. The 20th century left behind plenty of material. If the 21st century pursuer of intellectual dynamism doesn't make it into all the shops, doesn't sell thousands and thousands of copies, well, that'll only be a reversion to the norm. *Lila* didn't sell as well as *Zen* did, though I'd argue it's the superior work. Perhaps part of the problem is the title. *Zen and the Art of Motorcycle Maintenance* sounds like a self-help book. Its appreciation of the homespun craftsman in the face of rapid technological change felt timely. Though, for predictive insight, I think *Lila* will stand the test of time better. It's not quite as relatable to everyman (in no small part because Pirsig has already found success and fame with *Zen*) but as a work of cultural anthropology it finds a wholeness which, at least for me, has helped immensely to contextualize feelings related to society and intelligence. ∎

CHERYL HINDRICHS

Sounding Two Notes: Re-reading
Virginia Woolf and Elizabeth Bishop

Near the end of the first part of Virginia Woolf's novel *To the Lighthouse* (1927), "The Window," the Ramsay family and their invited guests have withdrawn for the evening after a feast of *boeuf en daube*—the children to bed, the guests to their rooms, and finally Mr. and Mrs. Ramsay to sit across from each other reading. Conscious of her husband's attention, Mrs. Ramsay wishes that he would not disturb her in this pleasant moment of reading but allow her to go on perusing lines of poetry at random and dreaming over them, that he would for once, for now, not demand her sympathy and attention. Woolf then changes the focus to Mr. Ramsay who is in a conciliatory mood, silently indulging his wife to go on but imagining she hardly understands what she reads. Mrs. Ramsay, granted this reprieve, reads a line of Shakespeare's sonnets to herself: "Yet seem'd it winter still, and, you away, /As with your shadow I with these did play" (123). Woolf writes,

> she read, and so reading she was ascending, she felt, on to the top, on to the summit. How satisfying! How restful! All the odds and ends of the day stuck to this magnet; her mind felt swept, felt clean. And then there it was, suddenly entire; she held it in her hands, beautiful and reasonable, clear and complete, the essence sucked out of life and held rounded here—the sonnet. (123)

This passage is an extraordinarily adroit observation of the strange pleasure felt when engaging with art—literature in particular. Further, as a scene about the powerful effect of reading, it signals Woolf's fascination with the ways in which our narrative horizons shape our lives. For Woolf, the narratives we are able to imagine are those we may be able to live.

This belief is why I have spent a life in school—teaching and reading literature with others. A book, an essay, a poem; these you turn to, live lives through, use to connect, use as foils and as sharpening steel. They hone our ability to imagine other horizons and other relationships.

When asked by new students why they should study literature or asked by new acquaintances what I do, I tell them that reading literature is a powerful skill to acquire and cultivate. If the listener seems dubious, I discuss how experiencing new narratives expands our intellectual and emotional horizons, thus making change possible in the world. I also often have recourse to the historical sense literature instills, a reliably attractive answer. However, my listener frequently accepts this proof of literature's value with an unspoken qualification—that studying "real history" might be a more valuable mental exercise in acquiring knowledge of a culture and time than studying fiction. Consequently, most often my testimony to the value of reading literature is that reading is creative work, and engaging with literature is the means for us to both see ourselves and connect with others.

For me, reading and re-reading have offered the richest prospects for such engagement, particularly Woolf's novels and Elizabeth Bishop's poetry. As a critic and a novelist, Woolf sought to rout the conventions of the novel—specifically those of the Victorian novel that preceded her—that had constrained both inner and lived narratives. In *To the Lighthouse*, Woolf breaks from generic expectations, takes up the inner voices of her characters, and creates self-reflexive scenes of reading in which readers become conscious of their own involvement in the work. Like Mrs. Ramsay, we are lifted out of our lives and enter into the art work or character while simultaneously engaging as an observing other. Woolf innovates the novel's form to get closer to what she saw as "life," to capture "the thing itself" which requires that we, as readers, create and experience it ("A Sketch of the Past" 72). In "Modern Fiction," Woolf asks how the writer can recreate in the reader "the thing itself" that is life if the writer is bound by the "thrall" of the novel's conventions to "provide a plot, to provide comedy,

Virginia Woolf

tragedy, love interest, and an air of probability embalming the whole" (160). She asks, "Is life like this? Must novels be like this?" (160). It is a thrilling revolt, and the novels that followed provide us with a stunning array of departures from convention with innovations that startle readers into taking up and creating the life through the exchange of reading.

Although I have long enjoyed dwelling on the revolutionary aspect of Woolf's innovations, here my point is to note that her profound quarrel with form—the quarrel that is the common denominator of modernism—is hardly a discarding or devaluation of form in and of itself. Rather, Woolf argued, the novel is a form that can and must do more to capture life. Each of Woolf's novels is a new experiment in the novel form, just as Elizabeth Bishop's poems are an evocation and subversion of poetic form. I would like to briefly consider a form that recurs within several of Woolf's multifarious works and explore how Bishop similarly uses form and repetition to create a powerful inner experience in the reader. In contrast to Mrs. Ramsay's sonnet reading, which is "satisfying" and "restful," elsewhere Woolf uses a simple formal device to convey the opposite effect—an echo. Specific-ally, the name of a character repeated.

In part three of *To the Lighthouse*, after ten years and a world war have passed parenthetically, Lily Briscoe has returned to the vacation house on the sudden invitation of Mr. Ramsay, who has invited that day's other visitors as well and is now attempting to recreate the trip to the lighthouse with his grown children James and Cam. The attempt at repetition, however, founders given the absence of Mrs. Ramsay, whose death readers have learned of in a subordinate clause in part two's description of time passing. Lily takes up the unfinished canvas she began ten years before, a post-impressionist scene of the home and garden. The presence of Mrs. Ramsay holding and reading to young James in the window had previously anchored the scene, signified by Lily on her canvas as a purplish triangle. Now the work as a whole remains unfinished, the vision incomplete. The power of Mrs. Ramsay's presence (influencing and directing all the lives of the characters) and now its absence unsettles the otherwise unattached, independent Lily. Preparing to paint she looks at the window where Mrs. Ramsay had sat, and her heart leaps: "'Mrs. Ramsay! Mrs. Ramsay!' she cried, feeling the old horror come back—to want and want and not to have" (205). When Mr. Ramsay confronts her briefly on his way to depart, demanding a sympathy she cannot give, Lily again, now silently, calls Mrs. Ramsay's name twice. This doubling, the call without an answer, engenders in the reader an unresolved tension—the empty space of the steps, mirrored on Lily's canvas, is an uncanny evocation of absent presence.

The opening pages of Woolf's *Jacob's Room* (1922) are likewise structured around an absent presence. Readers follow the life of Jacob Flanders from childhood to his death in the Great War through the point of view of women who have known him. At the end of the novel, Jacob's friend Bonamy stands in his bedroom and is overcome by his absence: "'Jacob! Jacob!'" cried Bonamy (176). Jacob's mother holds out "a pair of Jacob's old shoes," a material evocation of absence, asking, "'What am I to do with these, Mr. Bonamy?'" (176). Both Lily's silent cry and Bonamy's evoke a shift from major to minor—from protest to sorrow. The familiar made strange—doubled—is a hallmark of the uncanny, and a powerful conduit to the expression of grief in these two scenes.

The echo of that cry is haunting, and the repetition of the technique in Woolf's work suggests to me that she has hit upon some fundamental reality of human life: a particular, rhythmic vocalism that is both a call to the absent to become present and a signification of absence. It is at once fundamentally human and poetically resonant. The powerful affect this technique evokes has likewise drawn me to Elizabeth Bishop's poem "One Art," which achieves a similar emotional haunting. Here I'd like to consider how grief is both performed and recreated in a work of poetry that is, like Woolf's writing, an invitation to engage the reader in the power of form to capture life while simultaneously asking the reader to interrogate art's work.

Elizabeth Bishop's poem "One Art" (1976) is a perfect villanelle of six stanzas—five tercets with end rhymes a/b/a (excepting the fourth stanza which is c/a/b) and a final quatrain of four lines with end rhymes d/a/b/c. All of that is to say, the poem is pointedly following a form of the sonnet, a villanelle, and draws attention to the poet's recourse to it. Without saying "I," the poem immediately creates a powerful sense of who our speaker is. The opening two stanzas establish an insouciant voice:

One Art

The art of losing isn't hard to master;
so many things seem filled with the intent
to be lost that their loss is no disaster.

Lose something every day. Accept the fluster
of lost door keys, the hour badly spent.
The art of losing isn't hard to master.

Elizabeth Bishop

Here, we are on familiar ground, perhaps a bit charmed by the speaker's deprecation of loss as commonplace and unexceptional, and happily we read on for further absolution and perhaps commiseration. Having thus playfully established the "ease" of loss, the speaker continues in instructing the reader in the art:

> Then practice losing farther; losing faster:
> places, and names, and where it was you meant
> to travel. None of these will bring disaster.

There is a shift in tone here, as subtle as light on a blade or a wave. The hinge of "meant" dictates the downbeat of the next two words, "to travel," and as readers we must then pause and draw breath to complete the line. The imperative tone instructing us in how to practice this art reveals itself as subtly dark, but the abstraction of the examples of what is lost (places, names, intended journeys) and the nonchalance of the repetition in the last line ("None of these will bring disaster") carries us nimbly on to the next stanza. Here, however, the speaker gives quite specific examples of loss as evidence that belies the previous refrain:

> I lost my mother's watch. And look! My last, or
> next to last, of three loved houses went.
> The art of losing isn't hard to master.

For the reader, the unknowable meaning of the watch that was lost and the profoundly "loved" homes is a point of possible identification with a more personal voice. Further, it introduces a particular strain in that voice, which the repetition of the refrain attempts to check by asserting once again "The art of losing isn't hard to master." The stanza that follows opens outward toward the import of displacement, shifting the tone from an insouciant bravado to a more remote insistence.

> I lost two cities, lovely ones. And, vaster,
> some realms I owned, two rivers, a continent.
> I miss them, but it wasn't a disaster.

Of course, our speaker in no practical sense could possess any of these objects (cities, realms, rivers). Nonetheless, the lines speak to how our sense of self is rooted to time and place. What is remarkable, then, is that we are able to experience their displacement as not "disaster" but as integral to life's inevitable but survivable losses. It seems the "art of losing" is indeed simply part of any life's journey, and thus any loss can and should be surmounted by practicing the "One Art" masterfully. Yet, in the space between this penultimate stanza that has testified to the speaker's mastery and the next, the final stanza, a more deliberate pacing emerges and the bravado of the preceding lines wavers.

> —Even losing you (the joking voice, a gesture
> I love) I shan't have lied. It's evident
> the art of losing's not too hard to master
> though it may look like (*Write* it!) like disaster.

The weight of "you" shifts the open address to a personal one. However, whether the addressee of the poem will hear these words is unlikely. The poem's manner instead suggests a reading in which the speaker is addressing an absence, a "you" present only in memory. This moment of pain, revealed in the parenthetical details of "(the joking voice, a gesture / I love)," is nonetheless resolutely capped, not only by paren- thesis but also the insistence "I shan't have lied." The speaker reverts to the poem's original imperative tenor of instruction in a known art. As if having demonstrated a mathematical proof, the voice adds the flourish "It's evident" to the repetition of the opening line, "The art of losing's not too hard to master." Nonetheless, as if in the attempt to quickly complete the next before doubts or questions can arise,no period ends the line. In the final line, the speaker's stoicism cracks, as another parenthetical confirms. The tenor of its inclusion is protest, a determination to refuse the overwhelming tragedy of loss. Yet the second, final parenthetical in the stanza "(*Write* it!)" also sounds the speaker's sorrow. Together, the two parentheticals of protest and sorrow reveal the speaker's contrary emotions—on the one hand, to deny the grief of loss, and, on the other hand, to witness it.

Bishop's "One Art" and Woolf's *To the Lighthouse* capture a profound aspect of our living—how the experience of loss is a movement from protest to grief. The latter does not negate the former. Although the two notes (protest, grief) sound one after the other, the fact of their shared signifier recreates in the reader the haunting effects of absence and desire. The speaker of Bishop's poem and Lily in Woolf's novel express the haunting pain of that combination. They are able to do so through the formal use of repetition. Bishop's repeated insistence that the art of loss isn't hard to master parallels the two moments in *To the Lighthousee* when Lily calls Mrs. Ramsay's name consecutively. The sequential repetition in each instance evokes Freud's notion of the uncanny, a term originally known as the *unheimlich* or unhomely. These works are not only emblematic of our experience of absence and desire through the emotions of protest and grief, but also of our need to control and contain these emotions in the face of their inevitability given our relationship to time and place. The major to minor notes sounding sequentially captures the awful fact of present absences, the uncanny aspect of our lives. Form offers our only recourse; the work of art (that is, work in the sense of creative action, and work in the sense of a completed object) offers a means to articulate protest while simultaneously embodying and containing the formlessness of grief.

Woolf once theorized in her essay "Moments of Being" that if she had a "philosophy," it was that there is a "pattern" behind the "cotton wool" incidentals of daily life, claiming, "the whole world is a work of art; [...] we are parts of the work of art." Artists and their art are "the truth about this vast mass that we call the world [...]; we are the words; we are the music; we are the thing itself." Woolf's work, writing, is for her a means to master the formlessness of living. When dealt a blow, she no longer feels it as "simply a blow from an enemy hidden behind the cotton wool of daily life; it is or will become a revelation of some order" and by "putting it into words" she makes it "real" and its "wholeness" then revokes its "power to hurt me." This sense of triumphant wholeness life returns us to Mrs. Ramsay's scene of reading, in which she finds in "the sonnet" a sense "beautiful and reasonable, clear and complete, the essence sucked out of life and held rounded here" (123). Just as Mrs. Ramsay likens her reading to climbing a summit, achieving a revelatory view, Woolf herself attests to a "great delight to put the severed parts together." Woolf's reflection on her work as a writer here speaks to the consolations of form, even if form itself points obliquely to its inadequacy. It is for literary form's consolations and its self-confessed, necessary limitations that Woolf's and Bishop's works appeal to me. My ambition to understand how such works "work" for and upon us is perhaps a desire to understand something in the "pattern" of human life, a desire for revelation in the formlessness of day to day existence. Writing this essay, then, might suggest my own recourse to form in re-reading and reconsidering how these works continue to serve as haunting presences. Form enables us to "go on." It offers a means to both realize and contain an apprehension of our existential nature— the wonder that we live, the wonder that we die, the absurdity and the marvelousness of both experienced in love and loss. ■

Prospero's Cell

Lawrence Durrell

GROVE KOGER

Lawrence Durrell's Paradise Lost:
Re-reading Prospero's Cell

A s he completed his book about the island of Corfu, Lawrence Durrell remembered his years on the Greek island "with a regret so luxurious and so deep that it did not stir the emotions at all." Could his words, he wondered, "ever recreate more than a fraction" of what he had seen and experienced there? It was a rhetorical question, of course, but one worth asking, then (mid-1944) as well as now, three quarters of a century later.

Just what fraction *did* Durrell recreate? And how much did he choose not to?

Thanks to the recent PBS series *The Durrells in Corfu*, the public now knows quite a bit about Lawrence and his extended family, and especially about the island that he and his younger brother Gerald celebrated years ago. But the series is a fictionalized version of events, and the books it's based on—Gerald's trilogy of *My Family and Other Animals* (1956); *Birds, Beasts, and Relatives* (1969); and *Fauna and Family* (1978)—are another fictionalized version, while Lawrence's own 1945 account, *Prospero's Cell*, is another one still.

The basic facts are these. The Durrell Family was Anglo-Indian, and like many English families living on the subcontinent who could afford to, they sent their sons "back home" to England to attend school. That was Lawrence's unpleasant fate at age eleven in 1923, but the remaining members of his family—mother Louisa, brothers Gerald and Leslie and sister Margo—followed him to England when the *paterfamilias* died in 1928.

While budding naturalist Gerald found excitement in every suburban garden, the adjustment was more difficult for Lawrence and his mother. They both longed for the vivid life they had known in India and Burma, and Louisa eventually spiraled into a gin-fueled depression. Lawrence himself loathed the dour weather and the stultifying strictures of what he would later vilify as the "English Death," so when a friend wrote him in 1934 about the delights of life on Corfu, the enterprising young man set to work persuading his family and his bride-to-be, artist Nancy Myers, to make a bold move.

Now married, Lawrence and Nancy arrived in Corfu from Italy in mid-March 1935, and were followed a few days later by the rest of the family. Subsequently the six shared a series of dwellings at various locations, but despite what you might gather from Gerald's books or the television series, Lawrence and Nancy actually spent most of the next few years on their own. Their most notable residence was a fisherman's house—the White House—in the little seaside settlement of Kalami in rugged northern Corfu opposite the Albanian coast. Lawrence and Nancy took two rooms there and subsequently paid the owner to add a second story, and it was to be their base of operations until late 1939, when war drove them away.

*****

One of the first things you notice about *Prospero's Cell* is how demanding it can be of the reader's patience. Two such demands appear in the extended title itself: *Prospero's Cell: A Guide to the Landscape and Manners of the Island of Corcyra*. If you're not up on your Shakespeare, you may not know that Prospero is the sorcerer in that strange, late romance, *The Tempest*. Prospero lives on an island that he regards as

Lawrence and Nancy Durrell, 1930s

a prison cell, but its location is unspecified, and scholars have wondered whether the playwright had a real one in mind and what sources he may have drawn upon. In any case, one of Durrell's characters proposes, well into the book, the intriguing theory that Shakespeare was thinking of Corfu, and that "perhaps he even visited it." Durrell actually drops a hint about these matters in the epigraph—"No tongue; all eyes; be silent."—to the book's opening chapter, and proceeds to identify *The Tempest* as its source.

Then there's Corcyra, an even more obscure reference. You're not likely to find it on any map you have easy access to, but an online search, the route most of us would take these days, reveals that it's an archaic name for the island known as Kerkyra to modern Greeks and as Corfu to the rest of us. (In fact, several recent editions of the book have quietly altered the geographical reference in the subtitle.)

The first chapter of *Prospero's Cell* opens with a brief overture that includes one of Durrell's best-known sentences: "Other countries may offer you discoveries in manners or lore or landscape; Greece offers you something harder—the discovery of yourself." The remainder of the chapter is taken up with journal entries, the first dated April 10, 1937, and right away it's clear that we're not reading an ordinary travel narrative. "It is a solipsism to imagine that there is any strict dividing line between the waking world and the world of dreams," he writes. "N. and I, for example, are confused by the sense of several contemporaneous lives being lived inside us; the sensation of being mere points of reference for space and time." But the chapter also includes concrete details about the couple's new life, including a vivid account of swimming in a tiny cove beneath a red brick shrine to Saint Arsenius.

Among the many fascinating friends that Durrell made on Corfu is the polymath doctor Theodore Stephanides, who also plays a key role in Gerald's books. Then there are Constant Zarian (who claims "with firmness and modesty" to be "Armenia's greatest poet") and "celebrated recluse" Count D. The Durrells join them frequently for food and drink and especially talk, and the trio's learned commentary leavens the book. Another good friend (and important character in Gerald's books) is the larger-than-life taxi driver Spiro Halikiopoulos, known widely by the surname "Americanos."

While most of the chapters of *Prospero's Cell* are made up of dated entries, they proceed by subject as well as chronology. "History and Conjecture," for instance, gathers scraps of the island's "chequer-board" history—its role in the Crusades, the prosperity it enjoyed under the Venetians (who paid the Corfiotes to plant the island's myriad olive trees), its occupation by the British in the nineteenth century—and bits of unlikely but tantalizing lore. Could it have been on one of the island's shores, for instance, that Odysseus encountered Nausicaa? It's in this chapter too that the erudite Count D. raises the argument about Shakespeare. He finds, he says, a resemblance between the landscape of Corfu and of Prospero's island. And after all, the mother of the half-monster Caliban in *The Tempest* was named Sycorax— "almost too obvious an anagram" for Corcyra, he explains in triumph. And so on …

Several of the other chapters are more focused. "Karaghiosis: The Laic Hero" describes the beloved protagonist of innumerable Greek shadow plays and embodiment of the national character—"full of boasts, impatient of slowness, quick of sympathy." "Landscape with Olive Trees" celebrates Corfu's famous olive groves, and is punctuated with more observations by Durrell's friends. It also includes what may be the most widely quoted passage that Durrell ever wrote:

> The whole Mediterranean—the sculptures, the palms, the gold beads, the bearded heroes, the wine, the ideas, the ships, the moonlight, the winged gorgons, the bronze men, the philosophers—all of it seems to rise in the sour, pungent taste of these black olives between the teeth. A taste older than meat, older than wine. A taste as old as cold water.

Set for the most part in September 1938, the book's penultimate chapter, "The Vintage Time," describes the hallowed rituals of picking and crushing grapes, and strikes an appropriately autumnal note in richly toned prose. The last entry is dated January 1, 1941, and consists of a postcard greeting from the Count, who importunes Durrell with the plea, "Don't forget us." Then, in a short, undated "Epilogue in Alexandria," Durrell poses the question I cited in my first paragraph.

*****

Durrell scarcely refers to other members of his family. Nor does he mention that his first novel was published in 1935, or that he wrote his second while living in Corfu. Likewise, he makes only passing reference to American writer Henry Miller, whose explosive book *Tropic of Cancer* had recently been published in Paris by Jack Kahane's Obelisk Press. Durrell read the book in 1935 after borrowing it from a friend, and wrote Miller an enthusiastic fan letter soon afterward. *Tropic* would prove to be a defining influence, and Durrell's third, breakthrough novel, *The Black Book*, which he also wrote in Corfu and which was published by Obelisk in 1938, bears its stamp. But Durrell omits mention of these facts too.

Durrell's biographers have pointed out that despite his account of a circumscribed, almost halcyon existence on the island, he and Nancy were often on the move. Besides visits to Athens, there were trips to Paris (the first, in 1937, to meet Miller) and London, and interludes of camping on the island of Ithaca and skiing in the Austrian Alps. In fact, the two seem to have been extraordinarily busy. Adding to the already hectic mix, Miller himself visited the couple. More ominously, Durrell was growing emotionally abusive. He and Nancy quarreled frequently and would eventually divorce, hence the cipher that she becomes in her husband's book, both elusively present and hauntingly absent.

With the approach of war, most members of the Durrell family fled Corfu for England in June 1939. Lawrence and Nancy found their lives increasingly disrupted, and were themselves finally forced to leave. Durrell began writing *Prospero's Cell* in late August 1940 in Kalamata in southern Greece, where he had been posted by the British Council to teach English and direct an institute for English studies. But the Council closed the school in February 1941, and on April 6, German troops invaded Greece. Later that month, Lawrence and Nancy boarded an overloaded *caïque* bound for Crete, and, on the last day of April, an Australian ship heading further south. The next day, May 1, they set foot in Alexandria, Egypt—the city that would be the setting for the series that made Durrell a contender for the Nobel Prize, *The Alexandria Quartet*.

*****

Lawrence Durrell at 70, at Le Dome Café, Paris

Inspired by reading *Prospero's Cell*, my first wife and I traveled to Corfu in 1972. We had flown to Luxembourg aboard Icelandic Air, sharing a lumbering plane with other young travelers, all of us embarking on voyages of self-discovery. What we didn't learn until much later was that the low-cost line was popularly known as the "Hippie Express," and that another of its passengers during that heady period was Bill Clinton.

After making our haphazard way through Central Europe to Greece, we leased a villa in Nissaki, a few miles down the coast from Kalami. (Something else we didn't realize at the time was that our agent was the son of the Durrells' good friend Spiro!) The slope overlooking the rocky shore was covered with succulents, and among them we found dozens of tiny, newly hatched praying mantises—a sight that would have delighted young Gerald. And every evening, as night drew in, we sat on the villa's terrace watching the carbide lamps of boats fishing the narrow waters lying beneath what Durrell called the "dark bulk of the Albanian shadow."

It's nearly six hundred miles from Alexandria—where Durrell wrote *Prospero's Cell*—to Corfu. And it's a little over six *thousand* miles from Boise, where I'm writing these words during the Pandemic of 2020. But the Corfu that Durrell came to love in the 1930s and that I experienced for a few weeks in 1972 is a lot farther away than that. As Tom points out in Tennessee Williams' *Glass Menagerie,* "time is the greatest distance between two places."

However, I was able to revisit Corfu in July 2000, when my second wife and I attended On Miracle Ground, the biennial conference of the International Lawrence Durrell Society. On the most memorable day of the event, we all climbed aboard a caïque to sail northward across the bay from Corfu Town. We anchored for a time below the little shrine of Saint Arsenius for a swim, and from there proceeded to Kalami, where we enjoyed an *al fresco* lunch. But rather than actually touring the White House afterward, Maggie and I went swimming again with a few other errant souls off Kalami's rocky beach. I'd like to think it's what Lawrence Durrell himself would have done. ∎

UPSTREAM

FLY FISHING IN THE AMERICAN WEST

CHARLES LINDSAY   THOMAS McGUANE

APERTURE

ROBERT DeMOTT

McGuane's Other Fishing Book

I n our era, few people have written as brilliantly about the art and sport of fishing as Thomas McGuane. Whether in generation-defining fiction such as *The Sporting Club* (1968) and *Ninety-two in the Shade* (1973), or in non-fiction essays, including *Live Water* (1996), his Forewords to Nick Lyons' *Full Creel* (2000), Mike Lawson's *Spring Creeks* (2003), and Luke Jennings' *Blood Knots* (2012), and especially in 1999's *The Longest Silence: A Life in Fishing* (released in an expanded paperback edition in 2019 with seven previously uncollected chapters), McGuane excels and dazzles. His life-long writing and sporting crony, the late Jim Harrison, claimed ". . . no one writes better about fishing than Tom McGuane." I'm not one to disagree.

None of McGuane's writing, as far as I can tell, is in the how-to mode, so you can read his work end to end and not necessarily increase your store of technical angling ability. But if you believe in honoring certain existential pieties, reading him *will* make you a better angler because with eyes open and mind receptive, you will absorb much of value—though often intangible—about our sport's most enigmatic and enduring properties: "Angling," McGuane says in his Foreword to *Blood Knots*, "is a training in mystery."

And yet even those who know McGuane's extensive body of fishing prose might be surprised to realize that one work of his continues to fly under the radar. In 2000, in tandem with photographer Charles Lindsay, he brought out *Upstream: Fly Fishing in the American West* (New York: Aperture). It is a 96-page, large format, quarto-plus sized book featuring 56 of Lindsay's startling black-and-white photographs and thirty-one pages of lyrical angling prose by McGuane. It gets my vote as the least-known text in his sporting canon and one that I think deserves wider attention.

Upstream: Fly Fishing in the American West is one of the handful of angling books I carry with me on my annual Montana fishing trip each summer. I learn something from it every time I pick it up. It is a book that invites being mused over, ruminated about, delved into, even talked back to. To my mind, it accomplishes that rarest of ends: it teaches a posture, an attitude, a way of being different from what many of us normally encounter in angling books.

If fly fishing literature is rich in anything, it is rich in tradition. That ubiquitous and undefinable quality is both its strength and its weakness. Screw with tradition, propriety, or form, the critical master tale goes, and you risk apostasy. And yet not to put too academic a point on this matter, the ironic fact remains that, aside from everything else regarding content we can say about them, all fly fishing texts— particularly centering on the classic act of angling for trout in streams— seek to redefine the tradition. Whatever else they imagine themselves doing, each new work that comes down the river refines the possibilities of the genre, negotiates its own place in the historical line of descent. What is Norman Maclean's novella *A River Runs through It* (1976) or David James Duncan's *The River Why* (1983) but intertextual riffs on Izaak Walton's *The Compleat Angler* (1653). Or think of Richard Brautigan's *Trout Fishing in America* (1976), or John Lurie's hilarious film series *Fishing with John* (1991). They signified moments when the door swung open, however narrowly, toward a less traditional, less overly-determined form of fly fishing representation that entertained marginal views and odd angles, and quirky and unexpected piscatorial visions.

Upstream is in that revisionist style. Despite its size and heft, it is not standard coffee table fare. Certainly it is in the tradition of literate, specialized niche photo/text books, such as Larry Madison's and Nick Lyons' *Trout River* (1988), Charles H. Traub's *An Angler's Album: Fishing in Photography and Literature* (1990), and Grant McClintock's *Fly Water: Fly Fishing Rivers of the West* (2010), to name three exemplary works in the genre. But in the unprepossessing simplicity and starkness of its visual images and in the more or less under-stated elliptical style of its prose, the Lindsay/McGuane volume departs radically from that class of color photo books which presents perfectly framed and gloriously lighted scenes of huge, mind-blowing trout caught (and presumably released) in exotic far-flung landscape and privileged destinations.

For better or for worse, and with notable exceptions, many of those desire-inducing, hyper-glossy books don't simply enshrine beauty but fetishize it as a material fantasy and a longed-for commodity.

What I worry about in this streamlined, polished-chrome anglingscape, is that the contextual surround of angling, the daily layered presences that make up so much of fishing's undramatic weight and heft, its quotidian, ho-hum, day-to-day ordinariness, that marks the bulk of our fishing lives, will be neglected or relegated to antiquated baggage in favor of the sexier, primal, go-for-broke hook-up moment alone.

Upstream assuages my fear. It reverses the normalizing trend. I don't mean that it revels in deliberate ugliness—far from it—but it does have a kind of nervy, street-wise attitude and stripped-down point of view, a now-you-see-it, now-you-don't arc of attention. "I've reduced my camera equipment to a Rolleiflex with a fixed normal lens, the simplicity of which parallels the fly rod itself," Lindsay claims in an "Afterword." McGuane adds, "In defense of my going afield rod in hand and especially with reference to those pointed questions as to why I don't simply absorb and enjoy those wonders of nature and especially riparian nature about which I am ceaselessly nattering, I have sometimes quoted Antoine de St. Exupéry: 'A spectacle has no meaning except it be seen through the glass of a culture, a civilization, a craft'" (55).

McGuane's prose accompanies Lindsay's photographs, but is independent of them and can stand alone as an entity in its own right. (His contribution would make a fine, stand-alone short book by itself or the beginning of a yet-to-be expanded future narrative.) Written text and visual images are not directly or intentionally matched to each other—McGuane told me recently that he wasn't sure there was any connection whatsoever between Lindsay's photos and his prose—so it is left in each reader's lap to navigate the borders between them. Some words and images resonate with each other, some don't. They do not depend on each other for clarity, context, or explanation; rather they mutually enrich each other.

McGuane's prose commentary has its own stop-and-start trajectory; Lindsay's moody, jangly photos have their own random gravity. Words and images sometimes seem at odds with each other, and yet at the edge between them there is a relational dance, a dialogue about what is of value in the process of looking and being attentive, the impact of which is to defamiliarize fly fishing rituals and scenes, strip them of their cant and commodity, make them fresh again in so far as that is possible.

Photographer and novelist want us to forget everything we know about stock-in-trade representation—majestic panoramic views of landscape, pastoral images of riverine geography, or sensational accounts of catching trophy fish that inhabit such sexy, wet dream-inducing places. In fact, even though all of the photos were taken in the North American West, they so purposely eschew geographical spectacle that they could have been shot anywhere. Search as hard as you can, you won't discover a single image of that commercial stock-in-trade "Big Sky" Montana.

The locale of McGuane's prose, too, travels all over the place. With few exceptions he rarely mentions a geographical place or the name of a river he's fishing. He's not interested in travelogue. He offers instead a set of loosely linked meditations on angling in situ rather than a time-bound narrative with a definable chronology and recurring symbolism. McGuane wants us to put aside rote, culturally inflected notions of "beauty" and "professionalization of sport" (24) in favor of a view of angling as a form of "play" that involves neither mastery nor conquest, but rather, as he proposes "... an unaccidental journey toward a direct involvement with nature" (24). Angling, he continues, "ends with natural history."

For McGuane, insofar as that involvement is possible, it is best achieved through treating fly fishing as context, an awareness of the totality of its environment: "I was too cognizant of my surroundings to fish seriously," he confesses at one point in his otherwise fishing-obsessed life (30). And in a later anecdote, he writes of spending a day in Paris "ferreting out a tiny fly-tier's atelier in some godforsaken corner of the Right Bank. Looking at the

Thomas McGuane

seemingly haphazard but intuitive flies that wouldn't sell for a nickel in North America but were used to supply restaurants from hard-fished public water, I knew there was much more to learn, even if this wasn't the Louvre" (68).

Of Lindsay's 56 photographs, only a handful actually have fish in them, and only one of those, titled "Salmon," shows a fish being held by a human (84). Lindsay is more apt to be synechdocical and to provide an oblique or partial view--a fin, back, mouth, or tail--rather than, say, an entire brown or rainbow trout. The effect of this calculated erasure is both unnerving and memorable. There isn't anything else quite like it in angling's photographic record as far as I can tell. Lindsay's photos achieve their startling power by focusing on small, unexpected, and seemingly inconsequential or often unphotogenic objects—submerged boulders, a fallen log, an artificial fly—a Muddler Minnow—under water, a section of tangled fly line, or ubiquitous, mesmerizing river hydraulics, all darkly lit and often framed against ominous backgrounds.

McGuane's métier is the anecdote, the small suggestive episode, the cool reflection, the restrained emotion. "Under a ledge, a big trout fed, sending ripples of such substance out from his lair they took my attention away from the several nice fish that worked in approachable parts of the stream. I tried to skip my fly up under the ledge to the hidden beast and of course it didn't work. I put the normal feeders down for good. *Finis*" (41). And sometimes there is a world of portent just beyond his field of vision that doesn't necessarily bode cheery but cannot be neglected either. "Snags, hooking bush or branches, are parts of angling and fly-casting and are more than mere annoyances," McGuane states. "Finally, a snag is the suspicion that, while you have been casting, the old trees behind you have been creeping forward and that the general animation of nature is even more persistent than you had suspected" (41). Such moments are the undramatic building blocks of angling experience, the seemingly inconsequential moments when a "leisurely riparian saunter accompanied by the ceremonial movements of fly and line suddenly coalesces in trance" (13).

These are routine elements many blithe fly fishers ignore or take for granted, though doing so, both artists suggest, is to reduce attentiveness, to limit exposure to a side of life "not previously experienced" (81).

One Lindsay photo, called "Molt," taken in Montana in 1997, shows the empty nymphal cases of half a dozen large salmon flies still clinging to a bare willow branch long after, it is supposed, the nymphs metamorphosed into winged adults and flew away (83). The salmon fly shucks are the only objects in focus—the tree branches are slightly blurred, the river beneath them is a rush of pale grey. The effect is other-worldly, eerie, and bespeaks an unseen and unacknowledged rawness, even violence, in nature as well as unparalleled bounty. Peering at just-seined nymphs, McGuane writes that each "transforming nymph—and there were some pupating ephemerella duns with still-collapsed wings emerging from their thoracic cases—with its ancient genetic code, its sidereal photo-programming, its infinite engineering of body parts, in its complexity and completeness made *Finnegan's Wake* seem like a comic book"(48).

As with many hybrid tandem texts, meaning lies as much in the unseen and unsaid as in the obvious and apparent. That is one definition of mystery. We must imagine that a world of activity goes on in the liminal spaces. "When I'm casting on this perfect water" McGuane says of a small spring creek, "the sudden appearance of my line on the surface, the only straight line in view, is too emphatic. The water is so silky, the small boils of subsidiary springs and other small hydrological mysteries so unknowable, that drag materializes along the line imperceptibly; just when things seem perfect, the fly skids on its hackles making a faint V and I am no longer actually fishing" (66). River as text, text as river: "reading the water," which is the fly fisherman's modus operandi, has particular relevance in this book and carries beyond the stream. "Dawn and dusk, crepuscular light, is an open book and fish are emboldened by their own shadowlessness. The angler becomes still, watchful. Something is about to happen" (12).

And though I wish it were otherwise, as unique and genre-bending as it is, *Upstream* is not for everyone. I get that. It will have its detractors, its nay-sayers, its disbelievers, even its pooh-pooers, who, desirous of a more traditional and conservative view of fly fishing, will "go from room to room, drawing the blinds until the whole house is dark" (15). But they will be the poorer for that, perhaps even "impoverished" (24), and in their distrust of mystery will leave the fishing and the reading to the rest of us happy anglers waiting with McGuane for the next riverine thing that most assuredly is about to happen, even though we cannot yet guess what it will be. ■

THIS HOUSE OF SKY

Landscapes of a Western Mind

IVAN DOIG

RICHARD ETULAIN

Re-reading Ivan Doig's This House of Sky

R eading Ivan Doig's first well-known book *This House of Sky* (1978) was like a flashback to a remembered past. He knew what I had experienced growing up on an isolated sheep ranch. I quickly recognized, too, how much Doig was smitten with "characters," like his dad Charlie Doig and his grandmother Bessie Ringer. And Doig was a literary artist, with a range of words, old and newly created, like a well-stocked, innovative thesaurus.

A second reading more than forty years later proves that a moveable feast remains before us in *This House of Sky*.

Doig opens his appealing memoir with Doig family backgrounds, the traumatic death of his mother on his sixth birthday, and his father's knockabout, unending search for the best ranch owner and ideal job. When Charlie's quick, ill-planned second marriage leads to disaster, he has to make the toughest of decisions. Desiring a homemaker and support for his only child, Charlie invites his mother-in-law Bessie Ringer into their home. It was a difficult request because they disliked one another. But need, growing appreciation, and finally love gradually melt away the oppositions and forge a new kind of family. While Charlie still searches for the ideal position and Ivan races through schools, Bessie provides diligence and stability. The final chapters relate Ivan's college years at Northwestern, his marriage to Carol Muller, and his gaining a PhD in history from the University of Washington. In the closing pages, the story reverses itself: Ivan is called upon to help Charlie during his failing health from emphysema and after that Bessie's decline. Ivan has learned from these two worthies how to be worthy in return.

Ivan's story was unusual, a young guy still in his thirties already writing his memoir. In several ways, he stories the monthly turn of a sheepman's year. First, the lambing season early on, still in the frozen months of winter. Then forward a few weeks to shearing time. In spring, sheepherder sons like Ivan had to go through one of the traumas of woolly life. Tail-cutting and "docking" meant even preteens held a lamb's legs while their fathers or other men cut or burned off a lamb's tail to protect it from infectious diarrhea. Even more traumatic, little male lambies had their scrotum cut and the testicles removed. After a few weeks of healing, the sheep were trailed to the mountains for the greener, more luxurious grasses of the high meadows. The cycle completed when the new crop of lambs was shipped east in early fall in time for high holidays feasts.

But dramatic weather changes could, like unwelcome visitors, disrupt and sometimes nearly destroy a sheepman's well-planned schedule. Savage storms throughout the winter and even the spring and sometimes into early summer could whip down from the Rockies or south from Canada blanketing Doig's home country of central and northcentral Montana with clotting snow and dangerous icy surfaces. The upsetting impact meant herders and helpers had to perform like magicians to keep their herds safe and fed. Thankfully, wished-for, more-than-welcome, warm-air chinooks from the north could funnel in change, renewal, and hope.

Many of Doig's inviting pages overflow with these diurnal details of the sheepcamp. For the uninformed, the sketches and descriptions are moments of illumination. For the veterans of sheep camp life, these are cherished remembrances.

In his memoir, Doig the literary artist might have taken as his motto "character counts." His characters, their personalities, and their ideas and actions grab and hold readers. His father Charlie is pictured as a never-tiring foreman, herder, and trail boss on dozens of Montana ranches—and as a warm, supportive father. After the crushing death of Ivan's mother Berneta, Charlie tried to be both parents. The failed marriage to "Ruth" and, afterwards, the arrival of Berneta's mother Bessie Ringer, reveal much about the characters of Charlie and Bessie—and Ivan. The evolving and "cording" relationship among the new three-person family powers Ivan's story like a self-charging engine.

Surrounding these major characters are a passel of supporting figures. There are the drinkers at the town's saloons, the ranch owners and hired hands where the Doigs reside, and dozens of town men and women. One of the most memorable is Frances Carson Tidyman, a superb English teacher at Valier High School, where Ivan shines like

Ivan Doig (photo by Marion Ettlinger)

an emerging academic beacon among fellow students. Mrs. Tidyman, who loved literature, Latin, and most of all diagramming sentences, built on Ivan's reading addictions, his "knack for knowledge," transporting him from comic books and popular paperbacks to the joys of the classics.

Small Montana burgs, their social configurations, and physical layouts serve as still other characters in Doig's intriguing memoir. In White Sulpher Springs and Ringling in southcentral Montana near the Little Belt and Big Belt Mountains and then north in Dupuyer next to the Blackfeet Indian Reservation, Doig describes the houses that he, his father, and grandmother crammed into. The ramshackle hotels, public buildings, and taverns also play bit parts in Doig's narrative. The histories of these towns and buildings link the pasts and presents of the places that shaped Ivan's early years and later memories.

Settings and characters are indelibly etched in readers' minds through Doig's word wizardry. Later, the writer explained this marriage of ingredients to achieve his central goal: "If I have any creed that I wish you as readers, necessary accomplices in this flirtatious ceremony of writing and reading, will take with you from my pages," Doig wrote, "it'd be this belief of mine that writers of caliber can ground their work in specific land and lingo and yet be writing of that larger county: life."

Doig assembles his characters by combining their words and his. In one illuminating conversation, Charlie, the saloon stool philosopher, tells everyone in hearing, "I decided I'd be damned if I'd scratch along on a dab of a place." Here is another example of what Ivan says about his father, trying "to chant himself into a rightness about what he was doing." Or another description from Ivan: "the quickest part of his [Charlie's] brain, and they were several, mostly had to do with ranchcraft." Charlie boasted of another ingredient: "I'm awfully little but I'm awfully tough." Combined, these words and hundreds of others furnish a revealing portrait of Charlie Doig.

So too for grandma. Bessie "only chored on," Ivan tells us. She "went along as alone and unaided as a tumbleweed." Yet when needs came, Bessie shone: "her ability to prop other lives with her own" was her hallmark. Her lifetime philosophy comes into focus when she lines up the future for her grandson: "But we got these others [details] to get through." Bessie, lover of dogs, cooking, ranch duties—and Ivan—shines as brightly as Charlie.

Novelist and historian Ivan Doig would have embraced William Faulkner's statement "the past is never dead. It's not even past." Ivan and his characters had a foot in each world, leading them to "both-and" rather than misleading "either-or" thinking that led to out-of-kilter actions.

Doig's conceptions and uses of memory blanket his story. He first defines memory as "a set of sagas we live by" and then as "the near-neighbor of dream" and "almost as casual in its hospitality." Later, he adds, however, that "memory is a kind of homesickness, and like homesickness, it falls short of the actualities on almost every count." Understanding these fault lines undermining his memories, Doig interviewed dozens of people who knew his father and grand-mother, who worked with them, and who lived in their time.

He also researched, at the University of Washington Library, the historical record of Montana as the state stumbled through his boyhood years. Memory could be added to, corrected, and strengthened through diligent historical research.

This House of Sky boomed onto the western and national literary scene in 1978. Reviewers celebrated its appealing characters, scenic descriptions, and encouraging dramas of human relations. Doig's first important book was a finalist for the National Book Award and launched a career of more than a dozen novels. Altogether, many came rightly to view Ivan Doig as the rightful inheritor of Wallace Stegner's mantle, as "the dean of Western writers." ■

*"Late Summer Morning Run at Military Reserve" by Rachel Teannalach,
oil and wax on linen, 36" x 48."*

FROM THE ARCHIVE

Nancy Stringfellow and her daughter Rosalie Sorrells, 1990 (photo by Rosemary Ardinger)

REPORT FROM GRIMES CREEK
AFTER A HARD WINTER

Nancy Stringfellow

Introduction by
Rosalie Sorrels

NANCY STRINGFELLOW

Social Security

Editor's Note: *With this 2021 edition of* The Limberlost Review, *we thought we'd add a new section reprising some excerpts of works published by Limberlost Press over the last few decades.*

The following essay, "Social Security," is from a slim volume we first published in 1990 as Report from Grimes Creek after a Hard Winter, *a chapbook by Nancy Stringfellow, comprised of several short essays, a couple of poems, and a 1972 letter to her daughter, folksinger Rosalie Sorrels, our friend and neighbor, who chose the selections and pulled them together from her mother's larger, unpublished memoir,* Up Grimes Creek without a Paddle. *Nancy wrote her memoir after she retired from many years managing* The Book Shop *in Boise, Idaho, and moved around 1972 from her Boise home to the family's small summer cabin in the mountains about 30 miles north of town.*

In her concerts across the country, Rosalie wove between songs her stories about her mother and the family's log cabin, built by her father Walter and brother Jim, as an idyllic mountain refuge next to the ever-roiling Grimes Creek, near the town of Idaho City.

Rosalie had committed excerpts from her mother's memoir to memory, and later issued her own album of songs and spoken word titled Report from Grimes Creek *(Green Linnet Records, 1991). The cabin would be Rosalie's home for decades as well, a refuge she longed to return after months on the road, and a fabled place of memorable feasts and gatherings.*

Nancy's chapbook appeared in honor of her 80th birthday, and when Boise's Public Radio reporter Jyl Hoyt produced a story about the book that landed on NPR's Morning Edition, *orders from all over the country flooded in to quickly exhaust the first edition.*

Nancy died in 1994, but her little book continued to sell well at all of Rosalie's concerts, and copies are still available from Limberlost Press. "Social Security" remains a favorite, especially among those who come of age to receive the benefit.

April, laughing her girlish laughter, is upon me. The water is completely gone from the basement. Old Grimes is threatening the lane, and I park my car outside the gate, lest I get trapped by a sudden surge of water. Everything is coming up with a whoop and a holler. The earth shimmers with movement. Mysterious jeweled bugs venture forth. Ants stream over the ground in columns. Spiders pop in and out of holes, sidle along twigs, cast lines into the wind and swing out like the Flying Wallendas.

Lichen doily the rocks, and in every crevice green fingers of moss are reaching toward the sun. So beautiful and strange. Some are thick green velvet pincushions, some mounds of green stars. Scallops of soft green hair betray the Nereids peeking from their granite catacombs. Sit down and look at a patch of moss, and suddenly you are in Tolkein land, wandering in a green forest, strange branches waving above you, soft carpets beneath your feet. Sometimes a star flower erupts in the midst, terrifyingly tall, blindingly white. And tiny insects are wending their way through the trees to their Promised Land, following their own special star.

The birds are coming on strong now, the whole place has been divided up among them like a checkerboard, and every bird is in its own private square, hollering Mine! Mine!

*****

April is also the month my Social Security payments begin. Such a lovely little brown paper envelope, meaning, indeed, security. I remember other days. In the raw new land of Southern Idaho it was shove and scrape, and if you had bad luck or lost your strength you were done for. I was raised in mortal fear of disability or of some natural disaster. We walked a thin tightrope with no net. Two years of crop failures could wipe out the savings of ten years. That of course was part of the reason for large families. More hands to work the land. Someone to help you when your strength was going. Children were sometimes your only security against dying in a ditch. There was no cushion.

*****

I remember the bewildered old ladies, widows who had lost their husbands, and whose small hoard of savings had been swept away by illness and death. Sometimes they had no one left to turn to, and then it was the County Poor Farm, with bare endless corridors and echoing board floors. Cheerless charity. Sometimes they had children or relatives who took them in and sheltered them, but the extra mouth was a burden, and they knew it. Old ladies sitting in the far corner of the room when company came, thinning hair dragged back into a tight bun, knobby hands folded in aproned laps. Soft list slippers slit to ease the painful bunions. Apologetic, silent, arthritically awkward. Or drudging from one task to another, pathetically anxious to please a harried daughter-in-law. Relicts, they called them. Flotsam from an earlier culture, bleached dry, juiceless, and helpless. Women who had once been strong and beautiful, and suffered from that memory.

And there were the ones who still had a measure of strength, but were trapped in that dreadful bind that women were trapped in so little time ago. Not enough education to teach, too old to be a clerk or a waitress. There was little other opportunity. Poverty was a sandpit, and they could not scale the walls. They fought, sometimes gallantly, sometimes bitterly, but mostly they lost. Their lives subsided into an empty endless waiting. Even when their families cared for them and kept them safe they still lacked their independence. For as much as your people cared for you, and you for them, absolute financial dependence is a terrible, a crippling, thing.

Social Security helped change that. It gave the elderly a measure of dignity. Not to have to ask for little things, silly little things that made you remember you were still a woman. To be able to buy a lipstick, to ease your drying skin with pot of cream. And a small but solid contribution to the monthly bills. Enough so that you could have a room of your own. With luck, a place of your own.

Here in my mountains I am remarkably fortunate. Living is cheap. I have seven acres of room. Room for dignity and freedom, privacy to cry when I am sad and dance when I am gay. It all comes in that little brown paper wrapper, and it lets me spit in anybody's eye. ■

"Eventful" by Janet Wormser, oil on canvas, 12" x 16."

Judith Root, Oregon coast, last photo by Gerald Costanzo

JUDITH ROOT

We note in our Editor's Note (pg. 15) that since the appearance of the last
Limberlost Review *in the spring of 2020, we lost a few great friends of*
Limberlost Press and to literature. One of those friends, Judith Root, of
Portland, Oregon, who had poems in the 2020 Review, died in August of 2020,
three days shy of her 81st birthday. Her gentle, modest delivery reading her
work was betrayed by her hearty laugh. We'll miss her poems, her laugh, and
we'll miss her phone calls too.

She published several books and chapbooks, and her work appeared
in many great literary journals. Limberlost Press letterpressed a collection
of her poems, Free Will and the River, *in 2005. We thought we'd give*
Judith the "Last Word."

Free Will and the River

Every street in town
ends at the tanker
where the river used to be.
Without Alaskan oil the ship
rides high, blocks wind,
blocks light angled through clouds
releasing rain so slowly
the drops seem to turn around,
rise and fill the clouds again.

Year after year the process
repeats itself until we count on it
like we count on the salmon
whose return to spawn
determines when men fish,
when they drink.

If I were part of this cycle,
I'd pour beer at Charlie's Place,
chalk birthdays (Dutch—Aug. 11,
Spook—Aug. 20) on the board
behind the bar and stuff my tips

in hard finger rolls,
the clink of coins backing up
the jukebox bass shuddering
in my apartment wall.

Someday, I'd tell myself,
the difference between tips
and rent will pay my way
downriver to the city where
windows in tall buildings
throw back sunlight
and someone, safe from nature's
whims, controls weather
with metal discs, pipes and fans.

Once in a glass tank there,
I watched a tiny albino
catfish bob like a hypnotist's
charm, skin translucent
in artificial light that lulled me
back to clouds gathering
at the river's mouth, racing
the tanker out to sea, playing tag
with all my expectations.

"Untitled" by Jinny DeFoggi, ink on paper, 9" x 12."

"Happening" by Janet Wormser, oil on canvas, 16" x 20."

"Daybreak in the Sawtooth Valley" by Rachel Teannalach, oil and wax on linen, 38" x 81."

CONTRIBUTORS

SHERMAN ALEXIE has published 26 books including his recent memoir *You Don't Have to Say You Love Me* (Little, Brown). He has won the PEN/Faulkner Award for Fiction, the PEN/Malamud Award for Short Fiction, a PEN/Hemingway Citation for Best First Fiction, and the National Book Award for Young People's Literature. Born a Spokane/Coeur d'Alene Indian, Alexie grew up in Wellpinit, Washington, on the Spokane Indian Reservation. He's been an urban Indian since 1994 and lives in Seattle with his family. *A Memory of*  *Elephants,* a letterpress-printed, limited edition chapbook of his poems, was published in the summer of 2020 by Limberlost Press.

PETER ANDERSON is the author of the novel *Follower* (Limberlost Press, 2020) and the founder, with his wife Jeanne, of the independent bookstore Dark Horse Books in Driggs, Idaho. His essays and fiction have appeared in numerous regional and national publications, including *The Limberlost Review* (2019 and 2020). A second novel is forthcoming. He and Jeanne have performed extensive public service in Idaho's arts and humanities communities.

SANDY ANDERSON is the author of *Jeanne Was Once a Player of Pianos*, a letterpress-printed chapbook of poems from Limberlost Press. She was the longtime organizer and inspirational force behind CityArt, Salt Lake City's longest-running literary reading series (currently presenting 25-30 readings a year), and which also delved into small press publishing. She also edited *Fragile Constructions,* an occasional anthology of creative work that evolved from writing workshops she conducted and participated in. She has been a mentor to many and a tireless promoter of the Utah writing community.

JONAH ANDRIST is the author of a collection of short stories, a play, and a novella, *The Town of Books,* which is available as an audio book. He runs a freeform literary podcast with Pocatello, Idaho, writer and Walrus & Carpenter Bookstore owner Will Peterson called *Western Thought.* Jonah lives in Pocatello.

JOHN BERTRAM was born in Berkeley, California, in 1946, majored in urban planning at the University of Washington, and directed the Boise-based consulting firm Planmakers from 1977 to 2017, offering city planning, historic preservation, and urban design studies. As president of Preservation Idaho, he oversaw the preservation and restoration of many historic buildings and structures. Influenced by partner JanyRae Seda, he travels to art shows all over the  west, exploring museums and galleries at every opportunity. In 2017, he built and opened Bertram Studio, creating collages and mixed media art works.

MARY CLEARMAN BLEW has written or edited 15 books of fiction and nonfiction. The University of Nebraska Press has published four of her novels, *Jackalope Dreams* (2008, winner of the Western Heritage Award), *Ruby Dreams of Janis Joplin* (2018), Sweep Out the Ashes (2019), and her latest, *Waltzing Montana* (2021). Her short fiction collection *Runaway* won the Pacific Northwest Booksellers Award, as did her memoir *All But the Waltz: Essays on a Montana Family*  (Viking, 1991). She's also the author of a memoir *This Is Not the Ivy League*. She lives in Moscow, Idaho.

ROD BURKS graduated from the University of Wisconsin-Madison in 1979 with a degree in Art Education. He taught in Kalispell, Montana, for one year, then accepted a position with the Herrett Center at the College of Southern Idaho as an Exhibits Curator. Eventually he joined the family Agriculture and Construction Equipment business in Twin Falls and Caldwell, where he's worked for the past 35 years. After a 40-year lull and encouraged by friendships with numerous  artists from Boise's James Castle House Residency Program, he began painting again in 2020.

BOB BUSHNELL was raised in Wilder, Idaho, and attended the University of Idaho, Stanford University, and the University of Washington School of Law. He returned to Boise in 1972 to practice law before becoming a full-time businessman and a single parent, nourished by a membership in the Boise Great Books Club for four decades. He now devotes his time to reading, writing, and cultivating old and new friendships.

DENNIS & JINNY DeFOGGI are two Boise-based
artists who have been passionately dedicated to their art for
more than a half-century. Encouraged by mentor artist and
friend Ray Obermayr at Idaho State University in the 1960s,
they have in turn been great encouragers of writers, artists,
readers, thinkers, and creative believers and welcomed them
into their home and their fold. They've had many shows
together, and both have exhibited at the Boise Art Museum's
juried Idaho Triennial shows of outstanding work by the state's contemporary
artists. Dennis' work again was featured in the Boise Art Museum's 2020 Triennial.

ROBERT DeMOTT'S recent books are *Angling Days:*
A Fly Fisher's Journals (essays, Simon & Schuster, 2019),
Conversations with Jim Harrison, Revised and Updated (inter-
views, University Press of Mississippi, 2019), and *Up Late*
Reading Birds of America (prose-poems, Sheila-Na-Gig
Editions, 2020). His poetry has appeared in many journals,
including *Ontario Review, Georgia Review, Southern Review,*
Hiram Poetry Review, Southern Poetry Review, Lake Effect,
Windsor Review, and elsewhere. From 1969 to 2013 he taught at The Ohio Univer-
sity. He serves on the editorial board of *The Steinbeck Review,* and directorial board
of *Quarter After Eight*, a literary journal. He lives in Athens, Ohio, with his partner
Kate Fox, a poet and editor.

JIM DODGE is a Taoist dirt pagan and practicing panthe-
ist who may have been born enlightened but pissed it away
through thousands of sweet attachments and too many
random acts of sheer folly. As he dwindles into decrepitude,
he splits his time between an isolated ranch in the coastal
wilds of the Gualala watershed and the semi-settled Eureka
peninsula. Editor's Note: He is also the author of three novels,
Fup (Simon & Schuster, 1984), *Not Fade Away* (Atlantic
Monthly Press, 1987), and *Stone Junction* (Grove Press, 1998), and a collection of
poems and prose, *Rain on the River* (Canongate Books, 2002).

RICHARD ETULAIN is Professor Emeritus of History at
the University of New Mexico. He's the author or editor of
60 books, most of which deal with the history and literature
of the American West and studies of Abraham Lincoln.
His best-known works include *Conversations with Wallace*
Stegner, Beyond the Missouri: The Story of the American West,
and *Thunder in the West: The Life and Legends of Billy the Kid.*
He has been president of both the Western Literature and
Western History Associations. He grew up on an isolated sheep ranch in eastern
Washington, about which he is currently writing a ranch memoir.

REBECCA EVAN'S writing revolves around living with
disability and overcoming trauma. She served eight years in
the United States Air Force and is a decorated Gulf War
veteran. She now mentors teens in the juvenile system.
She is the co-host of *Writer to Writer* podcast on Radio Boise.
Her poems and essays have appeared in *The Rumpus, Entropy
Literary Magazine, War, Literature & the Arts, 34th Parallel,
Blue Mountain Review, Survival Lit,* and *Collateral Journal,*

among others. With an MFA in creative nonfiction, Evans is finishing a second
MFA in poetry at Sierra Nevada University. She has served on the editorial staff
of the *Sierra Nevada Review* and lives in Idaho with her sons. She's just completed
a memoir.

GARY GILDNER says he "threw far too many curveballs
in his youth, grew up to break bread in Paris, gave underground readings behind the Iron Curtain, and survived
Transient Global Amnesia in the arms of a ballerina in the
foothills of the Santa Catalina Mountains of Arizona."
He lived for 25 years in the Idaho panhandle before moving
to Arizona. He's the author of numerous books of poetry,
memoir, and fiction, and winner of the Walt Whitman Prize

and the William Carlos Williams Prize for poetry, the Iowa Prize for memoir,
and other awards. He's also the recipient of Fulbright Fellowships to Poland
and Czechoslovakia.

DIDI SHARP (AKA Diane Graves) says, "I consider myself
a kitchen table artist. What that means to me is that I am
untrained, but just love to make things. I spent many an
hour as a kid with my Grandpa Graves in his wood shop.
He thought me to use a jig saw and other tools. That's where
I learned to love making things with my hands. I started out
as a weaver. That went on for a number of years. When I
moved to Seattle in1980 I started making jewelry, mostly

from found objects. Then I started making lamps of found parts and an etched
copper line I made with my bff David Farnsworth. I started a group of women
lighting designers called Wired Women and we did a number of shows together
here in Seattle. Finally in 2018 I started making paper collages. I love to cut. I love
taking an image and creating something completely new with it. It still thrills me
every day (on Etsy @ didisharpcollages)."

SAMUEL GREEN'S most recent collection of poems is
Disturbing the Light (Carnegie Mellon University, 2020). With
his wife Sally, he has been co-editor of the award-winning
Brooding Heron Press on Waldron Island, Washington, since
1982. He has been a visiting professor at multiple colleges
and universities, and taught as a visiting Poet-in-the-Schools
for forty-six years. In 2008 he was selected as the first Poet

Laureate of Washington State. Honors include an NEA Fellowship in Poetry, an Artist Trust Fellowship in Literature, a Washington State Book Award in Poetry, and he was awarded an Honorary Doctorate from Seattle University. From 1966-1970 he was in the U.S. Coast Guard, with service in Vietnam.

SHAUN T. GRIFFIN is the co-founder and development director of Community Chest, a rural social justice agency serving northwestern Nevada since 1991. Southern Utah University Press released his *Anthem for a Burnished Land*, a memoir, in 2016. *This Is What the Desert Surrenders: New and Selected Poems* came out from Black Rock Press in 2012, and Limberlost Press released his letterpressed chapbook of poems *Driving the Tender Desert Home* in 2014. His most  recent books include a collection of essays, *Because the Light Will Not Forgive Me* (University of Nevada Press in 2019), and *The Monastery of Stars* (poems, Kelsay Books 2020). He lives in Virginia City, Nevada, in the shadow of the former home of novelist Walter Van Tilburg Clark.

CHUCK GUILFORD is a winner of the Western Litera-ture Association's Willa Cather Memorial Award and the author of the novel *Spring Drive: A North Country Tale*; *Altogether Now: Essays on Poetry, Writing, and Teaching*; and the collection of poems *What Counts*. He is also the creator of two popular websites, Paradigm Online Writing Assistant (powa.org) and Poetryexpress (poetryexpress.org). He taught  literature and creative writing at Boise State University for more than two decades and founded BSU's Idaho Writers Archive. His poems, stories, essays, and reviews have appeared in a many magazines and anthologies, including *Poetry, Kansas Quarterly, Coyote's Journal, Redneck Review of Literature, Crab Creek Review, Idaho Humanities*, and elsewhere. A collection of his poems is available at https://www.forthislife.org.

VINCE HANNITY studied English, with minors in class-ical Greek and Latin, at Gonzaga University some 50 years ago. Since then, he and friends of like mind have continued an informal education, studying the world's classic literature through the Great Books Club of Boise. He published *From Savagery to Civilization: The Power of Greek Mythology* in 2018. Simultaneously over the years, he pursued a rewarding busi-ness career with Boise Cascade Corporation, from which he  is now retired. He has served on a number of nonprofit boards, including as chairman of both the Idaho Humanities Council and Idaho Commission on the Arts, as president of Idaho Business for Education, and as chair of The Cabin, Boise's nonprofit literary center.

RON HATZENBUEHLER earned M.A. and Ph.D. degrees in history at Kent State University, and taught at Idaho State University from 1972 until his retirement in 2013. In addition to his teaching career, he's also written and lectured to the general public on migration and population trends and the legacies of presidents. Over the years, he has served on the advisory boards for Idaho State Univer-  sity Press, for ISU's magazine *Rendezvous*, and for the Idaho State Historical Society magazine *Idaho Yesterdays*. In 2006, he published '*I Tremble for My Country*': *Thomas Jefferson and the Virginia Gentry* (University Press of Florida) to much critical praise. In 2008, he received the award for "Outstanding Achievement in the Humanities" from the Idaho Humanities Council.

JIM HEYNEN was born on a farm in northwest Iowa and received his first eight years of education at one of the state's last one-room school houses, Welcome #3. He's the author of several collections of poems, including *A Suitable Church* and *Standing Naked* and several collections of stories, including *You Know What Is Right, The One-Room Schoolhouse*, and *The Man Who Kept Cigars in his Cap*. His most recent  collection of stories is *The Youngest Boy* (Holy Cow! Press, 2021). Since 1992, he has been Writer-in-Residence at St. Olaf College in Northfield, Minnesota.

CHERYL HINDRICHS teaches literature and critical theory at Boise State University. Her passion and research is in transnational modernist literature, film, and culture. She received two M.A.s and a Ph.D. at the Ohio State University, and occasionally pines for the forests of the Midwest where she grew up and her family lives. Having lived in Boise since 2006, she continues to be delighted by the sky and its fine artistry at dusk and dawn on the foothills. When health allows, walks through the city and along the river, in com-  pany if possible, is a joy. As the chair of Lit for Lunch and various book groups, she finds her greatest happiness in the brilliant individuals who make literature a part of their full and varied lives.

JENNIFER HOLLEY fell into love of history, antiques, old movies, and stories from summer-long visits with her grandmother Bertie on the east coast as a young pig-tailed girl. Growing up in Boise, her mother threw in some great art appreciation and decent cocktail making skills, dad gave her the wherewithal to know that baseball is America's game, and step-dad rounded out the edges with the right training in politics, boy advice, and how to order a Drambuie at TGI  Fridays. For 20 years she has worked for the Idaho Humanities Council, currently as Director of Programs and Development, where she edits the newsletter *Idaho Humanities*. Her essays have appeared in *Sesquizine: Commemorating Boise 150* (Boise City Arts and History Department, 2014) and *Dishrag Soup and Poverty Cake: An Idaho Potluck of Essays on Food* (Idaho Humanities Council, 2006).

BETHANY SCHULTZ HURST is the author of *Miss Lost Nation*, winner of the Anhinga Poetry Prize and finalist for the 2016 Kate Tufts Discovery Award. Her work has been included in *Best American Poetry* and she's published in *The Gettysburg Review, Gulf Coast, Narrative, New Ohio Review, Ploughshares,* and *The Limberlost Review* (2019). A recipient of a Literary Arts Fellowship from the Idaho Commission on the Arts, she teaches creative writing at Idaho State University in Pocatello.

JAY JOHNSON is a lawyer and writer working in Moscow, Idaho. After college, he lived in Oregon, Colorado, Washington, and California before settling in Idaho in 1995. He repaired automobiles and logged for twenty-five years prior to law school. Most of his law practice is criminal defense, generally for indigent clients. His fiction has appeared recently in *The Limberlost Review* and *Talking River Review.*

WILLIAM JOHNSON is Professor Emeritus of English at Lewis-Clark State College in Lewiston, Idaho, a former Writer-in-Residence for the state of Idaho, author of *A River without Banks*, a collection of essays from Oregon State University Press, and several collections of poetry, including, most recently, *Dogwood* (Limberlost Press). He lives with his wife Cheryl and their cat Manu in a house surrounded by trees, flanked by the Lewiston hills and sky.

GROVE KOGER is the author of *When the Going Was Good: A Guide to the 99 Best Narratives of Travel, Exploration, and Adventure* (Scarecrow Press, 2002), and Assistant Editor of *Deus Loci: The Lawrence Durrell Journal.* He has published fiction in such periodicals as *Cirque, Danse Macabre, The Bosphorus Review of Books, La Piccioletta Barca,* and *Punt Volat,* and blogs at worldenoughblog.wordpress.com.

MARGARET KOGER is a Lascaux Poetry Prize finalist living near the river in Boise, Idaho. She taught English at Boise's Borah High for many years and served as a Poet-in-the-Schools. Her work has appeared in numerous journals, including *The Amsterdam Quarterly,* the *Writers in the Attic* series, *Red Rock Review, Collective Unrest, Burning House, Tiny Seed, The Chaffey Review, Forbidden Peak, Déraciné, Ponder Savant,* and *Gravitas.*

ALEX KUO has lived and worked for most of his adult life in the American West, writing and teaching writing. His first book, *The Window Tree*, a book of poems, came out in 1971, the first volume of poetry published by an Asian American writer. He has since received multiple National Endowment for the Arts awards, a Rockefeller Bellagio residency, and the American Book Award for *Lipstick and Other Stories* (Soho Press, 2002). His next book, the novel *Cadenzas*, will be released in September of 2021.

DAVID LEE is the author of more than two dozen books of poetry. His collection *News from Down to the Café* was nominated for the Pulitzer Prize in 1999, and in 2001 he was a finalist for the position of United States Poet Laureate. He served as Utah's inaugural Poet Laureate from 1997-2002 and later received the Utah Governor's Award for lifetime achievement in the arts. His poems have appeared widely in literary journals, including *Poetry, Ploughshares, The Missouri Review, Narrative Magazine*, and *JuxtaProse Literary Magazine*. His first book of poems, *The Porcine Legacy*, was published by Copper Canyon Press in 1974, and he is the subject of a PBS documentary *The Pig Poet*. A former seminary student, semi-pro baseball player, and hog farmer, he served for 30 years as Chairman of the Department of Language and Literature at Southern Utah University.

JON D. LEE is the author of several books, including *An Epidemic of Rumors: How Stories Shape Our Perceptions of Disease*. His poems and essays have appeared or are forthcoming in *Sugar House Review, Sierra Nevada Review, The Writer's Chronicle, Connecticut River Review, The Laurel Review, The Inflectionist Review*, and *Oregon Literary Review*. He has an MFA in poetry from Lesley University, and a PhD in Folklore. He teaches at Suffolk University, and lives with his wife and children in Massachusetts.

ED MAROHN was a captain in the US Army (Airborne and Ranger trained) and served in Vietnam with the 101st Airborne (Airmobile) Division, commanding a combat unit and awarded three Bronze Stars and one Air Medal. He retired as an executive from International Fortune 500 companies and was elected to a four-year term to the Idaho Falls City Council. He has written numerous newspaper columns and has published fiction and non-fiction. As a volunteer VA facilitator for PTSD veterans and his return to Vietnam some forty years after the war, his novel, *Legacy of War*, took root.

JERRY MARTIEN left southern California at the beginning of the 1960s, spent that decade in the east and Midwest, and returned at its end to a still habitable part of the state. He considers his five decades in the Humboldt Bay region a bioregional experiment: if a person moves somewhere, invests one's life and art in its geology and weather, its human and biotic community, what might be the outcome? A school for the children, jobs as a book clerk, teacher,  carpenter; an environmental center, a coop and a clinic, a book store and a print shop; cultural events to mark the movements of politics and seasons, and a bar with good music—all the necessities of life. And surprisingly, two books about money and gift exchange, and several chapbooks and collections of poems, which Rosalie Sorrels, traveling lady of song, would carry from the bar back to Boise and eventually to the attention of the editors of this publication. "Geology of the Eastern Sierra" is from a recent collection, *Infrastructure* (available at northtownbooks.com), "John Ross Returns" is from a work in progress.

RON McFARLAND retired from the University of Idaho English department in 2018 after "47 years of blithe self-indulgence." He's the author of 20 books and served as Idaho's first State Writer-in-Residence (1984-1985). Current projects include a new collection of poems tentatively titled "A Variable Sense of Things" and a book-length study of the poetry & prose of Chicano writer Gary Soto. His most recent book is a biography of Colonel Edward J. Steptoe (1815-1865), *Edward J. Steptoe and the Indian Wars* (2016).

MARY ELLEN McMURTRIE is a poet who has had the good fortune to share her passion for language and literature with students in Idaho City and Meridian, Idaho. She lives on an old placer mine where she has spent much of the last thirty years trying to heal the stripped down land that the miners left behind when they rushed off to other gold fields. Her latest passion is a wild game camera which she checks each morning to see who came to visit during the night.  McMurtrie's poems and fiction have appeared in a variety of local and national literary journals.

E. ETHELBERT MILLER is a literary activist and author of two memoirs and several poetry collections. He hosts the WPFW morning radio show *On the Margin with E. Ethelbert Miller* and hosts and produces *The Scholars* on UDC-TV. Most recently, he received a grant by the D.C. Commission on the Arts and Humanities and a Congressional Award by Congressman Jamie Raskin in recognition of his literary activism. Miller has two forthcoming books: *When Your Wife Has Tommy John Surgery and Other Baseball Stories* and *the little book of e*.

ALAN MINSKOFF moved to Boise, Idaho, from New York in 1972. He lives in Boise and teaches at the College of Idaho. The author of *Idaho Wine Country* and *The Idaho Traveler* (both from Caxton Press), he's also the author of two chapbooks of poetry from Limberlost Press, *Blue Ink Runs Out on a Partly Cloudy Day* and *Point Blank*. His essays have appeared in *Harper's*, the anthology *Where the Morning Light's Still Blue*, and elsewhere. His contribution to this issue of *Limberlost* is an excerpt from a memoir-in-progress.

HANK NUWER is a prolific journalist who made his living during the heyday of slick-magazine journalism from the 1970s to the 1990s, interviewing people as diverse as writers Jim Harrison and Kurt Vonnegut and baseball greats George Brett, Don Mattingly, and many others. His main in-progress projects include a sweeping 175,000-word treatment of hazing in American culture, a forthcoming biography of Kurt Vonnegut, and his second historical novel set in the American West. He recently retired from teaching at Franklin College in Indiana.

FRED OCHI (1913-2007) was one of Idaho's most prolific watercolor artists, a plein air painter most remembered for his rural landscapes. Born in California, he maintained and operated a popular sign painting and graphic arts business and studio in Idaho Falls, Idaho, from the 1940s until his death. His work was exhibited widely in his lifetime, and is held in many museums and private collections. He received recognition and numerous awards in his lifetime for his painting and teaching, including a Governor's Award for Excellence from the Idaho Commission on the Arts, as well as recognition during Idaho's 1990 state centennial as one of 100 Idahoans "who made a difference" to the cultural life of the state through his art and by his activism promoting acceptance of racial and cultural diversity. Many hope that a family project to establish an archive of hundreds of his paintings will result at some point in a retrospective exhibition.

GAETHA PACE grew up in South Dakota to the north and east of Nebraska's fabled Sandhills country. Four generations of her family are buried on both sides of that Nebraska-South Dakota border. Until recently her writing has been submerged beneath careers as Special Assistant to a Governor, Director of the Idaho Commission on the Arts and as Director of the Idaho Heritage Trust. *I Taught Myself Denial* and *I Taught Myself Hope* are the first two novels in her "Little Bluestem Mysteries." She's working on a third: *I Taught Myself Desire*. The inspiration for her story "I Don't Know" was picked up cross a kitchen table in small town Idaho.

GAILMARIE PAHMEIER teaches creative writing at
the University of Nevada and in the MFA program at Sierra
Nevada University. She is the recipient of three Artist Fellow-
ships from the Nevada Arts Council. She is the author of
The House on Breakaheart Road and *The Rural Lives of Nice
Girls,* and three chapbooks, one of which, *Shake It and It
Snows,* won the Coal Hill Chapbook Award from Autumn

House Press. A new book, *Of Bone, Of Ash, Of Ordinary Saints,* appeared from
WSC Press in 2020. She has received the Governor's Award for Excellence in
the Arts from the state of Nevada, has served the City of Reno as its first Poet
Laureate, and she has been recognized by Nevada Humanities as an Outstanding
Teacher in the Humanities.

JOY PASSANANTE'S collection of stories *The Art of
Absence* and her novel *My Mother's Lovers* were finalists for
several national awards. She has also published a fine-press
book of poems, *Sinning in Italy,* with Limberlost Press. She's
the recipient of Idaho Commission on the Arts Fellowships
for poetry and fiction and an Idaho Humanities Council
Research Fellowship for nonfiction. She taught literature and
creative writing at the University of Idaho for 38 years.

Through a Long Absence: Words from My Father's Wars (2017), her first book of
narrative nonfiction, won a Foreword INDIES Book of the Year Award. She's
currently working on a collection of essays. She has lived with and collaborated
with Gary Williams for half a century.

LORELLE RAU is a contemporary collage artist, who
pieces together snippets of found paper and appropriated
imagery to create linear vistas and abstract scenes that coor-
dinate color, texture, and shape with balanced intention. Her
process is guided by her intuition for which these elements
come together, bringing line and detail into play within the
landscape. Rau earned her MA in Arts Administration from
the Savannah College of Art and Design; BA in Studio Art and

a BS in Arts Management from Appalachian State University. She currently lives and
works in Boise, Idaho.

ROBERT LEONARD REID is the author of five books,
four works for the theater, and some 150 magazine articles,
short stories, and essays. His essay collection *Because It Is So
Beautiful: Unraveling the Mystique of the American West* (Coun-
terpoint) was one of five finalists for the 2018 PEN/Diamon-
stein-Spielvogel Award for the Art of the Essay. The keyboard
player in several northern Nevada bands, Bob has written and
staged three satirical revues and the 24-song *Bristlecone Mass.*

He has received two Artist Fellowships in Literary Arts from the Nevada Arts
Council. In 2018, he was inducted into the Nevada Writers Hall of Fame.

KEN RODGERS is a poet, writer and filmmaker who lives in Idaho. Both a Pushcart Prize nominee and a Best American Short Stories nominee, Ken's stories, poems and essays have appeared in a number of fine journals. His published books include a collection of short stories, *The Gods of Angkor Wat* (BK Publications), and two collections of poems, *Trench Dining* (Running Wolf Press) and *Passenger Pigeons* (Jaxon Press.) Along with his wife Betty, Ken co-directed and co-produced *Bravo! Common Men, Uncommon Valor,* a feature-

length documentary film about Ken's company of Marines at the Siege of Khe Sanh in 1968. Betty and Ken's latest documentary, *I Married the War*, about caregivers to combat veterans, is scheduled to be released in 2021. Ken blogs fairly regularly at KennethRodgers.com.

JUDITH ROOT (1939-2020), during a lengthy career, taught at universities in El Paso, Columbia, Boise, Des Moines, Long Beach, and in the Summer Seminars in Prague. Her collections of poems include *Little Mysterie* (Stone Press), *Weaving the Sheets* (Carnegie Mellon University Press), and *Free Will and the River* (Limberlost Press). Two of her poems appeared in *Limberlost Review* 2020.

BRANT SHORT was born and raised in southern Idaho. He attended Idaho State University and studied communications and history at Indiana University. He taught at Southwest Texas University, Idaho State University, and Northern Arizona, where he currently teaches communications. His work has focused primarily on environmental topics. He's the author of *Ronald Reagan and the Public Lands Debate in the United States* (Texas A&M Press) and editor of *Democratic Demise/Republican Ascendency? Politics in the Inter-mountain West* (Idaho State University Press).

GINO SKY is the author of the novels *Appaloosa Rising* (Doubleday, 1980) and *Coyote Silk* (North Atlantic Books, 1987), the story collection *Near the Postcard Beautiful* (Floating Ink Books, 1994), and a dozen collections of poetry, including *Wild Dog Days* (Limberlost Press, 2015). He was an editor of the legendary 1960s literary magazine *Wild Dog* that began in Pocatello, Idaho, and moved on to Salt Lake City, and then to the Haight-Ashbury district of San Francisco prior to the Summer of Love, publishing many of the great

poets of the day. He and his wife Barbara Jensen currently live in Salt Lake City. An interview with Gino appears in the 2020 edition of *The Limberlost Review.*

LARRY SMITH is a native of the industrial Ohio River Valley, and he's published six books of fiction and eight books of poetry. He's also the author of two literary biographies of poets Kenneth Patchen and Lawrence Ferlinghetti, and he wrote and produced two documentary films about poets James Wright and Kenneth Patchen. As editor-publisher of Bottom Dog Press in Ohio he has guided over 215 books through publication since its inception in 1985. A retired professor of humanities from Bowling Green State University  at Firelands College, Smith and his wife Ann live along the shores of Lake Erie in Huron, Ohio, and are active grandparents and founders of the Converging Paths Mediation Center there. His most recent book is *Mingo Town & Memories* (Bird Dog Publishing).

NANCY TAKACS is the recipient of the Juniper Prize for Poetry and a Pushcart Prize. A Utah poet, she also spends time in the north woods near Lake Superior's Apostle Islands. A lover of the outdoors, during the 2020 COVID-19 summer, she became interested in foraging for mushrooms there each day, and began an extensive catalog of identifying them and preparing them. Takacs has taught workshops at the Price, Utah, senior center for ten years. She is the current poet laureate of Helper City, Utah, and is an emerita faculty of Utah State University Eastern.

RACHEL TEANNALACH is a contemporary landscape painter based in Boise. Originally from northern New Mexico, she graduated from Scripps College in Claremont, CA in 2003. She also studied at the Glasgow School of Art in Scotland, and Studio Art Centers International in Florence, Italy. Prior to following family to Idaho, Teannalach lived in Marin County, California. Each of these places contributed to her love of enjoying nature through landscape painting. Teannalach is represented by Capitol Contemporary Gallery  in Boise, Echo Arts in Bozeman, Simon Breitbard Fine Arts in the San Francisco Bay Area. Her work is characterized by bold, gestural brushstrokes and her ability to evoke the emotional quality of the places she paints. Teannalach has lived in Boise since 2008, where she and her husband are raising their two young daughters, Mairead and Saoirse. Learn more at www.teannalach.com

MARTIN VEST "The poet Tu Fu says, 'Clear the mind of common horses.' I try to do that." Editor's note: Martin also the author of the letterpress-printed collection of poems *Ghost in the Bloody Show* (Limberlost Press). His work has appeared in numerous literary journals, including *The New York Quarterly, Slipstream, Rattle, The Chiron Review, Pearl* and many others. He has received several Pushcart Prize nominations from various literary magazines. He currently lives near Idaho Falls, Idaho.

O. ALAN WELTZIEN, longtime English professor at the University of Montana Western (Dillon), retired from teaching in 2020. He has published dozens of articles and nine books, including three poetry collections and a memoir, *A Father and an Island* (2008). He's just published a biography of neglected Montana novelist Thomas Savage with the University of Nevada Press.

GARY WILLIAMS taught in and for many years chaired the University of Idaho's English department until he retired in 2015. A Montana native, he migrated east (St. Louis) and then farther east (Ithaca, NY) for his education before bringing his Midwestern bride Joy Passanante to Idaho in 1973. He's published on Hawthorne and Cooper before launching a long investigation into the life and works of Julia Ward Howe. His study of Howe's beginnings as a writer, *Hungry Heart,* appeared in 1999, followed by an edition of her fragmented manuscript novel *The Hermaphrodite* in 2004. He's a former board member of the Idaho Humanities Council, for which he served as Vice-Chair in the early 1990s.

JOHN NEAL WILLIAMS was born in Iowa and attended high school at the American International School in Vienna, Austria, and college studies at the University of Minnesota/Mankato and Washington State University under the tutelage of Alex Kuo and a friendship with Sherman Alexie. After 40 years in the Pacific Northwest, he returned to Iowa. He's a double cancer survivor (three years).

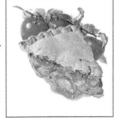

MIKE WOODS was encouraged by his parents at an early age to draw and paint. He holds BFA and MFA degrees in art from Boise State University and Idaho State University respectively. During the Vietnam War he served in the U.S. Navy for three years, after which he studied graphic arts at ISU, where he also taught drawing, painting, and sculpture for the Department of Continuing Education. He worked as a graphic artist for a magazine publishing company in Hailey, Idaho, in the 1980s, and then worked for 28 years for the Boise Department of Parks and Recreation. He's been creating art since 1990 from his "Blue Iris Studio" in his home in Boise.

BARON WORMSER is the author of eighteen books. He has received fellowships from the National Endowment for the Arts and the John Simon Guggenheim Memorial Foundation. From 2000 to 2005 he served as poet laureate of the state of Maine. In June, 2020, *Songs from a Voice, Being the Recollections, Stanzas and Observations of Abe Runyan, Songwriter and Performer*, a fictional consideration of the early years of Bob Dylan, was published. He lives in Montpelier, Vermont, with his wife Janet.

JANET WORMSER is a self-taught painter who has been painting for decades and has exhibited in Maine, Vermont, and elsewhere. She says her painting is "tied up with my spiritual journey, which is about my effort to be present to my life from moment to moment. This applies to my relationship with paint, particularly watercolor because it is not easy to control . . . I encourage the paint to spread, wander and pool by soaking and/or spraying the paper." More of her work can be seen at www.janetwormser.com.

ROBERT WRIGLEY is Distinguished Professor Emeritus at the University of Idaho and the author of eleven collections of poetry, including *Reign of Snakes, Lives of the Animals, Anatomy of Melancholy, Beautiful Country, The Church of Omnivorous Light*, and *Box* (all from Penguin). Tupelo Press in April of 2021 released *Nemerov's Door*, a collection of personal essays about poetry and the poets who inspired his own life and work. He's won numerous awards, including a Pacific Northwest Book Award, the San Francisco Poetry Center Book Award, the Kingsley Tufts Award, and fellowships from the National Endowment for the Arts, the Idaho Commission on the Arts, and the Guggenheim Foundation. He lives in Moscow, Idaho, with his wife, the writer Kim Barnes.

ATTENTION WRITERS!

Call for Submissions for

Into the Lavas
An anthology of writing on the Idaho Great Rift and Craters of the Moon

SPATTER CONES CRATERS OF THE MOON, IDAHO—5

Walrus and Carpenter Books of Pocatello is seeking stories (fiction and nonfiction), essays about personal adventures, and poetry about the Great Rift and Craters of the Moon to be published in an anthology to appear in commemoration of the centennial of the Craters of the Moon National Monument in 2024 (established by President Coolidge in 1924).

Epiphanies, mistakes, revelations of the subliminal, and appropriate metaphors favored for selection. Good writing and proof of having been there an essential feature. Submissions 2,000 words or so. New work, old work, previously published or unpublished considered.

Questions and Submissions by 6/30/2022 to:
Tom Blanchard, 208-788-4450, tjblanchard@svskylan.net

NEW FROM LIMBERLOST PRESS

A Memory of Elephants
A New Chapbook of Poems

By Sherman Alexie

A Memory of Elephants is a deeply reflective, introspective, and confessional collection of poems that explore the mysteries of a mental disorder, regret for things left unsaid to parents before their passing, tribal identity, raising sons in the urban world, the power of love, questions to God.

Printed on Mohawk Superfine paper and folded and sewn by hand into Stonehenge wrappers with illustrations by Erin Ann Jensen.

A Spokane/Coeur d'Alene Indian, Sherman Alexie grew up in Wellpinit, Washington, on the Spokane Indian Reservation. He has been an urban Indian since 1994 and lives in Seattle with his family. He is a poet, short story writer, novelist, and performer, and he has won the PEN/Faulkner Award for Fiction, the PEN/Malamud Award for Short Fiction, a PEN/Hemingway Citation for Best First Fiction, and the National Book Award for Young People's Literature.

He's published 26 books, including his recently released memoir, *You Don't Have to Say You Love Me*, and young adult novel, *The Absolutely True Diary of a Part-Time Indian* (all from Little, Brown Books); *What I've Stolen, What I've Earned*, a book of poetry, from Hanging Loose Press; and *Blasphemy: New and Selected Stories*, from Grove Press. Limberlost Press published letterpress-printed limited editions of his poetry chapbooks *Dangerous Astronomy, The Man Who Loves Salmon,* and *Water Flowing Home. Smoke Signals*, the movie he wrote and co-produced, won the Audience Award and Filmmakers Trophy at the 1998 Sundance Film Festival.

Letterpress printed in a limited edition of only 500 copies during the COVID-19 summer of 2020 on Mohawk Superfine paper and folded and sewn by hand into Rising Stonehenge wrappers.

$20 (*plus $3 Media Mail shipping; Idaho residents please add 6% sales tax*) from www.limberlostpress.com, or send check to: Limberlost Press, Rick & Rosemary Ardinger, Editors, 17 Canyon Trail, Boise, Idaho 83716

NEW FROM TUPELO PRESS

Nemerov's Door
Essays by Robert Wrigley

In his youth, Robert Wrigley had little interest in poetry; you even could call it an active *disinterest.* Then, at the age of twenty-one, after being drafted into the army during the Vietnam War, after receiving an honorable discharge on the grounds of conscientious objection, and feeling otherwise adrift, he took, on a lark, a class in poetry writing, and that class altered the trajectory of his life.

Nemerov's Door is the story of a distinguished and widely celebrated poet's development, via episodes from his life, and via his examinations of some of the poets whose work has helped to shape his own. The book is a testament to what matters most in this particular poet's life: love, nature, wild country, music, and poetry. Essays on James Dickey, Richard Hugo, Etheridge Knight, Howard Nemerov, Sylvia Plath, and Edwin Arlington Robinson are interwoven with essays about the sources of poetry; arrowheads; wild rivers; and the lyrics of a song from *My Fair Lady,* among other things. In the essay about Richard Hugo, Wrigley engages with a single poem by his great mentor, whose influence on Wrigley and many other poets of his generation has been enormous. "The Music of Sense" extrapolates from Frost's notion of the "sound of sense," and fuses it with Hugo's notion that the poet, forced to choose between music and meaning, must always choose music. As though to offer his own proof of that notion, one of Wrigley's other essays here is a poem.

"Robert Wrigley has been one of my foundational poets. Each of his books has taught me how to live in this world. And now this welcome essay collection brings a fresh slant of light on the trail. This is wonderful work. I'm grateful for it."
— Luis Alberto Urrea

Robert Wrigley is Distinguished Professor Emeritus at the University of Idaho and the author of a eleven collections of poetry. He's won numerous awards, including a Pacific Northwest Book Award, the San Francisco Poetry Center Book Award, the Kingsley Tufts Award, and fellowships from the National Endowment for the Arts, the Idaho Commission on the Arts, and the Guggenheim Foundation. He lives in Moscow, Idaho, with his wife, writer Kim Barnes.

$19.95, 180 pages. Order directly from Tupelopress.org or from your favorite independent bookstore.

NEW FROM UNIVERSITY OF OKLAHOMA PRESS

Tuesday Night Massacre:
Four Senate Elections and the
Radicalization of the Republican Party

By Marc C. Johnson

How did our politics become so partisan and polarized? Why has the U.S. Senate gone from "the world's greatest deliberative body" to dysfunction? Why does "outside" money have such an outsized role in every Senate election? A major part of the answer to those questions has its origin in four Senate races in 1980 where "independent expenditure" campaigns targeted four Senate liberals.

Marc C. Johnson explains how Senate races in Idaho, Indiana, Iowa and South Dakota in the pivotal political year of 1980 continue to shape American politics. Drawing upon archival research,interviews and a deep understanding of political campaigns, Johnson charts the decline in American democracy and a radicalization of the GOP that has its roots in places like Boise and Sioux Falls, Cedar Rapids and Fort Wayne.

Connecting the dots between the Goldwater era of the 1960s and the ascent of Trump, Tuesday Night Massacre follows the change that has deeply —and perhaps permanently—warped the culture of bipartisanship that once prevailed in American politics.

Marc C. Johnson has worked as a broadcast journalist and communication and crisis management consultant and served as a top aide to Idaho's longest-serving governor, Cecil D. Andrus. His writing on politics and history has been published in the *New York Times*, *California Journal of Politics and Policy*, and *Montana: The Magazine of Western History* and appears regularly on the blog *Many Things Considered*.

$26.95 paper, $45 hardcover. Order directly through University of Oklahoma Press www.oupress.com or from your favorite independent bookstore.

John Thomsen & Friends: Songs from Loafer's Glory
AUDIO CD

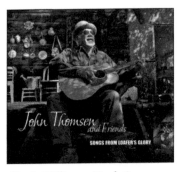

In commemoration of his 80th year, Limberlost Press has released a CD by longtime Idaho folk musician John Thomsen, of Idaho City, featuring an impressive list of musicians from the region backing up their musical mentor, friend, and collaborator. *John Thomsen & Friends: Songs from Loafer's Glory* features an array of favorites by Hank Williams, Hank Snow, Roger Miller, Tex Ritter, Sean McCarthy, and others, as well as a couple of Thomsen originals. Despite decades of making music at folk festivals, weddings, birthdays, political events, plays, dances, funerals, and backyard barbecues, *Songs from Loafer's Glory* is Thomsen's first CD.

Recorded by Sam Aarons of Idaho City Sound over several daylong sessions, the long overdue recording offers a sampling of Thomsen's musical versatility. The CD, which includes a colorful booklet of photos and tributes by admirers, features Thomsen's own "Idaho Spud," a bitingly satirical song-story about nuclear waste, the Atomic Energy Commission, and raising kids on "nuclear taters."

Limberlost Press publisher Rick Ardinger likens the recording to the work of Smithsonian folk music preservationist Alan Lomax, who saved from obscurity so much American folk music during the 20th century.

"Johnny has set the bar for being an authentic folk treasure. I am very fortunate to have had so many great times with 'the Golden Voice of the Boise Basin.'"
—*Dave Daley, fiddle player and longtime More's Creek String Band collaborator*

"I have never failed to be impressed by his repertoire and his abilities on guitar, concertina, and Dobro. He was, and is, the complete folklorist and musician. His wit and sense of humor are unmatched."
—*Jake Hoffman, veteran musician, and lap steel guitar artist*

"Johnny is a walking library of songs. He knows so many verses and choruses and the stories that go with them that he has to keep his interest by rewriting some with words most clever and slightly scandalous . . . I've been honored to play along, harmonizing on the fly."
—*Beth Wilson, Idaho City folk musician and collaborator*

$12 (*plus $3 Media Mail shipping; Idaho residents please add 6% sales tax*)
**from www.limberlostpress.com, or send check to: Limberlost Press,
Rick & Rosemary Ardinger, Editors, 17 Canyon Trail, Boise, Idaho 83716**

FROM LIMBERLOST PRESS

This Morning's Joy
By Ed Sanders

Here is a collection of anti-war poems that also offers elegies to friends (Allen Ginsberg, Robert Creeley, Harry Smith, Charles Olson), and reflects on memories of revolutionary times and the joys of carrying on despite "war-mongering sleaze" of governments.

Born in 1939, Ed Sanders is a poet, inventive musician, publisher, and founding member of "The Fugs" rock and roll band. Student of Greek, participant exorcisor during the 1967 March on the Pentagon, founder of the Investigative Poetry movement, editor/publisher of *Fuck You* magazine ("published from a secret location on the Lower East Side"), editor of the online *Woodstock Journal*, husband of Miriam R. Sanders for more than a half-century, he carries on poetically and politically, bridging the Beat generation to the Hippie generation, to a contemporary insistence that poetry matters and will change the world.

**350 copies letterpress printed and
sewn by hand into paper covers.**

$20 (*plus $3 Media Mail shipping; Idaho residents please add 6% sales tax*)
**from www.limberlostpress.com, or send check to: Limberlost Press,
Rick & Rosemary Ardinger, Editors, 17 Canyon Trail, Boise, Idaho 83716**

FROM LIMBERLOST PRESS

Of Your Passage, O Summer

By John Haines

Of Your Passage, O Summer is a collection of poems from the late-1950s and early-1960s thought lost, then found by the poet decades later, and published by Limberlost in honor of the poet's 80th year.

John Haines, once the poet laureate of Alaska, homesteaded in the wilderness near Fairbanks, working and living off the land. Written in relative isolation, the poems in this collection reflect news of the time — the Cuban missile crisis, confrontation with the Soviet Union, the threat of nuclear annihilation, the early stages of the Vietnam War.

Influenced by his readings of classical Chinese poets, Haines' poems quietly confront great questions about the very nature of existence, a plea for survival from a solitary survivor on a vast, beautiful, lonely and formidable landscape. Haines dedicates the book "to the time, the place, and the life lived—that which gave me the poems— and now to the reader of them."

"Dear Rick Ardinger: In publishing John Haines' Of Your Passage, O Summer, you have performed a very great service to the whole world of art and literature. His poems are beyond beautiful; they are important, uniquely valuable, and a destination for the hopes and ambitions of us all."
— Hayden Carruth, Unsolicited Letter, November 24, 2004

500 copies letterpress printed on Mohawk Superfine paper and sewn by hand into Stonehenge paper covers.

$20 *(plus $3 Media Mail shipping; Idaho residents please add 6% sales tax)*
from www.limberlostpress.com, or send check to: Limberlost Press, Rick & Rosemary Ardinger, Editors, 17 Canyon Trail, Boise, Idaho 83716

FROM LIMBERLOST PRESS

Juniper
By Nancy Takacs

This collection of poems is infused with sage and juniper, images of the Great Basin, a horizon edged by mountains, where every word is measured and matters. Here is a poet whose lines grip the page like desert plants, windblown and enduring, whose quiet stories of family and wild-life and gardens are as if from a friend who logs the arrival of birds and shares coffee in a kitchen on a winter afternoon.

    A former wilderness studies instructor and creative writing professor at the College of Eastern Utah, Nancy Takacs lives in Wellington, Utah, and is the author of a half-dozen books of poetry, including *Pale Blue Wings* (Limberlost Press, 2001), which was a finalist for the Utah Book Award and sold out quickly. She's the recipient of several awards, including The Nation/Discovery Award. She's held residencies at the Ucross Foundation in Wyoming and Vermont Studios. Her work has appeared recently in *Diner, Red Rock Review, Cutthroat, Plainsongs, Adirondack Review, The Spoon River Poetry Review,* and *Weber Studies.* She holds an MFA from the University of Iowa.

"Add Nancy Takacs's name to the list of Utah's best-kept secrets. These are beautifully crafted, well-made poems drawn from deliberately lived, introspective experience . . . Her truths are clothes in the silk of well-drawn imagery and are revealed in a manner that produces a life enhancing afterglow."
    — David Lee

400 copies letterpress printed on Mohawk Superfine paper and sewn by hand into Stonehenge paper covers.

$15 *(plus $3 Media Mail shipping; Idaho residents please add 6% sales tax)*
from www.limberlostpress.com, or send check to: Limberlost Press, Rick & Rosemary Ardinger, Editors, 17 Canyon Trail, Boise, Idaho 83716

FROM LIMBERLOST PRESS

Complete your collection of
The Limberlost Review revival
with the 2019 and 2020 editions!

Together featuring more than 600 pages of poetry, fiction,
essays, memoir, and artwork.

Interviews with Clay Morgan and Gino Sky

Poetry by Ron Padgett, Ed Sanders, Sherman Alexie,
Jennifer Dunbar Dorn, Greg Keeler,
David Lee, William Studebaker, Nancy Takacs, Robert Wrigley,
Kim Stafford, Alan Minskoff, Shaun Griffin, Raúl Zurita,
Bethany Schultz Hurst, Martin Vest, Gary Holthaus,
Robert DeMott, and more . . .

Fiction and essays by Mary Clearman Blew, John Rember, Jim Heynen,
Gary Gildner, Judith Freeman, Tom Rea, Joy Passanante, Leslie Leek,
Peter Anderson, Vardis Fisher . . .

Re-readings by Grove Koger, Marc Johnson, Michael Corrigan,
Jim Hepworth, William Johnson . . .

Artwork by Dennis & Jinny DeFoggi, Greg Keeler, Royden Card,
Nancy Brossman, Ray Obermayr, Glenn Oakley, Alberta Mayo, Jackie Elo . . .

And more

Get them today through
www.limberlostpress.com
or send check to: Limberlost Press, Rick & Rosemary Ardinger, Editors,
17 Canyon Trail, Boise, Idaho 83716

What's next for

The Limberlost Review
A Literary Journal of the Mountain West

2022 Edition

**NEXT DEADLINE
October 1, 2021**

Re-Readings

Have a favorite old book you've read more than once?
Consider submitting a "Re-Reading."
Who were you when you first read it?
How did it have an impact?
Why should we read it?

Remembering

Remember a friend, a writer, a journey,
an experience . . .

What's in store so far for LR 2022 . . .

Re-readings by
Bill Woodall on Henry David Thoreau
Baron Wormser on Nathaniel Hawthorne
Alan Minskoff on John Dos Passos
Dan Popkey on Muhammad Ali

Essays by
Kelli Parker on 'Remembering Tom Trusky'
Alex Kuo on joining the U.S. Forest Service, 1957

Poems and stories by
David Lee, Diane Raptosh, Jim Dodge,
and more poetry, fiction, essays, and memoir.

Send new work to editors@limberlostpress.com

"Dream Scrapbook: I Wouldn't Be Like This If I Knew How Not To Be Like This" by Didi Sharp, paper collage, 8" x 10."

COLPOHON

The Limberlost Review body copy is set in ITC BERKELEY OLD STYLE, based on Frederic W. Goudy's beautiful 1938 typeface. It is a serif font inspired by "old style" (pre-18th century) type, especially the "Fell Types," a collection of fonts used by Oxford University Press in the late 1600s. Originally, this typeface was titled "University of California Old Style," which Goudy designed for exclusive use at the University of California Press at Berkeley. He extolled the design virtues of the face he created, stressing its legibility in particular, for academic work. Goudy's typeface, however, was not available to the public because it was commissioned solely for private university use. After Goudy's death in 1958, the typeface was re-released by Monotype, which reissued it as "Californian." In 1983, Tony Stan redrew the family for ITC as "ITC Berkeley Old Style." Stan redrew the font to include a greater variation of weight, italics, and caps. Although no longer the "corporate font" of the University of California Press or System, Goudy's typeface is widely used in academia, as well as book and magazine publishing and advertising.

The Limberlost Review header font is TRAJAN PRO, a more modern all-caps font designed for Adobe by Carol Twombly in 1989. The design is based on inscribed Roman capital letters on column bases, such as those on the Trajan Column. Twombly designed this in all-caps-only because the Romans didn't use lower-case letters. Calligrapher and type designer Edward Johnston once wrote in 1908, "Roman capitals have held the supreme place among letters for readableness and beauty. They are the best forms for the grandest and most important inscriptions." Trajan letterforms are often used for display text, large-format printing such as posters and book covers, and on public buildings.

The Limberlost Review is designed by Meggan Laxalt Mackey of Studio M Publications & Design in Boise, Idaho, in collaboration with Rick and Rosemary Ardinger of Limberlost Press. Since its inception, *The Limberlost Review* has celebrated the spirit of excellence in writing, artwork, typography, and book design.

"Vardis Fisher" by John Bertram, cut paper on canvas collage, 24" x 36," 2020.

CPSIA information can be obtained
at www.ICGtesting.com
Printed in the USA
JSHW032224240621
16184JS00001B/1